ON FALCON'S WINGS

Lisa J. Yarde

I0727874

ON FALCON'S WINGS
Copyright © Lisa J. Yarde 2010

ISBN-10   1939138116
ISBN-13   978-1939138118

This is a work of fiction. The names, characters, locations, and incidents portrayed in it are the work of the author's imagination, or have been used fictitiously. Any resemblance to actual persons living or dead, locations or events is entirely coincidental.

All rights reserved.
No portion of this book may be transmitted or reproduced in any form, or by any means, without the prior written permission of the Author.

www.lisajyarde.com

Cover design by Lance Ganey
www.freelanceganey.com

ALSO BY LISA J. YARDE

On Falcon's Wings (2010)

Sultana (2011)

Sultana's Legacy (2011)

Long Way Home: A novella (2011)

The Burning Candle (2012)

The Legend Rises – HerStory Anthology (2013)

Sultana: Two Sisters (2013)

ACKNOWLEDGMENTS

I am very grateful for the support of everyone who has read various drafts of this novel, the members of my critique groups, especially Anita Davison, Bill Greer, Jen Black, Laura Hogg, Mirella Patzer, Pamela Maddison, Richard Warren Field, Rosemary Rach, Sheila Lamb, and Wendy Laharnar. Your knowledge and patience inspires me. I could not have finished my edits without Candice S. Watkins' timely and thorough proofreading. As I said, Candice, you are brilliant and I am very appreciative.

To my loving family, thank you for encouraging me to fly far with my dreams.

For Eunice, who always inquired and encouraged.

To Anita, Mirella and Gemi, the truest friends anyone could have.

CHARACTERS

In Flanders

Avicia: the niece of Count Rudolf of Aalst, from Normandy

Edric of Newington: only son of Tunwulf Grim of Newington and Lady Emmeline, from England
Emmeline: Edric's mother, from Flanders
Father Alwine: Edric's great-uncle, from England

*Count Baldwin V of Flanders: son of Count Baldwin IV of Flanders
*Matilda of Flanders: only daughter of Count Baldwin of Flanders and Countess Adele of France

*Count Rudolf of Aalst: Avicia's uncle
*Countess Gisele of Luxembourg: the wife of Count Rudolf of Aalst

*Brithric Meaw: grandson of Earl Leofric of Mercia, ambassador to Flanders

Biota: Avicia's childhood nurse, from Normandy

Thiedard: a falconer at Lille

In England

Tunwulf Grim of Newington: Edric's father, son of Leofsige of Newington and Eanflaed of Tickenhurst

Eanflaed of Tickenhurst: Tunwulf's mother, Edric's grandmother

Cynwise of Elham: Edric's wife

Leofsige: Edric and Cynwise's eldest son
Wynflaed Thorkelsdatter: only daughter of Thorkel Redbeard, Leofsige's handfasted wife
Aelfred: Leofsige and Wynflaed's son, Edric's second grandson
Gytha: Leofsige and Wynflaed's daughter, Edric's eldest granddaughter

Leofflaed: Edric and Cynwise's eldest daughter
Heahstan of Elmton: Leofflaed's husband
Edric of Elmton: Leofflaed and Heahstan's son

Cenweard: Edric and Cynwise's second son
Eanflaed: Edric and Cynwise's third daughter

Deorwynn: Edric and Cynwise's second daughter
Cyneburh: Deorwynn's daughter, Edric's second granddaughter

*Earl Godwin Wulfnothson of Wessex: son of Wulfnoth Cild, *thegn* of Sussex, the first Earl of Wessex
*Countess Gytha of Wessex: Godwin's wife, mother of his sons Harold, Sweyn, Tostig, Gyrth, Leofwine and Wulfnoth, and his daughters Queen Edith, Gunhild and Gunnora

*Abbot Aelfwig Wulfnothson of Winchester: son of Wulfnoth Cild, *thegn* of Sussex, Godwin's brother

*Earl Harold Godwinson of East Anglia: son of Godwin and Gytha, later Earl of Wessex and King Harold II of England

*Edith the Fair of Nazeing: Harold's handfasted wife, mother of his sons Godwin, Edwin and Magnus and his daughters Gunhild and Gytha

*Ealdgyth of Mercia: daughter of Earl Aelfgar of Mercia and Countess Aelfgifu, Harold's queen, mother of his sons Harold and Ulf

*Earl Sweyn Godwinson of Hereford: son of Godwin and Gytha

*Haakon: Illegitimate son of Sweyn and Abbess Edgiva of Leominster

*Earl Gyrth of East Anglia: fourth son of Godwin and Gytha, later also Earl of Cambridge and Oxford

*Earl Leofwine Godwinson of Kent: fifth son of Godwin and Gytha, later also Earl of Essex, Middlesex, Hereford, Surrey and Buckinghamshire

*Wulfnoth Godwinson: sixth son of Godwin and Gytha

*King Edward of England: wed to Queen Edith, eldest daughter of Godwin and Gytha

*Archbishop Robert Champart of Canterbury: first Norman archbishop of Canterbury, former abbot of Jumieges, advisor to King Edward

*Bishop Stigand of Winchester: advisor to King Edward, later succeeds Archbishop Robert Champart of Canterbury

*Alwin of Buckland: a *thegn*, Edric's friend

*Aethelwold of Teston: a *thegn*, Edric's friend

Thorkel Redbeard: a Danish *huscarl*, father of Wynflaed Thorkelsdatter

Wulfstan: steward of Newington

Odgiva: Emmeline's cook, from Flanders

Hallveig: a Danish midwife in London

In Normandy

*Hugh II de Montfort-sur-Risle: son of Hugh I de Montfort-sur-Risle, advisor to Duke William de Normandy
*Alice de Beaufort: Hugh's wife, mother of his sons Hugh and Robert, and his daughter Alice

Philippe: illegitimate half-brother of Hugh, Avicia's husband
Geoffrey: Philippe and Avicia's eldest son
Baldwin: Philippe and Avicia's second son
Simon: Philippe and Avicia's third son
Thorbert: Philippe and Avicia's fourth son
Cecilia: Philippe and Avicia's daughter

*Duke William de Normandy: also known as William the Bastard, illegitimate son of Duke Robert de Normandy and Herlette de Falaise
*Bishop Odo de Bayeux: second son of Comte Herluin de Conteville and Comtesse Herlette de Falaise, William's half-brother

*Roger de Montgomery: son of Roger de Montgomery, advisor to Duke William de Normandy
*Mabel de Belleme: Wife of Roger de Montgomery, and mother of his sons Roger, Robert, Hugh, Philip and Arnulf, and his daughters Emma, Matilda, Mabel and Sibyl

*Archbishop Maurille de Rouen: Primate (senior clergyman) of Normandy, consecrated Rouen cathedral in 1063

*Abbess Beatrice de Montivilliers: illegitimate daughter of Duke Richard I of Normandy, great aunt of Duke William de Normandy
Sister Felice de Saint Pols: Philippe's mother

Marian de Vernon: childhood friend of Philippe

Turstin: a barber-surgeon
Torfida: a midwife, Turstin's wife

Gunnora: a wet-nurse

PART I – CHAPTER 1

Lille, Flanders
April 1048 CE

The red hide leather whip arced and bit deep into Avicia's flesh. A warm trickle joined the crimson rivulets already staining the remnants of her robe. She struggled against the pain. Her teeth chattered behind lips tightly pressed together. When another cruel blow snaked across her shoulder, raw, guttural sounds escaped her. She jerked against the splintered wood and clung to the whipping post with trembling fingers.

Defiant, she stared straight ahead. Her gaze locked with Edric's own. When they had first met, his eyes reminded her of the pale shade of a robin's egg. Now, they flamed bright blue with frustration and anger. The whip tore across her back once more. Her gaze faltered. A hot wave of blinding pain overwhelmed her. In the blink of an eye, she surrendered to the darkness.

❧

Edric's stare never wavered throughout Avicia's punishment. As the whip shredded her flesh, it also battered his soul. She endured a punishment he should have received instead. It was his fault.

When she sagged, battered and bloodied, her cheek pressed against the whipping post, he studied the unrepentant faces of her tormentors. Matilda, the selfish daughter of Baldwin, the Count of Flanders, bawled beside one of her attendants. She remained inconsolable over the death of her beloved falcon. Her reddened face held no sympathy

1

for the girl who suffered. Avicia's uncle, Count Rudolf of Aalst, gave her one last narrowed gaze. Then he spat in the dirt, turned on his heel, and stalked off with his shoulders squared. None of them helped her.

Edric moved toward Avicia, but sharp fingernails dug into his arm. He followed a lily-white hand from where it disappeared under a billowy green sleeve until he met the strict scrutiny of his mother.

"Do not think to help her now, not when her actions have shamed all of us this day."

✺

Harsh, ragged sobs filled the chamber, where Avicia wept on a pallet in the corner. Her nurse Biota tended her with gentle care in the dim light of a tallow candle. The brutal whipping had shredded the top half of her robe, which now hung in tatters around her slender hips. Wisps of fabric clung to the torn flesh. She winced and shuddered as Biota peeled cloth fibers from the raw skin.

The linen curtain at the entrance rustled and cold air intruded. Gisele of Luxembourg, Countess of Aalst entered the room and padded across the earthen floor. Her dark blue garments shuffled the dank straw on the ground. The folds of her headdress framed her heart-shaped face. Two gold plaits peeked beneath the cloth. She pressed her fleshy lips firmly together, before she exhaled in a huff.

"How could you risk my husband's good name, and your place in the household of Baldwin of Flanders? You dared take Matilda's favorite merlin from the mews and fly it with the English boy. The bird was worth more than you could imagine, and now it is dead, because of you."

Avicia buried her face in her hands. When Biota applied a cold poultice of crushed marigold and fresh comfrey leaves, she whimpered, though Biota tried to soothe her.

"Hush now, my lambkin. The worst of it is over. This poultice shall prevent infection and reduce the threat of fever. Your scars shall fade with time."

"Do not coddle her!" Gisele snapped at Biota, who hung her head, before she turned her cold stare on Avicia again. "You have shamed my husband before Baldwin." Her cheeks flamed. "Have you forgotten all he has done for you? We raised you after the deaths of your parents. By Rudolf's good graces, you have resided here as one of Matilda's attendants. Yet, you betrayed his trust."

"Edric wanted to see the bird. When we took it out, I did not know there would be a goshawk in the sky."

"You thought only of the Englishman's wishes. You did not think of the offense against my husband, or Matilda, or the punishment that awaited you. You are a selfish, stubborn child. Only a fool takes such risks, in a vain attempt to impress a boy. "

"Edric is not just a boy."

Gisele rolled her gray eyes toward the timber ceiling. "Saint Jude, grant us hope. I blame Rudolf. He would not listen when I advised against taking you in as a child. He has spoiled you overmuch, girl. His love for his sister has made him sentimental. He has allowed you too many freedoms and indulged your every whim, in the hopes you might prove useful to us. Now, he shall see the truth."

Avicia moaned softly. She could not risk banishment from court. Where would she go?

"I am sorry, milady. I know I would not be here without Count Rudolf's generosity."

"You should have remembered that before this foolery occurred. By some miracle, you have survived your punishment. Be thankful Baldwin did not cut off your hand, as he should have ordered. Be grateful you still serve among Matilda's attendants, though I do not know if she shall ever forgive you. You shall remain here and do your duty to Rudolf. Do you understand me?"

Avicia lowered her gaze and nodded. Biota bound the poultice with clean cloths and patted her arm, but the comfort of her nurse's familiar touch diminished neither her pain nor humiliation.

She shook her head, recalling her foolhardiness. At the time, she had thought of it as fearlessness, another clandestine visit inside the mews, for a glimpse of its newest resident - a prized merlin. When she discovered Edric there, his compliments on her skill with the falcon emboldened her. His bold desires manipulated her foolish decision.

"With the betrothal negotiations concluded for Lady Judith," Gisele interrupted her thoughts, "the English shall return home. This Edric of Newington goes with them. He is an English lord's son. His home is far from you. Put him from your mind."

She paused and knelt beside the pallet. Her talon-like fingernail scraped across Avicia's brow and her lips curved in a smirk. "Remember that he encouraged you, but you bore the punishment alone. He did not suffer for his role in such foolery."

Avicia met her eyes. "Edric suffered, too. I saw the pain in his eyes when they lashed me."

Gisele drew back and dug her fingernails into her palm. "Pray there are no further consequences of your folly. If you have damaged our relations with Baldwin, you shall be sorry."

She glared at Biota. "Leave her be and let her consider the consequences of this day."

Biota followed her from the room, pausing briefly at the entrance. She looked over her shoulder and shook her head, her gaze full of compassion and sadness.

Alone, Avicia turned her face toward the wall. The tears she had struggled against during Biota's ministrations now trickled down her cheeks. "Oh, Edric."

In misery, she kept her face pressed against the timber. Then, another draft pervaded the room. Heavy, familiar footfalls crossed the floor.

She raised herself up on one elbow. Hellfire blazed along the seams of shredded skin on her back. She tucked the front of the tattered robe under her arms for modesty, before she dared look up. Count Rudolf of Aalst towered over her.

His eyes searched her face.

She shrank back against the wall, despite the pain stabbing her back. She hoped, if she spoke first, the intense anger in his expression might diminish.

"Forgive me, milord, I acted without thinking."

"Why did you do it? Do you know what your foolery might have cost me?"

He advanced on her with fists firmly closed. She whimpered in terror. Then, he stopped and clenched his fingers tightly. Harsh breaths tore from his chest.

"I have never endured such shame before today. Do you know the value of just one of Baldwin's hunting birds? He acquired the creature as a special gift for his daughter. Now, it is dead because of your carelessness! Why did you touch her? The boy made you do it. Your behavior with him has almost ruined me. Baldwin's daughter told us everything!"

Avicia gasped. Matilda's enmity and fury knew no bounds.

Now, she regretted that Edric had convinced her not to flee Lille, when the opportunity presented itself. Instead, they had returned with the dead bird and admitted their wrongdoing. His status as a guest protected him. He had earned little more than stares of condemnation. She suffered alone for what they had done together.

Rudolf continued, "Matilda told me how he looked at you when he first arrived. His eyes followed you everywhere. You encouraged his attentions! Little whore…."

"I am not!" Her breath escaped in a ragged sigh, tinged with fear. "I swear on my mother's soul, I never encouraged him in anything."

"Do you deny he met with you alone in the mews today? Did you arrange your meeting beforehand?"

"It did not happen that way. I often went to the mews and found him there in these last weeks. We have always spoken in the presence of the falconer. Edric shared my love for the fine birds in the mews. Today, he wanted to see the new merlin. I told him she belonged to Matilda. He knew I was one of her attendants. I should have refused him. Please, do not blame Edric, milord."

"Oh, Edric is it? You have grown overly familiar with him!"

He grabbed her wrists and dragged her from the pallet, hauling her up against him. Pungent ale soured his breath. With massive arms, legs and a barrel-shaped chest, his strength overwhelmed her.

"Hold still, damn you. What did you do with him in the darkness of the mews? Did he touch you?"

Her shock outweighed the pain-filled flames blazing across her torn flesh. She lowered her gaze. Could he know all that had happened? Did he suspect Edric had kissed her earlier? One brief, stolen kiss that had distracted her while the merlin flew toward its unforeseen end.

"You cannot look at me because your eyes would reveal the truth."

He grasped her chin and forced her gaze upward. "A midwife shall examine you tonight. I must have the truth. If he has ruined you, not even Godwin of Wessex shall protect him from my wrath."

He left her without another word.

Avicia shuddered and collapsed in despair on her pallet. She had shamed her family with her dim-witted actions. She acted the fool for a boy who would never see the agony and humiliation she now endured.

In the chapel at Lille, Edric turned from the Crucifix at the altar and looked toward his mother, Lady Emmeline. She paced the length of the nave again and stirred the rushes in her wake. A silk girdle wound about her hips and smoothed the lines of her garments. A silver filigree circlet held her headrail in place, which concealed hair the same color as Edric's own.

At his father's insistence, he had accompanied his mother to Flanders six weeks before, in the retinue of Aelfwig Wulfnothson, abbot of Winchester and younger brother of Godwin of Wessex. Before her marriage to Edric's father, Lady Emmeline had attended the half-sister of Baldwin of Flanders, Judith. Now, Godwin wanted a marriage between his third son Tostig and Judith. Tunwulf Grim, Edric's father believed his wife could persuade a reluctant Judith to accept the marriage.

Since their arrival, Emmeline had spoken only Flemish, despite her fluency with the Saxon tongue. She wanted Edric acquainted with his Flemish heritage, but since the disaster with the merlin, he believed she regretted their visit.

She halted her relentless pacing and strode toward him, placing her bejeweled fingers on his shoulders. Worry etched itself in the lines of her heart-shaped face.

"I forgive you. You are a *thegn*'s son. Women of loose morals shall always seek your company."

He shook his head. He did not want, or seek her forgiveness. Only Avicia could absolve him of his misery.

"Mother, is the girl's punishment not enough? Must you call her whore, too?"

She continued, "I saw your regard for her while she stood at the whipping post. The infatuation is beneath you. What did you do in the mews, alone with her?"

His silence seemed all the answer she needed. The intensity of her green-eyed glare made him ashamed. Before, he had felt remorse about only one thing. Avicia took the punishment meant for him. He had convinced her no one would see them leave the mews with the merlin. He had not anticipated what would happen afterward, or how she would suffer for it.

"I have told you the truth of our encounter."

Guilt slammed him in the stomach. Something else had happened. He had kissed Avicia in the meadow, an impulsive act that made her gasp and release the merlin's jesses. Then, it flew toward its doom.

He began again. "Neither of us meant for the bird to die. It was an accident, Mother. Avicia should not suffer the blame alone."

"You shall not speak her name again!"

A low growl escaped his throat. When he turned from her, she stroked his shoulders.

"Dearest, you know the value of a hunting bird. The girl is fortunate she did not lose her hand. Only her relationship to Count Rudolf of Aalst prevented it."

Edric spun and looked at her, incredulous. "I cannot believe you would condone such brutality."

She gave a flippant wave of her hand. "The girl learnt her lesson. I believe you learned from this incident, too. Consequences ensue for every action in life. Now come, it is time for dinner."

"I am not hungry."

Her thin lips brooked no refusal. "Edric of Newington, you shall not shame me further! Dine with us and forget the girl."

He stared her down and never flinched. When she returned his gaze steadily, he sighed. "Allow me a moment's peace, Mother, and I shall follow directly."

After she had left him, he expelled a heavy, weary sigh. He cupped his face in his hands with a groan. "Avicia."

"It does no good, young master, no good at all."

He turned at the voice of his father's chaplain, Alwine of Newington, who spoke in their native Saxon tongue. Father Alwine had accompanied them across the Channel. No harsh criticism reflected in his doe brown eyes. Edric never expected it. Father Alwine was also his paternal granduncle and personal tutor.

Pain knifed Edric's heart. "The girl took the whipping for my sake."

Father Alwine clasped his shoulder in a gentle grip. "Do not lay blame upon yourself or the maid. There shall be pain and penitence enough for both."

Edric followed him toward the hall, bustling with activity. The aroma of roasted boar and stewed pheasant mingled with the smell of tart, ripened cheeses and freshly baked breads.

The Saxon retinue sat at the trestle tables. Edric strode toward them. He studied the thick, timber-framed trusses supporting the roof. Woven tapestries hung on the wall. Servants scurried past him with jugs of wine and beers.

His desperate attempt at avoiding the expected stares of disapproval failed. The courtiers, his fellow Saxons, and Rudolf of Aalst watched him relentlessly.

Two vacant seats at Emmeline's right waited for the chaplain and Edric, who took his seat with Father Alwine beside him.

Edric fought against retching urges with every swallow. If his mother noticed his discomfort, she gave no indication. Her slender fingers picked the bones from the pheasant. The slippery game meat barely soiled the tips.

Though little discussion occurred at their table, other courtiers showed no such reserve. Over the din of their exchanges, hounds yelped and scrambled for scraps from the table. Some of the dogs snatched a few choice morsels from an unfortunate diner's hand.

An hour later, Count Rudolf stood. His lips touched a chalice, encrusted with jasper and bloodstone, and he downed the wine in one gulp. When he scanned the room's occupants, his steely gaze pinned Edric. The reproach in his eyes spoke volumes of his displeasure.

Edric ducked his head and sopped up the last of his stew with a piece of bread. He lingered even after the meal ended. The servants removed the remnants of food and wiped down the trestle tables. When they eyed him pointedly, he left the hall.

He walked without direction and stumbled on a stone in his path. He kicked it aside in frustration. He stood in front of the mews where he had first met Avicia. Here, he shared his passion for the peregrine and fell in love with her.

He clenched his fists. The sky darkened and villagers hurried off into their homes. The rain broke through the clouds and pelted him with heavy drops. He stood immobile and turned his face toward the sky. The rainwater mixed with his tears.

CHAPTER 2

Kent, England
May 1048 CE

When Edric disembarked with his family at Dover, the cold morning dampness of his birth country chilled him. On the five-day voyage home, he had endured his mother's complaints about the rotten fish and the sluggish pace of the ship.

Now, she fretted, "Why did we come here? We should have landed closer to home, at Hythe."

"Mother, we arrived here only at Father's command. We shall rendezvous with Wulfstan since he is here for market day."

She ignored his explanation and issued terse instructions for their servants. She admonished them for their brutish handling of the travel trunks and satchels.

He stared out across the blue-black waters, lost in reverie.

She intruded again. "My lord, attend me if you please."

He groaned and clapped his fist against the lean muscle of his thigh. She insisted on formal address whenever the servants stood nearby. Her behavior infuriated him. Surely, their servants knew of his status.

He stalked to her side and helped her into the sidesaddle of her gray palfrey, while a stable boy held the reins. Father Alwine mounted his dun-brown mare.

Another stable boy brought Edric's stallion, Elfhar. Edric touched the white patch beneath the horse's forelock. The horse nickered in warm response before he nosed his master's hands and the folds of his damp, linen cloak.

Edric murmured, "Sorry boy, nothing today."

The horse's head drooped with disappointment.

Overhead, the kek-kek-kek of a peregrine falcon echoed through the clammy air. Edric studied the sky expectantly, waiting for a glimpse of the bird through the mist, but the falcon never reappeared.

With a sigh, he turned and admired how dawn illuminated one of the most stunning vistas in Kent. The white, chalky escarpment at Dover dominated the landscape. Black flint streaked the cliff face. A few trees dotted the ridgeline, but rock samphire with its little yellow florets thrived along the edges. On the east cliff, the church of Saint Mary-in-Castro stood beside the ancient Roman lighthouse, the octagonal Pharos. A stockade of stakes, set upright around the wooden fort, formed a barrier along the edge of the sand ridge.

"My lord? My lord, we must leave."

Edric ground his teeth together at his mother's command. Father Alwine coughed loudly behind his hands, smothering his laughter.

Wistful, Edric looked toward the Channel, before he patted Elfhar's shoulder and mounted. At the dock, servants packed the last of the trunks on the wagons. The belfry at the Pharos marked Prime.

Two servants and six men-at-arms coalesced around their party, as they rode from the beach toward the gatehouse. Edric paid the toll at the gate and they rode uphill. Four guards shielded them at the forefront, while the rest protected the mule-drawn wagons with their trunks and satchels. The party approached the river Dour.

Emmeline said, "My lord, might we slow the horses a little? I cannot appear windblown when your father sees me."

Father Alwine coughed loudly again. Edric turned in the saddle. He wished she might appear windblown and harried for once, if only it altered her usual composure. Still she sat resplendent in her sidesaddle, the epitome of elegant nobility. A silver circlet festooned with cornelian and sardonyx kept her headrail in place. Her green mantle, trimmed with ermine fur, remained wrinkle-free even after days spent on a dank ship.

They approached the market, set at the intersection of two main thoroughfares. Their steward Wulfstan, who stood with his arms folded across his chest, watched while the blacksmith shod a horse. Wulfstan had served the family at Newington since his youth, in the days of Edric's grandfather. Now, he uncrossed his arms with an audible grunt and approached them. "Welcome home, my lady. Lord Edric, Father Alwine."

Emmeline gave a barely perceptible nod.

Edric scowled at her before he smiled at Wulfstan. "Are you well?"

With a generous grin, Wulfstan replied, "Indeed, my lord. All has been well here in its usual manner,"

A lively twinkle glistened in Emmeline's eyes as she surveyed the marketplace.

"You do not object, my lord, if I purchase some textiles for your bride?"

She spent more coin and bartered with greater skill, better than anyone he knew, and he anticipated more of the same now.

He sighed. "Surely the heiress of Elham has enough."

Emmeline rolled her eyes. "I do not understand why you must be so disagreeable, my lord. I pray you reserve your ill temper for others more deserving of it." She paused and shied her horse a distance from him. "Heavens, but you do possess the boorish nature of my lord Tunwulf at times. You behave worse than your father in one of his foul moods."

"My father has an iron-will, Mother, but so do you. You can hardly fault me if my nature is less than malleable. I do not want Father blaming me for any delay."

"He shall not, for I shall tell him I ordered it."

Edric looked at Wulfstan, who said, "The blacksmith needs more time. I have asked for a new lock for the mews at Paddlesworth."

Father Alwine leaned forward in his saddle. "I shall accompany the lady."

Edric tugged Elfhar aside. His mother smiled at him before she nudged her palfrey onward. She, the chaplain, and two guardsmen maneuvered the crowded streets. Merchants besieged the party, with their offers of woven baskets and glass bowls, vessels and containers, metal utensils, cauldrons and pans. Emmeline waved them off and urged her mount toward the textile stalls.

Timber-framed buildings with wattle walls buffeted the marketplace. A few stone structures juxtaposed among them were the homes of wealthy merchants and landowners. The stench from rubbish pits ensured the rich and poor alike shared the same fouled air. Wild pigs nosed about the refuse in the streets.

A grime-covered criminal hung in despair at the pillory. His grizzled head and spindly arms drooped from holes in the hinged wooden boards, padlocked together. A placard at his side indicated the crime: theft. Edric shook his head. Sharpness Cliff, a place of execution, awaited the condemned man.

Emmeline returned with burdensome sacks while Wulfstan completed his business. The sun peeked through the mist as the riders took the old Roman road at the fringes of the Andredsweald forest, a vast mass of trees covering nearly two-thirds of southeast England.

Edric remained alert for danger despite the company of his father's loyal men-at-arms. Years before, his paternal grandfather had died in an ambush near the outskirts of the Andredsweald. Toward late evening, he glimpsed familiar patches of bracken. He quickened Elfhar into a steady gallop, escaping his mother's incessant conversation with Father Alwine.

Nestled in the midst of trees of holly, rowan, sweet chestnut, willow, birch and the ever-present oak, stood Newington's tiny village. Edric's great-grandmother had inherited the property at the deaths of her parents. Since then, the family prospered. The villagers' single-roomed homes dotted strips of land, some with a small patch for cultivating wild garlic or mint. The fields and pastures grew barley, wheat, oats, rye, and beans at intervals.

Edric cheered. "Home!"

His exultant cry scattered the birds nestled in the trees.

Guardsmen stood stalwart at the opened gate of the timber stockade. The stakes enclosed an acre. Edric slowed his pace, and matched his mother and Father Alwine.

The blacksmith and his apprentice at the forge bowed in greeting. Penned cattle and two oxen lowed in their enclosure. Edric eyed the boughs of holly that decorated the wooden chapel. His family usually worshipped there, instead of Saint Nicholas' church in the village. The newly built bower-house, constructed for his father's guests and retainers, reminded him of the fate that awaited him. Directly ahead, stood the hall and at its solid oak door, the lord of Newington waited.

Edric studied his mother. He often wondered how she endured such a formidable man as his father. No fear or hesitation showed in her expression. Her emerald gaze flickered and her cheeks brightened.

Father Alwine dismounted first and exchanged pleasantries with his lord. Then Tunwulf Grim glared at Edric with eyes more frigid than the North Sea, until he slid from his horse's back.

The only son of Leofsige and his widow Eanflaed of Tickenhurst, Edric's father earned his appellation "Grim" for his eternally stone-faced expression. Four jagged scars ran almost the extent of his face from his left eye to his chin, the mark of an encounter with a bear in his youth. Tunwulf's matted, yellow hair and beard gave him a somewhat grizzled appearance. His sturdy frame supported powerfully built arms and legs. A thick barrel chest coupled with club-like hands warned of his prowess. Bronzed flesh glowed with vitality.

Edric bowed stiffly then straightened. "I pray you are well, Father."

Tunwulf made no reply. Instead, he took Emmeline by the waist and aided her dismount, setting her gently on her feet. A spark of satisfaction filled his gaze. Not a word passed between them for a length of time.

Then, she whispered, "The sight of you pleases me greatly, my lord."

In a gruff baritone, Tunwulf replied, "I thank God for your safe return, my lady."

A heavy undercurrent of emotion beneath the polite exchanges charged the air. Their mutual gazes held more than quiet admiration.

Edric stubbed the ground with the tip of his shoe. He always felt like an interloper in the presence of his parents' accord. A jolt of envy struck him. His heart longed for Avicia. He remembered her heart-shaped face, her melodic laughter, the gracefulness of her hands while she handled the merlin at Lille, and the feel of her lips beneath his. Memories flooded his mind.

Tunwulf Grim asked, "Did our son comport himself well in Flanders?"

Edric shook his head and focused on his mother. He frowned at the question, but also dreaded the answer.

Emmeline glanced at him. Purpled skies framed her image in a severe, foreboding backdrop.

"He behaved in his usual manner, my lord."

He worried whether she would reveal the truth later. Though fearful and uncertain, he fell into step beside Father Alwine, behind his parents.

Newington's hall had existed unchanged since the time of Edric's grandfather, until Emmeline ordered divisions of the hall with screens.

A passageway led from the pantries, larder, and kitchen area at the eastern end. The living space and sleeping rooms occupied the western end of the house. The aromas of fresh bread in the pantry and roasted meat in the larder permeated the hall.

A fire crackled in the central hearth. Smoke escaped through a hole in the roof. Two large windows at the northern and southern ends of the hall allowed the only natural light into the structure. Sparse furnishings filled the hall, home of Lord Tunwulf and his family, which also included Edric's grandmother, Eanflaed, who preferred her solitude. Benches and tables, which were routinely set in place at mealtimes, now lined the walls. Interspersed among them were a few linden chests and two small cupboards.

Edric shuffled his feet and sighed, hesitant about joining his parents at the table.

Father Alwine urged him on. "Wulfstan assured me that Odgiva saved one of her delicious pigeon pies for our meal."

Edric slept poorly and woke long after dawn on the next morning. He searched for his parents but instead met Wulfstan in the hall, who told him Tunwulf and Emmeline had ridden off just after Mass at the chapel.

"Do you know where they went, Wulfstan?"

With a curious smirk, the steward said, "They went to the woods. My lady mentioned her desire for wild nuts."

Edric shook his head, puzzled, but he knew of only one clearing in the woods where nuts and berries grew. He saddled Elfhar and rode through the timber gate toward the south, past the village and fields.

Shortly after he entered the forest, he sighted his parents' horses, but he saw neither of them. Then, the deep rumble of a male groan and an answering feminine giggle echoed from a clump of trees at his left. He dismounted and crept forward. Through the thicket, he spied his parents and almost fell backward in shock.

Emmeline sat astride his father with her torso bared, her skin flushed pink and her head thrown back in abandonment. Her curly golden locks cascaded over her husband's muscular thighs. Tunwulf's burly hands kneaded and stroked her pale breasts. She caressed her husband's bared, broad chest. Her nails rippled across the hard mass of muscle along his belly. With her skirts hiked up, she exposed slender legs up to the tops of her thighs.

Tunwulf said, "When you suggested an early morning ride, I should have known your intent."

She laughed again. The rich, throaty sound startled Edric and made him uncomfortable. Their behavior in presumed privacy shocked him, since they always acted so decorously before others.

Embarrassed, he backed away, but his father's baritone voice made him stop. "When Godwin arrives later this month, we shall have no time to ourselves."

"He comes so soon, husband?"

Edric tried secreting himself behind a nearby bush, but rustled the shrubbery.

Tunwulf sat up and pressed Emmeline close with a burly hand.

"What is it?" she whispered.

He said, "Hush. I thought I heard something."

"Be still, husband, it was likely some woodland creature."

Edric held his breath until she nuzzled Tunwulf's bearded cheek and drew his full attention again.

"I confess, Emmeline. Our son's future concerns me. This marriage to the heiress of Godwin's choice troubles me."

The admission stunned Edric. His father had never showed an interest in him, and instead tolerated him, at best.

"She brings our son the estate at Elham," Emmeline said. "The king has approved the match for over a year. Why should it concern you now?"

"Godwin of Wessex is the most powerful magnate in England. I hate how he foists his goddaughter off on us. The girl is a widow of one of his *thegns* and has been his son Sweyn's mistress. The dishonor tarnishes her forever. Is this woman a good match for our son? Can he tame her wild nature?"

Fury roiled in Edric's stomach. First, his parents forced him into this marriage, now he discovered the girl was no better than a common whore was.

Emmeline shook her head. Golden curls shimmered in the morning sun. "Tunwulf, you cannot believe Earl Sweyn's version. Cynwise of Elham lost both her parents at barely eleven years old. She became a wife and widow in short order at age sixteen. She had no protection. Only she and Sweyn know the truth, but I think he took advantage of her. You know enough of his nature. By the rood, Tunwulf, he took Abbess Edgiva of Leominster for his mistress and sired a child with her. Now, Godwin has approached our king and bartered his goddaughter in marriage. Yet, it is better she should marry our son than be subject to Sweyn."

"I would have preferred Edric's wife chaste, her maidenhood assured."

"Godwin and his family always do as they please, my love, whether in the abuse Cynwise suffered, or our son's hasty marriage. It has been so since the time of your great-grandmother. She fared worse than Cynwise of Elham."

Edric hung his head in shame. His great-grandmother Leofflaed had allowed Godwin's grandfather, Aethelmaer Cild, to entice her into a handfasted marriage, which the Church had not recognized. Leofflaed had borne him twin sons, Edric's grandfather Leofsige and his granduncle, Father Alwine, before he abandoned her. Blood bound Edric's ancestors to the most powerful family in England. Whenever Godwin's forbearers had acknowledged the bond in the past, Edric's kin always acquiesced to their demands. Now, Godwin forced him into a marriage with his wanton goddaughter.

Emmeline's voice returned him to the present. "Worry for our son later. We must take this time for ourselves."

She nipped Tunwulf's jaw line. Her pink nipples brushed against his bronzed chest. When he raised her hips, she leaned back with a languorous sigh, exposing her throat. She rocked against him. His teeth scored her breasts.

While his parents remained engrossed in each other, Edric led Elfhar out of the woods without a sound.

CHAPTER 3

Lille, Flanders
May 1048 CE

A gentle shake on her shoulder stirred Avicia from sleep. Biota stood at her side. "Rouse yourself and dress. Matilda shall be furious if you are late."

She rose from her pallet in the corner. "Then it is true, nurse? I am still one of her attendants?"

Biota's pale blue eyes brimmed with joy. Avicia hugged her while ignoring the dull ache in her back. She washed her face and readied for the day.

While her nurse braided her hair in two plaits, Gisele entered the room. "You are not ready yet!"

"Soon, milady," Biota answered. She draped a large square of linen over Avicia's head and held it in place with red twine.

"Cover her ears!" Gisele snapped.

Biota pulled the cord tighter and secured the headcloth.

With her back to Gisele, Avicia rolled her eyes heavenward. The Church's teaching about the sensuality of a woman's ears of all places seemed ridiculous. Surely, no one believed the Virgin Mary conceived through her ear for the preservation of her chastity.

Biota bowed before she took the bedding outdoors.

When Avicia turned, Gisele reviewed her appearance. "Do not think Matilda's displeasure has abated. She allows your return to her service because of my influence. Keep your mind fixed upon your duties. It helps that the English have left us."

Avicia stabbed her feet into the leather turnshoes.

"Do you hear me, girl? They went north on one of the Flemish merchant ships. Now, you may do your duty without further distraction."

Avicia said nothing, brushing the folds of her garment.

Gisele grasped her chin, nails digging into the flesh. "He has left you, forever. You shall never see the Englishman again."

When she released her grip, Avicia skirted around her and left the room.

More than a week after the whipping, pain flared along her shoulders down to her tailbone, though lessened. Halfway down the hall, she paused and looked behind her. Gisele had not followed her.

With a deep intake of breath, she took familiar steps toward the mews. A light mist hovered over the ground, evidence of the first morning rain. The waterlogged earth squished beneath her turnshoes. She treaded carefully through the men-at-arms and villagers already at their toil before dawn. With a silent prayer to Saint Catherine, she hoped no one marked her progress.

A sharp sensation tingled along her spine. She ignored it and fled inside the mews. The door creaked on its hinges.

"Who goes there?" the old falconer asked over his shoulder. The winged occupants of the room chorused their alarm. The birds demanded quiet in their domain.

She drew the heavy oak door closed and leaned against the portal. Her heart hammered in her chest.

The timber-framed mews housed peregrine falcons, blue-grey goshawks, long-winged harriers and the fierce merlins caught late last fall at the time of their migration. The falconer's brown kestrel also enjoyed the comfort of the mews. Two slated windows allowed enough light and air in, keeping the birds comfortable.

Opposite the enclosures for each type of raptor, an eye-level bow perch stood in a darkened corner of the room, with the worktable in the middle of the space. Eyes downcast, Avicia avoided the enclosure where a single merlin sat. The female had died because of her actions, but the male with his slate-blue wings remained. When he sighted her, he echoed a short, sharp vocalization. She wondered if he recalled her secretive entry inside the place, where she had taken the female from its enclosure.

Then, she shook her head and dismissed the notion, but her cheeks heated again with the memory of her indiscretion with Edric. She had thought of him often in her days of rest. He had known as much about falconry as she had.

"I said who goes there?" The falconer's voice stirred her from idle thoughts. With Edric returned home, she must forget him.

She cleared her throat. "Thiedard, how do you fare?"

The lure fell from his hands. Then, he bent and retrieved it from the floor of packed dirt and sand.

"Milady, you should not be here."

"I had to come." She licked dried lips before moving to his side.

He swerved toward her. She halted in her tracks and drew back. His face bore fresh, reddened bruises beneath the eyes and around his nose. A jagged, puckered scar gouged across the pockmarked surface of his cheek.

"Thiedard, what happened to you?"

"They punished me, milady, for your offense. Count Rudolf ordered it. He said if I had secured the mews, you could not have entered."

She hung her head in shame. "You suffered because of me. I am so sorry."

He turned from her. "I am a peasant and you are a noble. You should not feel sorry for me. You should not be here. We may both be in trouble if you stay."

"I was careful that no one saw me."

"I pray you were more careful than last time."

The sharpness of his voice rang through the mews. A chorus of broken cries issued from the raptors before they quieted again. Her head drooped in despair. He resented her with compelling reason. He had indulged her fascination with falconry from the time of her arrival at Lille five years before, and she repaid him now with treachery.

At ten years old, she and Biota had been the only survivors of a fire in which her parents, Thurston de Manneville and Godalinda, perished. In the past, Count Rudolf must have thought it advantageous if his younger sister wed the third son of a minor Norman lord. Avicia doubted her uncle still believed the marriage benefited his interests, for Godalinda had produced only four stillborn sons before Avicia's birth.

With a sigh, she recalled how her father had introduced her to falconry. Six years old and perched high on his shoulders, she loved nothing better than watching the birds in flight. Her mother often chided Thurston for his behavior, but for Avicia, those childhood memories were the happiest of her existence. The fire had changed everything.

She looked at Thiedard again, who selected two strips of cow leather from a bucket. First, he pulled hard on them and then laid the hide on the worktable. With a thin charcoal reed, he traced an outline of four pieces, which he then cut from the leather. He selected one pair and wielded the knife, slicing a hole in the strips. He removed the cloth cover of a wooden vat and dipped his hand inside. When he withdrew it, greasy, yellow wool fat coated his fingers. He worked the mixture into the leather.

She cleared her throat. "Can I watch you make the new jesses and anklets for the merlin?"

"You should not be here. What if someone sees you?"

Her gaze darted toward the merlin's enclosure again. Guilt stabbed at her. The coldness of his voice heightened her pain. He blamed her for his misery, and she deserved his reproach.

"Do not make me go just yet. Please."

He sighed for she already knew the answer from him. "You are a noble. I cannot make you do anything."

His clipped tone betrayed his continued resentment. Yet, she lingered at his side. She drew hope from the fact that he would not make her leave. Perhaps, she could remain a little while. Surely, Matilda remained abed and never missed her.

He drew on a long leather glove and covered his forearm. He reached into another cask and withdrew a bloodied piece of meat.

She leaned forward. "Is that skylark?"

"It is." He opened the cage and swept the meat just under the bird's beak. When it darted forward, he drew back.

She nodded. "I remember how you first let me feed one of them. You once told me skylark was the merlin's favorite."

He said nothing, only passing the flesh under the bird's beak again. Whenever it reached for the morsel on the glove, he drew back. Falconer and bird repeated their movements until the merlin alighted on the glove. He pecked at his reward.

She stared at the floor. Shame overwhelmed her again. She had lured the other merlin out of her cage with the same methods.

With the merlin on his forearm, Thiedard affixed the bird's jesses, the swivel and leash. The merlin looked past him and watched her with a wary gaze. Entranced, she edged closer, but the falcon raised its wings and opened its beak. Its dusky eyes locked with hers.

"When he is fearful, he opens his beak," Thiedard murmured over his shoulders.

Guiltily, she stepped back. He was right to chastise her. She had already caused enough trouble in the mews.

He soothed the bird with a gentle touch of his hand. Soon, it lowered its wings, though the tiny head bobbed and darted. Occasionally, it eyed her. She shifted her stance.

"I know you do not want me here, Thiedard. I am sorry for all my uncle and his men did."

"It is the lot of a peasant to bear the punishments God delivers."

"God had no hand in it!" All the birds trilled noisily at her heightened tone. She crept closer and whispered, "Count Rudolf is cruel. He let them whip me. He did not have to hurt you, too."

"He is a nobleman. He has every right."

Thiedard swept past her without another word. He opened the door and went outside. He set the merlin down on an eye-level block perch made of stone. It alighted on the leather-covered surface, an inverted triangle. He affixed the leash to a ring at the base of the stone spike.

Then he returned to the mews. "You should leave now and never come back. I do not want Count Rudolf or his men to find you here."

She nodded and stumbled to the doorway, wiping tears of regret. She would never visit the mews again. She could not risk it, for Thiedard's sake.

Outside, myriad hues of blue and gray still colored the sky, but dawn approached. Thiedard hefted a cask of fresh water on his shoulder. He gazed at her briefly before he shook his head and re-entered the mews.

"Why are you here, Avicia?"

She jerked at the harsh sound of Rudolf's voice. He closed the distance between them in long strides, his retinue of guards behind him. Though his proximity made her tremble, she stood her ground. He looked beyond her toward the closed door of the mews. His gray eyes darkened like a fierce, gathering storm.

"I knew you possessed your mother's bold nature, but must I question your sanity, too? You dared visit the mews once more, after what happened?"

"Please, milord, let me explain."

"Do not lie to me! Thanks be to God I posted one of my men in the courtyard."

She looked past him at the men-at-arms who idled, attuned to their conversation.

"Everyone blamed Thiedard for my actions." She paused and drew back, meeting Rudolf's fearsome visage again. "I did not think you would have your men beat him."

His hand closed on her arm. "He got what he deserved."

"Does Baldwin of Flanders know what you have done to his falconer?"

His hold tightened. Pain flared along her forearm. A whimper rose and died in her throat. If the heartless brute could harm an innocent man, she expected no better treatment from him.

"Even if he knew, he would consider it the right course," he said. He released her with a hard jerk. She stumbled in the mud but righted herself.

"I sent Gisele to wake you. Did you not see her today?" he asked. His gravelly voice chilled her. Though fearful, she returned his stare.

"I woke earlier," she whispered. "When she arrived, I was already dressed."

The corners of his mouth crinkled. He stepped closer. "I can believe it. You are so like your mother. She always roused herself before dawn for prayers."

His nostalgic look betrayed his affection for his sister. She stared at him, surprised at the depth of emotion he revealed. Godalinda had never spoken with affection for him.

His gaze hardened. "Do you know Matilda requires your service?"

"I know, but she does not often rise before Tierce. I shall attend her now."

"Contemplate the great favor she shows you while you wait upon her today. She could have dismissed you from her service. Where would you be then? Without her favor, you would return to Aalst in disgrace and burden me."

She lowered her gaze. "Then, I am only a burden to you. My mother was your sister. Why did you raise me if I am such trouble?"

He pinched her arm. "You were no trouble until you became willful and deceitful. I placed you here, so I might have an ear to the events at court. What other purpose could you have possibly served? Yet, you have failed. You are not clever enough for Matilda of Flanders to share her confidences."

Now she knew the truth. He wanted a spy in the Flemish court. He placed her here only for that purpose. He had not cared for her at all, except for what she gained for him through her service.

He continued, "Gisele influenced Matilda's decision. She pleaded for your return to service. You should be grateful to her, too." He glared at her, as though his wife's generosity came at a heavy cost.

She clasped her hands together, fighting the urge to slap him across the face. "I am thankful for Countess Gisele's efforts, milord. I am happy Matilda has forgiven me."

He scowled. "She has not absolved you of blame. You must earn her clemency. Keep from the mews. If ever you forget my command, I shall ensure the falconer does not."

He stalked away from her, intent on the mews.

Bitter tears of frustration stung her eyes, but Avicia swiped at them. Her impetuousness meant more trouble for Thiedard. She must learn better control, or others would always suffer for her mistakes.

CHAPTER 4

Newington, Kent, England
May 1048 CE

Within two weeks of Edric's return, Tunwulf announced the imminent arrival of Earl Godwin Wulfnothson. Bedlam descended on Newington. Curses bellowed across the courtyard and led to unrestrained fights. Odgiva, Emmeline's Flemish cook, often boxed the kitchen boys' ears.

One morning, Edric pushed aside the heavy leather skin that partitioned his sleeping area in the family quarters. His mother swung toward him and smoothed her pea green kirtle. Her arrival appeared planned, with a purpose in mind. He shook his head, his lips quivering against a smirk. She had not deceived him.

"Good morning, my lord." She cupped his jaw line where new growth sprouted. "Did you not sleep well? You look haggard."

In truth, he had scarcely slept all week. Concerns about the marriage and Avicia's fate remained. His heart rebelled against the thought that he would never see her again.

"Your father wishes to speak to you," Emmeline said.

"Why?"

She frowned at his gruff voice. "Have you forgotten your betrothed arrives with the Earl of Wessex?"

"How can I? It is all you and Father can speak of these days."

When she exhaled, the weary exasperation in her voice amused him.

"My sweet son, please go to Tunwulf. He waits at the stables with Bavo and Elfhar saddled."

He left her with a stiff nod, just before the cook barreled in their direction.

"Good morning, Odgiva," he said, with a smile. In her usual manner, she snarled and bared her teeth at him.

Edric grinned as the anticipated fight began behind him. "My lady, the fennel roots are rotten! How am I to make braised fennel without them? There is no ginger either…."

He emerged in the courtyard under the pale light of morning, whistling cheerfully with a casual stride until he reached the stables. Tunwulf waited with the two horses and his ever-present frown in place. Edric quickened his pace.

"You took your time." His father tossed him Elfhar's reins and mounted Elfhar's sire, Bavo. Edric settled into the saddle in resigned discomfort and followed his lead.

They passed villagers at their toil in the wheat fields. Broad pasture bordered the cropland and the dirt road north. Under holly and rowan trees, they rode in the direction of Paddlesworth, a hamlet that the family had held for three generations.

The thick, awkward silence maddened Edric. Yet, he preferred it more than a conversation with his father. The sun glinted through the canopy of leaves. His mind drifted toward satisfying thoughts of his yearly escape to Paddlesworth, where he and his mother would go hawking.

Discomfort weighed upon him, and though the frigid glint in Tunwulf's eyes warned him, if he tried for conversation, perhaps their time together would pass quickly.

"I look forward to our annual visit, Father. I hope the falconer shall be ready for us."

"I suspected some idle desire captured your mind." An irritated sneer rippled across his father's face. "That is one of your faults, always in a daydream, your mind never on the things which should occupy you."

Tunwulf nudged Bavo into a gallop. The distance between the pair mirrored their emotional divide.

Edric called out, "What are my other faults, my lord?"

His father slowed his horse, which matched Elfhar's canter.

"What did you say to me, boy?"

"I asked, what are my other faults?"

"You dare repeat it."

Tunwulf's blow landed with a brutal thud against Edric's right temple. His head jerked in response, but he never swayed in the saddle.

He pinched the bridge of his nose and squinted, before focusing on his father's cold stare. "I ask again, what are my other faults?"

Shock glazed Tunwulf's expression. His thick, golden eyebrows flared upward. When he chuckled, his voice thickened with contempt. "You are too impulsive. You let your emotions dictate your actions without careful forethought. Second, you accept everything without question and never wonder if you should do as commanded. Except for this new display, I would think you had no spine at all."

Though shamed, Edric never hesitated. "You count these as my only faults?"

His father spat on the ground between the two horses. "I never said you possessed only two faults. Those two came foremost to mind."

"May I defend myself against your accusations?"

"I do not ask you to defend yourself."

"Yet, you judge me every day, my lord. You measure me by your standards of manhood and find me inadequate. You say my mind is always idle. Yet I dream grand visions, my lord, of a better life in service of the king, beyond that of a mere *thegn* who answers for two or three holdings. If I am impulsive, it is because my heart guides my actions. I accept without question because I am loyal and respectful of those who command me."

When his father cocked his head, as if he mulled the words, a small measure of satisfaction filled him. Then, Tunwulf nudged Bavo into a gallop again. Edric rubbed his throbbing temple and followed his father.

When they reached Paddlesworth, the reeve met them at the outskirts of the hall. While he and Tunwulf spoke, Edric idled between Bavo and Elfhar. The black stallion snorted and nudged his master with his muzzle. Edric held the reins and patted his horse's forelock. He felt more affinity for the animal than he had with Tunwulf Grim.

Later, the pair returned to Newington in the usual silence. When his father slowed Bavo, Edric also reduced Elfhar's gait.

Tunwulf said, "I wanted you with me to understand the administration of the estate you shall hold at Elham."

Edric nodded.

His father halted Bavo. "You shall be responsible for a large property, yet you say nothing. The burden does not concern you?"

"God shall guide my actions. I shall not fail you."

"Listen well, Edric. My father kept me underfoot. I had no influence in the management of Newington. His death thrust me into the role of landowner, unprepared for the responsibility. I would not have you meet with the same difficulties. If I am harsh with you, it is because I expect more of you than I was able to accomplish at your age."

Edric gaped in stunned silence. He never knew until now, how much Tunwulf resented Leofsige. "As I have said, I shall not disappoint you, my lord."

Emmeline awaited them at the door of the hall. Concern flushed her face a faded pink. "Where have you been, my lords? Godwin's messenger has arrived. The herald enjoys the comfort of our hall. He told us Godwin is a short distance from Newington."

She wrung her hands. "Two of the kitchen boys fell ill, and the boar meat is rancid. My Odgiva has been after me all morning. She is such a difficult woman."

"I do not know why you brought her from Flanders," Tunwulf grumbled.

Emmeline frowned. "My father insisted on it."

Tunwulf grinned. "Wretch, she inflicts her foul moods upon everyone and none may be happy until she is so." He wheeled his stallion around and nodded toward his wife. "Tell Odgiva she shall have her boar within the hour."

Edric watched his father until he disappeared behind a line of trees just outside the gate. Then he dismounted and turned his horse over to a waiting stable boy, before following his mother into the house.

Father Alwine sat by the hearth with Godwin's messenger, an East Anglian bard. While Emmeline listened to the recitation of the battle of Maldon, an epic about a Saxon clash with the Norsemen, Edric said to the chaplain, "Please come with me to the chapel."

Outside, village women hung more boughs of holly at the chapel door. Mothers admonished their young daughters who looked on their future master with admiration.

Father Alwine opened the doors and Edric followed. He closed the portal behind him with a heavy thud. Near the altar, they sat on the lone, long bench reserved for the family.

Edric began, "I have concerns about this union. I fear the lady shall not be a good wife. I shall resent her past behaviors."

Father Alwine nodded. "You speak of the gossip about Lady Cynwise and Sweyn of Herefordshire. Give no ear to those stories."

"I have heard he bedded her."

"Did you know, my lord, last autumn I went to Elham, and counseled the lady and heard her confession?"

Edric frowned. "Where was I when you made this journey?"

"You were at Paddlesworth. You and Lady Emmeline were gone for a month. I sojourned with Lady Cynwise for three weeks. Confession is a sacred trust. I cannot tell you what she said. However, I caution you. Do not believe all you have heard."

Father Alwine leaned closer. "Other thoughts occupy you. You still worry for the girl at Lille."

"I cannot put her from my mind!" A ragged sigh tore from Edric's throat. "I still recall our first encounter. I went to the mews for the peregrines. Instead, I found Avicia."

When her brilliant beauty filled his thoughts, his whole body ached with a desire he could not restrain. She had stood at the enclosure, which held two merlins. Her profile to him, she remained intent on the birds, unaware of his scrutiny. He marveled at her striking loveliness, her pale brow, and the delicate, pink curve of her cheek. She had caught him unaware as she turned her gaze on him. Her pert nose flared and amusement danced on her lips. He lost his heart to her, a girl he could never forget.

The bench creaked under Father Alwine's weight. "Did you love this girl, my lord?"

"With all my heart I love her still."

"Then you must let her go."

Edric's heart pitched inside his chest. "That is your sage advice? I should let her go?"

"Either you shall accept her loss, or rail against it until bitterness consumes your heart. Do not sour your recollection with regrets."

Father Alwine rose and patted his shoulder. "I would see you spared such bitterness, good son. Meditate on this matter in peace. I must prepare the Mass."

Father Alwine disappeared inside the adjacent room, where he kept his vestments.

Edric stared after him. Could he do it, forget Avicia? Memories of her fired his blood. He seethed at the cruelty of a world that kept them apart.

❧

Before Sext, he returned to the house. He donned long trousers and cross-gartered them with strips of leather. He paired the green garment with a thigh-length tunic of the same color. Over this, he pulled on an over tunic with a key-shaped neck and girded it at the waist. His red linen cloak covered his shoulders in a half-circle shape with two yellow lines along the border. He grasped a round, bronze, cloak fastening, dotted with green and red jasper.

When Emmeline had offered it to him on the previous evening, she said, "For gentleness and love."

He pinned the mantle at his right shoulder, and wondered if he could expect such sentiments from his new bride.

Images of Sweyn and Cynwise abed whirled in his mind. He clenched his fists. "I shall have her fidelity and naught less."

He put on his turnshoes and left the room. He willed courage into every step. At the entrance of the hall, his father, mother, and Father Alwine stood, dressed resplendently. Tunwulf's green linen mantle billowed in the breeze.

Edric looked beyond them. In the yard, their guests reined in their horses. Godwin Wulfnothson dismounted first. His Nordic blue gaze scanned his environs with an icy glare reminiscent of Edric's father. Then Godwin swept Tunwulf into a bear hug. Companions of old, they embraced like friends. Yet Edric wondered how a friend could bully another into a marriage of convenience.

In height, Godwin and Edric's father matched each other. Except for the scars on Tunwulf's face, he and Godwin would have shared the same impressive features. Godwin's hair and beard gleamed white in the sun. He draped his commanding figure in the attire of a king. His long tunic and cloak, embroidered at the hems and cuffs with gold thread, were each in dark, sumptuous blue and red colors. His sword belt gleamed in the sunlight, festooned with a gold clasp and studded around its width.

When his father signaled him, Edric drew a deep breath and shuffled forward.

Godwin eyed him with a lazy smile.

"Your heir has grown in the last two years. The hairs on his chin are new." In a deep baritone, he addressed Tunwulf, though his stare lingered on Edric, who felt like a prized stud.

Tunwulf gestured toward Emmeline. "You know my lady."

Just before Edric's gaze fell, a dainty pair of shoes came into view, the leather dyed red and decorated with tiny gold bells. The shoes met the embroidered hem of a yellow kirtle, which disappeared under a cream-colored *gunna*. A belt studded with enameled gold cinched the waist of the *gunna*, which suggested full hips below and rounded breasts above. A red mantle draped the woman's shoulders. Her startled, dark blue eyes widened at the sight of him. Their color reminded him of the nighttime waters of the Channel.

"This is your intended, boy, Lady Cynwise of Elham."

At the sound of Godwin's voice, she dipped into a deep curtsey. Waves of raven-black hair strayed from beneath her headrail.

When Tunwulf cleared his throat, Edric groaned before he muttered, "Welcome to Newington, my lady."

"Thank you my lord," she replied, her voice inflectionless.

Godwin's laugh soon broke the interminable silence that followed. "I have known more warmth on a winter's day."

He patted Tunwulf's burly shoulder and chuckled. "I pray it is not years before they give you a grandson."

Edric's father made no reply but introduced his wife to Cynwise. The women shared a warm welcome and spoke with ease. His mother must have said something funny, because Edric's betrothed giggled. However, he frowned. The cold exchange between him and his future bride portended an unhappy union.

"Shall we retire to the hall?" Emmeline asked. "My cook prepares a fine feast. Earl Godwin's bard has promised to recite poems for our entertainment."

"I assumed we would unite these two young people now," Godwin said.

Edric's father and mother met Godwin's gaze with careful expressions. Cynwise's fair skin took on a chalky appearance. Her eyes filled with dread.

Emmeline began, "My lord earl, the marital feast is not ready."

Godwin dismissed her concerns with a wave of his brawny hand.

"Your chaplain is here. There is no reason we should wait."

Godwin signaled his traveling companions. Among them, four young women dismounted from their palfreys. Godwin took Cynwise's pale, slim hand in his and led her forward. Edric looked at his father, who placed his hand on his back, and shoved him onward.

At the door, the small party gathered. Tunwulf, Edric, and Godwin stood on the right while Cynwise with her four attendants and Emmeline gathered on the left. All the noise in the courtyard ceased. Wulfstan and some of the household servants idled near the door of the hall.

Father Alwine made the sign of the Cross. He grasped Cynwise's bare hand in his and held it aloft. Edric hesitated but then took his place. He hardly heard the chaplain's words. His gaze remained on the reluctant bride. She stared at the ground resolute, except for the tremors at the corner of her mouth. When Father Alwine tapped his shoulder, he jerked his gaze away from her.

The chaplain cleared his throat. "I said, Edric of Newington, do you take this woman Cynwise of Elham for your wife?"

Edric nodded but his father nudged him. He muttered, "I shall."

Cynwise's eyes misted. She stood rigid with terror.

Father Alwine instructed, "Repeat after me, my lord. I take thee, Cynwise of Elham now as my wife, in the name of the Lord. Amen."

Cynwise stared catatonically while he spoke. Then the chaplain followed the ritual with her. Strange how the fear betrayed in her countenance and actions never resonated in her voice. She spoke in a dull monotone, not the raw whimpers Edric had expected. For a wanton, she seemed passionless. Might there be some truth in Father Alwine's advice about her?

Her gaze jerked to his. He could not fathom why or how, but knew in an instant that she wanted something from him.

Godwin proffered the ring. At the baptismal font in the corner of the chapel, Father Alwine blessed and sprinkled the silver metal with holy water. He gave the ring to Edric who looked down at the band inlaid with crystal. The chaplain gave Cynwise's hand over and instructed him.

Edric moved the ring in turn from her thumb and index finger to her long finger, while he said, "In the name of the Father and of the Son and of the Holy Spirit."

He released her trembling, ghostly-white hand with haste and knelt with her before the chaplain, who blessed them. Father Alwine entered the chapel before returning with two tallow candles. When they stood, he gave one each to Edric and Cynwise. He led them, their relations, and the bride's attendants into the chapel, beyond a curtain separating the nave and chancel.

At the bridal Mass, Edric remained silent throughout the prayers, hymns, and biblical verses. His heart hammered inside his chest. He married a woman he could never love.

His mind echoed with the thought even while Father Alwine began the bridal benediction. Then he realized Cynwise knelt before the altar and glared up at him.

Father Alwine leaned forward. "My lord, please kneel."

His knees buckled. A square of linen came over his and Cynwise's heads, which the bridal attendants held. With his head down, Edric ignored the woman beside him.

"O Lord, your blessings upon your servant Cynwise," the chaplain intoned, "that she should be agreeable to her husband like Rachel, able like Rebecca and loyal like Sarah. Let her be fruitful, pure, and guiltless."

Edric turned toward his new bride sharply at those words. She met his stare and that damnable question filled her eyes again. After the benediction, the communion Mass followed.

Then, the attendants withdrew the linen cloth. Edric and Cynwise shared the cup of communion wine. She turned the vessel, and thereby avoided where his lips had touched the cup. He frowned at her.

Father Alwine gave him kiss of peace. In his turn, Edric leaned toward Cynwise. She offered her cheek, but he pressed his mouth against her fleshy lips. Her murky eyes flew to his.

Father Alwine solemnly said, "I now pronounce you man and wife."

CHAPTER 5

Lille, Flanders
January 1049 CE

In the bitter cold, Matilda of Flanders attended Mass. Afterward Avicia waited and shivered, while Matilda spoke with the English envoy, Brithric, the young grandson of Earl Leofric of Mercia. Heavy snowfall blanketed them. Matilda and the other women had donned their hooded linen cloaks lined with fur. Avicia enjoyed no such comfort. The wet and wintry precipitation chilled her to the bone in her short cape.

She stared at the pale-faced Brithric and wondered whether Matilda could not also see his sheepish expression and half-hearted shrugs, which answered all her inquiries. Whatever Matilda's regard for Brithric, Avicia knew he did not find her appealing. He finally begged her leave and hurriedly reunited with his entourage. Matilda sighed and clasped her hands over her heart. Avicia rolled her eyes heavenward.

The next day, she sat with her head bowed over her embroidery, in a corner of Matilda's room. Since her arrival at Lille, the other attendants had treated her with disdain. Each of the young, unmarried women came from the oldest and noblest of families in the country. They looked down upon her because her father had held no lands of his own.

"Lady Avicia!"

She looked up and found six pairs of expectant eyes on her. She blinked rapidly and wondered what she had done wrong now.

"You are not finished, while the other ladies and I have completed our tasks. Are you so useless, even at embroidery lessons?"

Matilda's melodic laughter filled the chamber. Her attendants joined in. Then Matilda rose from her cushioned stool. All the women of the Flemish court envied her subtle beauty and petite frame. Brilliant blue eyes rivaled her indigo colored garments. Her headcloth, secured with a gold and sapphire diadem, concealed flaxen hair except for a few stray strands.

Avicia coughed and the sound rattled deep in her chest. "I am sorry. If milady recalls, we were out in the cold yesterday. Now, I am unwell."

She swayed in her seat, as a sudden, dizzying wave of heat overwhelmed her.

"Your illness is not my concern." Matilda dismissed her words with a wave of her hand. "If your uncle cannot provide you with warmer garments, it is not my fault."

When she turned from her, Avicia said, "I would not be sick if we had not waited outside the church for so long. Had I not stayed with you, I would be well. In the end, Lord Brithric barely spoke with you before he rushed to re-join his retinue."

Matilda's stony gaze returned. "You dare blame me for your weakness. Tread carefully, or I shall warn your uncle of my displeasure. You should be grateful you remain at court. Do not think I have forgotten the trouble you caused me last spring."

A pained wheeze escaped Avicia. She cringed at the memory of the incident with Edric and the dead merlin. Though seven months passed, Matilda had often remarked on it.

Matilda covered her mouth and nose with her pale hand. "I shall send my physic to you. Perhaps bloodletting may cure you of this sickness. When I receive his report of your condition, you may return to my service but not before."

She swept from her room and her attendants followed. Avicia glared in their wake before she left.

Outdoors, she gathered her woolen cloak tighter about her shoulders. Brutal cold descended with ferocity this winter afternoon, a few days after the New Year. The bleak landscape at Lille mirrored her health and fortunes. Baldwin's stone fortress towered over her head, near the Duele River. Massive gray fortifications protected it on almost all sides. Within the courtyard, men-at-arms, servants, and nobles jostled each other. Despite the fetid smell of dank earth and gray clouds, the open air offered the freedom and serenity she had never found in anyone else's company, except perhaps with one person.

She closed her eyes and inhaled deeply. She should not have spoken so bluntly to Matilda. She should not have blamed her for the illness, or reminded her how Lord Brithric barely tolerated her.

Gruff demands for entry echoed beyond the gatehouse. The wooden entrance groaned before a band of riders galloped into the courtyard. Count Rudolf rode at the forefront of them. He had returned to Aalst last spring, and since then, he sent no word to her. A sense of foreboding warned her that his return would affect her.

The familiar dress of the men with him sparked memories of her father. One among the new arrivals stared across the courtyard at her with such familiarity, it bordered on rudeness. He was a yellow-haired man with a ruddy face, who wore the robes of a clergyman, yet he carried a sheathed sword. His beady eyes fixed on her, a hawk trained on its prey.

She jerked her face away and met the relentless gaze of another man.

Suddenly entranced, she studied his sculpted face with a cleft chin, high cheekbones, an aquiline nose and a mouth set in a thin, dry line. He wore black hair severely shaved at the back and sides of his head. Her eyes drifted downward. His red linen cloak covered chainmail. His deep, throaty laugh drew her gaze to his face again. He obviously took pleasure in her scrutiny. She blushed.

"Avicia, do not dare turn from us! Attend me."

Rudolf dismounted and met her on the steps.

She curtsied. "Milord, welcome to Lille."

"Why are you not with Matilda of Flanders?" His gruff voice betrayed his displeasure.

"She dismissed me for the day because I am unwell."

Rudolf groaned and rolled his eyes heavenward. "Can you do naught to please her?"

When she made no reply, he shook his head. "Where is she, in her chamber?"

"I am not certain, milord." She looked past him. Both the clergyman and the black-haired man eyed her boldly.

"Who are those men in your company, milord?"

He scowled at her question. "They are knights from Normandy."

She gasped. "Are they my father's relations? Have they come for me?"

He sniggered. "Why should anyone in Normandy care for you? They showed no concern for your welfare when your mother and father died. I inherited the burden, a thankless task. You have done little in these last five years."

She blinked away tears at his cruelty.

"Why have the Normans come then?"

"Their duke seeks an alliance with Baldwin."

"Why would he ally himself with a Norman, milord?"

He assumed his usual posture of superiority. "William the Bastard is Duke of Normandy. His father proclaimed him heir before his pilgrimage and subsequent death. William is a powerful man. Flanders would do well in an alliance with him. I shall convince Baldwin of this fact. They shall seal the alliance with the betrothal of William and Matilda. When they marry, the Normans shall remember my role in forging this union and reward me."

"Milord, what if Matilda does not want this bastard duke?"

"Have you lost what wits remain you, woman?" he asked. "Who cares what she wants? Matilda shall do what her father tells her!" He jerked his head toward the riders. "I have brought William's envoys to Lille with gifts. When she receives such inducements, she cannot reject William's claim. I shall ensure it."

She peeked at the men. Rudolf followed her gaze.

The black-haired Norman grinned again. The yellow-haired clergyman continued his scrutiny. His appraisal bothered her more than the first man's own. Rudolf's stare swung back to her, accusation in his eyes. She recoiled from his glare and fled inside.

She bypassed Matilda's room, where the door creaked slightly on its hinges. A shrill scream echoed beyond the wall and Avicia halted in her tracks. She returned to the door and peeked inside. Matilda sat on a stool. She ripped the threads from the tunic she had been embroidering earlier. Pink blotches marred her face and her eyes were puffy and red-rimmed.

She looked up. "Get out!"

Avicia jerked at the mournful sound of her voice, but she lingered in the doorway. Matilda tossed the ruined cloth aside and advanced on her.

"Did you hear what I said?"

"Milady, forgive me, but you are overwrought. Is there naught I can do to help you?"

"You? Help me!" Matilda laughed as she mimicked her tone. "You are useless! You could never help me. Leave me, and do not return until after you have seen the physic."

She stumbled backward and collapsed on the stool, before burying her face in her hands. Heavy sobs shook her slim shoulders. Avicia's heart cleaved, pity warring with her natural inclination to leave the selfish girl to her suffering. After all, Matilda had stood by and watched her whipped for a careless mistake.

"Why do you stand there? Do you stay only to torment me?" Matilda's eyes lit up with fiery accusation. "You take such joy in seeing my misery?"

"I do not, milady. I wish to help you. Shall I call one of your other attendants?"

"So they can laugh at me? They already whisper that I am a fool behind my back."

"Surely not!"

"I have heard them! I do not give you leave to contradict me."

Avicia edged closer. "If they cannot help you, then let me do so, milady. I shall not fail you, again."

Matilda hiccupped and wiped a hand across her nose. "Would you be willing to do something for me? To deliver a missive for me? It is not for prying eyes, especially not your own. If you betray me…."

"I shall not. You have but to command me, milady."

❧

Within minutes, Avicia loitered in the shadows of the church. She watched the entryway, as congregants entered and left in succession. The biting cold nipped at her flesh through the short cloak, but she dared not leave before she had completed her duty to Matilda.

At last, the English delegation exited the church. The envoy Brithric trailed them, as they crossed the courtyard, headed for the fortress. He had drawn a hood over his head, nearly down to his eyes, but thin hanks of his white hair escaped the folds of cloth. Just as he reached the steps, she approached him.

He smiled at her tentatively. Before he moved on, she clutched at the rich wool of his mantle. He jerked aside in surprise.

"I do not mean to startle you, milord," she whispered.

"Then remove your hand, milady. Mercy. Are all you Flemish women so forward?" Accusation embittered his tone and he sneered at her.

"I serve the purpose of another." She handed him a rolled parchment. "Please, will you take it?"

He drew back the hood. "What is it?"

"I cannot say. I have not read its contents."

When he snatched it from her, she drew back and clenched her jaw stiffly. He seemed rude and hardly worth Matilda's interest.

He broke the seal and read the letter. She stared at him expectantly. When he finished it, he tossed it at her and rushed to re-join the other Englishmen.

Avicia returned to Matilda, who sat alone on her stool. Her head cradled in her hands, she looked up. Then, on shaky legs, she rose to her feet. Her gaze drifted to the rolled parchment Avicia carried. She took the missive and noticed the broken seal. A sob escaped her. She shook and stumbled slightly.

Avicia grasped her shoulders before she tumbled. She did not resist as Avicia drew her near, resting her chin atop the diminutive girl's head.

❧

Brightly colored tapestries hung along the walls of the Flemish court. Beneath them stood a multitude of people dressed in deep hues of varied colors. In the audience chamber, the rulers of Flanders outshone them all.

Baldwin wore a gleaming gold crown slightly askew on his yellow hair. A broad smile softened his ruddy face. His wife Adele, daughter of the king of France, clasped her slim, bejeweled fingers in a pose of sedate modesty.

Avicia hovered in the recesses of the room. Her uncle approached with the Norman envoys.

A herald announced their arrival in a strident voice. "Count Rudolf of Aalst and the envoys of Duke William of Normandy may draw near."

"Welcome to Lille, my lords." Baldwin's voice squeaked. He held out his pudgy hand. Each finger except the thumb bore a ring set with a ruby or sapphire.

Rudolf kissed the hand he proffered. "You honor me, Count Baldwin with your gracious welcome."

The Normans bowed, though Avicia thought their movements stiff and reluctant.

"Why have you come?"

"Duke William seeks friendship. I pray you shall hear his envoys and accept a token of his house."

Rudolf snapped his fingers. One of his retainers set a wicker enclosure on the floor and removed the linen cloth. The peregrine falcon inside chorused her alarm immediately. Her long, pointed wings thrashed against the cage. Her black head bobbed. She revealed her white throat from which a short, sharp vocalization issued. The bird's obvious distress pained Avicia, but she kept her distance from the cage.

Baldwin leaned forward on his gilded throne. "It is a fine gift you have brought, Count Rudolf."

"It is but one of many from William of Normandy intended for Matilda."

"Indeed? Then news of your niece's carelessness with my daughter's prized bird has reached Caen? Did Duke William think one falcon might replace another?"

Avicia pressed back against the wall. Though no one took any note of her, shame filled her at Baldwin's reference. Rudolf's visage darkened, but he never looked in her direction.

"I should not make sport of the issue," Baldwin sobered. "It is in the past. Let William's emissary make his address."

Heavy booted steps sounded. The man who approached seemed a larger version of the black-haired Norman Avicia had admired. He possessed the same cleft chin and aquiline nose. Despite the craggy lines and crinkles at the corners of his eyes, the resemblance was uncanny. She wondered briefly at their connection and then shook her head. She should not concern herself with the Normans at all.

The envoy said, "I am Hugh of Montfort-sur-Risle. His Grace the Duke of Normandy is a friend to Flanders."

Baldwin's loud guffaw interrupted him. "His forbearers were not!"

"The duke desires friendship and peace with Normandy's neighbors." Hugh continued without an acknowledgment of Baldwin's comment. "Duke William would seal the peace with Flanders through a royal marriage. He proposes himself as the bridegroom and the prospective bride, your noble daughter Matilda."

Baldwin rose from his seat. "William the Bastard thinks much of himself to claim my daughter."

"Indeed, Father, for I am far too high-born to marry a man of such low birth."

Matilda entered the audience chamber, her attendants trailing. Restored to her usual outward cheer, she glided across the room in dark red garments. A bejeweled chaplet encircled her headcloth. Rubies set in gold sparkled on her fingers. Her garments rustled lavender and honeysuckle bulbs strewn on the floor.

Baldwin came down from the dais and took her hand. "I present my daughter Matilda of Flanders."

A grim frown marred Hugh's visage. "Count Baldwin, perhaps your daughter does not understand the great honor my lord William shows her."

Matilda giggled. Tears sprang to her mirthful eyes, which she dabbed at with an embroidered handkerchief.

"A descendant of the noble King Robert Capet of France," she began, "and of the great King Alfred of England shall not sully her body with the seed of a Norman bastard. Return to Caen and tell your duke I shall never have him for a husband."

She withdrew while her attendants trailed behind her. Her laughter pealed along the length of the corridor.

Baldwin dismissed the courtiers and trailed after his daughter, with his wife at his side.

The crowd bustled from the audience chamber and swept Avicia along with it. When an iron hand closed on her wrist, she stifled her natural reaction.

"Prove your worth." Her uncle's foul breath washed over her. "You shall learn the true reason Matilda refuses this match. Come with me and I shall tell you what to do."

CHAPTER 6

Lille, Flanders
January 1049 CE

One week after the disastrous presentation of the Normans, Avicia visited the physic. While she doubted bloodletting might help her, she worried whether Matilda would learn of her disobedience.

The physic cut her forearm and drew a long trickle of blood. He checked its thickness and temperature. He dipped his finger in the bowl and licked it. His wife, the village healer, boiled rose petals and sage in water over the central hearth. With her eager counsel, Avicia drank the bitter, pungent brew and left the physic.

The Normans had just entered the courtyard on horseback. Hunting dogs bayed and struggled against the leashes their pages held. Blood stained their muzzles and coats. The black-haired man who had admired Avicia rode near the forefront.

In the week since his arrival at Lille, she had seen him every day. Now, his silvery eyes found her in the crowd. She met his stare and held it for the first time. A lazy grin dimpled his cheeks. She admired the way he sat his brown palfrey. His lean, muscled thighs gripped the horse with precise control.

She shook her head and turned from him. A flush of heat on her face cast aside the frigid coldness of the day. She hardly fathomed the pangs of emotion inside her whenever she looked at him. They had never spoken. She should have ignored him further but found the task difficult. When he watched her in the way he had just now, she could not breathe or think. He possessed a strong allure that held her enthralled with just one look. She found his gaze again.

He broke their fevered contact first and spoke with his companion Hugh, who glanced in her direction and nodded. Then, the black-haired Norman dismounted and walked toward her in a lengthy stride.

With a gasp, she whirled and headed for the steps. People thronged on all sides. She vied and jostled with them, offering murmured apologies. The door and the familiar shelter of the fortress' walls loomed.

"Demoiselle, wait. I command it."

The Norman French of her father sounded strange after five years. Compelled, she turned toward the voice echoing behind her.

A snort escaped the man's horse. Then the beast broke free from the young squire who had held its reins. The palfrey stamped before it charged in her direction. Terrified shouts leapt in the courtyard. The black-haired man grabbed and pulled her against him. The horse bucked its hooves. Her rescuer dove away with her in his arms, while the squire and Hugh grabbed the reins of the skittish animal.

The weight of the man atop her pressed her into the cold, wet mud. He fingered her cheek with a furtive caress. "Demoiselle, are you hurt?"

"Please, release me, I pray."

Long black lashes shuttered his silver gaze. His lean arms slid under her and hefted her up. In the space of another breath, she stood before him. Her mud-stained cape slipped from her shoulders. His fingers loosened the red linen cloak over his shoulders and draped it around her. She gazed in awe at his gentleness and courage.

Hugh joined them. "Brother, are you injured?"

Avicia stared back and forth between the men, understanding at last their resemblance to each other.

Her rescuer replied, "I am well though it appears the little fright has scared this lovely demoiselle."

His husky voice washed over and enveloped her in exquisite warmth. Under hooded eyelids, she glanced at him. His presence overwhelmed her. She swayed slightly. His hand closed on her shoulder. The flesh beneath her garments tingled where his hand alighted. His grin returned.

Hugh said, "She seems dazed. Does she need help? Perhaps someone should attend her. How can we tell her so? She does not understand what we say."

"She understands us plainly. Is that not the truth, demoiselle?"

"How would you know, Philippe?" Hugh asked.

Avicia stared at her rescuer anew, now that she knew his name. Philippe's unabashed grin widened.

"When we arrived here, I inquired after her from our host, Comte Rudolf." He continued smiling at her, though he addressed Hugh. "This girl is his niece. She is also the daughter of Thurston de Manneville-sur-Risle and his Flemish-born wife, Godalinda. She lived at Manneville until five years ago."

"So, you are the child who survived the fire?" Hugh seemed taken aback. "It killed everyone except you and the heir of Manneville. Your cousin is Hugh de Manneville. I am his godfather. He bears my name. I fostered him after his father's death."

Her heart leapt. She had more relations other than Count Rudolf of Aalst, still alive in Normandy.

"Look how she colors. She recognizes the name. It is certain she is de Manneville's cousin. A very beautiful cousin." Philippe reached for her cheek but halted just before his hand made contact.

She removed his cloak and returned it to him, despite his protests. She snatched hers and left him without a backward glance.

❧

At the dinner hour in the afternoon, Avicia sent Biota with word for Rudolf that she suffered from female concerns.

Instead, she escaped into the quiet afternoon. Just after midday, the sun set the sky aglow. Laughter and music drifted from the hall. Whatever his resentment of the Normans, Baldwin had proved a generous host.

She rubbed her shoulders and hugged herself tight. The arrival of the Normans had changed more than just the court life at Lille. They offered connections to her past.

At first, her heart soared with the knowledge that one among her father's relatives still lived. On the terrible night in which she had lost her parents, her paternal grandfather, uncles, and their families also died. She remembered her cousin Hugh, just a few years older than her. Her childhood memories could not conjure the name of the family who fostered him at the age of seven. Hugh de Montfort-sur-Risle could have raised him. She realized Hugh de Manneville must be a knight now. Would he remember her? Would he care that she still lived?

She shook her head and dismissed the misguided notion. The heir of Manneville had held no affection for her in the past. Their blood ties might mean nothing now. Perhaps he would offer her worse treatment than Rudolf, who harangued her daily for information on Matilda's continued rejection of the Norman ruler. Avicia knew Matilda's refusal lay in her infatuation with Brithric Meaw, but thwarted Rudolf by keeping the secret from him.

If only she could hide away from all of them for a time, alone with her thoughts. Perhaps she might have that time now, since Matilda had dismissed her until the physic pronounced her well again. Only one place in Lille could comfort her. The forbidden mews beckoned.

The door creaked on its hinges. Dim light filtered through the slated windows at the top of the building. Darkness enveloped its recesses. She knew the layout and found her way with ease.

She stood at the center of the room for an interminable time, her eyes closed. Then voices at the door jerked her back to awareness. She scrambled for the back of the room and found refuge in the shadowy darkness. The door creaked. The burly profile of a man filled the entryway.

"Get in here."

She did not recognize the brusque tone. The man stepped inside. He pulled a smaller, shapely woman behind him. He turned and hauled her against him. His strength forced his companion against the wall. A throaty moan escaped her mouth and died, as he covered her lips with his own. He reached between their bodies and pawed at her breasts. The woman laughed in a husky tone.

"Such passion burns inside you, milord bishop. Are all Frenchmen so hot blooded? I would never have guessed at the power of your lust, when Rudolf introduced us."

Avicia clamped a hand over her mouth and stifled her cry of shock. The woman was her uncle's wife, Gisele.

"Shut your mouth and spread your legs."

"Milord, stop!" Gisele shoved him off. She stepped closer and although Avicia could see little of her, she recognized the voice. "Odo, there is someone in the room. Did you not hear someone?"

"There is no one here, but us. Come now, you have admired me since dinner. I saw the lust in your gaze. You shall not deny me any longer."

Gisele struggled against his hold. "I cannot. If someone knew…Rudolf would kill me!"

She gathered the folds garment and fled the mews. With the door ajar, sunlight illuminated the recesses of every corner. The birds chorused sharp calls at the intrusion of the light.

The obsidian gaze of the yellow-haired bishop fell on Avicia. She shuddered against the wall. He stepped toward her. When she gasped, he halted.

"You are an unexpected, but welcome delight. I know you, lady. You stood on the steps when I first arrived. Comte Rudolf spoke to you. Where have you been all week, pretty bird?"

She made no reply. Perhaps if he thought she had not understood the Norman language, he would leave her unmolested.

A wry smile slashed across his features. "He is your uncle. He told me of your heritage. You do not speak. Have you forgotten the language of your birth?"

Avicia expelled her breath with a loud sigh. "We should not be here. I should go to my uncle."

She darted forward. He blocked her path and the beckoning sunshine. She could not escape him. Her nostrils flared at the scent of fetid wine on his breath. Fear rippled along her spine. His eyes glowed in the dimness.

"I am Odo, brother of William of Normandy. Tell me your name."

"I am Lady Avicia," she whispered. "Please let me pass."

She glanced at the open door and edged a step closer to it. His fingers clamped on her wrist in a powerful hold.

"Release me, I pray."

His smile widened. His arms encased her in a solid grip. He hauled her against his meaty frame and she yelped in surprise.

"Not just yet, milady. Countess Gisele is gone because of you."

"I recognized her. She is my uncle's wife. If you let me pass, I shall not speak of what I have seen happen between you and her."

Odo chuckled. "Petty threats do not frighten me. You have spoiled my afternoon sport. No matter, one woman is just as good as another for my purpose."

He mashed his wet, sloppy mouth over hers. He pulled at her headcloth. He gripped the length of her hair without mercy and jerked her head back. She screamed in shock and outrage, as his teeth bit her throat. Her tiny fists pounded on his back. A wave of dizziness overcame her when he lifted her off her feet and moved further back into the room. The short, sharp cries of alarm from the birds mirrored her screams.

He ignored her desperate pleas and struggles, and tossed her down on the hard floor. His bulky weight imprisoned her beneath him.

"If you please me, you may find my attentions welcome in the future."

"You cannot have me!"

Her cry died in her throat. His fist smashed into her mouth. He wrenched her clenched hands away and tore her garments to the waist. She screamed until fire filled her lungs.

Then, suddenly, the crushing pressure of Odo's body dissipated.

Another man's voice bellowed curses. Then two heavy grunts followed, before a loud thud sounded. She rolled on her side and gasped for air. Her gaze flew to the sight of Odo prone in a heap on the floor. Philippe stood between them. He glanced at her attacker and then eyed her steadily.

He said, "I did not see you in the hall, milady, and went in search of you. I heard your screams from the courtyard. He might have ravished you and no one would have been wiser."

His gray gaze studied her. "A beautiful blossom like you should not be crushed."

He offered his red cloak. This time, she covered herself and snapped it closed around her shoulders.

She frowned at Odo. "Is it true that William of Normandy is his brother?"

"Although Odo is legitimate and William is a bastard, they are brothers."

"He shall not forget this insult, yours, or mine."

"Do not worry demoiselle. I shall protect you."

❧

One week later, at the hour of Vespers, Avicia crossed the courtyard, intent on the church. An orange and purple sunset flamed overhead. One of Rudolf's retainers approached her.

"His lordship sent me to fetch you."

She followed him inside, her heart pounding. Had Rudolf discovered her secret visit to the forbidden mews, or Odo's assault? Biota had questioned her about the small bruise on her throat but she hid her shameful secret. If she spoke of it, Rudolf would know she had been in the mews again, and she would not hide what she had seen of Gisele and Odo. His perverted lust made her fearful. She feared ever seeing him again. If she incited unruly lust in men, she could not blame them. The fault must lay with her.

She walked down a dank hallway, where torches glowed in brackets along the wall. He knocked at an oaken door.

Rudolf's voice beckoned. "Enter."

She followed his command. The retainer closed the door behind her. Eyes on the ground, she avoided Rudolf's gaze. Her turbulent emotions shamed her, even after a week.

"You know the knight in the Norman retinue, Sieur Philippe?"

Her heart thudded when Rudolf mentioned him. Since the incident in the mews, he hovered near whenever she stepped outdoors or into the hall. Despite his respectful distance, her senses always tingled and alerted her to his presence before she ever saw him.

"His liege lord Hugh has spoken with me. Sieur Philippe wants to marry you. I am your lord, so I shall allow the match. You are to be Philippe's wife. Baldwin has given his consent, too. I shall even allow you to take your nurse Biota. She shall likely welcome the return home."

Avicia gaped in stunned silence before her breath quickened. Deep inside, her stomach contracted into a tight ball. She dug her nails into her palms and her throat grew constricted.

"I shall not leave Lille. You cannot make me marry a stranger. I do not know this Norman."

Rudolf sighed and cocked his head. He regarded her like a recalcitrant child. "You are Norman. You should be with your people."

"But one of them attacked me. Odo is no man of God. He found me alone and tried to hurt me."

In rapid strides, he rounded the table where he had sat. He grabbed her wrists in one hand, tighter than the bishop had. "When did he do this?"

"A few days ago," she paused, filled with dread, "in the mews. He bit my neck and cuffed me. Sieur Philippe rescued me, my lord."

His gaze narrowed. Her flesh throbbed in his painful grip. He grasped her chin and turned her cheek upward, exposing the purple bruise on her throat. "He found you in the mews, a place where I warned you never to go?"

When he released her suddenly, she stumbled backward.

"You wretched girl, I am well rid of you. You defy me and accuse William's brother of rape. You shall not jeopardize my rapport with the Normans. You shall not speak ill of Bishop Odo."

She gasped. "It happened. I swear it upon all the saints' bones."

"Why should I believe you?"

"Ask Sieur Philippe, who rescued me from the bishop's vile attentions."

"Then you were alone with two men in a darkened mews?

"It did not happen that way." She clasped her hands together in supplication. Rudolf shook his head, but she continued, "If you refuse to help me, I shall seek Matilda's protection. I serve her."

She did not know whether she could rely on Matilda, especially now that she knew the girl's secret. Perhaps, she would prefer her gone from Lille too, now that she had exposed her deepest desire to Avicia.

"You are useless in your current role." Rudolf's voice issued with incontestable command. "I wed your mother to the Mannevilles' third son and hoped the alliance might benefit me. Godalinda failed me, but perhaps you may best her. You shall marry Sieur Philippe. You dare not defy me."

She drew a deep breath and summoned her courage. "You think I am willful and you want to be rid of me, but I am no more trouble to you than your own wife."

He stared coldly at her. "What do you mean?"

"When I went to the mews, she followed…."

"Likely to stop you! She knew you could not be trusted to keep from the place."

"She went there with Odo. He kissed her, touched her…."

He grabbed her arms and shook her. "You dare accuse my wife?"

"Let me remain at Lille. Do not send me to Normandy with these strangers. If you allow me to stay, I shall never speak of what I saw happen between your wife and Odo."

He shoved her from him. "Speak of it and I shall personally remove your tongue. You shall do as I say and marry Sieur Philippe. Best to get you gone from my sight before you cause more trouble, and even better that the Normans should go with you, especially that pig Odo. I shall have the truth of what you have said from Gisele. I pray for her sake that you have lied."

He left the room. She paced back and forth. Her heart warred inside her. She should welcome the prospect of escape from Lille, but she hardly knew Philippe. How could they marry?

When she fled toward the church, she met him in the courtyard. Even his warm smile could not soothe her.

She glared at him. "You want me without regard for my wishes. You hardly know me. How can you marry me?"

"I cannot return to Normandy and leave you behind," he protested. "Since I first saw you, I knew we belonged together."

She shook her head at his impassioned plea. He drew her toward the side of the fortress, into the shadows of evening. She struggled against his sinewy frame but he held her close.

"You feel it, too, Avicia. We belong together. I cannot return to Normandy without you. I promise you my heart, my love, and my fidelity."

"I do not love you!"

Hot tears stung her eyes. She swiped at them and turned her back on him. His hands trailed along her spine. She sucked in her breath at the sudden warmth, which coursed through her belly. Could a man's touch alone produce such aches in a woman?

"You shall grow to love me."

He held and turned her in the circle of his arms. One hand cupped her chin. She stared wordless into the dark pools of his eyes. With such conviction in his gaze, how could she doubt him?

"Marry me, Avicia. Become my wife and you shall never regret it," he whispered.

Her heart flip-flopped and she leaned against him. Resistance drained from her body. With his resolve alone, he compelled her. How else could she explain why her heart soared when he made his pledges? He had made her dream of the promise of love, again.

"Be my wife," Philippe insisted.

His blunt fingers skimmed along her spine and trailed beneath her headcloth. His hand rested at the back of her neck. Powerless against the lure of him, she pressed closer. Her fingernails pressed into his forearms. The muscles beneath his flesh tightened in response.

"Why do you make me feel the things I do?" She wondered whether she asked the question of him, or herself.

His eyes loomed closer, incandescent. Candor, fondness, and adoration filled his gaze. Her heart beat so loud, he must have heard it. She inhaled the scent of leather, horses and another aroma, distinctly masculine, uniquely Philippe.

The feather light touch of his lips made her believe she imagined his kiss. On her next inhalation, their breaths melded together. She melted against him and pressed against the hard resistance of his chest. His hand swept downward in one rapid, fluid motion to her waist. A wave of heat crisscrossed her belly. Their intimacy changed. The demand of his lips would only accept surrender from her. Her arms encircled his shoulders.

When they drew apart, she shuddered against him.

"Avicia, marry me. I shall always protect you. You shall want for nothing."

Philippe released her. She stood in a daze. Her mouth trembled and ached for another embrace. His thumb stroked over her lower lip.

"What is your answer?" He grasped her hand.

Her heart hammered, and she sagged, defeated.

"If you want me, I shall be your wife."

He kissed her fingers. "You shall never regret it. You shall love me one day, as I love you now."

She tugged her hand from his hold and fled inside the church. By God's mercy, no one acknowledged her. She dropped to her knees and begged God's forgiveness for her inconstancy.

Philippe stirred her heart, which she once vowed would belong to Edric of Newington forever. His dark visage had begun replacing Edric's face in her mind. Images and memories she once thought would have stayed with her grew fainter with each day. Edric's smile and laugh, the texture of his hair, even the exact shade of his eyes faded from easy recall. She felt the same rush of happiness in Philippe's presence as she once experienced with him. How could that be, when she had pledged herself to Edric forever?

CHAPTER 7

Rouen, Normandy
February 1049 CE

"For over a hundred years," Philippe informed Avicia, "Rouen had been the capital of Normandy and the residence of its dukes for the last fifty years. Now Caen is Duke William's seat though he is often at Rouen. Much of the court remains here, the wives and children of the knights and men-at-arms. After we are wed, you shall see more of the city."

She whirled from the view of the ships along the river Seine and stared at him, blushing at the prospect of their marriage. When he smiled, his dimples showed.

Winter clouds heralded the overcast day. Hugh feared they would not reach Rouen before the rain fell and urged them onward. Their horses galloped in a column of nearly twenty, which had left Flanders weeks ago.

Avicia rode near the forefront on Philippe's white palfrey while he sat his destrier. Biota traveled by boat rather than brave the jarring journey overland. Hugh had provided her passage and offered two of the Montfort retainers for protection.

Odo had left Flanders by boat a few days beforehand. Avicia almost wept with joy when Philippe informed her of his early departure. She dreaded a reunion with such a lustful man.

She had once thought no other place could rival Lille, until her first glimpse of her new home. Two thick walls of stone encompassed the city, built on sloped countryside. Immediately within the confines of the second wall, half-timbered structures lined the slick, mud-covered streets. In the marketplace, which spilled haphazardly along the river, the scent of raw fish tainted the air.

"Do you like oysters and flatfish?" Philippe asked.

"I have never eaten them."

"You shall experience many new things when you become my wife."

His witty tone and persistent smile held her entranced. With a blush, she dragged her attention to the gray façade of a stone edifice up ahead, surrounded by walls of the same material.

"What is that building?" she asked, her arm outstretched.

"It is the *donjon* of Rouen."

Her gaze scaled the height of the escarpment. "Your duke must have many enemies."

"Why do you say so?"

"If he needs such a strong defensive building, he has many enemies."

A gatehouse barred their way. Admitted past it, the riders crossed a bridge slung over a low-lying ditch. Avicia ducked her head and pinched her nostrils closed at the fetid scent of dank water. Filth skimmed its surface. Philippe chuckled beside her.

"You shall grow accustomed to the scent."

She shook her head. "I could not bear the foul stench again."

"You must bear it at least twice more today. We wed this evening at St. Ouen church. Afterward, we shall enjoy a fine feast. Then we shall enjoy each other."

The breath caught in her throat, but not just because of his carnal promise. "We marry this evening? How can it be? Can you marry me without consent from your duke?"

"Hugh sent a messenger ahead with news of my intent. Duke William shall not deny me, since my message indicates that I have abducted you from the Flemish court."

Her cheeks flamed. "You did not. We had no secret union."

"Hugh shall swear an oath on holy relics if he must. I am more than just the captain of his knights and the lowborn son of his father. Hugh and I share a strong bond. He would do anything for my sake. Do not worry. No one shall interfere or ever know the truth of our hasty union."

Her fears warred with the thrill of anticipation. They must pretend he had already bedded her, so Duke William would accept their union as a fact. Would the women of the ducal court regard her as a woman of ill repute? Yet, she felt she could bear the scandal with Philippe at her side. He had vowed eternal protection.

Then, a thought occurred to her. "What about the wedding night? If we have already consummated our union, some may question the virginal blood tomorrow."

He chuckled. "You inspire such ardor in me. No one shall inquire about it. I have dreamt of the pleasures we shall share." When she blushed further, he laughed harder.

"I can send word to Hugh de Manneville of your arrival," he said.

Avicia shook her head. "Please do not tell him I am here. He has not bothered about me for five years. You and our children shall be my family."

They entered the confines of the bailey. She remained on horseback while Philippe and Hugh dismounted. The pair strode toward the steps, where a pale, thin woman awaited them. She wore a dark red robe with elbow-length sleeves. A girdle sewn with gold thread girded it around the waist. Fine linen concealed all her hair and fell over her right shoulder, secured with a silver circlet with a garnet gem at its center. Her richly colored attire stirred memories of Avicia's mother.

Philippe greeted her, just after Hugh had. Then he returned and lifted Avicia down from her palfrey. When he tugged her hand gently, she followed him. She mounted the steps with her eyes averted. The dainty feet of the woman appeared before her.

"This is the demoiselle who has captured my dear Philippe's heart?"

Avicia's heart hammered at her soft, melodic tone of endearment. The woman dared speak with Philippe on such familiar terms. On closer inspection, Avicia realized she appeared older. Despite it, unexpected jealousy flared inside her. Her gaze rose to the woman's face, where an angelic smile played on her lips.

Philippe made the introduction. "Alice de Beaufort, my intended, Avicia." He turned to her. "My heart, Alice is Hugh's wife."

Alice interposed herself between Avicia and Philippe. "Leave us. Philippe, I shall take your wife away and see her settled."

Before Avicia could protest, Alice curtsied and then tugged her through their environs with haste up to the third floor. Those whom they bypassed stared with amusement or puzzlement in their expressions. The pair entered a windowed room with two stools beside the casement. Alice gestured toward one of the seats.

"First a bath, for you cannot be a travel-worn and dirtied bride," she began. "A meal, you must eat, or you should eat and then have a bath."

She paused and reviewed Avicia. "My hips have borne children, but I have garments you can wear and my maid can dress your hair. Shoes! Yours are entirely too muddy. *Non, non,* you cannot marry in those dirty shoes. I think your feet may be a little bigger than mine are...."

She drew breath and sank down on the other stool. "Philippe told me you were born at Manneville though you lived in Flanders, lovely country, but unlike Normandy. My dear, you have not said a word. What is the matter?"

Avicia burst into tears. She hid her face behind her hands. Alice's arm draped her shoulder. "Philippe is a wonderful man and he shall be a good husband." Her gentle voice provided little comfort.

"I know...but how shall I be...a good wife...to a man I do not know?"

"None of your tears now," Alice admonished. "I first met Philippe when I prepared for my marriage to Hugh. He escorted me from Beaufort to my new home. The prospect of marriage frightened me, but Philippe soothed my concerns. He spoke of the bravery and kindness of Hugh. When we neared the end of the journey, he confessed his blood ties to my husband. Has Philippe told you the story of his birth?"

Avicia shook her head. Alice continued, "My husband's father also bore the name Hugh. He died in defense of the young Duke William. He came from a rich and powerful lineage. His father Thurston de Bastembourg later became the Seigneur de Pont-Authou."

"Where's Pont-Authou?"

"Oh, the 'where' does not matter now, it is the 'who' which is important. Philippe is bastard-born, sired on the widow of his father's best friend. Soon after Hugh the elder's wife died, Philippe's mother Lady Felice de St. Pols also lost her husband. She comforted Philippe's father for a time. She became his *leman*. Later, she hid her pregnancy and Philippe's birth from him."

Avicia listened while Alice explained how Philippe's mother had raised him among nuns until his father took him. She wondered how his low birth affected his youth. Had other fostered children in his father's household teased him for it? The thought made her realize how much she cared for him. She vowed he would never suffer pain at her hands.

⌘

Avicia remained in Alice's care. Although Alice weaved a conversation faster than a bumblebee, she seemed warm and genuine at least. Through her good graces, Avicia worried less for her marital prospects.

When the bells for Nones pealed in the afternoon, she dressed in one of Alice's fine white chemises. Over this, she wore a yellow and green robe. A girdle sewn with gold thread belted her waist. She sat beside the shuttered window while Alice's maid arranged her hair.

"I wonder what Matilda of Flanders would think if she saw me in such rich garments."

Alice turned from the third-floor window. "Philippe mentioned you lived at the Flemish court. So you knew the lady our duke wishes to marry?"

"I knew her well. I served as one of her attendants."

The maid's hands stilled at the nape of her neck. Over her head, Alice glared at the young girl, who returned to her work.

"In a position of honor, I am sure?" Alice asked. When Avicia nodded, she continued, "You must understand many of the highborn ladies here might not think so well of your duties."

Avicia sighed, but Alice patted her hand. "You do not have to worry for me, I care not. You may find the wives of Norman knights are often too idle."

When the servant finished, fine linen concealed Avicia's braided hair. Alice topped the headcloth with a gold circlet inlaid with citrine and green jasper, and kissed her cheek. "Lovely."

❦

The afternoon passed in a blur. Avicia remembered the stink of the moat on the ride to St. Ouen church. Alice and Hugh accompanied them. The wedding ceremony happened so fast. When she blinked, she stared down at the silver ring on her finger with some surprise. Then the wedding party returned to Rouen's *donjon* for the marital feast.

Seated at a trestle table, Avicia shared a trencher with Philippe. Alice sat on her right. A cacophony of noise surrounded them, the guests being the Montfort's retainers. She wondered aloud why the wives of these men were absent.

Alice lowered her cup of clove-spiced wine. "The wedding occurred with such haste, not everyone could attend."

"But we are the only women here. Where are the others?"

"My dear, I do not mean to be unkind," Alice paused and patted her hand. "Yet, you must appreciate how Philippe's low birth and the unusual circumstances of your union might concern some of the nobler families. You have resided in the Flemish court. You know how other women can be."

Avicia nodded and stared at her plate. Though freed of Matilda's displeasure, she might have no more friends here than at the Flemish court. Would the Norman women despise her status and her lowborn husband?

Philippe often turned from his discussion with Hugh and watched her. She met his continual appraisal with a forced smile, given the nervous flutters in her belly. However, the last time he looked at her, it sent a thrilling ripple through her flesh. His eyes loomed larger, like the silvery glow of a full moon. She remained transfixed until a strident voice broke the spell.

"Allow me to congratulate the bride and groom."

Philippe offered her his hand. She slipped her long fingers into his grasp and stood. A thickset, tall man with dark hair strode into the room. Other men followed, dressed in fine attire paired with precious gemstones. Their leader moved with confidence and purpose.

"Milord." Hugh stood and inclined his head. "You come upon the marital feast of my brother Philippe. I thought it of little note to you, but I did send word to your seneschal."

"My seneschal FitzOsbern just reminded me." William of Normandy's baritone voice rumbled through the room. "I intended to pay my respects."

Avicia curtsied before him, not in the pretty way Alice had, but it came close in her mind. When she raised her face, William admired her.

"She is a beauty. You are congratulated, Sieur Philippe."

"Thank you, my duke." Philippe bowed.

"Indeed, a lovely demoiselle."

At the unexpected praise, Avicia's gaze found the speaker. Odo stepped out from behind his burly brother. His black eyes took in her visage.

She clutched at Philippe's arm. He placed a hand over hers and patted her fingers.

"Where were you married?" William questioned Philippe.

"At St. Ouen, my duke."

"Odo arrived in Rouen this morning. He could have officiated."

"I do not believe so, brother."

When William turned and looked over his shoulder, Avicia's hold on Philippe's arm tightened. William's face reddened with displeasure.

"Why ever not, brother?" he asked.

Odo smirked. "It would have been unseemly, for he is a bastard."

William scowled. "I hope you do not suggest, Odo, that Sieur Philippe's bastardry concerns you."

Without waiting for Odo's answer, his gaze returned to Philippe. "We bastards must defend each other in this world." With a grin, he punched Philippe's left shoulder, a blow that would have laid a smaller man flat on his back.

The same grin split Philippe's face into a warm smile. Then, he favored Avicia with it.

Her heart soared at the tender look in his eyes.

Hugh handed a goblet of wine to William, who raised the silver metal. "To Sieur Philippe and his lady."

The Montfort retainers repeated the toast. William drank with them. Then he reached for Avicia's hand. "I would salute the bride, also."

Tension radiated in Philippe's sudden, rigid stance. William must have noticed it, too. "I only claim her fingers for a kiss, man."

At Philippe's nod, she offered her hand. William kissed her fingers lightly and winked at her. He turned on his heel and left the room with his retainers, except for one.

Odo glared at her. Philippe nuzzled her brow. Odo's sneer intensified.

Over his shoulder, William demanded, "Brother, surely you have Mass to celebrate? Let these people enjoy their revelry."

With a final, smirking appraisal, Odo followed.

❧

Later, Avicia shivered naked under the soft woolen coverlet on a pallet.

Alice stood beside her. "I have heard Philippe is a thorough lover."

She scowled. "Who told you so?"

Alice kept her silence. Raucous laughter pealed in the hall. The Montfort retainers propelled Philippe between the opaque curtains that partitioned the room. Avicia pulled the coverlet up to her eyes and cowered under the eager gazes of the men. They left after much protest when Alice ordered them out. With a wink and smile for Avicia, she and Hugh followed.

Avicia closed her eyes and listened to Philippe's grunts, curses and mutters. She peeked over the coverlet's edge. He swayed into her view. He hopped and twirled on one foot while he dragged the tunic over his head. She stifled a giggle, but it escaped in a snort. She still chortled when he settled beside her.

"Laughter? I shall teach you to make sport at me."

He tickled her waist. She squealed and slipped from his grasp, but not for long. His fingers dragged across her belly, down to her hips and swept up again. He no longer teased her. He desired a different response from her body. The ripples of a slow flame trailed in the wake of his caresses.

"Open to me, *pucele*."

Her thighs parted of their own volition. Thought surrendered to sensation. His lean-muscled body settled between her thighs. She sighed languidly and closed her eyes.

His voice rumbled in her ear and urged her caresses. Her fingers trembled, and she hesitated before she touched his chest. He threw off the coverlet and revealed them both as God fashioned. Her nails scored his shoulders. Braced above her, he stared down at her pale body. His warmth of his gaze told how much he relished the sight of her. He caressed each place his eyes alighted. Myriad sensations overtook her. She welcomed his touch.

His eyes glowed and he kissed her again, possessively this time. She surrendered to him, the will to deny him anything long gone.

He rested his brow against hers. "Lord, how I have desired you, woman. I would taste your passion, but I need your trust."

She looked into his warm brown gaze. "I trust you. I shall always trust you."

She pulled him closer and sought his warmth. She returned his nips and kisses along the length of her neck with chaste pecks at his arm and his shoulder. In the union of their bodies, she stiffened at the anticipated pain, but soon her breath came in shallow pants. She held him tighter still, clung to him. He gasped and chanted her name. She cried out for him. An ache swelled deep inside her with great intensity. Then he fell against her, and she welcomed the full weight of him.

When she opened her eyes, he looked down upon her. She shied away from his stark gaze. He cupped her cheek and brought her gaze back to his. His tender expression puzzled her, until the words she whispered in the midst of their passion came back to her.

Her hand trembled against his chest. His heart pounded. She whispered, "I spoke the truth. I do love you, Philippe."

He kissed her nose, then her forehead, her chin, her eyelids, everywhere but her lips. She longed for the feel of his mouth and framed his face between her hands. He kissed her palm. When his lips pressed against her skin, she shivered.

"I thank you, for your willingness to love me. I swear you shall never regret it."

She smiled and kissed him. Her trust in him made her bold. This time, he surrendered.

CHAPTER 8

Newington, Kent, England
July – September 1049 CE

Edric arrived at his father's hall just before dusk fell. He reined in Elfhar, slid from the black stallion's back, and stared in bewilderment at the sight in the courtyard. Godwin's men, a few of whom he recognized, sat on their mounts with faces illuminated by torchlight. He cast the folds of his blue linen cloak over his right shoulder and strode toward the hall entrance. Halfway, he halted in his tracks. His father and Wulfstan exited with heavy strides. A fresh breeze descended and quelled the summer's unusual heat. Tunwulf's red mantle billowed behind him.

"What took you so long to come from Elham?"

Accusation ripened in Tunwulf's gruff tone. However, nothing his father could say today would dampen Edric's spirits.

"With Mother's help, my wife delivered of a son, a fine and healthy heir. You became a grandfather today."

The age lines, which marred Tunwulf's brow, smoothed for a moment.

Edric continued, "I have named him Leofsige, for your father."

Tunwulf nodded. "It is a good name. See he lives up to it."

His father would never change. He always expected the best of everyone around him because he demanded it of himself.

Edric asked, "Why did you summon me? Why are Godwin's men here?"

He followed Tunwulf a short distance away from the riders. Edric scrutinized his father's face for clues. Uncertainty shadowed Tunwulf's expression.

He said, "I travel with these men to Sandwich, Edric. From there, we sail for Pevensey. We protect Godwin and his family against the king now."

Edric's jaw dropped, the breath strangled in his throat. When he regained his composure, he asked the one question brimming in his mind. "Is this because of Earl Sweyn?"

Tunwulf looked at the men who awaited him before he nodded. "In truth, the king's men are after Sweyn on suspicion of the murder of his cousin, Earl Beorn. The king has demanded the full wergild in repayment for Beorn's life. Sweyn fled rather than submit and pay his cousin's family."

"Sweyn is an outlaw and no man should give him aid." Edric bridled at the thought of the arrogant Sweyn, who had bedded and abused Cynwise.

Tunwulf jabbed his arm. "Heed those among us who are loyal to Godwin that they do not overhear you. I am also his man. I give you no leave to insult Sweyn in my presence."

"Father, everyone knows he bears the guilt. He lured his cousin Beorn to Bosham and killed him. He has sinned against God and man's laws."

"I stand with Godwin, who has gone to London, seeking the king's pardon for his son. He fears Edward cannot forgive. He shall strike out at Godwin's family and estates."

Edric spat on the ground. "Godwin makes a fine gesture. Sweyn once claimed his mother an adulteress and his father a cuckold by King Canute. Yet Godwin forgave him."

"Fathers do anything for their children, even forgive them grave dishonor, at the risk of their own pride."

Some indiscernible emotion crossed Tunwulf's face. Before Edric could question it, he continued, "You shall understand when your own son grows. Does my grandson favor you or his mother?"

"He has her black hair," Edric said, "but his eyes are the blue of his father and grandfather."

"I must part you from him for now. Stay here, and bring your wife and child when she can travel. Protect Newington."

"I shall hold your lands, Father, until my last breath."

Tunwulf nodded and gripped Edric's shoulder. He mounted Bavo and leaned toward Wulfstan, who held the stallion's reins.

"Proclaim the news and let the village rejoice. My son has sired a fine and healthy heir of his own. By God's favor, I pray our fortunes shall increase."

Cheers erupted in the courtyard.

Tunwulf nudged Bavo into a slow canter toward Edric. "When I return, I shall hold your boy high. For now, tell him his grandfather shall return. Tell your mother, I take my leave of her only for a short time."

Edric nodded and bowed at his father's side. Tunwulf rode out at the head of Godwin's men. His linen cloak became a blur of crimson flame in the light until he faded entirely from view.

"Godspeed, Father," Edric whispered.

Within days, one hundred of Godwin's men went into the blue-black waters of the Channel. Their ships struck submerged rocks, just outside Pevensey on a stormy night. The dead included Edric's father.

In the weeks that followed, some at Newington whispered of divine punishment for Godwin over his argument with the king. However, none dared say this within earshot of their new lord.

Two months onward and a dark pall of grief enshrouded the village. Edric of Newington sat at a trestle table alone at midday. His long fingers gripped a wooden cup. He sipped the ale inside and pronounced it bitter swill. With a dark scowl, he shooed the maidservant who hovered, offering more drink. He glowered in her direction long after she fled. When he pounded the cup against the table with a sharp thud, the vessel cracked and spilled the brew. He jerked back in disgust when the ale trickled to the edge of the table and soaked his knee-length tunic.

He buried his face in his hands. Nearly two weeks growth of hair covered his jaw and chin. It scratched at his palms.

"My lord husband."

"What, lady?" He turned abruptly at the plaintive sound of his wife. Cynwise halted in her stride, her blue eyes wide and startled. In her willowy arms, she held their son Leofsige, who whimpered softly.

Edric unclenched his fists and reached for the baby.

"I am sorry." He dampened the tightness in his voice. "I forgot I asked you to bring him to me."

Cynwise hesitated as her lips trembled.

He grimaced. "Why do you recoil so? I would never hurt my own son."

She shook her head. "Since we received word of your father, you have not been yourself. How can I trust you?"

"You dare question me. Tunwulf Grim is dead! Do you wonder why it has changed me?"

With a shudder, she handed over their son. He cradled Leofsige close. Dark curls peeked from beneath the woolen cap on his head. Edric stood and crooned to the baby while he circled the room.

"I shall go to the chapel to pray with your mother," Cynwise said behind him. He had almost forgotten she remained there.

Alone again, he studied his son's face. The same raven-black hair as Cynwise, but pale blue eyes and ruddy skin marked Leofsige for Edric's son. He smiled and held him close. "You are all mine."

When he had first married Cynwise, he refused her bed until after her monthly show of blood appeared. His mother chided his mistrustfulness. His father warned him against inciting Godwin's displeasure. Their admonitions fell short. Approximately two months had passed after his marriage before Edric knew Cynwise did not carry Sweyn's child. Yet he hesitated. It annoyed him that he remained a virgin, instead of his wife. Intimidated and aggravated, still he had been unprepared for Cynwise's response. In truth, he could not call it a response since she had initiated it. His body alone reacted, but her furtive movements scarcely inspired him or brought much pleasure.

For weeks, they repeated the act, until the morning she tossed up her porridge in their chamber pot. When the midwife at Elham confirmed the pregnancy, Cynwise refused her marital duty. Edric had not missed her half-hearted passion. Yet he wished his marriage gave him greater joy.

The soft, even rasps of his son's exhalation drew him from reverie. He tucked the blanket snug around the baby.

"You remind me of your grandfather. Leofsige used to rock Tunwulf to sleep, too."

His grandmother Eanflaed of Tickenhurst tapped her heavy walking stick. With stiff and slow movements, she shuffled across the hall. For all her fifty-six years and the aches and pains, she remained a striking woman with russet locks and few signs of gray.

She sank into a chair near the hearth. "Bring my Leofsige and set him on my lap."

Reluctant to part with him, Edric said, "He sleeps."

Eanflaed silenced him with an impatient tap of her walking stick. He shook his head and laid the baby on his grandmother's bony knees.

Leofsige sighed deep in slumber. She stroked a gnarled hand over his head and rustled his cap. Edric moved it back into place. The elderly woman stabbed him with a sharp glance. He bowed and strode toward the hall door. The midday sun glinted down on his face.

"You and your wife argued again," Eanflaed commented.

He glared at her for eavesdropping and faced the entryway again. "We argue about many things."

"It is not good. Your grandfather and I lived in peace. Your mother and father did, too."

He sighed. "The lady and I do not get on well."

"Still, you have a son by her. You must have peace or the land shall fail."

He shook his head. Again with the damnable, old prophecy.

"You do not believe, but Lady Leofflaed's curse is strong. She brought it down upon herself."

"I have heard this story before."

Eanflaed ignored his comment. "After your great-grandmother Leofflaed took Aethelmaer Cild to be her lover, and bore her two sons by him, she came to know regret. If ever Aethelmaer loved her, still he abandoned her and her children. He denied her claim of hand fasting, knowing the Church would never recognize his Danish wife. Leofflaed pledged herself God's faithful servant if He would grant her wish. *'When there is peace between lord and lady, so shall Newington thrive.'* Your grandfather and father lived by her pledge. You must do the same."

"How can there be peace with a woman I do not love, who does not love me?" Edric pounded his fist on the doorjamb and turned to her in exasperation.

Eanflaed shook her head. Her opaque eyes watered. "Then blood shall flow, and God shall curse us. Unless you and your lady have peace in your union, we may all suffer the consequences of your discord."

PART II - CHAPTER 9

Rouen, Normandy
August 1051 CE

An hour after dinner, Avicia heaved the contents of her stomach into a chamber pot. Biota and Alice stood on either side of her.

"Send for the physic, nurse. I am dying." She groaned and heaved again.

With a sigh, Alice said, "Breeding women do not die so easily. Otherwise, no woman would endure her man's hands upon her."

Avicia looked from her to Biota. "Could it be?"

Biota nodded. "Two full cycles of the moon have passed since you last had your monthly courses."

Alice nodded. "It is plainer than winter's day, at least to me. You are with child. Your breasts are fuller. Surely, your husband has noticed. Breeding women are always thus. Oh heavens, do not tell me Philippe makes love to you in the dark or with your clothes on!"

Avicia ducked her head, but not in time, for she saw Biota's blush. Her nurse often slept behind a thin partition next to the space she shared with Philippe. Heavens only knew what Biota had overheard in the darkness.

Alice continued. "You complain of headaches, and you are always sleepy, too. Remember how I woke you when you dozed off during Odo's Mass last week?"

"His sermons could make any person weary."

The women looked at each other and laughed, before Avicia sobered. "I am with child. Philippe shall be so pleased."

"You must first consult with the midwife, Torfida. She keeps all the women's secrets, so yours shall be safe."

Avicia straightened. "I want to tell Philippe now."

"You must wait until you have spoken to Torfida," Alice cautioned.

Heedless, Avicia scurried down the stone steps to the outdoors. The familiar sights and sounds of the bailey greeted her. Blacksmiths pounded metals with their hammers. Stable hands bellowed to each other while they toiled with horses and hay. The animals in the barns chorused squeals and grunts.

Near the gatehouse wall, Philippe and his men remained on the practice field.

Giddy with a bubbly mood inside her, she broke into a run. Astonished villagers and men at-arms gaped at her, but she ignored them. Her heart soared at the anticipation of Philippe's happiness. The guffaws and cheers of the men on the practice field alerted her husband.

She halted in her tracks. His handsome visage tightened in a narrow gaze, his lips pressed tightly together.

"Avicia! Proper Norman wives do not run around with skirts hiked up to their knees for all to see. How is it that you cannot understand what I expect of you?"

She blushed at the unexpected chastisement, but her husband only glared at her. Beyond him, came the rude stares and smirks of several of the other knights. She turned on her heel and fled.

❧

She went to Torfida, who examined her and confirmed her suspicions that she carried Philippe's child. Afterward she lapsed into quietude. Not even Alice coaxed her from willful melancholy. Petty stubbornness kept her silent. After dinner, she lingered in the hall alone, with her head bowed.

Philippe entered with heavy footsteps. He leaned against a wall with his eyes closed. Though resentful and reluctant, she gathered her skirts and approached. When she neared, he pulled her into his arms and rested his chin atop her head. Normally, she might have relished such an embrace, but his earlier rebuke chafed at her.

Still, the rapid pulsation of his heart told her something troubled him. She gazed up at him. His eyes were murky, the color of the sky when a storm approached. He heaved a sigh.

"I must leave you."

She stepped back in the circle of his arms and searched his narrow face. "What do you mean?"

"William visits with King Edward of the English. Hugh and others among the court shall accompany him. Therefore, I must go. The voyage across the Channel can be treacherous. I prefer to leave you here."

"Take me with you!"

His eyes widened at the vehemence in her plea, but he shook his head. She threw her arms around his neck. "Do not leave me alone while you are gone so far."

"Why are you so insistent on this? The strong winds of the Channel can drive ships against hidden rocks. You shall be well here. Are you afraid to be without me?"

She nodded and though she regretted the lie, she could not reveal the source of her disquiet, which had nothing to do with her pregnancy. She knew Philippe would never believe her awful premonition about the death awaiting him in England.

In the first months after her marriage, nightmares plagued her. Most were short, meaningless images except the torturous dreams of several days ago. In it, she saw Philippe's body, bloodied and stiff on a shallow valley floor. The standards of Norman and English warriors fluttered in the breeze over the corpse. In her nightmare, she recognized the English round shields she had once seen in Flanders, and knew the frightening vision offered her a glimpse of England, a place she had never visited and never thought she would see, until now.

"Take me with you," she pleaded again.

He shook his head. She sighed deeply and with the movement, her bosom brushed against her husband's chest through his tunic. Her nipples tightened under the cloth. He looked down at her. Desire sparked in his gaze. She reveled in the strength she possessed, but did not understand, feminine power, which stirred his blood.

"Do not leave me alone. Please, let me come with you," she whispered.

Her hands trembled slightly while they roamed the expanse of his chest. Muscles bunched beneath the fabric wherever she touched. Her hand slid around his neck. Her fingers threaded through the dark strands of his hair.

"Avicia." His voice carried a cautionary tone. She ignored it and focused instead on the ragged breaths he expelled. On tiptoe, she pressed soft kisses at his throat. Her other hand splayed across his belly, inched down and moved up under the tunic.

"You shall do anything to be with me?" His harsh gaze held hers.

"Do not leave me. Must I wait here, week after week, for your return? I love you."

Her impassioned words created the effect she craved. He hauled her up against him. His lips bruised hers. Her thighs gripped his waist, while he pushed the ample skirts of her robe up. Blunt fingers tugged the short ends of the linen girdle around her waist. The girdle slipped to the floor when he tugged her chemise around her hips. Nails scraped at his scalp and scored the breadth of his shoulders. His hands trailed across the backs of her thighs. Desire surged inside him so strongly that he hardly cared for the impropriety and would take her in the hall. She relished his wild abandon.

Before sanity fled, she whispered against his ear, "Take me to England."

His answer muted against her heated skin, she tugged at his hair again, and nibbled at the apex of his shoulder and neck. "Say it. Tell me."

"I shall take you with me," he muttered, fingers at the drawstrings on his hose. "I shall do it because I cannot bear to be without you."

She arched her back as he lifted her, fitted her against him. She delighted in his words more than his fierce passion, and promised herself he would know about the baby after the voyage.

❧

"Your husband told you of the court's journey to England?" Alice asked, later.

Avicia nodded. "I shall accompany him."

Alice's delicate face flushed with happiness, but in the next instant lines marred her brow. "Is it wise given your condition?"

Avicia fingered her stomach wistfully and smiled, but made no reply.

At a glance, she found Alice stared at her with a look of appraisal. "Is there something wrong?"

"I am curious. Why do you want to go to England?"

"A wife belongs at her husband's side. Why do you question my desire?"

Alice replied, "A wife should always concern herself with her husband's whereabouts, for when we do not, their eyes and all else wander. Lord knows my Hugh cannot keep from other women. He has his *lemans* here and at Montfort-sur-Risle. I wondered instead about your anticipation. Do you imagine you shall again see the young man from England?"

Avicia turned from her. Just after her marriage, she had confided to her friend about the year before she left Flanders. Three years had passed since she last saw Edric. She tried summoning his image to mind. All she recalled were his eyes, the blue of a robin's egg.

Alice asked her, "Do you harbor some hope of seeing him?"

She smoothed the folds of her garment over her stomach. "It is unlikely to happen."

"Avicia, please answer me."

She regarded Alice again. "Do not question my loyalty to my husband. I shall never betray Philippe for any man. That includes Edric of Newington."

Her friend shrugged. "If you are certain."

"Why do you persist? Are you accusing me? Have I ever given you reason to believe another man holds sway over my heart?"

She turned to the wall. Alice grasped her shoulders. "You have not. Please do not be angry with me, but I sense you are not telling me the truth about your reasons for going with Philippe." When she groaned, Alice added, "If it is not because of the Englishman, then why do you insist? Your need must be great to risk your babe."

"I do not risk the child! I would never willingly hurt my baby." She cradled her stomach with a trembling hand. "I cannot let Philippe go, not yet."

"Let him go? England is not so far. You speak as if…you speak as though you fear he shall die. You cannot think that, for surely he is as hale and hearty as I have ever known."

"I do!"

Silence stretched between them before Alice asked, "Why do you believe this?"

"I do not know, but dreams have plagued me of late."

When she turned to Alice, who made the sign of the Cross, she frowned. "Do not do that! I am no witch or seer to foretell the future."

As she described her nightmares, Alice's face whitened. "But you have never even seen England! You cannot know your dreams have meaning." Her breath came raw and ragged before she calmed herself. "Put those thoughts far from your head and never speak of them again. England and Normandy are not in conflict and shall never be. Philippe shall never have to fear death in some distant land."

Avicia nodded and wished with all her heart that she could believe Alice, but her dreams told her otherwise.

CHAPTER 10

Newington, Kent, England
August 1051 CE

Edric narrowed his eyes at the man across the trestle table from him. The glare of the beeswax candle illuminated the youthful visage of Earl Harold Godwinson of East Anglia. His thick, golden hair and beard gleamed. His powerful frame and attire reminded Edric of the man's father.

Edric sipped his ale. "I do not understand why you and Godwin want me at the king's court. I am a minor Saxon noble with a few estates and seven men-at-arms at my command."

Harold's dark golden lashes swept down when he took a long draw of the ale. He wiped his mouth and beard on the cuff of his marigold-colored tunic. He returned Edric's stare.

He had arrived with a retinue of *huscarls* after everyone went to bed. When Wulfstan alerted the hall with news of his arrival, Edric would have called him a liar, if Harold had not entered.

Godwin's children bore their father's pride. Edric shook his head, hard-pressed at the thought of the blood bond that aligned him with these people.

"We are kin and I rely on your support. I do not ask you to appear before the king, only aid in my protection. We must stand firm against the threat the Frenchmen pose. Our fortunes shall rise. Rise with us."

Harold seduced with his rich timbre tone, but Edric remembered how old Godwin had used the same tone with Tunwulf Grim when he brought about Edric's hasty union with Cynwise.

"Shall I rise or fall with you? Are those my only choices?"

Harold cocked his head with a thoughtful expression in his gaze, signaling a change in tactic. "Do you fear proximity to my brother Sweyn, on account of your wife? I assure you, he shall trouble the lady no more."

Edric bridled at the mention of Sweyn and snorted. How had Sweyn obtained the king's forgiveness and returned from exile in the year before? The thought of Godwin's manipulation of the matter angered him.

In the past, Aethelmaer Cild had stolen his great-grandmother's virtue before abandoning her. Godwin's conflict with King Edward had resulted in Tunwulf's death. The family abused its power, whether in influencing a king or browbeating poorer relations.

"I could force you," Harold stated. "Remind you of the loyalty your family owes mine. Blood binds us, though I suspect you have grown tired of that reminder. Be assured, my memory is long. I do not forget those who thwart my plans. Nor do I overlook those who help me."

Edric swirled the contents of his mug. "Persuasion is better than brute force, but your intentions remain the same. The matter does not concern me."

"Think on it," Harold urged. "What would you do for your father's sake?"

Edric's lips curled in disgust. "Yours is an odd question. It comes from the son of one who took my father from me. Edward affirmed my rights to Newington. Why should I care for Godwin's or your demands? You can do nothing to deprive me of my holdings."

Harold lowered his cup. His free hand went to his sword belt, festooned with a gold buckle and studded around its width by carnelian. A dagger glittered in its sheath, next to Harold's long sword.

"My father served yours loyally for all his days," Edric muttered. "His reward was a watery grave in the Channel. Godwin remains my overlord. However, his quarrel with the Frenchmen in the king's retinue does not concern me. My loyalty foremost is to England and its king. If he keeps Frenchmen at his court and invites their duke here, it is his will. No man may sway me against it, not even Godwin's son. I remain unmoved."

Harold's visage became the dark scowl of some foul beast roused to fury. "You speak of loyalty to the king, but you forget the duty you owe my family, because we are kin. My great-grandfather's blood binds us together. Would you spit upon the memory of Aethelmaer Cild?"

Edric stared into the candlelight for a time. "As he spat upon the love my great-grandmother bore him? He pledged himself in a handfasted marriage and lived openly with her as his wife. Not a full year had passed before he disavowed her and the sons she gave him, to wed a woman of rank. Why should I care for him, for any of you?"

Harold leaned forward. One burly hand gripped the edge of the table. "At dawn, my men and I rally others to my cause. You are my kin. I demand your service. If I do not see you and your men assembled, I shall have your answer. I caution you, think about your choice. Whatever you decide, Godwin shall know of it."

He downed the last of his ale in one swallow. He slammed the cup down on the table. It hit the wood with a heavy thud and splintered across its base. He strode from the hall. His *huscarls* followed hard on his heels.

Edric tapped his fingers on the trestle table. In the weeks after he had received word about his father, he half expected Tunwulf Grim would stride into the hall and demand his son get off his bench. He would have welcomed even an unkind word from his father, if it meant he lived again.

He stretched his long legs out. "What would you do, Father, if you were here?"

"Do you talk to the shadows, my dear?"

He turned at the echo of his mother's voice.

The delicate grace in her had faded. Emmeline wore no finery except for her wedding band. She had withered after the death of his father, a wilted flower without the sunlight warming its petals.

"I thought you were asleep." He reached for her hand.

When she settled into the seat beside him, her willow-thin frame shook. "I was abed while you and the earl talked. You were rather abrupt with him."

"You have often said it is not polite to overhear conversations."

"I am sure I was not the only one who listened."

Edric mused that every ear in the hall had probably strained for their exchange.

"Mother, do you think it wrong of me not to support Harold's cause?"

Emmeline sighed. "It is dangerous, but not wrong."

"I miss Father. He would be certain of the course."

"Dearest, you lived in his shadow for so long. Now, you are a man of twenty years and lord of this place. You must decide for us all."

Silence descended on the darkened hall. The beeswax candle had burned to a stub before Emmeline rose. She trembled with the movement.

Edric stood and draped his linen mantle over her narrow shoulders. "Are you cold this night?"

"It is the old ache, the one which time cannot heal."

He sighed. Her grief and sense of loss over his father mirrored his, except she lost the love of her life. Their family had endured tragedy at each generation since his great-grandmother's time. His grandfather Leofsige ambushed and killed. His father drowned in the blue-black waters of the Channel. He worried for his fate if he joined Harold Godwinson.

When his mother's slim fingers cupped his bearded cheek, she drew him from reverie. His stoic visage reflected in eyes now the color of grass. Their jewel-like spark had faded with Tunwulf's death. "Dearest, do what your heart tells you. Let your decision be for the good of Newington."

Edric kissed her lined brow before she shuffled off to her bed. He hefted the bench atop the trestle table. With the candle in hand, he followed in his mother's wake to the lord's chamber.

He placed the candle on the flat top of his clothing chest and removed his garments. His clothes went inside the chest, the shoes beside it. Beside his pallet now, he sank down and pulled the feather-filled coverlet up to his shoulders. With his hand tucked under his head, he closed his eyes.

"My lord?" Cynwise's plaintive voice sounded.

He sighed. "What it is, lady?"

Silence followed and thickened with each moment. He groaned and rolled on his back, staring at his wife. She swallowed audibly and scooted back on her pallet. Her fear disgusted him, palpable in her terror-stricken voice and shaky body.

He rolled his eyes heavenward. "Do you wish to say something?"

"I hoped you might share," Cynwise began, "that is, you might tell me what you decided about Harold."

He rolled and dragged the coverlet over his shoulders again. "Do not concern yourself. Whatever happens, you, Leofsige, and our baby daughter shall be safe. If Harold or Godwin moves against me, I shall send you to my mother's relations in Flanders."

"Please tell me what you decided to do."

"What difference does it make?"

"If you go to London, I must accompany you."

He turned to her with a long look. He sought the truth behind her intent in her gaze. Her cheeks turned pink under his scrutiny.

"This is no pleasure excursion, wife. Leofsige and our Leofflaed need you here."

"Your mother can care for our children, for she loves them dearly."

He raised an eyebrow and pinned her with his stare. "Do you miss your lover so much? Do you anticipate a reunion in London?"

The breath caught in her throat. Cynwise's face whitened. Her lips trembled and she turned from him. At the sight of her pained expression, he half-regretted his harsh accusation, but pride ruled him.

"I told you the truth of our relations, husband. Yet, you cannot forgive me."

Edric groaned. "You said he flattered you. You were young and his advances overwhelmed you."

Cynwise sat up and the coverlet fell to her side. "I meant he forced me! After he arrived at Elham and informed me of my husband's death, he forced himself on my body. He returned many times afterward. He raped me! When he wanted no more of me, he brought an old midwife from Hereford with her foul potions to rid me of the child he had planted in my belly. How could I ever want him? He was no better than my first husband who beat me because he could not get a child upon me. When he died, his brother claimed his estate and called me barren. Both of those men ruined me."

Her words ended on a harsh sob. She buried her face in her hands. Edric shook his head. She despised men because of what Sweyn and her first husband had done to her.

"I wanted the child so much," she whispered, "though Sweyn was the father. I knew if I had a child, he might be my husband's heir. Sweyn took my child from me. I hate the sight of him. Yet I do not want you to journey alone."

His hand alighted on her arm. She flinched and pressed against the timber wall behind her. He knelt in front of her and raised her face to his. She cried out fearfully, but he wanted the truth.

"Why do you care, Cynwise?"

She shook her head and lowered her gaze. He asked again, even gentler this time and she whispered, "You are a good man, Edric. You deserve a better wife than me, one who does not, who cannot love you."

He returned to his position beside her and rolled on his side. Her even breathing soon followed. The candle flame sputtered.

He frowned into the darkness. She did not love him. In truth, he did not love her either. Still, he wanted more from his marriage.

The faint brush of her hand on his back alerted him, but he ignored it. Yet, her furtive touch on his hip made her intent clear. He refused a response.

"Please, Edric."

He hated the soft entreaty in her voice. "I am tired. Go to sleep, Cynwise."

Her fingers circled on his hip and stroked downward. "My lord, I wish to give you more children. How can I if you turn from me?"

"You tell me you do not love me. Your only wish is to bear my children. It wounds a man's pride when his wife does not care for him."

"I am sorry. I wish I could love you, as you deserve. I have given you my fidelity and obedience. That must satisfy you."

Her unemotional tone sparked his anger. If all she wanted of him were his children, he would give her the sons and daughters she craved. He forced her back onto the coverlet. A silent plea in her eyes glimmered in the dim candlelight. He raised himself above her. When he mounted her, for all her wiles, she lay stiffer than a plank of wood under him. With each thrust, her brow furrowed. Her lips trembled until she bit them. An impassioned cry torn from the very depths of her soul filled the room. His body responded in kind, but he closed his eyes and blotted out the sight of her.

When he raised his head, she cried softly in her hands. He tugged at her wrists. "I did not hurt you. You wanted it. Must you weep each time?"

She waved him off and recoiled from his touch. He turned from her in disgust.

❧

At dawn, Harold and his men assembled in the courtyard. Edric waited at the door of the hall. If he stepped beyond the threshold, he committed himself to Harold's cause. He feared the consequences.

He gave a start of surprise when his mother appeared at his side. She draped a wolf skin pelt around him and pinned it with a brooch in the shape of a wolf's head. Emmeline regarded him.

"Your grandfather and father wore this in times of worry. They believed the spirit of the wolf protected our family. I pray it shall protect you."

He kissed her brow. Cynwise and his grandmother Eanflaed approached. His wife carried their baby girl, only four months old. Their two-year-old son clutched at his great-grandmother's skirts. Emmeline reached for her granddaughter.

"May you both go with God," Eanflaed said.

The small family embraced. Outside, he and Cynwise grabbed the reins of their horses. He rode Elfhar while hers was a dun brown mare with which Elfhar sired a foal last year. Four of his men accompanied them, with three left behind for the security of the family. At Harold's command, his company moved out. The sun blazed behind the low clouds. Edric nudged the stallion onward and followed Harold to London.

<u>CHAPTER 11</u>

London, England
August 1051 CE

Edric admired Harold's byplay with his minions throughout the rapid-paced journey. In such moments, he saw the charm of Godwin of Wessex emerge, whether in Harold's banter with his *thegns* or his Danish *huscarls*. Edric surmised Godwin's hopes for his family rested on Harold, the second son. The eldest son, Sweyn, possessed an unpredictable personality, and lurched from scandal to scandal.

Just after midday, their party drew abreast near a ferry crossing that forded the river Thames. Within London's old Roman walls, trade flourished. A moat protected the city. In the fields, the small wooden houses of London's inhabitants spilled out toward the king's palace on Thorney Island, an islet on the western bank of the Thames River.

The arrival of another set of riders drew Edric's attention. His wife gasped at their abrupt appearance. He grabbed the reins of her mount, the mare suddenly skittish. Cynwise's eyes became deep, unfathomable pools, which mirrored the depth and expanse of the river. The horsemen charged along the bank toward Harold's party.

Edric's gaze darted to the man at the forefront of the newcomers. He recognized Earl Sweyn by his strong resemblance to Harold. Two boys rode directly behind Sweyn. Their likenesses made Edric wonder if his sons would favor the Godwinsons' features.

Harold and Sweyn nodded to each other. Sweyn spoke in a rough baritone. Though Edric never overheard his words, whatever they were, Harold reacted badly.

He slapped his thigh and spoke in a gruff bellow. "God gave you no common sense. For the whim of two boys, you brought them here. This is a journey with grave purpose. I have business with the king. Haakon and Wulfnoth should have stayed at your home."

The youths shrank visibly in the saddles of their geldings. Sweyn colored.

"Haakon is my son, Harold, and Wulfnoth is our brother. They have an interest in what happens to our lands."

"Wulfnoth is but a child. Haakon is your bastard! How can they help?"

Sweyn smoothed his hand over his golden hair. Cynwise's mare snorted loudly and moved closer to Elfhar. Sweyn directed his gaze toward the sound. A grin rippled across his features. Edric looked at Cynwise, whose bottom lip trembled. He edged his horse even closer. Sweyn's widening smirk slashed across his face.

Harold spoke again. "You must send them home with the *huscarls*."

Sweyn stared him down. "I need my men with me."

"You are a fool!" Harold railed. "You did not foresee the inherent danger? You can risk your bastard all you want, but Wulfnoth shall not remain here. Mother would kill me if anyone harmed him. You always act on a whim. You never care for the consequences. You are a selfish, stupid man. I shall not endure your foolery any longer! Not when you put our youngest brother's life at risk."

Sweyn grabbed the reins of his horse. He dug his heels into the beast's side. His retainers followed, returning on their chosen path.

"Damn you, you cannot mean to leave them behind?" Harold's cries died under the hooves that hammered the earth.

He tore his gaze from his brother's image across the distance and cursed again. Then he looked to Edric.

"You, take charge of these children my brother has abandoned here."

Elfhar nickered and shifted under his master's weight. Edric patted the stallion's neck, certain his horse sensed the tension in him. "Why choose me?"

Harold nodded toward Cynwise. "Your wife is here. What better use of her?"

She whispered, "If you wish it, my lord earl."

"I do not wish it!" Edric thundered.

Harold's face purpled, heralding his descent into a maddening fury. He closed the distance between Edric and him, but Cynwise moved her mare between them. "Give over, husband. Truly, it is no burden for me."

"One of them is Sweyn's son!" He pitched his voice lower. "I know you care for children, my lady, but can you bear the sight of Sweyn's child?"

"Please, Edric, he is just a boy." Cynwise's dark eyes pleaded for his indulgence. He bridled at the thought of her discomfort. He looked at Harold, who glowered at him. Cynwise's hand alighted on his forearm. He nodded in surrender.

Edric's lips pressed into a thin line. Harold signaled the two boys, who placed themselves on either side of Cynwise. The eldest of the pair swiped wavy light brown hair off his forehead and smiled at her.

She returned the gesture. "Are you hungry, Haakon?"

The boy nodded with youthful eagerness. Cynwise reached into her satchel and tore off a hunk of crusty bread. She divided it between the pair, who ate it with obvious appreciation. Harold jerked the reins of his stallion.

With the addition of Wulfnoth, three of Harold's five brothers were present. Edric had never met Gyrth or Leofwine Godwinson before. Tunwulf Grim once remarked they least resembled their father. Seeing how they looked like Harold, Edric understood from this that his father meant they had never possessed Godwin's arrogance.

Gyrth's youthful appearance under a neat trim of facial hair marked him as the elder of the two. Leofwine seemed an even-tempered, thoughtful member of the family.

The riders crossed to Thorney Island on river barges. A streambed bounded the island and beyond, a marshy stretch. Edric followed Harold, his kin, the other *thegns* and the Danish *huscarls* ashore. The fertile land abounded with willow and oak trees, and deer and rabbits darted over the green fields. Edric did not understand the chosen name of Thorney Island, when there were no brambles. The construction of the new west minster, distinguished from St. Paul's east minister, dominated the approach.

Narrow slits for windows with rounded arches punctuated the abbey's rough, grey, stone façade. Near the top of the western wall, workers toiled under the open sky. The king had begun the abbey last year, in honor of St. Peter. Harold eyed the construction, before he spat on the ground. Edric wondered why he showed such disdain for a holy place.

Another building towered above the trees. The dense cover obscured most of the structure, but Edric believed it must be the Benedictine monastery on the island. The royal residence of King Edward rose behind a palisade.

A stout man in religious vestments waited at the gates. He held a copper gilded staff aloft. Garnet surrounded by gold shimmered at the center of its ornately carved head. Huscarls on horseback surrounded him.

When Edric recognized Abbot Aelfwig Wulfnothson, he stared hard at Harold's back. Edric worried whether it was right for the Church to take sides in the confrontation between a nobleman and the king. He bristled at Harold's brilliance. By strength in supporters and with the sanction of an influential clergyman, Harold would compel King Edward.

Harold dismounted. When the monk drew back his conical cape, he revealed a sheathed sword. It hung from a sword belt tightly coiled around his girth.

When Harold gestured, everyone else dismounted. All followed him and Aelfwig. The prelate demanded entry at the gate. After some time, the guardsmen acquiesced. Twenty *huscarls* guarded Harold and Aelfwig. Gyrth and Leofwine Godwinson followed, with the *thegns* loyal to Harold or Godwin behind them.

Guardsmen admitted the group into the long, great hall. They treaded across floors strewn with heather and sweet scented herbs. At the head of the hall, Edward, the king of England, slumped on a gilded chair.

Edward's hair, almost white in its fairness, curled at his nape. The rose pink of his cheeks contrasted against the pale, almost translucent face, its lower half covered by a long, white beard. He possessed slim, almost feminine hands, which gestured to another man who sat beside him. The king wore a long robe, dyed a heavy purple with decoration at the cuffs and hem, partially covered by a crimson and purple mantle. He and his courtiers stared when Harold approached. The king's rheumy eyes widened. A cold sneer splayed across the face of the other man, dressed in the rich robes of a high clergyman.

The attire of the courtiers marked their distinction and rank. Edric noted the presence of the king's *huscarls*, which outnumbered Harold's men. If trouble occurred, he might die in the resultant massacre. He turned from morose thoughts to the exchange between the king and Harold.

"By God's grace and favor, I bid you welcome, Earl Harold," Edward said. He extended his arm. Gold rings inlaid with precious stones gleamed on three of his fingers. "Do you offer the kiss of peace?"

The prelate at the king's side intended anything but peace. Waves of fury emanated from him. He looked at Harold with the scorn reserved for a manure pile.

Harold answered the king. "I shall offer peace when the king gives it." Gasps of outrage followed.

The angry prelate rounded the trestle table. "You dare bandy words of peace? You and your family do not know the meaning of the word! Your father usurped church lands at Canterbury! Your brother Sweyn defiled a bride of Christ and kept her a slave to his carnal desire! He slew your kinsman Bjorn Estrithson these two years past."

"The bishop of London knows I am not Sweyn or my father. I am Harold."

"Had you been welcome at court, you would know that I am the archbishop of Canterbury now."

When the archbishop assumed a posture of superiority, Harold's lips curled in disgust. He drew closer but the king said, "I have no quarrel with Harold Godwinson. His Grace Robert the archbishop of Canterbury shall withdraw."

Robert Champart, former abbot of Jumieges, had come to London from Normandy at the king's ascension. He remained Edward's close confidante.

When he stepped back, Harold continued, "The king cannot offer my family peace when he offers English tenancies and ecclesiastical lands to outsiders. How can England's nobles support a ruler who threatens our hold on our own country?"

Edric wondered which outsiders Harold meant. Men dressed in the Flemish style of his mother's people filled the court, along with others in French dress.

Tension rippled through the air. Yet the king continued smiling. His countenance brightened, if it were possible. "So you have brought kith and kin, making demands of me?"

When Harold frowned, Abbot Aelfwig put his hand on his nephew's elbow. Harold looked at him. Something indiscernible passed between the pair before Harold continued.

"My king, I do not demand. I make a plea for reconciliation. My father wants to seal the breach between our families, but he needs to understand why the king shows such constant favor to outsiders. In particular, you prepare for a great party of Frenchmen from William the Bastard's court, who are even now on their way to London."

Edric looked at Archbishop Robert of Canterbury, whose face colored an angry red. Mutters pervaded the chamber, some in angry tones, but others nodded in agreement with Harold. The king's smile vanished and he slunk further in his chair.

"Only Godwin's son dares question the king," the archbishop began. Edward turned rheumy eyes on him. "Robert, be silent!"

Edric wondered why everyone thought the king a monkish man, for he did not behave so now.

Edward continued, "I have made no secret of William's imminent visit. However, it should please you to know he shall not be present. Others of his retinue shall soon arrive."

"Why does William the Bastard remain in Normandy?" Harold asked.

Everyone else stared at him wide-eyed or slack-jawed. Silence descended again before Edward muttered, "I believe it is a personal matter."

If Harold intended more questions, Aelfwig's hand on his shoulder prevented it. Instead, Harold bowed before the king, who settled back in his cushioned chair.

"You and yours are welcome to remain our guests while the Frenchmen are present. Queen Edith shall be pleased to see you and the rest of her family."

Harold snorted at this, but he sketched a bow. "You may command me, my king. We accept your gracious invitation."

CHAPTER 12

London, England
September 1051 CE

Avicia accepted Philippe's hand when he helped her disembark from the barge on the Thames River. She draped the folds of her mantle against the coolness of the air and surveyed the landscape.

"This is the English capital, husband?"

Behind her, Philippe replied, "*Non*, dearest, the capital is at Winchester where the king keeps his treasury."

Alice moved beside her. "I think it is a dismal, gray place. A storm approaches. Look at those clouds."

"The landscape reminds me of Flanders."

"Does the foul smell also evoke memories of home?"

The friends turned at the female voice tinged with menace. Avicia ground her teeth at the sight of Mabel de Belleme, the new wife of William's trusted advisor Roger de Montgomery. Since the black-haired, green-eyed beauty arrived at Rouen in the weeks after her marriage, she showed disdain for all those whom she believed beneath her. Avicia's husband held no lands and lived by the generosity of his half-brother. Mabel deemed them too low for her interest and made bitter remarks whenever possible.

Avicia clasped her hands together lest she drove her fist into the woman's face. "All rivers have unpleasant smells, milady. The Thames is no more unsavory than the Seine."

A green flame leapt in Mabel's eyes. Avicia remained undaunted by the ferocity mirrored in her nemesis' expression. Philippe took her hand just when Mabel's husband appeared. Roger de Montgomery grasped his wife's slim fingers and kissed the tips of her talon-like nails. "Has my dear little hellion unsheathed her claws again?"

The woman's gaze raked over Avicia's face before she favored her husband with pursed lips. "*Non*, Seigneur, I unsheathe them only in our quarters for your pleasure."

Her husband gave a carnal laugh. Mabel glared at Avicia before she trailed him.

"Be mindful of her, dearest," Philippe murmured.

"Mabel de Belleme does not frighten me," Avicia replied. "She reminds me of a fierce passager at Lille, a peregrine that refused the glove."

"What happened to the peregrine?"

"The falconer flew her against a grouse one day. He did not know there were other hunters in the area. A fierce little merlin appeared. In the tussle for prey, it tore at the peregrine's breast. The larger falcon died."

Philippe chuckled and kissed her brow. "I trust Mabel de Belleme shall think twice before she troubles my little merlin again."

He joined Hugh and the Montfort retinue. Alice looped her arm with Avicia's own. "Come, dear. Let us see the rest of what your London has to offer."

"It is not my London," she replied. "Husband, what is this port called?"

"Ethelred's Hythe is what the ship's captain said. Hythe is the English word for a port. We must hire horses to take us to the king's residence. It is on the island upriver there." Philippe pointed.

Avicia followed his direction to a marshy thicket in the distance.

After she mounted a white palfrey with her husband's help, she remarked, "Why are we here if William is not?"

"His business keeps him across the Channel," Philippe said.

"William woos the daughter of Baldwin of Flanders." Hugh maneuvered his bay stallion beside his wife's mount.

Alice frowned. "Oh, by the heavens, not the haughty Flemish girl again!" She looked at Avicia. "I meant no offense to you."

She laughed in response. "Why should I care? I never liked Matilda. Is it true, milord Hugh? He still pursues Matilda?"

"The very same," Hugh replied. "He has heard she spent the past summer in Bruges. He intends to press his suit in person."

"Why might he fare better than his envoys? The lady is very proud."

"The daughters of counts can afford to be proud, even at a duke's expense."

Everyone chuckled at Hugh's comment on the ride to the royal residence.

Alice chatted the whole way, so Avicia paid scant attention to their environs. The horse jostled her and made her nauseous. Illness plagued her throughout the Channel voyage. Philippe never questioned it, since she had never traveled by boat at such length before.

They entered the grounds of the royal residence. It seemed no different from Rouen. With Philippe's aid, Avicia dismounted and joined Alice.

The squeals of a woman caught their attention. She crossed their path, her skirts held above her ankles. She ran in the direction of some men in English dress, who emerged from the main building. She launched herself at the tall, yellow-haired man at the forefront. When she hugged him, he spun her around in his arms. The woman leaned back. He nuzzled her graceful, long neck and she laughed.

Although Alice gaped at the strangers so engrossed in each other, Avicia felt a sudden pang of jealousy at their open affection. Philippe would never have embraced her so passionately in front of others.

She drew Alice aside. Their husbands called for the pages, who rubbed down the horses. They marveled at the peaceful beauty of the king's island abode.

"I suspect the English queen shall host many fetes for her husband's female guests. Imagine us in the presence of a queen." Alice's eyes were aglow. "She had her education at a nunnery. She speaks English and the Danish tongue of her mother."

"I do not speak any of those languages!" Avicia whispered.

Alice smiled and patted her hand. "You shall be with me. I shall teach you what to say before we make our presentation before the queen."

Avicia's gaze drifted toward another man who spoke with the tall Englishman and his beautiful companion. Though long yellow hair hid most of his features, he drew her attention. He introduced a woman beside him, who curtsied before her richly dressed counterpart, and beckoned two boys who hovered nearby. Then, he retrieved saddlebags from a black stallion.

Suddenly, he looked up and straight across the courtyard in her direction.

Her curiosity melted. From a face glazed in shock, his eyes, the pale blue of a robin's egg, held hers in a tight gaze. Her heart slammed against her breastbone. The breath came raw in her throat. The woman beside him turned and stared in the direction he did, a frown creasing her brow. He stepped forward once before halting.

Alice touched her arm. "You are pale! Are you cold?"

Avicia shook her head. She struggled for a reply. "Edric. Edric of Newington," before she crumpled in a heap at Alice's feet.

❧

When she became aware again, Avicia noted the voices, raised and furious. Some words she understood, others were incomprehensible.

"Shall she recover?" Alice's voice trembled with concern.

Unintelligible words followed from another woman.

"What about the baby?"

She recognized the male's voice instantly. With some effort, she sought Philippe's face. Her action proved a mistake. An intense throb flared up, centered between her eyes. She stifled a heavy groan.

"Oh, she is awake!" Alice scrambled to her side, knelt, and took her hand. "Avicia, how do you fare? By the heavens, you gave me such a fright. I thought you might die. You hit your head on a stone, you see, there was blood everywhere. Reminded me of when little Hugh fell from his pony. Do you remember how he cried? It was dreadful. I feared for my boy."

"Alice," Avicia groaned.

Her friend patted her hand. "Philippe is here to comfort you now."

"Where am I?" She blinked rapidly in the harsh candlelight. Knowledge of her surroundings eluded her. It felt so much better when she rested on whatever pillowed her head.

"Why, you are in London. Oh dear, have you forgotten what happened? After you fainted, well we could not leave you there in the dirt. We found someone to examine you, a midwife."

"Am I hurt badly, Alice? My head aches so much. Is the baby well?"

Her voice trailed off. Alice said, "Your baby is well, the Danish midwife has assured us the child suffered no harm. God favored you. Indeed, by His grace, the fall did not hurt the child."

Philippe moved beside them. "Alice, my wife needs her rest. I ask you to leave us for a moment."

"I shall visit with her later."

Avicia's gaze swung back to Philippe. She licked her dry lips and forced a smile. For all her efforts, a sharp pang of fear dug into her belly.

"The woman cleaned your wound and bandaged it. She says you are not hurt otherwise." His monotone voice belied his expression. His sculpted face became a dark mask, the lips drawn tight in a thin grimace. Gray eyes harder than stone regarded her without sympathy.

"Philippe, I meant to tell you soon, tonight."

He avoided her eyes, but waves of disapproval emanated from him. "You kept news of our child from me. It was deceit. I refuse to accept it from you."

"Please, if you would only listen to me. I did not want to hide it."

His gaze swung toward her again, his brow wrinkled in vexation. "You cannot excuse your behavior. You put my heir in danger, lady!"

Tears stung her eyes and tracked watery lines down her face. "This is my child, too. I shall never put our baby in danger."

"Yet you did! You made the journey when you knew you carried my child. You risked his life."

She closed her eyes and turned from the fury in his voice. Suddenly, his grip closed on her forearm none too gently. She winced in pain.

"Do not shutter your gaze when I speak to you. You are willful, but I shall not tolerate it. Stay here and rest. You shall remain here until the midwife assures us of the child's health. Do you understand?"

Fear stifled the words in her mouth.

He wrenched her arm and jerked her toward him. The veins throbbed at his temple and his mouth contorted grotesquely. His eyes bulged from their sockets.

"I said do you understand?" he demanded.

"I do, husband."

He released her. She rubbed the flesh and shuddered softly, her gaze averted.

Philippe smoothed his hand through his hair. "I shall send Alice to you. Remember what I said, Avicia. Stay and rest."

"I shall rest. I shall do naught to harm your precious child!"

He leaned closer. She stiffened with fear at the thought of his cruel touch, but anger emboldened her. "You only care about your child! You wish only to be certain my foolery has not endangered the health of your heir. You have yet to ask me if I am in pain. All I am to you is your broodmare."

She closed her eyes again, blocking out the sight of him.

His even breaths filled the space. "Avicia, I never meant it. I was so frightened, I did not think."

She rolled on her side. The movement sent another dizzying wave of pain through her skull. "*Non*, you did not think of me, you thought only of your baby. Now leave me be. Send Alice, I need her."

"Please forgive me. I did not mean to hurt you."

She ignored the sudden strain in his supple voice. "Go away, Philippe."

It seemed a long time passed before his footsteps retreated, and the door closed shut. When tears threatened again, she swiped at them. A sob escaped. Her voice exploded in a howl of agony.

When she stopped crying, she rolled on her back and looked around. Tie beams supported the roof above her. She felt around her surroundings tentatively. Wisps of straw clung to them. She rested on a pallet in a small windowless room. A bedraggled animal skin hung over the door in tatters, against the draft. Though unused to the humble appearance of the house, within its comfort, she pretended the world would not intrude.

Had she imagined Edric of Newington in the courtyard of the English king's residence? When he had left Flanders, she never expected to see him again.

From the moment he had emerged from the whitewashed palace, an animal skin draped over his square shoulders, he drew her gaze. He had changed over the years. He seemed taller, more self-assured than the young man she remembered. His hair seemed a little longer, too.

Many things about him were new, along with the woman at his side. Perhaps she was his wife, the girl who had awaited him back in England. Who were the two boys? Both possessed Edric's light-colored hair, but in truth, they seemed too old to be his sons.

Why had he stepped forward when he saw her? Why had he stopped? Had he wondered at her arrival?

She sighed. It did not matter. Philippe's mercurial display of temper aside, she loved him. His earlier cruelty pained her so much. Yet, the terror her nightmares inspired would not let her remain in Normandy without him. She feared for his safety, knowing with certainty, his life would end in England.

Alice entered the room with the Danish midwife on her heels. Avicia envied her friend's competence with several languages. The Dane gave instructions, which Alice translated before she knelt beside the pallet.

When the midwife withdrew, Alice glanced at the moss-covered walls with some disdain. Her nose upturned, she grasped Avicia's hand.

"Is Philippe still angry with me, Alice?"

Alice shook her head. "He was so afraid when you fainted. He rushed to your side, held you in his arms. Everyone was shocked. Mabel de Belleme laughed but Roger de Montgomery slapped her for it, after my husband chided her bad manners. We could not find anyone to staunch the blood. Hugh's squire learned the midwife lived at the outskirts of the city. We brought you here. When she told Philippe you were with child, he seemed thunderstruck. He stayed while she examined you. He did not leave your side. He feared for the baby, but also for you. He loves you, Avicia, never forget."

❧

Avicia followed Alice's counsel and forgave her husband, who remained vigilant, attentive, and kind in every way. The midwife, a stout Dane named Hallveig, possessed Torfida's thorough manner. In her care, on the fifth day after Avicia's arrival in London, she mended.

Muscles stiff from disuse, her legs wobbled a bit when she first stood. Philippe returned her to the king's abode via a small riverboat. She gripped his arm at every bump. On dry ground again, she breathed a sigh of relief.

"Where is Alice?" she asked.

"She and Hugh are here this morn," he answered. They walked with others toward the royal residence. Within the palisade, a flurry of activity ensued. Pack animals and men-at-arms converged in the courtyard.

"What is happening, Philippe?"

"The court moves westward to the city of Gloucester. We join King Edward. With good weather and good roads, it shall take four or five days before we reach our destination."

"I did not expect we might travel further. It is over land?"

He smiled at her. "Indeed, dearest heart, no more boats for you. Even the short journey along the Thames troubled you?"

"I can wait until eternity before traveling by boat again."

She halted at the entrance to the king's hall.

Philippe took her elbow. "Why do you stop? Are you unwell?"

"I am well." Despite her assurances, she trembled. She feared seeing Edric again.

CHAPTER 13

London, England
September 1051 CE

Edric knew the moment Avicia entered the room. Sensation crept up his spine. He watched as she walked from the recesses of the king's hall, with one of the Frenchmen at her side, toward a man and woman. He recognized the black-haired man who had cradled her after she fainted. He could not understand why she might be in England, instead of Flanders.

Her appearance remained the same after three years. The shortened sleeves of her pale blue and yellow garment showed a white cloth underneath. Yellow linen wound about her waist. His eyes lingered on her belly, slightly thickened. His gaze darted to the man beside her, whose hand cradled, even caressed her elbow.

She and the woman beside her engaged in an animated conversation. Then she rose on her tiptoes and whispered to the black-haired man. He confirmed their intimacy when he patted her belly. She belonged to him and carried his child.

"My lord, are you unwell?"

Cynwise's voice sounded beside him. In truth, he had forgotten she stood with Wulfnoth and Haakon at her side.

"Do not concern yourself, lady."

Cynwise drew back and her eyes widened at his sharp tone. He cursed inwardly. The sudden tension in him was not her fault, and he regretted his harshness.

"I am sorry, lady. I wondered about Harold, why he takes so long. He told us to await his arrival this morn. I did not anticipate this delay."

"My brother meets with our family before he talks to the king today," Wulfnoth volunteered.

Edric's gaze swung to the boy who often overheard much and understood even more. He dropped on his knees in front of him. "What more do you know of Harold's plans, Wulfnoth?"

The boy flashed a grin and puffed up his chest with a sense of self-importance. "Harold says he shall confront the king."

"Did he say naught more?"

"Things I did not understand. My lord, what does 'confront' mean?" Wulfnoth shuffled the dried herbs under his boot heel.

Cynwise grinned but Edric stifled his smile. "It means when you are face to face with someone, or something you do not like, you are bold and brave about it. You do not run from it. You face the thing or person you fear."

Wulfnoth nodded. "That's my brother Harold. He is very bold and brave."

"And you are a very wise young man." Edric tousled his curls. The child flushed with a look of delight, which colored his cheeks pink.

"You look like my brothers. Are you kin to us?" the boy asked.

Edric glanced at Cynwise with a startled gasp, unsure of his response. She nodded toward him, a beatific smile on her lips. For a moment, he stared at her entranced. Wulfnoth tugged on his hand and asked the question again.

He hesitated. After his father's death, he had resented Godwin and his family, and the havoc they played with the people of Newington since the days of Aethelmaer Cild. Lady Leofflaed, his father, even Cynwise and now him, all held in the sway of this ambitious family of nobles. He had not thought of himself as one of them.

He smiled at Wulfnoth. "We are kin."

He had never experienced a strong bond with the Godwinsons until now.

A sudden flurry of whispers made him stand. Harold approached with his family and at his side, strolled the woman he loved, Edith the Fair whom he had married in the Danish custom of hand fasting.

Edric saw her first on the day of their arrival in London. He recalled the memory of her skirts held high, the turn of her ankles on display when she ran toward her lover. She and Harold met some years ago at Nazeing in Essex. Tunwulf Grim had repeated the story of their love to his family. At the time, Edric had not believed in such emotions. A man who loved a woman forever upon his first sight of her seemed impossible. Now, he understood how it might happen. He had loved Avicia upon sight.

Wulfnoth and Haakon scrambled to their feet. They bowed with Cynwise and Edric when Harold stood before them.

"We began to think you might never arrive," Edric muttered. Cynwise put a hand on his forearm.

Lady Edith's arm wound about Harold's waist. "My lord Harold regrets our delay. I trust you and your lady slept well, Lord Edric."

The melodic tinkle of her conciliatory tone soothed his annoyance. "We did, thank you for your concern. My lord earl, what do you intend?"

Harold scanned the hall. Many stared in his direction, among them, the Frenchmen. Across the room, Avicia spoke with her female companion, but when she saw Edric, she reached almost blindly for her friend's hand. Edric averted his stare.

Harold said, "I shall speak with the king today and hear his excuses."

Edric frowned at his answer, which boded nothing but trouble.

They waited until mid-morning when the king arrived. At his side were his *huscarls* and the archbishop of Canterbury, Robert of Jumieges. The king moved at a slowed place. He walked to the forefront of those assembled. When he sank into one of the chairs, Edric thought his actions mimicked those of someone twice his age.

A man leaned in, whispering to the king. When he straightened, Edward nodded and beckoned the archbishop forward. They spoke in muffled tones. Then Robert de Jumieges stepped back.

The king's herald said in a harsh voice, "The king shall hear the Earl of Wessex."

Edric gaped at Harold in stunned silence. They intended on arguing in full view of the court. He glanced at Wulfnoth and Haakon.

When Harold bowed before the king, Wulfnoth slipped between Cynwise and Edric, who put his hands on the narrow shoulders of the boy. Wulfnoth offered him a quick smile.

Harold spoke in Latin. Edric did not know whether he did it for the benefit of the king's guests but if so, he hoped Harold intended no insult.

From across the room, Avicia's stare jolted him. Their gazes locked and neither broke the intent look.

Lost in her rapt gaze, sudden raised voices jarred him back to awareness.

"Be silent, I command you!" Edward shouted above the fray. When the room's occupants quieted, he continued. "We have heard Earl Harold's concerns, but I do not favor the Frenchmen in my realm more than any Englishman. Can the son of Godwin say his family has always shown me loyalty?"

When Harold made no reply, a broad smile lightened the king's purpled features. "Still, I do not want to quarrel with Godwin or his son."

The archbishop of Canterbury interrupted. "Your Grace, Harold Godwinson and his father have insulted you. They have reviled your honorable guests. Edward, they are responsible for Alfred's death! Have you forgotten how your brother died?"

Harold shouted, "The *witan* cleared my father of such accusations, twice!" His hand went to his sword belt. "I shall meet any man who makes such a claim again, be he the lowest commoner or the highest churchman in England!"

"My lord earl, please. Robert, calm yourself. I forget naught." Edward appraised them with a stern gaze. Both returned to their previous positions.

Focused on Harold again, Edward continued. "I pledge to meet Godwin and discuss this matter in peace. I want assurances he shall do the same."

The king followed up his words with a nod toward Harold's family.

Edric shrank back and pulled Wulfnoth with him.

Harold asked, "What assurances can I offer?"

"Your sister Edith tells me your brother is here, your father's youngest Wulfnoth, and there is your brother's bastard Haakon, too," Edward said.

A collective gasp arose from most of the Saxon nobles in the room.

Cynwise put a hand on Haakon's shoulder but he shrugged it off.

Wulfnoth looked up at Edric. "My lord, the king said my name. Why?"

Edric did not answer because Harold shouted, "You cannot mean for these boys to become hostages. I shall not do it! They are children. Damn my sister! Edith would not do this to one of Tostig's children. He was always her favorite."

"Lord Edric, what is a hostage?" Wulfnoth asked.

"We are prisoners," Haakon grumbled. "We must stay with the king."

Wulfnoth turned around, wild-eyed when he regarded Edric. "I do not want to stay! Please, my lord, my brother cannot let them take me, can he?"

Edric dropped on one knee before the boy who trembled. The king's *huscarls* approached. He gripped Wulfnoth's shoulders. Tears brimmed in the boy's eyes.

"Do not cry. Do not be afraid," he said. "Your father is a powerful earl. He shall not let the king hold you for long. You are a brave and bold son of Godwin, like Harold."

When the shadows of the *huscarls* fell, he patted Wulfnoth's head. "Brave boy."

"Come along with me." One of the Danes tugged at Wulfnoth's tunic.

"Give him a moment for farewells to his family," Edric pleaded.

The *huscarl* grinned and showed his ugly, yellowed teeth. He grabbed Wulfnoth's arm, and wrenched the boy toward him. Wulfnoth squealed and struggled, but the man's grip remained firm. Edric stood and touched the *huscarl's* forearm. "You need not be so rough with him. He is only a small boy."

The man aimed his fist. Edric anticipated the blow but it grazed his cheek. Wulfnoth scuttled away briefly before another of the king's guards grabbed him.

The embittered *huscarl* brandished his axe against Edric. Cynwise dragged Haakon back with her. The king demanded the withdrawal of his man, but he seemed intent, as he swung his axe in the air.

"Edric, *non!*"

He ducked in time and drew his sword in the next instant. His agility annoyed the *huscarl* who growled. The Dane's axe whistled through the air again.

"Have you lost your wits? How dare you raise your weapon against one of the Godwinsons?" One of the *huscarl*'s cohorts grabbed his arm in mid-strike.

The king came forward, his expression purple with rage. He struck the Dane full across the face. "Get him out of my sight."

The other *huscarls* dragged off Haakon and a frightened Wulfnoth, who cried piteously into his hands. Cynwise stared, her expression transfixed in shock.

Astonished, Edric sought out Avicia across the room. He had recognized her voice over the din. She called his name in such alarm when the *huscarl* attacked him. Now, the black-haired man took her arm. In heavy strides, he dragged her from the room.

CHAPTER 14

London, England
September 1051 CE

In the shadows outside the hall, Philippe released Avicia. He wrinkled his brow once again in irritation.

She leaned against the timber wall behind her, with eyes averted. When he stepped closer, she shrank from him. Tension rippled through the length of her body.

Philippe folded his arms over his chest and exhaled slowly. "I am beginning to question everything you say. Why did you cry out for that man in the hall? Who is he?"

His voice thickened with insinuation. Toes curled in her shoes, Avicia released her pent-up breath. The question had hung in the air, since she foolishly called out Edric's name, in such abandon.

She dared regard Philippe. The veins in his neck stood out in livid ridges. The breadth of his shoulders and chest beneath the wool tunic reminded her of his strength. She scanned the courtyard around them. One nobleman scurried inside the hall. No one else stood nearby who might rescue her from Philippe's anger. She never feared the possibility before that he could seriously hurt her.

"I await your answer." An edge of impatience sharpened his tone.

She swallowed loudly and hesitated. "He is Edric of Newington. I met him three years ago. I told you about him after we married. You must remember it, Philippe."

He drew back, with upraised eyebrows. "You mean the little English lord, the one who first kissed you?"

Embarrassed, she recalled how Philippe laughed when she confessed her folly with Matilda of Flanders' bird. Pity filled his eyes when she explained the resultant scars on her back. The memory gave her courage now. Her pain had saddened him. He had kissed her scars and promised he would always protect her.

She placed her hand on his clasped arms. "He is not so little. He is tall like his kinsman, the son of Godwin. Bold like him, too."

"Indeed, Harold Godwinson was reckless to insult our people," Philippe replied. "He forgets the debt King Edward owes us. We sheltered him and his family."

"Harold Godwinson appears to be a proud Englishman. He fears losing his holdings to others. Any man would defend a claim to title and land."

"You think well of your friend because he supports this Harold Godwinson?"

"Lord Edric is not my friend. I do not think of him at all."

Yet, her heart had cleaved in two with fear when she envisaged a Danish axe buried in his chest.

She continued, "I understand his loyalty toward Harold Godwinson."

When Philippe said nothing, she added, "I have met Lord Edric before, it would be impolite to ignore him now. Do you object?"

"You may greet him if you please, as long as I am with you. You did not expect to see the Englishman when you arrived here?" Philippe asked.

Avicia perceived his fears instantly. He wanted the truth, but he feared hearing it. He could not hold such poor faith in her love, but if so, she must reassure him. She rubbed his shoulders. The motion calmed him. His breaths became even.

"Lord Edric left me without a farewell. I expected none. I never thought I would see him, again."

Philippe cupped her cheek and raised her face for his inspection. She met his steady gaze. Surely, he detected the pounding of the heart beneath her breast.

"What did you feel when you saw him again?"

She buried her face in the woolen comfort of his tunic. "He means naught to me."

Philippe chuckled and hugged her close. Her eyes brimmed with unshed tears. She had lied to him for the second time.

❧

When Edric emerged in the daylight in Harold's wake, he blinked harshly against the mid-afternoon glare. He glanced around the courtyard. Harold spoke with two of his *huscarls*. Edric scarcely overheard their exchange. The *huscarls* bowed before their lord, mounted their horses, and urged the beasts out of the palisade.

Harold turned, his face pale, features fallen.

"Edric, I thank you for your kindness with Wulfnoth."

His wooden, distant tone belied the praise he offered.

Edric answered, "Your brother is a brave boy, my lord earl, a fine son of Godwin. If I may ask, what shall happen to him and Haakon now?"

"They shall remain with the king's court, ensuring Godwin's cooperation. My sister Edith shall take charge of them. She must keep them safe, or answer to me."

"And what of the *huscarls* who left here?"

"One goes to Hereford with word for my brother Sweyn. The other goes to my father and mother. I shall meet Father and Sweyn at Beverstone. I leave within the week. You shall accompany the rest of my family north to Gloucester with the court. Beverstone is less than a day's ride from the king's lodge. Grant me this boon. Be mindful of Haakon and Wulfnoth. You may see them."

"I shall try, my lord." Edric bowed and returned to the king's hall. A few of the royal guests and some of Harold's men lingered. He wondered if Avicia and her man might return.

Cynwise had wept when they led the children off. Edith the Fair still comforted her. She and Edric smiled in sympathy with each other before she departed. Edric bent on one knee before Cynwise.

"The court moves to Gloucester. We shall accompany them. Harold intends to meet his father and Earl Sweyn at Beverstone. We must prepare for our leave-taking."

Cynwise swiped at her wet cheeks. With his help, she stood. They left the hall side by side in silence.

On the left were storehouses where servants loaded sacks onto ox-drawn carts. Cynwise packed their possessions. Edric went to the stables, and saddled Elfhar and the mare beside the stallion. His mind strayed to thoughts of Avicia again.

Would she accompany the king's court to Gloucester, too? He should not care where she went. She seemed happy with her man.

In truth, things were not so terrible for him with Cynwise. They did not love each other, but he reasoned there must be others who simply tolerated their spouses, except he did not know any such couples. He focused his mind on Cynwise's better traits. She was an admirable woman. She possessed courage and gentility. She had proved a dutiful mother to their children. He still wanted the love a wife should bear a husband, but perhaps he expected too much from her.

With a grunt of irritation, he heaved the saddle onto Elfhar's back. The horse snorted and stamped in fury. Edric tugged the reins gently and calmed the stallion. "Sorry, old boy. Be at ease, I meant no harm."

He reached for Elfhar again but the horse nickered and shied from him. When he tried once more, Elfhar settled. Edric patted and rubbed the stallion's neck. Once saddled, he led both horses into the courtyard. Cynwise waited there, her face upturned to the sky for a moment, before she handed him his satchel.

"You are a good man, my lord."

He looked at her. "How is that, lady?"

"You were good to Wulfnoth and Haakon, though you resented how Harold foisted them upon us. You were kind with Wulfnoth. You comforted him when he was afraid. Even his brother could not console him."

"I would do the same for any man's son. I vow, my lady, I shall never allow any man, king or earl, to use our children in such ways."

"I know you would not, my lord." She smiled shyly and turned back to the horse.

Edric stared at her for a moment. He wondered why her words gave him no satisfaction. Why did he still want more from a wife than she gave? He realized such brooding did little good. Those thoughts only led in a direction he could not go.

❧

The Saxon court journeyed to Gloucester in five, uneventful days. They progressed under fair skies through the fertile beauty of the Severn valley.

Edric retreated to idle thoughts. He wanted no share of the conversation between Edith the Fair and Cynwise. When either of them looked to him for comment, he struggled with a response. After the second day, his wife gave up. He tried focusing on the gentle hilly landscape they traveled over, but the throaty laughter of one woman frequently interrupted his reverie.

The Saxon and French magnates of England rode in a cluster behind the king, flanked by his *huscarls* on all sides. His guests followed. Edric, along with other minor Saxon nobles trailed them.

His position afforded a view of every move Avicia made. Her peals of mirth drifted from up ahead. Muscles in his jaw twitched each time she gazed at her husband with eyes that twinkled. The knight hovered beside her, enthralled as Edric had been, or remained.

Resentful, he stopped watching them, and found Cynwise and Edith the Fair studying him. Then, Harold's wife looked eastward, beyond the hawthorn trees where the ridge of a steep escarpment loomed.

Cynwise's eyes probed his in a slow stare. "Perhaps you did not hear, but Lady Edith said we approach the hunting lodge at Kingsholm."

"Good, I shall be glad to take a proper rest."

Cynwise continued regarding him. His face warmed. She gave him a last sidelong glance before resuming her discussion with Edith the Fair.

The king's herald announced their arrival in the early evening. At the outskirts were several small cottages. A ditch-and-bank enclosure topped with a timber fence greeted them. The king and his party rode through the whitewashed, timber-framed gatehouse. Guards who stood at attention eyed their approach. Two others leaned out of narrow windows in the structure.

Edric slowed Elfhar after he came through, and marveled at the extent of the space. The size of his home at Newington could never compare with Kingsholm.

People thronged around the courtyard. He identified a small stone chapel, the royal stables and mews, the blacksmith's area thick with smoke, and the bake house and brewery. In the midst of the outlying structures, the roof of the king's long hall belched smoke. Huscarls patrolled either side of the front entrance. Next to it stood another building half its size, which he assumed was the bower house. Two women emerged from it, their mantles caught in a light breeze. They greeted the queen.

Edith the Fair said, "I wonder how the king shall accommodate us all. We do not enjoy the comfort of London's guest houses here."

"The bower house seems large enough, my lady," Cynwise replied. "I hope we shall not be separated from our men."

Edric looked at her askance and her cheeks flushed pink. She held his gaze. He broke the contact first. Guilt haunted him.

CHAPTER 15

Kingsholm, Gloucester, England
September 1051 CE

On the evening of their arrival, Edric attended the prayer Mass at Vespers. He stood near the back of the chapel. Cynwise's melodic singing drifted up over the other women in the hymn of the Blessed Virgin Mary. Even her angelic voice gave his heart no peace of mind. He thought only of Avicia.

How dare she be so happy in her marriage? He claimed contentment but little more. Cynwise's demonstration of loyalty and her gentleness with their children aside, nothing else recommended her. She did her duty by the Church's laws, not because she loved him. Surely, the knight loved Avicia and, worse, she loved him.

His mouth crimped in annoyance at lascivious thoughts of them together. Her husband must take immense pleasure in her body at night, his fingers kneading her breasts with her thighs pressed against him. Edric bridled at the images in his mind.

His hands were tight fists at his side when he stalked from the chapel after prayers. He waited outside for his wife in the fresh evening air.

In due course, she came. "Husband, I did not see when you left, you moved so quickly. Lady Edith told me the king devises a royal hunt in the morn. One of his relations, his sister's husband Count Eustace of Boulogne, shall leave in three days. The king honors him tomorrow with a feast."

"I wonder why he rode to Gloucester with the king at all, if he leaves so soon," Edric grumbled. "I am hungry. Let us dine in the hall."

Congregants streamed out of the chapel, headed for the hall. Cynwise scanned the crowd for Harold's wife.

Avicia appeared, her arms interlocked with the black-haired man at her side and a woman on her right. She walked directly toward him and halted at his side. She and her female companion curtsied.

"Lord Edric, it pleases me to see you again."

He blinked with surprise at her flawless Latin. When they had first met at Flanders, she spoke only the Flemish language.

Now, she regarded him without a hint of emotion. By contrast, his heart raced at the sight of her. The same pert nose and mouth he remembered. Her golden brows flared while he studied her. An uneasy silence stretched between them.

Cynwise rested her hand on his forearm and curtsied.

Recalling his wife beside him, Edric whispered. "This is my wife Cynwise of Elham. Wife, this is the Lady Avicia."

Avicia said, "I present my husband, Sieur Philippe de Montfort and the wife of our overlord, Lady Alice."

Edric bowed before them, as each acknowledged him with a slight nod. He straightened. "Lady Avicia, you surprise me, in many ways. Your fortunes have improved vastly since we last met."

She arched her eyebrows at his statement. Though she seemed ready for a reply, Cynwise interjected, "How do you know my husband, Lady Avicia?"

Blood roared in his ears. Edric waited for the answer.

Avicia regarded his wife, who favored her with a pretty smile. "We met in Flanders three years ago, Lady Cynwise, when the retinue of Godwin of Wessex negotiated his son's marriage to Lady Judith of

Flanders. Milord Edric taught me some English words. Your country is very beautiful."

"I have heard much the same of Flanders," Cynwise said.

"I hold fond memories of it, but my home, my heart is in Normandy," Avicia replied.

Edric sneered inwardly. How dare she come in all her glory, parading her happy marriage?

He interrupted whatever his wife's reply might have been. "Indeed, Lady Avicia, much has changed since we last saw each other. Both of us married. You to a French knight. When last we saw each other, you held no lands or monies, and had no marital prospects. You were a mere attendant in the Flemish court. How you must relish your improved fortunes."

Avicia gaped in stunned silence, while her friend gulped. Wide-eyed, Cynwise's cheeks reddened.

"A lowly attendant?" A feminine voice intruded. "I am not surprised, for you do not possess the refinement of a true lady."

Edric looked toward the interloper. A black-haired, green-eyed beauty stood nearby. She tittered behind her hands. The brawny man beside her tugged her arm. "Come along, Mabel."

Avicia's husband pulled her close. "A pleasure."

He led her from Edric's side. Her friend glared at him, before she followed.

Cynwise cleared her throat. "You embarrassed her, my lord. Why does she inspire such cruelty?"

Lady Edith's arrival halted his reply. "Forgive me, for I tarried too long with the queen. She shall let me see Wulfnoth and Haakon after Tierce tomorrow. You may both come with me. I am sure Wulfnoth would be pleased upon seeing Lord Edric again. Oh, the hall must be very full. Shall we go in?"

"I have no appetite," Edric said.

Cynwise eyed him with an unwavering gaze. "You said you were hungry."

"Not anymore." He walked off into the dim evening alone.

⌘

Avicia sat beside Philippe on a long bench at the narrow trestle table. For the first time in which they dined together, she noted the coarseness of his table manners. He selected the thickest slices of venison for himself and piled thin scraps before her. He licked his grease-covered fingers. When he poured generous cups of wine for himself from the earthenware pitcher, much of it spilled on the white tablecloth. She sneered at his crude behavior and turned from him.

Across the hall and to her right, Mabel sat with two other women. Avicia could not remember their names, but knew they were also the wives of William's closest advisors. Mabel met her gaze and laughed openly. The other women bowed their heads and smothered their sniggers. Mabel challenged Avicia with an unrepentant stare. Her green eyes narrowed with disdain before she sniffed haughtily and whispered with one of the women, who laughed.

Avicia's stomach soured. Why had Edric embarrassed her? She had never experienced feeling ashamed of her service to Matilda of Flanders, but when he belittled it before her nemesis, she felt lower than dirt. No doubt, Mabel had shared the insult among her friends. Most of them already presumed they were her betters, because her husband possessed no land. Now, they likely thought of her as a servant who aspired for higher status.

Mortified at her humiliation, she barely stomached the food. The butter tasted rancid, or perhaps the onset of her pregnancy made her think so because Philippe spooned copious amounts on his bread. The leathery meat and its taste, or lack thereof, disgusted her. She had never liked lampreys and refused them now, steeped in wine and covered in cold sage.

Her husband's silence about the insult Edric had delivered hurt her. Philippe betrayed her trust and reliance on him. He devoured a leg of roasted pheasant with obvious relish. Not for the first time, she wished he might choke. He experienced no shame in his lack of action. How dare he act indifferent while she suffered?

"You do not eat." Philippe discarded his bones.

She rolled her eyes heavenward. "How observant of you, husband."

He raised one of his black eyebrows in a quizzical slant. "Why take such a tone with me? You became ill-tempered after you saw the Englishman…."

"Ill-tempered?" she sputtered. "Ill-tempered!"

Alice and others glanced at her, but she ignored their curious expressions. She stared at Philippe, with her lips pressed tight together.

"Avicia, I beg you do not scowl at me so. Lower your voice at the table." His visage hardened. "Do not be angry with me, if your reunion with the Englishman went badly. Why did you seek him out? He has the arrogance of his kinsmen the Godwinsons. If he was rude to you, why should you care for his opinion? You shall never see him again, after we leave England."

Although he acknowledged her suffering, he simply did not care about it.

He continued, "His actions do not matter. When we were in London, you said it meant so little to see the man again. Eat some food for the sake of our child."

She forced a smile. "You only care about your heir. You did naught while Lord Edric shamed me before Mabel de Belleme."

He chuckled and sought her hand. "She cannot harm you either."

She tugged her fingers from beneath his grasp and stood. "How can you be so blind to my misery? I must leave. I shall return shortly."

"You cannot wander alone in this strange place."

"Please, leave me be!" She stifled a sob and darted from the hall. High-pitched laughter chased her.

❧

Edric pressed his head against a timber post. He had behaved stupidly. Avicia's happiness rankled on two accounts. Her marital pleasure surely outmatched his. She had given her heart in full to her man, while his wife did not love him.

He and Avicia had known each other only for a short time. Still, it seemed a betrayal that she loved another. She had forgotten him.

His heart ached with nostalgia. She had found someone else who made her happy. Her disloyalty hurt. For years, he had kept memories of her afresh and alive in his mind and heart.

Still, she had not deserved a measure of his pain, but like a fool, he had belittled her, reminded her of her humble origins. He gained little for his trouble, except more cause for regret.

He sank down on the dank earth and tugged his grandfather's wolf skin pelt around him. Across the yard, a hound nosed for a few scraps in a heap. He emitted a baleful whine when he found nothing, before he loped off. Edric drew his knees up, rested his elbows on them, and slumped into silent misery.

❧

Avicia stumbled into the courtyard and headed for a dense copse of thick leaves. Her eyes watered with every step. She wiped the tears aside as soon as they fell, intent on the solitude the thicket offered.

"Avicia?" In her path sat the source of her embarrassment.

When Edric rose, she stepped back. He advanced and she put her palms up, warding him off. His fingers closed on her wrists.

"Get away from me! By your own recent observation, I am a lowly retainer, worth no one's notice."

"Stop this. I did not mean to hurt you."

She wriggled from his grasp, desperate for an escape. "Let me go, or I shall scream."

"You behavior draws unnecessary attention. The king's guards look at us."

Two *huscarls*, who warmed themselves by a fire, nudged each other with shrewd leers. One winked at her and gave a raspy chuckle before he whispered to his companion, who also laughed.

"Come with me," Edric urged.

She bridled. "Leave me be! How dare you?"

His hand clamped on her wrist. He dragged her toward a timber structure. Behind them, the sounds of laughter echoed.

He pried open the door and pushed her inside. Birds squawked in loud protest at the intrusion. They stood in the king's mews.

"I am the wife of a knight, not some peasant you can abuse. Let me out, my lord, or I shall scream this place down!"

He barred the door and stepped closer.

Her stomach fluttered and she licked her dry lips.

She wiped her clammy hands in her skirts before she balled them into fists. Her senses grew attuned to the sound of his even breath, the smell of horses and grass that lingered on him. Masculine power emanated in his square shoulders and powerful legs.

"I acted without foresight. I regret my earlier behavior, my lady."

"You regret it? You regret it! You embarrassed me before my friend, my husband, and a woman whom I despise. Yet you can counter my feelings with simple regret."

"Shall I fall on my knees and beg forgiveness? I shall if you want!"

As if giving proof of his words, he did so. His body hit the earthen floor with a heavy thud. She held his rapt gaze in silence. The king's birds quieted.

"Why did you do it?" Her eyes watered again.

"It was unforgivable. I was angry. I did not expect that you might marry, might love another."

"Should I have brooded forever in your absence?"

He smiled but it seemed insincere, forced. "Was it too much to hope?"

She turned her back on him. "You are an English lord's son. I lived by the whim of my uncle. Your status and mine dictated our fates."

"My father is dead. I am the lord of his lands now. Your fate changed for the better, too. You left Lille and your cruel uncle behind."

"Philippe rescued me."

Stillness descended in the room again. Stifling warmth grew and swelled in the enclosure. Edric's boots scraped the earth behind her. She whirled and faced him. He stood with arms rigid.

Perspiration glided down her back underneath her garments. She backed off, but he reached for her and held her firm.

"Do you love the Frenchman?"

"I married him."

He jerked her toward him. "That is no answer. Do you love him?"

His breath warmed her cheeks. His mouth drew her gaze for a moment before her eyes flitted back to his. "I love him! I carry his child. Did you believe I would never find love again, content with shallow memories of you? There is a great divide, which separates us forever. Hope forsook me when you told me you belonged to another. Philippe found me. He desired and loved me. I chose to love him, too."

Edric released her so fast, she stumbled a moment. He turned from her, his shoulders hunched. Waves of misery cloaked him. Her heart wrung with pity at the sight.

"Cynwise is no true wife," he muttered. "She does not love me. I married her because Godwin wished it. She tolerates me at best."

Avicia blinked back tears. His voice seemed so wooden, remote. With trepidation, she put a hand on his shoulder. Muscles bunched beneath her touch.

"I am sorry for you, my lord."

He spun around, his face a dark mask. "Do you think I want your compassion? Am I some object of your pity, scorned and ridiculed for my loveless marriage? Do you congratulate yourself for the happiness of your union with the Frenchman?"

"Please, I meant no such thing! I would never pity you, or think myself above you. You have confused me and made me say things I do not mean."

Edric captured her face in his hands, forced her gaze upward.

Her eyes traced the contours of his mouth. She remembered the pleasure of his lips on hers. Her heart fluttered in tiny ripples.

He loomed closer. "Did you forget me, Avicia?"

She tugged at her lips with her teeth. He inhaled sharply, desire warming his gaze.

"Please release me. I am a married woman, my lord."

"What did you feel when you first saw me? Why did you stare openly? Did you remember our days together? Have you missed me as much as I have missed you?"

"I love my husband. Edric, do not do this….."

His lips hovered dangerously close to hers. "You forgot to say 'please'."

She drew breath in one space. In the next, the feathery light touch of his kiss trailed across her mouth. So softly, her mind scarcely acknowledged it. She leaned toward him, seeking proof of the phantom caress. With a low, urgent chuckle, his mouth pressed against hers in full. She responded with keen insistence. Their lips and breath melded together. Her hands swept up his arms to his face. She held it firm between her fingers.

The distance and time between them faded. His kiss outmatched the hesitant, exploratory embrace of their past. He grew bold and brutal, possessive. She moaned when his hands slid down her waist, cupped her buttocks beneath the coarse wool and lifted her against him. He hardened beneath the layers of cloth, and pressed against her firm, rounded belly where the child grew inside her. Philippe's child.

She broke the kiss. "This is madness!"

Rushing for the door, she escaped into the evening air.

Alice whirled toward her in the middle of the courtyard. "Avicia! I have been looking everywhere for you! Philippe was worried and I…."

Her voice faltered when Edric emerged from the mews. Stiff-backed, he bypassed them in lengthy strides. Alice gaped at him before her gaze returned to Avicia.

They fell into step together. Near the hall door, Alice halted. Cold speculation frosted her gaze. "I shall not speak of what I have just seen."

"You saw nothing…."

"Do not contradict me! I know what I saw. I love Philippe, Avicia. He is dearer to me than my own brother is. I shall never let anyone deceive him, not even you."

"I love him, Alice! I would never betray him with Edric."

Alice frowned, her lips drawn tight. "I do not believe you. I do not know why you and he were alone together. You are my friend, but if Philippe ever suspects your fidelity to him, I shall not defend you."

"Naught happened, Alice!"

"I wish you spoke the truth. Yet, your lips are too full and moist, those of a woman who has just been kissed, passionately so."

Alice continued toward the hall. Avicia fell into place behind her. She touched her swollen lips and shivered.

CHAPTER 16

Kingsholm, Gloucester, England
September 1051 CE

The next day brought no word from Harold at Beverstone, and Edric brooded in concern. Instead of joining the hunt, he and Cynwise accompanied Edith the Fair to the bower, where they saw Wulfnoth and Haakon. Wulfnoth pestered him for stories, but cried when the *huscarls* took him back to Queen Edith.

A full week passed. In the afternoons, Edric kept himself occupied in the stables with his horses. Today, he brushed Elfhar and the mare's coats.

He had avoided Avicia since the night in the king's mews. His cheeks heated with shame at the memory of his actions and her response. His desires had never ruled him before now. He must control his passions. Yet, her allure made him forget his personal vows of faithfulness to his wife. He had never desired a woman more.

He leaned against Elfhar's neck and drew a heavy sigh. The stallion nickered and nuzzled his shoulder. He patted the horse's head and continued his work, looking up when footsteps sounded behind him.

Lord Leofwine Godwinson stood before him. He nodded to the horses. "You have no servant who tends them?"

"Elfhar prefers my touch." Edric patted the stallion's shoulder and brushed his hands together. "How may I serve you, my lord?"

"You saw my brother Wulfnoth earlier in the week. Tell me how he fares."

"He is a little afraid, but I suppose his blood ties with the queen help him fare the worst of it. I believe he would welcome a visit from you. Surely, the queen cannot object."

Leofwine never replied. Something else drew his attention and made him frown. Edric came around Elfhar and viewed the distraction.

Edward and a few of his courtiers emerged from the hall. Beside the king strode a broad-shouldered man, with heavy, reddened whiskers that obscured half his face. He embraced the king before he and other French knights mounted their horses. They rode to the gatehouse. Heavy hooves pounded the earth.

"Who was that?" Edric inquired.

Leofwine spat. "Count Eustace of Boulogne, who married the king's sister, the princess Godfigu."

Edric sensed his abhorrence of Eustace.

Leofwine smiled at him. "Can I help you with the mare?"

He drew back, surprised at Leofwine's generosity. "I would be honored, my lord."

The two men worked together. Despite his rogue's smile, Edric felt an instant affinity with Leofwine. An easy camaraderie developed between them. By the time he and Leofwine went into the hall for mugs of ale, he had gained a friend among his distant relations.

❧

By the middle of the next week, Edric worried about Harold still, but Leofwine told him no word had arrived.

"Father and Mother spent time in Flanders recently, only just returning this month. You mentioned your mother is also Flemish, Lord Edric. Have you ever visited Flanders?" Leofwine asked, while they returned from a mid-afternoon ride.

Edric mumbled, "Once."

"Are you familiar with the Flemish court?"

"My mother is. She attended Judith of Flanders."

"Is this the same Judith, wife of my brother Tostig?" When Edric nodded, Leofwine continued, "It would seem we have more connections than I thought possible. What do you think of the Bastard's negotiations for the hand of Matilda of Flanders?"

"I was not aware of it." Edric scowled at the memory of Matilda's cold-hearted refusal of forgiveness for Avicia. Count Baldwin's vain daughter had stood by and watched her whipped for a careless error.

"Father believes the Bastard is scheming. He does not scratch himself without a plan in mind."

Edric chuckled, but the topic of the Frenchmen did not interest him. "Tell me more of your mother, Countess Gytha of Wessex, if you please."

Leofwine alerted the sentry, who leaned out of the window up ahead. The man yawned and withdrew into the gatehouse.

"My mother is very beautiful, even in her advanced years and quite proud of her beauty," Leofwine continued when the gateway opened. "She is an intelligent woman, too, and she insisted my sisters received their education from the nuns at Wilton. Queen Edith especially is her match in languages and music. My mother is generous with her knowledge, compassion, and possessions. She is tolerant of my father in all things, except his adulteries."

Leofwine faltered and stared. Edric followed his gaze. A band of bedraggled Frenchmen surrounded Edward. The archbishop of Canterbury demanded silence. The Frenchmen shouted over each other's heads. Some brandished bloodied swords.

Stunned at the sight of the red-haired Count among them again, Edric asked, "Why is Boulogne still here? I thought he had returned to his lands."

They dismounted and a stable boy took their horses. Harold's wife and Cynwise approached. Edith the Fair drew Leofwine away and spoke with him in a hushed tone, while Cynwise bowed before Edric.

"Wife, what has happened?" he asked. He pointed at the Frenchmen. "What caused this argument?"

Cynwise put a hand over her chest, her breath ragged. "I can scarce speak of it. My lord, it is terrible. Count Eustace went to Dover and hired a ship for home, but he claims the townspeople assaulted him, a king's guest."

"What? Why would the townspeople do such a thing?"

"We do not know, but before dawn, Count Eustace came again to Kingsholm. The king has sent word to Earls Harold and Godwin at Beverstone. He has demanded Godwin punish the Dover men, in his capacity as earl of Kent."

Over the past weeks, Edric experienced a greater sense of loyalty to his relations. Cynwise's next words gave him no time for considering the extent of his emotions.

"Earl Godwin's reply was swift. He refused to do it. He and the king are at odds again. The king summons Earls Leofric and Siward. You know Earl Siward shall not support Godwin's defiance, not when Sweyn Godwinson slew Siward's father, Bjorn Estrithson. King Edward has summoned the *witan*. With his council, he shall bring charges of treason against Godwin of Wessex."

❧

Edric saddled Elfhar in the courtyard of the royal hunting lodge at Kingsholm. The afternoon sun beat down on his shoulders, while Cynwise pestered him.

"Why must you do this? You entrust me to strangers in the hopes of safe conduct, while you ride off to war with the Godwinsons against the king."

He fastened the girth for Elfhar's comfort. "Lady, blood binds me to them. I cannot turn from them. They are kin."

"This is madness!" Cynwise stamped her foot. "Edric, you hold your lands by the king's affirmation. You do not need to follow Godwin. You care naught for me or the fates of your children."

With Elfhar saddled, Edric sighed. "Wife, you are overwrought. The king must resolve this impasse with Godwin. The *witan* shall reject the charge of treason. Godwin shall return to court, and you and I may revel in the peace of our return home."

"What if you should die?"

Her voice dissolved in a whimper. He looked at her at last. Her face appeared pale, a look of mute appeal in the dark blue eyes. Tears tracked down her puffy cheeks. He put his hands on her shoulders, but she launched herself at him. She buried her face and her heavy sobs in his tunic.

He struggled for words at this torrent of emotion from a wife who did not love him. Worse still, a stab of guilt pierced his heart. He longed for Avicia, her warmth and passion in his arms again, instead of Cynwise with her forlorn tears.

He drew back. "Please, look at me."

She complied. He tucked a wavy black tendril of her hair under the headrail from which it came loose. She stared up at him, wordless, her face now scarlet and swollen.

"I make a solemn vow by St. Augustine. For you and our children, I shall return, I promise. Go with Lady Edith to Nazeing. From there, her retainers shall conduct you home again. Understand that I cannot turn from duty now."

"Edric, I do not want to leave you. I am frightened."

"Cynwise, do not fear. I gave my word. It shall suffice. Believe in me."

The members and retainers of the Godwinson clan gathered in the courtyard, some already mounted on their horses. Leofwine Godwinson maneuvered his bay stallion forward. His fierce, dogged look fell on Edric. "Are you ready?"

Edric nodded and vaulted atop Elfhar. Edith the Fair approached, her long slim fingers clasped together. She draped an arm over Cynwise's shoulder. "Do not fear, my lord of Newington. Your wife shall remain with me until it is safe. My household guards shall take her home."

"You are gracious and kind, a credit to your man," Edric said with a nod.

Cynwise's cool touch on his hand drew his gaze. She brought his fingers to her lips. "I hold you to your promise, my lord."

A sensation prickled his spine. Someone stared at him. Across the courtyard where many of Edward's guests milled about, the men watched with darkened gazes, the women in odd fascination. All, except one.

The breath hitched inside his chest. Avicia's gaze met his and remained, far longer than circumspect for both of them. Then, her forlorn stare fell. Her hand rested in the crook of her husband's arm. The black-haired man spoke with a larger man who resembled him.

Abbot Aelfwig Wulfnothson issued orders. Taking his leave with a bow, Edric left Cynwise, who stepped back. Edith the Fair consoled her with a hand on the shoulder.

Edith called out, "My lord Leofwine, tell my lord Harold I expect he shall keep his word, and return home in time for our Edmund's birthday."

Leofwine nodded and nudged his mount forward. Edric waved to Cynwise. She smiled though her eyes watered. He flicked Elfhar's reins.

At the last moment, he looked over his shoulder. Avicia's gaze met his again and stirred a maelstrom of emotions deep in his heart.

❧

The English nobles rode off in a haze of dust. Hugh crossed his arms over his burly chest. "Good riddance." He spat on the ground.

"Why do you say so, husband?" Alice asked.

"I believe they and this Earl Godwin are trouble. It is good they are gone."

"The English are aggrieved," Alice replied with a shrug. "None of us know the full circumstances behind Comte Eustace's charges. We did not witness the events at Dover. Those who did are either in Eustace's employ or dead."

Hugh raised a black eyebrow. "You favor the Englishmen in this dispute?"

"*Non*, husband, I favor no one. We cannot judge without certainty of the facts. Comte Eustace has presented his claim, but we have heard naught from the Englishmen at Dover. Lord knows what Eustace has done in truth. Even William judges him a brute."

While Alice and Hugh continued their discussion, Philippe stared at Avicia, who trembled under his scrutiny. Edric's sudden departure left her naked and exposed.

"Dearest, you were quiet all morning. Have you naught to say?"

He tipped her chin up with a gentle touch. "You look pale. Are you unwell?"

"The babe makes me tired."

Philippe smiled and his hand cupped her belly. She stifled the urge against pulling from his possessive touch. "I miss home, husband."

"We must return to Normandy." His hand lingered firm on her abdomen. "The English make war with each other. Winter must not trap us here. I want our heir born in Normandy."

Avicia wanted the same thing. So, why did her heart tear at the thought of her return home? If she did, she might never see Edric again. Twice the fool, she still cared for him. She had believed his words of continued devotion on their last night in the mews. Yet he avoided her afterward. He had not bothered offering farewells now, just rode off with the rest of the English nobles.

Worse, he had lied to her. She witnessed the proof of his dishonesty. Edric's wife followed him with greater eagerness than a hound desperate for attention. She cried her heart out in despair, clutched at him, and kissed his hands.

He had deceived Avicia about his unhappy marriage. She would be glad when they left England, where she might cast aside the memories of his faithlessness.

She fought against tears. She must forget him, forever. She belonged to Philippe and Normandy. Edric's fate bound him to the service of the English and his pretty wife. He and Avicia would remain apart, never more than a memory for each other. An empty ache filled her heart with the realization.

Beside her, Philippe mused, "I shall be glad when we return home. I suppose England has its charms, but not for me."

In his usual manner of late, he seemed oblivious to her turmoil. He rubbed her belly. She shrank from his unwelcome touch though he took no notice.

"What do you say dearest, are you ready to leave?"

Avicia stifled a sob. "Oh, I wish we had never come here."

She turned from Alice's sudden scrutiny. Waves of censure radiated from her, disappointment echoing in her narrow gaze and pursed lips. Alice had never spoken of the night she saw her and Edric exit the mews. She behaved with the same politeness and cordiality. Yet an air of suspicion clouded her gaze ever afterward.

Now she asked, "When might we be able to leave, Hugh?"

Hugh replied, "We shall remain far removed from this conflict, but our departure depends on William. He shall soon arrive here. He sent a messenger to Roger de Beaumont this morn."

"And how did his pursuit of Matilda of Flanders fare?" Philippe asked.

When Hugh shook his head, Alice chuckled. "The lady's continued refusal tests him. His patience is limited. Yet he is such a man who, when he wants a thing, wants it even more if he cannot have it. He shall never admit defeat. I suspect this Flemish girl does not easily admit defeat either."

Avicia cleared her throat. "Why does he want her so badly?"

Hugh replied, "She is rich and beautiful, and of a noble lineage. She even bears the bloodlines of a great English king, called Alfred."

"She may be of the noblest blood, but Matilda has a fine temper and she can be petulant. What I remember of her makes me wonder at her suitability as future Duchess of Normandy."

"Whatever do you mean, milady?"

"She was proud, overly so, milord. Beyond what our duke should tolerate in his bride. We have all seen his temperament. He is a strong man and could not abide this woman's haughty behavior for long."

"We are in agreement that the daughters of counts can afford to swell with pride."

"Our liege is also proud. Surely, there are other amenable heiresses from whom he may choose, within Normandy or France. Why does one haughty, little Flemish girl mean so much? What does he gain from a union with her?"

Something indiscernible passed in the look Hugh and Alice shared. When neither one answered her, Avicia touched Philippe's forearm.

With a soft chuckle, he replied, "Who can know the duke's moods? William wants what he wants and he is determined to get it."

His answer seemed evasive. Avicia asked, "What is his relationship to the king of England? Are they kin?"

Before Philippe spoke, Hugh interjected, "They are distant cousins. King Edward spent his minority in Normandy. Now come, the bells peal for Nones. Shall we attend the chapel?"

Alice rested her hand on his forearm and glanced at Avicia, who frowned. They withheld something from her about William and his earnestness for marrying Matilda, who, if she descended from an English king, might share kinship with the current monarch. Hugh had said William and King Edward were also distant cousins. Blood ties bound the three together, but the Church forbade marriages between relations of the seventh degree. Perhaps, William would escape the match and choose another. Avicia did not relish bowing and scraping before Matilda of Flanders again.

"Are you ready?" Philippe interrupted her reverie. She fell into step beside him. She refused the arm he proffered, and followed Alice and her husband to the chapel. The Mass might offer her some comfort.

CHAPTER 17

Beverstone, Gloucester, England
September 1051 CE

At the southern outskirts of the Cotswold area, the beech trees thinned. Dense woodland gave way to Beverstone. Just as the moon rode high and church bells marked the hour of Compline, Edric and the rest of the Godwinson *thegns* reached Godwin's encampment on sloped grasslands. The safety and warmth of torchlight and cooking fires beckoned in the darkness.

Beside Edric, Leofwine slowed his horse. "I shall find Father and Harold."

Edric nodded. "I shall wait nearby."

Leofwine frowned. His dark yellow eyebrows knitted together. "You are kin. Come."

Edric said nothing to Leofwine's acknowledgment of his association, though over the previous two weeks it weighed upon him. His horse trotted beside Leofwine's own through the encampment.

Brilliant stars illuminated the night sky though the earlier warmth of the day hung heavy in the air. Thegns sat together by firelight. Men-at-arms hefted double-bladed swords over their shoulders or carried bows and a quiver of arrows. Many of the *thegns* wore helmets and mail tunics. Would they lose all in a contest with the king? What role might Edric, a minor Kentish *thegn* play in the quarrel?

Leofwine halted outside a square-shaped tent, where his younger brother Gyrth stood. Edric reined in Elfhar beside Leofwine's horse and dismounted with the others in their company. A group of men stood outside the tent, deep in argument, Earl Sweyn the loudest among them.

Edric stared at Godwin, agape. His hair reflected the gray of old age and worry. His features were timeworn and weather-beaten. Firelight illuminated deep lines etched into the skin.

Harold roared over the other voices, "Be silent, damn you! Worse than the stalls at market day, I tell you."

Godwin's counselors fell into hushed whispers and mutters. When Harold's hot gaze swept over them, they were silent. Abbot Aelfwig Wulfnothson embraced his brother Godwin. Leofwine and Gyrth also hugged their father.

Beside Harold stood a rail-thin, petite woman in sea green garments, cinched at the waist by a leather belt of precious stones. Her murky gray eyes scanned the crowd, fell on Edric, and hung there for the space of two breaths, before she perused the rest of the company.

She glared at Godwin. "Where is my son Wulfnoth? Why is he not here with us?"

Edric turned from the stark pain in her voice and expression. Countess Gytha, wife of Godwin and mother to his sons, repeated her inquiry. Everyone avoided her baleful stare. Her lips crinkled in a sneer. She fled inside the tent. The flap snapped closed behind her.

Another moment of tense silence followed before Harold said, "Only close family may remain. My father shall speak with you again, if necessary."

"I shall wait out here, my lord," Edric said to Leofwine. A solitary beech tree beckoned. He turned Elfhar loose, sank down beside the tree, and waited.

⁂

The next three days passed dully. Many in the encampment waited for word. Edric briefly saw the Godwinson clan outside their tents. Leofwine alone greeted him every time. In one instance, Harold nodded in his direction before he rushed into his father's tent.

Edric perceived a change by the fourth morning, when the entire family gathered outside Godwin's tent. A messenger rode into the camp. Godwin's chief *thegns* surrounded him. All eyes were on the herald.

From Edric's position, he observed dark scowls marring the faces of Harold, Leofwine, and Gyrth. Aelfwig Wulfnothson and Sweyn argued in guttural tones. Countess Gytha clutched her throat and wailed, striking her breast with a tight fist. When her husband Godwin offered a kindly hand of comfort, she snarled at him, "This is your fault! I shall never forgive you, Godwin, never."

After the messenger left, Harold escorted his distraught mother inside the tent. The assembly of *thegns* dispersed, muttering among themselves.

Edric approached Leofwine. "My lord, please, what has happened?"

Leofwine spat on the ground near his boot. "The king persists with his demand. He insists Father punish the people of Dover. He refuses an inquiry. The *witan* convened and delivered a proclamation. We return to London where Father must appear before the full council on the day of the autumn equinox."

"The equinox shall fall on the twenty-first day of this month, in a few days," Edric said.

"Then, we must make haste, but I wonder, to what end?" Leofwine asked.

Edric did not like the answer that loomed in his mind, so he made no reply.

❧

London, England

Over the four-day trek, the party dwindled along the route to London. A number of *thegns* deserted Godwin during the nights. News from London indicated the growing strength of Edward's supporters, Leofric, and Siward chief among them. Earl Siward's position surprised no one.

With his support of Godwin, Edric jeopardized his future. He held his lands of the king. Yet even in such troublesome times, his concern often returned to Avicia. Her face appeared pale the morning of his departure. Breeding women were sometimes thus, but he wondered if she felt sorrow at his leaving. He prayed in the conflict between Edward and Godwin that she remained safe.

He cursed aloud and slapped his thigh. "I am a damned fool."

"You talk to yourself now, hmm?" Leofwine chuckled. "It is a sign of foolishness. I believe we are all a little foolish these days."

Up ahead, the silver arc of the Thames beckoned and on its north bank, a large host assembled. Leofwine pointed at them. "The king's men."

Few *thegns* remained with them, but Godwin's *huscarls* and men-at-arms stayed. The men set up camp at Southwark, where Countess Gytha sheltered inside her husband's tent. Within an hour of their arrival, a herald crossed the Thames and summoned Godwin to trial.

Godwin stood in the midst of his family. The weariness on his face dissipated. Resignation etched itself in the leathery lines of his complexion.

He greeted the king's messenger. "Tell His Grace Edward I shall attend if the exchange of hostages occurs. Only then can I assure my safe conduct in his presence."

The herald's face colored crimson. "The king shall not bear the insult."

"He took my son Wulfnoth from me! Tell that lily-livered monk I shall be damned if I see him without an arrangement for hostages." Godwin struck the rump of the messenger's horse with his hand. The beast reared and the man scrambled for the reins. The Godwinsons laughed at his troubles. Edric smiled, too.

Beside him, Leofwine put a hand on his shoulder. "I told Father of your kindness to Wulfnoth. He is grateful."

Edric looked at Godwin, who nodded before he withdrew inside his tent.

From the east came a small retinue led by a short man in religious garb. The sun shone down on his tonsure. When he entered their encampment, Gyrth, who stood closest to his father's tent, went inside. He soon reappeared with Godwin, who smiled. "Good Bishop Stigand!"

The men embraced warmly, lifelong friendship evident. Stigand, bishop of Winchester shared warm felicitations with Abbot Aelfwig. The bishop patted Godwin's arm. "I have heard of your troubles. How may I aid you?"

"You are very welcome here," Godwin replied.

He took Stigand and Aelfwig into his tent. While they talked, another of the king's messengers arrived. Again, Gyrth fetched his father. Edric considered the fate of the first man who had delivered Godwin's terse message. The new herald offered the king's terms. Edric turned to Leofwine, whose eyes could not meet his gaze.

"If your father must surrender all in his company before the negotiations can begin, what shall happen to us?" Edric asked.

Leofwine stubbed the earth with his boot. "Ride for the king's encampment. Edward shall not strike at you. The *witan* shall never allow it."

Harold and Godwin returned Edric's regard. His shoulders hunched, he tugged Elfhar's reins from a nearby post.

Edric, along with twenty other *thegns* followed the king's herald. After they bypassed the patrol at the gate, they crossed the Thames over the wooden bridge. He stared hard at those who witnessed their arrival. Scorn echoed in their narrowed gazes and sneers. One man booed them before a chorus of jeers followed. Throughout, Edric held his head higher than the rest of the *thegns*. He never experienced such pride at his association with the Godwinsons.

Edward's *huscarls* confined them to the northern edge of the field, far from any action. Edric never knew what transpired in the subsequent hours.

Before sunset, a man strode toward them. Edric sat on the grass with his chin buried in his hands. The man looked down his nose before he spoke.

"Our king in his wisdom has ordered your release, despite your treachery. You are to leave London at once and return home."

"What of Godwin?" one of the *thegns* asked.

The king's man stared them down with a harsh gaze. "The traitor Godwin and his family are banished. Thrice Godwin refused the king's summons to his trial. Now, his and his family's lands are forfeit. The king has given them five days grace for their leave-taking."

Edric scanned the horizon for the party on the Thames' south bank but the tents blocked his view. With the other *thegns*, he saddled his horse and rode toward the river. His heart sank. The men stared in dismay. Godwin and his family were gone.

CHAPTER 18

Newington, Kent, England
August – September 1052 CE

Edric looked up from where he sat among the rushes with little Leofsige, as Wulfstan the steward hustled across the hall. He returned early from his quarterly review of the estates, but Edric doubted trouble on his lands accounted for his steward's haste.

Stiff with age, the steward sagged into a bow before he flashed a gap-toothed smile. "Earl Godwin's come home."

Cynwise bolted from her seat beside Edric's mother. "Are you certain?"

"I am sure, my lady. His ship landed at Folkestone just before market day. He sought volunteers. Truth, if I were not so old, I might have joined them! They sailed to Dover the next day."

Edric sighed. "It is true. He and Harold are back."

Wulfstan continued, "Earls Ralph of Hereford and Odda of Deerhurst assembled a fleet of forty ships in preparation for them, but it made no difference."

Cynwise interrupted. "How did Godwin elude them?"

"Our Heavenly Father interceded. A storm forced him back across the waters to Bruges in Flanders," Wulfstan replied.

Cynwise glared at him. "It is blasphemy to say God would take the side of Godwinson."

"Hush, wife," Edric said. "Pray continue, Wulfstan."

"The king had given all of Sweyn's lands to Earl Ralph and Odda holds Cornwall, Devon, Dorset, and Somerset now. The earls know not what to do. They shall not get a second chance against Godwin. I think too many *thegns* remain loyal to him. He shall get back his lands and we shall be the better for it."

Cynwise stamped her foot. "He laid waste to the Isle of Wight! He cannot command loyalty if he does not deserve it."

Edric cut in. "He moved against his enemies who imposed themselves on the king."

Cynwise stared wide-eyed. "Do not tell me you would follow Godwin, again! He withdrew a year ago in disgrace. You cannot mean it. Do not forget you hold Newington from the king."

Wulfstan snorted, which drew a scornful look from Cynwise.

Before she might upbraid the steward for his boldness, Edric said, "Godwin shall reclaim what is his and drive the Frenchmen out for good, starting with Earl Ralph. Edward shall see reason."

Cynwise put her hands on her hips. "I never heard you say aught against Frenchmen until we made our journey to London last year."

Edric's gaze narrowed. Guilt stabbed at his heart. One person remained present in his thoughts. "What do you mean, lady?"

"When the queen mother died, the gossips said Edward refused her burial in the Old Minster at Winchester. If the king loved Frenchmen so much, why did he show such spiteful behavior toward his own mother?"

"Edward's quarrels with his mother had naught to do with her ancestry. Frenchmen hold Godwin's lands and those of his kin. I wish God Himself might cast them out of England."

Cynwise glowered at him, before she stomped off. He returned his focus to their three-year-old son.

Emmeline moved beside him, his daughter Leofflaed balanced on her hip. "Heed your wife's caution. She speaks so because she cares for your welfare and the safety of our family."

"She is too sensitive. Breeding women are ever thus."

"What?"

"She is with child again, told me last night."

"Remain mindful of her condition. Do not cause her concern. I mean it, Edric. Keep out of Godwin's intrigues."

"Mother, has he sought me out? In all the months where he and his family were in Flanders and Harold in Ireland, did we entertain Godwin's messengers? Did I miss their weekly dispatches?"

Emmeline glared at him. "Do not take such a caustic tone with me! I am your mother. Though you are a man with your own children, you shall give me the respect I am due. Lord, but I can hear your father when you speak so."

"I am glad! My father was ever Godwin's man and so am I. You and my wife shall remember the blood that binds me, and abide by the decisions I make. What are we, if not loyal to our kin? We cannot be as chaff in the wind, blown in any direction because the king is too weak…."

"What is this noise you make? No good for an old woman's ears." Eanflaed of Tickenhurst sank her aged body into the seat Cynwise had vacated.

Emmeline shared with her the news of Godwin's return and her concerns about Edric's attitude.

Eanflaed stopped her with a heavy thump of her walking stick. "Edric bears a heavy weight on his shoulders. The demands of kith and kin are a burden when he owes all to the king. He does not need you and a breeding wife lecturing him."

Edric swung toward her. "How did you know Cynwise is with child again?"

"I have ears and eyes still, and have borne children of my own. Now daughter, bring my grandbaby here."

Emmeline settled Leofflaed on her great-grandmother's lap. The child's plump hands were lost in Eanflaed's white hair, worn loose around her shoulders.

Edric and Emmeline shared an exasperated look about the old woman's continued immodesty.

"I see your stares. I am an old woman and shall wear my hair as I please, until the Lord tells me otherwise. Is that not right, my lambkin?" Eanflaed trilled for the child on her lap, gaps and timeworn teeth peeking through her lips.

Edric rolled his eyes heavenward.

&

Weeks passed in which Edric waited for news of Godwin. Silence and shrugs met his inquiries to other Kentish *thegns*. They hardly cared when there were hogs requiring feed in September. At last, heralds announced Godwin's reunion with the king, almost a year to the day since his exile. Edward offered the kiss of peace. He restored estates once belonging to Godwin and his sons.

Edric went to Folkestone, where many of his fellow *thegns* gathered on market days discussing the events of the late summer. He met Alwin, *thegn* of Buckland, and Aethelwold, whose chief estate lay at Teston. Both men were old friends of Tunwulf Grim.

The trio visited the blacksmith stall and collected Elfhar. The stallion had slipped his shoe on the journey to Folkestone.

Alwin said, "The king forgave but does Godwin reciprocate?"

Edric asked, "Do you mean because of the king's dismissal of Queen Edith? I am sure she has returned from the nunnery at Wherwell."

Alwin shook his head. "I do not mean the business with the queen. Robert Archbishop of Canterbury, with Bishops Ulf of Worcester and William of London fled from Essex to Duke William in Normandy. They took Godwin's son and grandson."

Edric stared dumfounded at his counterparts. "Are you certain they took the boys Wulfnoth and Haakon?"

His heart sank when he recalled the children. Wulfnoth had cried when the king took him from his brothers in London. Haakon, the proud, stubborn son of Earl Sweyn did not. "Godwin and Sweyn shall get the children back."

Alwin swore and scraped offal from his shoe. "Doubtful. He and Sweyn cannot sail to Normandy. Godwin would be Daniel in the lion's den."

Aethelwold grinned. "Daniel survived his encounter, but Godwin might not. Besides, Sweyn cannot help his father, since he is so far from here."

Edric frowned. "Flanders is no more than five days by boat."

When the men resumed their walk, Aethelwold replied, "Sweyn Godwinson is not with the family. He set out from Bruges last year, barefoot it seems, intent on a pilgrimage to the Holy Land. Do you think God shall forgive his sins?"

"Unlikely," Edric muttered. He resented Sweyn's role in Cynwise's past. If Sweyn had not ruined her, she and Edric might have been happy.

He left Aethelwold and Alwin, and rode homeward, his mind preoccupied with the fate of Wulfnoth Godwinson.

∽

Rouen, Normandy

April 1053 CE

Avicia smiled at the wet nurse outside her quarters. She took the bundle the young woman proffered. Her sleeping son nestled in the crook of her arms.

"Geoffrey was no trouble during the night, Gunnora?"

"Oh *non*, milady, he is a good baby," the wet nurse said.

Avicia handed her a coin and placed Geoffrey in his wood-carved cradle. She hovered beside him and hummed, until Alice arrived.

"Is this how I shall always find you?" Alice swept into the room. "You ignore me in favor of your little boy."

Avicia kissed his head. "William returns?"

"He and Matilda have stopped at the cathedral for Mass but most of the court has come here. What a blessed day, very fine weather for the duchess' entry to Rouen. They rode straight here after their union in the Notre Dame d'Eu. You should have seen it."

"Alice, you know full well why I remained here."

"To coddle your son, it seems. William looked resplendent and oh, his lady, the duchess is quite lovely. All brides are beautiful on their wedding day. Except for Garnier de Senlis' wife, do you remember her nuptials in the spring? Horrid, weepy girl, a lamb led to the slaughter it seemed."

Geoffrey drifted asleep as Biota arrived with fresh herbs for the floor.

"Do let your nurse stay with the baby. Come with me, Avicia," Alice cajoled.

Avicia sighed with a wistful look at Geoffrey in his cradle.

Alice rolled her eyes heavenward. "Oh, do stop! You shall spoil him. Philippe shall foster him out in seven years."

"Do not remind me of that barbaric custom, of sending children far from their parents to other families. It is cruel."

"Your husband and mine endured it, so shall your son. Come, it is very fine out."

"Must I leave Geoffrey? You have three children of your own."

Alice draped Avicia's blue mantle on her shoulders and tied the strings. "Hugh did not let me coddle either of our boys. Philippe indulges you too much."

Bells pealed the hour of Tierce. Alice grabbed her hand. "Hurry, we shall be late."

Onlookers stood outside Rouen's cathedral when they arrived. Guards protected the sanctuary. They allowed the women inside when Alice informed them of her husband's identity. Avicia stared at the solitary figure of the new Duchess of Normandy.

"I still cannot believe William received her consent," she whispered to Alice.

"True, for clobbering a woman in the hopes she shall turn compliant has never worked for many a father and husband I know."

At the conclusion of Mass, the new duchess and her attendants left the cathedral. Matilda of Flanders looked like an angel in white. The sapphires she wore could not rival the brilliancy of her blue eyes, which shone with pleasure. She bypassed Avicia and never noted her presence.

Avicia smiled, grateful. Matilda never liked her and truth be told, she had never liked her either.

Outside the church, she commented, "She still looks haughty. I do not doubt William's tale of his ride to Bruges where he beat her into submission. I think he must do more of the same if he wants her full obedience."

With a smile, Alice replied, "Our duke shall compel her. She married him after all, although she once vowed she would not."

⚘

On their return, Alice put a hand on her arm. "I have some news of England. You recall when we heard last autumn of Earl Godwin's return?"

Avicia remembered how Robert, the former archbishop of Canterbury appeared at Rouen afterward. He begged asylum from Duke William.

She thought it strange how the prelate fled, believing himself in danger, yet he managed the theft of two children in his hasty departure. One look at the children and dread overcame her. She recognized the smaller boy in an instant – the youngest of the Godwinsons.

"Earl Godwin is dead, Avicia."

She clutched her throat. "Dead? How?"

"Hugh and William talked of it most of the morn. Godwin feasted at the English king's Easter court, in Winchester. He swore an oath that if he had any hand in the death of the king's brother, God might strike him dead. He toppled afterward. I thought you might wish to know, since the man is a relation of your Lord Edric."

"He is not mine, Alice. Why should I care about the fates of his kin?"

Alice said nothing. Suddenly cold despite the warm, spring weather, Avicia clutched her mantle tighter about her. It did not matter what happened in England. Her life was in Normandy.

PART III - CHAPTER 19

Newington, Kent, England
March 1064 CE

Edric fastened the brooch in the shape of a wolf's head to his pelt. His mother approached with her vibrant, field-green eyes. He could not remember when he had seen such an animated expression on her face, in the last fifteen years since Tunwulf's death.

Her slim fingers skimmed his coarse, thick beard and reminded him he needed a trim.

"You are Tunwulf Grim reborn, my son."

"Do you believe so? Would my father approve?"

Emmeline measured his appearance in a long, slow stare and nodded.

Cynwise stood alone at the hall door. "Children! Come say your farewells to your father! I shall not call you again."

"If only my wife might do the same," he muttered.

Emmeline gripped his shoulder and heaved a sigh. "She does in her own way. She cares for you."

He shrugged. "Tell Grandmother I have gone. The old woman harangues me so when I rouse her before midday. I am loath to do it."

Emmeline batted his shoulder. "Coward."

Raucous shrieks and rumbles announced the arrival of Edric and Cynwise's five children.

He grinned when the youngest, six-year old Eanflaed dashed across the rushes in advance of her brothers and sisters, and launched herself at him. "Bring me a present from London, Father."

Edric kissed her wispy, black curls.

Behind her, nine-year old Deorwynn snapped, "Father meets Earl Harold at Bosham. He is not going to London."

"What shall you do at Bosham, Father?" Eanflaed asked. "Do you go to market day? I want a new spinning top, for you see, Deorwynn broke mine."

"I did not! Mother, tell Father I did not!" Deorwynn wailed.

"Oh, do be quiet, girls. Your father has more important concerns than your playthings." Cynwise crossed her arms over her chest.

"You promised me a new wooden sword. Please remember it, Father," said Edric's second son Cenweard. He stared up at him with his mother's dark blue eyes.

Edric tousled his thick golden curls before he noticed Cynwise's baleful stare. He offered an indulgent smile at little Eanflaed and a wink for the eleven-year-old Cenweard.

His eldest daughter Leofflaed glided into the hall. She twirled a bluebell stem between her thin fingers and hummed a wistful tune. Edric marveled at the sight of her. He anticipated Leofflaed and her betrothed husband Heahstan of Elmton might soon start a family, after their wedding in the summer.

Leofflaed noticed him. She kissed his cheeks, even with the heavy beard. "I shall miss you, Father, come home soon."

"I shall return before your nuptials," he said.

"If Harold Godwinson does not keep you with him overlong." Cynwise's shrill voice betrayed her annoyance.

Edric sighed and approached, taking her hand in his. She scowled at him.

He began, "I know you do not like this."

"Yet, you scorn my advice and leave anyway!" She wrenched her fingers from his grasp. "Harold Godwinson summons you to Bosham without an explanation. He did not say why he wants you there, when you might return and worse, you take Leofsige with you!"

"Woman, must I remind you our son is fifteen years? He is a good, strong lad, in the image of his ancestors. He shall be safe with me. Do you doubt that I, as his father, can protect him?"

"I doubt you can protect him from the Godwinsons! You have fallen in with their schemes, as your father before you. I want my son kept from them before they ruin his life!"

The object of their discussion strode into the room.

Edric's heart swelled with pride at the sight of black-haired Leofsige, virtually grown to a man. His eyes were the pale blue of his father and his grandfather Tunwulf Grim. A sword in its sheath banged on his leg. He twisted the belt and rested the weapon on his hip.

With a nod, he greeted his father. "I am ready."

So severe, the essence of his mother, yet Edric knew a playful, mischievous side existed in his heir. He encouraged it.

Behind Leofsige, Emmeline tapped his shoulder. "I think not, my grandson." She embraced him and kissed both cheeks. "Now, you are ready."

Edric looked down at Cynwise, again. Waves of condemnation blackened her blue-eyed gaze.

He inclined his head. "A kiss for me, too?"

She grabbed his hand and brought his fingers to her lips. Her mouth barely skimmed the flesh. Edric growled low in his throat. He pulled her against him and covered her lips in full with his. Her squeals and Emmeline's screech of disapproval followed.

"Oh, my lord, must you be so bold in front of your own children!"

With a grin of satisfaction, he drew back, still holding Cynwise captive in the circle of his arms. "This is my hall, and if I wanted to kiss my wife in the presence of God on His holiest day, I would do so without fear of His wrath."

Cynwise sputtered in outrage, but he said, "I know you shall think of me in my absence. Keep the peace of this house. I shall return soon."

"I do not care if you never come back!" She wrenched herself from his grasp and fled.

He called after her, "You shall when you are cold at night."

"Edric, you can be such a brute at times." Emmeline gathered her skirts and followed her daughter in-law. "Wait, Cynwise, he did not mean to embarrass you."

Leofsige's siblings wished him farewell. Wearied by their boisterous voices, Edric made them disperse.

He stepped outside and shielded his eyes from the mid-morning sun. Four men-at-arms waited with horses in the yard, along with Father Alwine.

The aged chaplain shuffled forward. A low grunt escaped him as he bowed. Edric helped him straighten.

Father Alwine said, "I wish I might accompany you."

"Remain here to comfort my wife and mother."

Edric took Elfhar's reins from a stable boy while Leofsige mounted Bavo, Elfhar's colt. Low gray clouds and rumbles of thunder in the sky portended seasonal rain. With a wave to Father Alwine, Edric directed his company out of the gates of Newington.

∽

Bosham, Chichester, England

Despite the rain and mud-slicked roads, Edric made the southbound journey to Bosham in three days. He and Leofsige shivered in waterlogged clothes. When they neared Harold's hall, the rain tapered off.

Edric groaned at the rain's timing, and then paused in admiration of the expansive view of Bosham's harbor.

"My lord of Newington!"

He wheeled Elfhar around at the greeting, and grinned at the man who hailed him.

Leofwine Godwinson rode toward him with a retinue of *huscarls*. The horsemen scattered villagers, who cursed in their wake.

"I knew you would come!" Leofwine's smile highlighted dimples under a heavy pelt of facial hair.

"My lord." Edric inclined his head.

Leofwine punched his arm. "By the rood, stop. I am not your lord. After so many years, I had hoped you considered me your friend. And, who is this young man who attends you?"

"My son, Leofsige. Son, my lord Leofwine is brother to Earl Harold."

"I have not seen him since he was a little boy. Now look to him, a man. He has the look of you and of our kin," Leofwine pronounced.

Leofsige sat a little straighter in the saddle.

Edric grinned. "I am proud of him."

"Come, Harold shall meet him and see you." Leofwine nudged his mount onward.

Edric and his son fell into place behind him and his guards. They approached the extensive hall. Leofwine signaled the *huscarls* who patrolled at the gatehouse. The spiked ends of the timber palisade appeared thick and unapproachable.

A beautiful woman waited in the courtyard with three boys.

"Lady Edith, how do you fare?" Leofwine saluted her.

"I am well, brother. Lord Edric, you are welcome here." Edith the Fair's eyes sparkled in the sunlight. The men dismounted.

"Where is Harold?" Leofwine asked.

"Your brother's in the hall and blusters at anyone who dares approach him," Edith said, with a flippant wave of her slim, pale hand. "He has asked for you at every moment. I grew weary of his temper and left him alone. I take our sons down to the creek. Godwin, Edwin, Magnus, present yourselves to your uncle Leofwine and our kinsman Edric."

"Why, they are almost as tall as Harold!" Leofwine exclaimed. The young men laughed.

When his son dismounted, Edric introduced him to Edith the Fair.

She smiled and curtsied before Leofsige. "He is hardly a year or two older than my Godwin and handsome, too. My lord Leofsige, shall you join us?"

The boy stared at Edith with his cheeks pink, his mouth wide open.

Leofwine thumped Edric's shoulder. "Our fair Edith bewitches most men. Best not let Harold see him stare though, for he is the jealous sort."

Edric shook Leofsige and drew his attention at last. "The Lady Edith asked if you want to go fishing with her and her sons. What say you?"

Leofsige barely nodded. Leofwine guffawed and gestured for Edric, who followed him.

Edith the Fair curtsied before she led his and her sons toward Bosham creek.

Edric and Leofwine entered a dimly lit hall, where smoke from the hearth stung Edric's eyes.

Harold sat at a trestle table. He gulped loudly from a mug. It landed with a heavy thud when he noticed their approach. "Leofwine, why in the hell did you take so long? What word do you bring?"

Leofwine winked at Edric. "The warmth of my brother's hall has diminished."

Harold barked for a serving maid and demanded two mugs of ale. He came around the table and grasped Leofwine's arms.

Edric frowned, puzzled at Harold's appearance. Dark circles and puffiness under his eyes suggested a lack of sleep.

"What news?" Harold asked Leofwine. "What does our mother say?"

"Countess Gytha is insistent. She holds you to your pledge. She shall not speak with you until you bring her 'baby' home. She awaits you at Wilton."

Harold groaned and scratched his head.

Edric looked to Leofwine for an explanation.

"Mother has harangued Harold for nigh on two months. She demands he secure our brother Wulfnoth. He is the youngest and her favorite, after Harold. Mother wants him back. When Robert Champart skulked back to his homeland, he stole Wulfnoth and Haakon. At Father's side, Harold swore a deathbed oath the boys would return home. Mother holds him to his vow."

"If William has them, what hope can your mother have? Lord only knows if they are alive after all these years."

"Do not say that!" Harold roared across the chamber and hauled him up by the scruff of his tunic.

Edric met his wild-eyed stare until Harold released him. Overwrought, he buried his face in his hands for a moment before he shouted, "Do not say it! He must be alive, he and Haakon."

He whirled toward Edric and stabbed a finger at him. "Both of them still live. I must get them back and you shall help me!"

Harold stalked from the hall, past the beleaguered serving maid with her mugs and a flagon of ale. He left both men speechless in his wake.

Leofwine reached for his cup and swallowed a mouthful. After, he wiped white froth from his moustache, he said, "Forgive him. He has not slept since Mother turned from him. She can drive a man to distraction with her demands, or, so my late father attested. Harold wants you with him. He trusts you and remembers your kindness to Wulfnoth."

When the servant girl offered him a mug, Edric waved her from the hall. Leofwine quickly retrieved the drink before she retreated. He downed the brew and with a wink at Edric, followed her. "Wait for me, Thyra. You still owe me a kiss."

"Go back to your whores, my lord. I'll have none of you." The girl's shriek echoed from the adjoining room, followed by her muffled giggle.

Edric's careworn sigh rippled through the room. "Cynwise shall kill me when she hears I am bound for Normandy."

In his heart, he knew Cynwise would be angrier if he dared take Leofsige with him.

On the evening before his departure with Harold, he waited for the boy near the *huscarl*'s practice field. Since their arrival, his son seemed fascinated by the Danish warriors. Except for when Edith the Fair enthralled him. One of the senior men among the Danes, a giant twice Edric's size named Thorkel Redbeard, appeared partial to him. Leofsige spent much of his time at Bosham with the aged *huscarl*.

Now he ran toward his father. Youthful excitement brightened his gaze.

"Father, Thorkel says he can train me, imbue me with the strength of a *huscarl*. Can he come to Newington?"

"Son, Thorkel belongs to Harold's retinue. He cannot visit you."

"I beg your pardon, my lord. I am but one of many among the old guard," said the hefty warrior who advanced on them.

Edric stood as tall as most men, and matched Harold's height, but the *huscarl* towered a full head above him.

Thorkel stroked his gray beard, which retained a hint of its former color.

"I have served the Godwinsons for long years now, since the days of old Godwin. Your boy is good and strong. He has quick reflexes and the mind of a warrior. I would train him and serve you with honor."

"My home is a tiny village in Kent. I shall not take you from your family."

"All three of my sons are dead in Earl Harold's wars with the Welsh. I have a daughter, Wynflaed. She cares for me, but she cannot replace a son."

Edric understood the *huscarl*'s affinity for Leofsige. "Truly, I am sorry you have no sons, but this boy is a *thegn*'s heir."

Thorkel's ominous stare barely affected Edric. Instead, he glimpsed Leofsige's face, so full of hope and enthusiasm. His heart shrank against disappointing him.

"Very well, I shall speak with Harold tonight. If he agrees, you may train my son, Thorkel Redbeard."

The old warrior nodded and hefted his heavy two-headed axe on his shoulder.

Edric patted Leofsige's arm. "Do not make him regret his choice."

They left Thorkel and walked to the meadow.

Sunset cast long shadows over the wet grounds. Edric stopped beside Leofsige. "If Thorkel shall serve me, return home under his protection while I make this journey."

"Father, I want to come with you."

"Leofsige, Normandy is a dangerous place, made even more so by Harold's quest. The Frenchmen cannot be trusted."

"I can fight."

"And you have much to learn about fighting, son. Be thankful Thorkel shall teach you what he knows."

Leofsige kicked up dirt with his turnshoes.

Edric grabbed his shoulders and shook him. "You shall heed me. Return to your mother."

Leofsige scowled. "What do I say when she asks about you?"

Edric struggled for an answer.

By morning, he still had not found words that might assuage Cynwise. At dawn, he exchanged farewells with Leofsige and Thorkel, the latter of whom Harold had released from his service. Edric imagined Cynwise's shock at the sight of the brawny *huscarl*, now part of the retinue of a minor *thegn*.

"Listen to Thorkel. Tell your brother and sisters to mind their mother. Tell Cynwise," he halted in consideration of his words, "I shall see her again."

Leofsige nodded and bowed before him stiffly. He chuckled and hugged the boy.

Harold did the same with his sons, while his Edith hovered nearby. Though she smiled winsomely, now tears sparkled in her gaze. Harold embraced her with fierce passion. Edric's heart ached with envy at the sight.

He remembered Avicia. Thirteen long years had passed since he last saw her. Would she recall him if they ever met again? She remained the only woman he had ever loved. What did that matter when they were destined to be apart?

Harold left Edith while Edric mounted Elfhar.

Leofwine, who would protect Harold's estates and his family in his absence, moved beside Edric. "Guard my brother well."

Their retinue included *huscarls*, but Edric promised Leofwine, "With my life."

Harold signaled their departure. Edric waved to his son before he fell into place with the riders.

An hour later, cold, drizzling precipitation stung his scalp. He remained mounted outside the Church of the Holy Trinity, which overlooked Bosham's creek. One windowpane swung open repeatedly before the blustery wind clapped it shut.

Harold emerged from the church and mounted again. At his direction, the party rode down to the harbor. Hounds bayed at the pitiless rain. Harold's hunting hawk, which clung on his master's glove, shook its feathers vigorously. Beyond the harbor crowded with ships, a mist enshrouded the Channel. Normandy awaited them.

CHAPTER 20

Rouen, Normandy
March 1064 CE

Avicia sank on the pallet, removed her turnshoes and rested on the coverlet, head cradled in her hands. Unbidden, tears of misery came again. She let them fall. She shuddered, her heart wracked with the pain of loss.

Her name sounded with alarm. Alice's plaintive plea came from beyond the opaque screen. "May I see you, dearest?"

"Go away!"

"I shall not! You behave badly, worse than the wife of Robert Fitz Erneis did. Remember how she cried over their son, young Robert."

"I am not like her!"

"You are and you know it! You cannot keep to your pallet and weep all day. What shall little Thorbert say when he sees his *maman* all red-faced, like a plucked chicken? Oh, I do wish Philippe might return soon from Eu. You cannot go on this way."

"Leave me be!"

"You have experienced this separation with two sons already! Now Simon is gone, but Thorbert still needs his *maman*. I dare not leave."

Alice's voice trailed off but Avicia remained unmoved.

Her life seemed bereft in the absence of her children. First, poor Geoffrey fostered to the Beaumont family six years ago, then his brother Baldwin three years later. Now, her Simon left her at barely six years old. She hated the cruel practice.

Dear Thorbert, such a fate awaited him, too. The thought drove her into deeper melancholy. Her lament lasted until she slept. Sometime later, she awoke when a voice called for her beyond the screen.

"Go away, Alice!"

"It isn't Alice, it is Gunnora, milady. I have Thorbert out here. He wants his *maman*."

The familiar whimpers of her fourth son sounded.

She roused herself and peeked between the screens. Gunnora stepped aside and Alice came into view, with Thorbert perched on her hip. Alice gave him the carved wooden ship she held at arm's length, and he ceased his whimpers. Gunnora mumbled something that sounded vaguely like an apology and scrambled off.

Her frown in place, Alice handed over the boy and swept into the room. "Disgraceful! You are not the first mother who wept when her children departed. Look at you, puffy eyes, and a red nose. Just like a plucked chicken you are. Well, this shall not do. Prepare yourself. Your Biota can attend you. Thorbert can stay with me. You know how much little Alice loves to play with him."

"I am not hungry, Alice."

Avicia set Thorbert down among fresh scented herbs. He scrambled across the floor, the carved boat forgotten.

Avicia said, "If you have come because the dinner hour approaches, I am not hungry."

Alice shook her head. "Your husband and mine have returned."

"What?"

"Oh, by St. Ouen, have you lost your wits? Our men have returned from Eu. William dashed off and met with Comte Guy but told no one, not even the duchess, why he left with such haste. They are returning now, a short distance from Rouen. So, you must rouse yourself and welcome Philippe."

Alice left the chamber.

Avicia looked at Thorbert, covered in tiny white flowers from the herbs on the floor. She forced a smile and sank down beside him.

"My darling son, they shall take you from me, too."

A short time later, Alice re-entered. "Here's your Biota."

She scooped up Thorbert from the floor, who promptly fretted. She settled him and nodded at Avicia's aged nurse. "Attend your mistress. Her husband cannot see her so forlorn."

With an imperious nod, she departed again.

Avicia washed her face and with Biota's help, tidied her appearance, donned fresh, unwrinkled garments and brushed her hair.

Alice barged into the room. "You must come with me!"

"What?" Avicia swung around. "Did something happen to Thorbert?"

"Heavens, *non*, he is with my daughter, but you must come."

Alice tugged her down the hall and outside. Many gathered, welcoming William's return.

He rode proud in his saddle, beside a stranger in a hooded mail hauberk, his gaze averted.

Avicia could not understand why the stranger's appearance intrigued her, but another sight quickly drew her gaze. Her husband lay prone on a litter with his arm bent at an odd angle. A profusion of sweat coated his brow.

"Philippe! What has happened to him?"

One of the knights answered, "The Englishman tried to escape but your husband stopped him, milady. The brute broke Sieur Philippe's arm."

"Englishmen!" Avicia glanced at the stranger riding beside William. "What are they doing here?"

The knight shrugged. "I know not, milady." He stabbed a finger across the bailey. "Look, the whoreson comes now. Pardon me, milady."

Other knights dragged a yellow-haired man across the muddy courtyard. Chains shackled his wrists together in front of him.

Her heart fluttered, as he swept the crowd with a look of contempt and spat. His filthy garments and rank odor pervaded her senses. Women reeled back when he passed near. Hugh's men forced him toward the *donjon*. Avicia stared long after he disappeared into an underground passage that led to a Roman sewer.

Alice came to her. "Did you recognize the man in chains?"

She nodded. "It was Edric of Newington."

❧

Avicia fled down the hall toward her quarters, with Alice hard on her heels.

"What shall you do?" Alice called out.

She spared a brief glance over her shoulder at the knights who trailed behind them, bearing Philippe on a litter.

"I shall attend my husband until the barber comes."

Alice's hand closed on her arm. "You know I do not ask after Philippe! What shall you do about Edric of Newington?"

Again, Avicia looked beyond her to the men and pitched her voice low. "My concern is for my husband. Edric is not my responsibility. For heaven's sake, Alice, he broke Philippe's arm. Edric is William's concern now."

Alice's gaze bored into her. "I do not believe you. You are worried for him."

"I care for my husband! Do not dare suggest I should worry for any other man when he is hurt. Now, let me go."

She pushed aside a linen screen. The men swept past her and set Philippe down. Her husband cried out in pain.

When Biota yelped, Avicia ordered her to bring the barber at once.

Alice loitered. "I shall return, after I speak with Hugh. I want to know why the English are here even if you do not."

Avicia edged close to her, hoping Philippe would not overhear. "I do not care why Edric is here. He injured my husband. He can rot in the *donjon*."

Later, after the others had left, she knelt at Philippe's side. "Husband, can you hear me?"

"My arm is broken. I am not deaf." He shifted his weight gingerly.

She bit her lower lip. After fifteen years of marriage, his casual responses to her concern wounded.

"Are you in pain?"

He glared at her. "My arm is broken! What else should be the result? I do not want you coddling me like a babe. Torfida's husband shall tend me."

She clasped her hands in her lap, unsure of her next words.

He frowned at her. "At the very least, offer me some water, woman."

She berated herself for her thoughtlessness, and poured a drink from the beaker she kept in the room. She cupped his head and tried aiding him.

"Damn you, woman, mind my head!" He growled when his neck left the pillow at an odd angle.

Surprised by his reaction, she jerked back. Water splashed on the floor.

He slumped against the pillow and winced.

"If you cannot help me, wait outside."

Before she could rail at his rudeness, the barber-surgeon arrived. She set the wooden cup beside the beaker with a heavy thud, and ignored her husband's scowl.

"Welcome, Turstin," she said to the barber. "I thank you. My husband's here, he is in pain."

"Well, let the man attend me already!" Philippe snapped.

She rounded on him, her patience at its end.

Turstin interrupted before she lost her temper. "I have heard all about your troubles, Sieur Philippe. I got some comfrey from my Torfida. You shall mend soon enough and be back on your horse in no time."

Behind him, she asked, "Turstin, may I help?"

"I think not, milady."

"Wait outside, Avicia," Philippe said.

She left the room, fists clenched tight in her annoyance.

How had it come to this? This day's events forced the truth on her. Where passion once bound her and Philippe in the past, now only icy tolerance remained. Their love lingered though a faded remnant of their torrid past. Her heart no longer pounded at the sight of him. She endured his touch, never reveling in it.

For his part, their lovemaking seemed a chore. After each of her deliveries, he withdrew to Montfort-sur-Risle for long months. His sons gave him pleasure, but not her.

She paced the hall, face downcast. Time passed without her notice.

Dainty turnshoes trimmed with ribbons appeared in front of her. Her gaze met the sharp, blue eyes of Lady Marian de Vernon.

"Lady Avicia, I am come to inquire after your husband."

Avicia frowned until her brow hurt. "He is with the barber."

"I heard those horrid Englishmen broke his arm. Poor, dear man," the red-haired woman replied. She frowned. "You left him alone?"

Avicia found the disdain and chastisement in her tone intolerable.

Lady Marian sighed with a wistful look. "I suppose the barber needs his privacy. Please, tell Sieur Philippe I was here."

"If you wish it," Avicia muttered.

The woman curtsied and smiled. She retreated down the hall, the over-sweet scent of cassia and lavender left in her wake.

Avicia questioned Philippe's fidelity. Seven years ago, he had returned from Montfort-sur-Risle with Lady Marian, newly widowed. Later, Avicia learned of their former friendship.

In his foster years, he had served Lady Marian's father and knew her from girlhood. It seemed only natural they renewed their friendship. Yet, Avicia envied the obvious closeness between them.

At times, she despaired of her jealousy. Philippe shared a rapport with Alice, but their closeness had never threatened Avicia's marriage. By contrast, she knew nothing of Marian de Vernon's intentions. Worse still, whenever Avicia grew heavy with child, Lady Marian's nimble steps beside her husband annoyed her. The woman's wide mouth always curved into a seductive smile, her laugh like a melody. Avicia kept her worries hidden, afraid everyone would think her a jealous shrew. Most of all, she feared voicing concerns, which might be true.

"Why are you out here?" Alice approached.

"Turstin is not finished with Philippe."

"Did the barber come only a little while ago?"

"*Non*, within a few moments after you left."

"Then he has been in there for more than an hour, for I went to Hugh just before the bell for Sext rang."

Avicia tugged at her lower lip and stared in silence.

After a while, Turstin came out.

She released the pent-up breath she held. "How is he?"

"He sleeps for now, milady. I have bound his arm with wood splints and cloths. Beneath is a poultice of comfrey, which shall heal him. He needs rest." Turstin tromped down the hallway. His baldpate glistened in the torchlight.

Avicia clutched Alice's hand. "Thanks be to God."

"We must be glad he is not gravely injured. Hugh feared he suffered. My husband explained what happened at Eu. A storm drove the English near the coast and Comte Guy de Ponthieu's men captured them."

"Why were the English on this side of the Channel?"

"I thought you did not care."

"Alice!" For the first time, she considered clobbering her friend in the face.

"Very well, I shall tell you if you must know. The Englishmen claimed the storm blew their boat beyond our waters. You know how terrible these sudden storms can be. Do you remember all those trade boats, which sunk at the mouth of the Seine last year? Terrible."

"Alice!"

"Oh, indeed, my mind does often stray, does it not?" A faint smile of amusement played on her lips. "Comte Guy surrendered the English and William ransomed them at Eu."

"Who leads the English? Who were the rest with Edric?"

"They are the retinue of Earl Harold Godwinson. Did you see him riding shame-faced beside William?"

Avicia nodded. "Why did Godwinson risk a journey here? He hates our people."

"You remember Wulfnoth Godwinson?"

"How could I not? He remains William's captive."

"He eats well and has his pick of the servant girls. I daresay he enjoys his confinement," Alice said, with a soft chuckle.

Avicia did not share her mirth. "A prisoner he remains. No less than four guards are always at his side. Likely, they stand outside his cell door while he is rutting with the kitchen maids. When I see him outdoors on a rare occasion, he looks in the direction of England. Robert de Jumieges stole him from his family. He has not seen them in years, except for the young man Haakon. Does Harold Godwinson seek a ransom for them?"

At Alice's nod, she sighed and considered the implications.

Edric desired the ransom of his kin. She recalled their initial encounter, so many years ago in Flanders. He told her of his kinship to the powerful family of Godwin. At the time, he spoke of his father's loyalty with scorn, but it seemed he had changed his opinion of the Godwinsons.

"Where is he?" she asked.

"Who? Harold Godwinson?"

She whirled toward Alice. "I meant Edric and you know it!"

Mischief glinted in her friend's eyes. "You said he could rot in the sewer."

"I meant it! Did Hugh's men take him there?"

Alice nodded.

"I must confront him."

"By the blood of St. Ouen, why? Besides, he is under guard."

"I do not care," Avicia said.

Alice gripped her arm. "Wait. What about Philippe? What if he asks for you?"

She glared at the linen screen. "He does not need me."

She shrugged off Alice's hold and ignored the puzzled look on her face.

Under blue skies with nary a cloud overhead, she walked with purpose toward the stone *donjon*, the heart of William's former residence.

Stairs led to the old Roman sewer, partitioned off as a cell for prisoners. She covered her nose with a hand. The place smelled worse than a cesspit. A streak of black fur scrambled past her and she yelped in fright, terrified of rats. Slick dampness covered the walls, highlighted by the glow of torches in their brackets. Two sentries waited at the end of the corridor, in front of a large door.

"I want to see the Englishman who attacked my husband, Sieur Philippe."

One guard, who wore keys hooked on his belt, glanced at the other. The first man shook his head.

"We cannot let anyone attend the prisoner without permission."

"He attacked my husband!"

"Yet, you risk a visit with such a dangerous man, milady." The bulky shadow of Odo emerged from the shadows, his ruddy face and beady eyes under a baldpate.

On instinct, Avicia stepped back and banged against the wall behind her. Whenever Odo stared at her, she recalled his attempted rape.

"Why is everyone barred from this man?" she asked.

A tic pulsed at the bishop's temple. "Why do you wish to see him?"

She tried bypassing him without an answer. When she pressed against the dank, dirty wall because of his bulk, his hand closed on her arm.

"I might permit you inside."

His wine-soaked breath nauseated her. Yet, he offered one chance for her to see Edric. "Say 'please' first."

"Please, may I see the prisoner? Alone?"

Odo signaled the sentry with the key, who opened the lock.

When Avicia moved toward the cell, Odo's fingers tightened on her arm. "You do not come to confession."

"I have naught to confess."

"If at any time you wished it, I would hear yours."

When he released her, her arm throbbed.

He left the corridor and when his footsteps faded, she turned toward the opened door. She stepped inside.

Fetters bound the *donjon*'s newest prisoner to the wall at his wrists, which allowed for perhaps an arm's span of movement. His face downcast, he avoided her gaze. She crept closer, but not too near. The stink of his clothes and environs sickened her.

His gaze locked with hers. Avicia drew back. When she had last seen those eyes, passion fired them a vibrant blue. Now their color evoked images of the North Sea, cold and unforgiving.

CHAPTER 21

Rouen, Normandy
March 1064 CE

Avicia stared at Edric. He stood before her, after thirteen years. It seemed impossible.

She licked her lips, suddenly dry in this dank, fetid place and smoothed the folds of her robe. She regretted the action and hoped he never noticed how she hid her sweaty palms.

"You need not be wary in my presence, milady. Indeed, you should not be here. Please leave."

Her eyes widened. He spoke Norman French. In the past, they had conversed in the Flemish tongue of his mother's family. Yet, he spoke her language with ease and ordered her departure.

"I do not want or need your pity, milady."

"You think I would offer comfort, when you have hurt my husband?"

"He lives and you should be grateful. You should be at his side rather than with the man who harmed him. Where is your loyalty, milady?"

The stare of condemnation in his gaze and the contempt in his voice infuriated her. She delivered a harsh blow to his cheek. His head reeled, which gave her some pleasure, but pain also shot through her hand.

His icy gaze flitted back to hers. He spat on the ground. The white blob landed at her feet.

"Do you feel better, milady?"

"You are full of pride and conceit. You do not care who you hurt. Thanks to you, my husband's arm is broken. I shall never forgive you for it."

When she reached for the door handle, Edric's voice sounded behind her.

"In truth, I did not know the identity of my attacker. His mail hood fell back while we fought. When I recognized him, I broke his arm quite happily. Pity I did not do more."

She rested her forehead against the door for a moment, and shuddered with suppressed rage.

She whispered the words she had said to Alice earlier. "You can rot in this *donjon* for all I care, milord."

She left the room and pulled the door shut behind her. Her skirts aloft, she walked up the narrow, musty corridor and reached the stairs. She broke into a run, despite the gapes of those whom she passed. She never stopped until she stood just outside the domestic quarter.

From behind the opaque screen, she heard Philippe's muffled snores. She sank down on the rush-strewn floor and cradled her head in her hands.

"I am naught but a fool!"

⇢

Edric thought the same thing, of himself. He lolled on the moss-covered wall. In his current misery, putrid smells assailed him. The image of Avicia tormented him.

She appeared more beautiful and spirited than their last encounter. With one look, the distance and years between them melted. He remembered his youth when he stood in the mews at Lille, desperate for her touch and embrace. Except this time, he was older and his traitorous heart wanted more than a kiss.

His wife and children waited for him at home, yet he marveled at how easily Avicia and his desires for her consumed him again.

His hatred for all Frenchmen vied with desire for one of their women. They were the enemies of his people. They still wielded influence within Edward's court, though much less since Harold and his brothers controlled most of the earldoms of England.

"I shall not be a fool for her, again. I am Saxon and she is French. I must get Harold out of here and get us home," he muttered.

He leaned against the wall and closed his eyes. Where were Harold and the others? Would the Frenchmen release him or kill him for the attack on one of their own?

He tugged at his chains again, though they still resisted his efforts. Soon, his limbs throbbed. No matter how he shifted his stance, the deep ache never ceased. The pain only increased his agitation.

The wooden door creaked on its hinges some time later. Light pierced the darkness of the cell. Edric recognized the outlines of two burly figures. When they stooped and entered, he eyed them warily. He knew the second man by his resemblance to Avicia's husband.

"So, this is he who felled Philippe?" William asked.

"The same, my duke," said the other man.

"I tell you, he attempted escape on my orders." Harold ducked and entered the cell. "If you must punish someone, it should be me."

Edric expelled his breath in a ragged sigh, grateful for the sight of Harold, who nodded in his direction before he addressed William. "I pray, release him."

"He harmed the brother of one of my best men here. He must endure some punishment for his actions." William scratched his chin.

"I shall bear it! He acted on my orders," Harold said.

William turned to the dark-haired man behind him. "Hugh, what would you have me do? After all, Sieur Philippe is your brother."

Edric scowled. The man Hugh returned his glare and flicked a glance over his shoulder at Harold. "His actions warrant a lashing."

"Agreed." William nodded.

He stared at Harold, one dark red brow upraised in a quizzical slant. Harold nodded.

William called for the men outside the cell. "Release him. He shall have his punishment now."

When the manacles came off, Edric rubbed his wrists. He looked at Harold. "Thank you for my release."

He spoke in their native tongue. William and Hugh frowned at this, likely, because they could not understand his words.

Harold replied in the Norman French language, "Do not thank me. We are indebted to Duke William for our rescue from the Comte d'Eu."

Edric said nothing. He hoped Harold's conciliatory tone helped them achieve their objective.

The French knights grabbed his arms.

Harold stepped between them and Edric, addressing William. "Please, he is my kinsman and I can vouch for him. He shall not attempt an escape again. He shall bear his punishment."

William studied Edric, before he dismissed his men with a wave. They left the murky cell with William and Hugh at the forefront. Harold, Edric and the men at-arms followed.

Scornful derisive gazes from the knights met Edric's first steps outside the prison. William called for someone. Soon, a barrel-chested warrior appeared, a redhide whip coiled at his waist. He and William spoke, before he favored Edric with his insolent grin.

The whipping post, nothing more than a timber staked in the ground, stood in a corner of the courtyard. Edric and Harold went to it.

Harold put his arm on his shoulder while they walked. "Have courage."

"Tunwulf Grim raised me well. I do not fear the Frenchmen."

He removed his grimy tunic, gave it to Harold, and advanced on the whipping post. He offered no resistance or protestation when two men grabbed his hands, and tied them to the stake. His forehead rested against the thick timber. He waited.

The first lash fell after an interminable time. He shuddered when the leather bit deep into his skin and tore at the flesh. With each stroke, his heart hardened with hatred and mistrust for the Frenchmen. Their duke would not let Harold see Wulfnoth or ransom him. Edric felt certain that William wanted something first.

He did not realize his punishment ended until Harold appeared at his side, and sliced through his bonds. "It is finished."

Edric muttered, "It shall never be finished. We are prisoners here."

"I spoke with William earlier and told him our purpose." Harold pitched his voice low. "I asked after Wulfnoth. He is not here."

"Why does this duke keep us here if your brother is gone?"

"William said Wulfnoth went to Mont St. Michel on the coast and would not return for a month. My brother wishes to become a monk."

Edric spat in the dirt and frowned.

Harold nodded and brushed aside the last of the knots that bound him. "I do not believe it, either. I reached a compromise with William. I shall write to Wulfnoth at Mont St. Michel. William promised he would send a messenger."

Edric rubbed his wrists. "Do you trust the Bastard?"

Harold never answered him.

❧

For three weeks after his return, Avicia stayed at Philippe's side. His cross tone and constant complaints tested her patience, but she stayed with him. They hardly spoke unless she initiated the conversation. He seemed weary of her.

Yet he engaged in animated discussion when Hugh and Lady Marian visited. Avicia found Lady Marian's gaze lingered for too long, and her sighs of pity irritated her.

Although not fully recovered from his injury, Philippe planned to accompany Hugh to Montfort-sur-Risle, where they would remain for a month.

On the morning of their departure, he winced when he handed his squire a saddlebag. Avicia stood beside him in the bailey. She wrung her hands in frustration.

"Husband, your arm has not fully mended. Turstin believes this journey is ill-advised." She shared the same sentiments but kept her silence. Philippe disregarded her opinion these days.

He offered her a weary sigh. She touched him lightly at the elbow.

"Damn woman!" he roared. "Mind yourself!"

She cringed at the fury in his tone. Such a light touch could not have caused him serious pain. She swallowed against the lump in her throat and clasped her hands together.

"I am sorry, I do not mean to leave you," Philippe said with a ragged sigh. "My duty is to my liege. I shall be gone but a month. Alice and all your friends can keep you company."

Avicia sniffled and groaned in misery. He remained oblivious to her life in Rouen. He never knew that Alice alone maintained her friendship.

He continued, "I shall return with word of our Geoffrey. We shall enjoy one night's sojourn at his lord's castle of Beaumont le-Roger."

Hugh approached, Alice's arm locked with his.

Avicia stood beside her while the knights mounted their horses.

"Did you hear the news?" Alice whispered. "There shall be a hunt tomorrow. William has organized it for his guests. All the courtiers shall share in the revelry. Matilda is excited to fly her new merlin."

Avicia said nothing when Philippe jerked the reins of his horse and saluted her with a wave. Alice and Hugh made no exchange of farewells. He appeared eager for the journey. The horses charged out of the bailey in a flurry of grit and dirt. Avicia stared long after their hoof beats faded.

❧

The next morning, hounds and hunting birds on their perches crowded the bailey at Rouen. The dogs yipped and leapt, keen for the chase, despite their handlers tugs on the leashes. Stable boys and pages darted between the horses. They fastened saddles on the beasts' backs.

Beside her horse, Avicia stared at the different types of raptors. Falconers readied fierce peregrine falcons, merlins, and goshawks for the hunt. For the court ladies, the merlin remained the hunter of choice. William flew an eagle, a rare and prized killer. After the last hunt, Alice described the bird's ferocity while it tore the heart from a grouse, its white plumage smeared in blood.

Alice appeared radiant. A stable boy followed with her white palfrey already saddled. At her gesture, he attended Avicia's horse.

"It is a glorious morning," Alice commented.

Avicia nodded inattentively.

William appeared with Matilda at his side. For a woman so small in stature, she dominated any space she entered. Her brilliant blue eyes scanned the bailey. The duchess tiptoed and spoke with her husband, who stood more than a foot taller than her. His baritone laugh filled the air. She bestowed affectionate kisses on the cheeks of their seven children.

Avicia sighed. "I should not be here. Matilda intends to join the hunt."

Alice groaned. "You cannot leave the bailey now, you would only draw scrutiny. You cannot hide from her forever. You have always avoided her whenever she and the duke visited from Caen."

"I wish they would return there."

They will, soon, but for now, stay close to me and pray you escape her notice."

"You need not warn me against her. I have never sought her out."

William and Matilda led his retinue forward, which included the Englishmen.

For the first time since their horrid reunion in the *donjon*, Avicia saw Edric again. A sudden gust of wind blew his yellow hair back from his face. His haggard appearance startled her. Dark circles shadowed his eyes. He avoided her gaze.

"It is impolite to stare at other people," Alice warned. "It is also unwise. You never know who is also watching you."

With a nod, Alice gestured across the bailey, and Avicia followed her direction.

Odo's beady eyes lingered on her, as did the emerald glare of Mabel de Belleme.

William mounted his courser, a horse smaller than a destrier. At his signal, the hunting party left the bailey in a long train of lords and ladies, servants and animals.

At the rear, Avicia rode in silence beside Alice. A good distance separated her and Edric. She longed for his gaze upon hers, but he never acknowledged her. She wished she could easily dismiss him, as he did with her.

❧

Edric ignored the animated conversation Harold and his companions shared. How long would they affect this pretense? The Frenchmen held them against their will. The truth eluded Harold, but Edric acknowledged it.

He calculated the weeks without word from Wulfnoth. The young man had spent thirteen years apart from his family. Surely, any message sent to Mont St. Michel would result in a response, a desire for reunion. Unless, as Edric suspected, William had lied to Harold. Perhaps he never sent the letter.

In the meantime, the Frenchmen feted and entertained them. Edric joined them today only at Harold's insistence. For weeks, he had refused. He rebuffed their hospitality, but also avoided Avicia.

When he emerged in the bailey, he had immediately spotted her. Her eyes never left him, until she noticed the duke's brother, Bishop Odo, staring at her. Edric did not wonder at Odo's fascination. He suspected a lascivious intent on the clergyman's part, for she remained lovely. Another woman with hard green eyes also watched Avicia with a sneer. She seemed familiar, but Edric could not recall when he had first encountered her.

Harold's thump on his shoulder drew him from his contemplation. "Have you heard a word I said? We have arrived."

"Forgive me." He slowed his horse beside Harold's mount. The group halted near a copse of trees. Cool mist shrouded them and hung over wetlands in the distance.

William dismounted. He spoke with those whom Edric assumed were his huntsmen.

"I wonder what quarry they try for at this time of the year," Harold commented to no one in particular.

One of his *huscarls* said, "Small game is likely. It could be foxes or rabbits, my lord, too late in the season for boar, too early for roebucks."

Harold shook his head. "If I know the Bastard well, and I have come to know him very well, he is ambitious and will never be satisfied with trifling prey. He will hunt the bucks, though they have already shed their horns."

Edric noted the arrival of the ladies with William's diminutive wife Matilda at their lead. His stomach soured at the sight of her, for he remembered her cold vanity. Avicia rode at the rear of their company, keeping her distance. The pages lit fires that kept everyone warm.

Most of the men were eager for the chase, and as Harold anticipated, William sought the roebucks. Harold joined them and entreated Edric to do the same.

"This sullenness does you no good, Edric. Enjoy this day," Harold cajoled.

"How can you pretend all is well here?" Edric whispered.

William huddled in the midst of his advisors. Some eyed Harold's retinue with suspicious looks.

Edric ignored their questing gazes. He continued, "Go on without me. I shall remain with the women and pages, my lord."

Harold scowled. "I could force you, but I shall not. Surely, your wish has naught to do with the comely lady who stared at you earlier. It was impossible not to see her interest in you. Who is she?"

"She is unimportant to me." Edric looked off into the distance.

Harold laughed at him and nudged his horse into a short canter, joining the others.

The duchess and a few others wished to fly their hunting birds, though Edric thought it a waste. As he expected, Matilda's bird fared poorly. She berated the hapless falconer for the merlin's failure at every turn.

When the falconer cast the raptor from his glove again, Avicia leaned toward her friend who hovered nearby. "She shall never find prey, her pitch is too low."

"What is the pitch, my dear?" the woman beside her asked.

"It is the height at which she flies to find her quarry. The mist is moving closer. It would be impossible, even for the sharpest hunter to see anything…."

"You, there! What do you know about falconry?"

Avicia whitened when the duchess addressed her.

"Who are you? You seem familiar," Matilda continued.

Edric shook his head. How was it possible that she did not remember Avicia, who had attended her in Flanders? Had they never interacted again, before the hunt today?

Avicia's friend interjected, "Your Grace, if I may, this is Lady Avicia, the wife of Sieur Philippe."

The duchess frowned and leaned forward in her sidesaddle. "I knew an Avicia in my girlhood. I had heard a Norman knight abducted her. She once destroyed a perfectly good merlin of mine. She was an incompetent attendant who never learned her embroidery and was good for little else. Could you be her?"

"Surely she must be, Your Grace, for she has never shown any talent since her arrival from Flanders. It is a wonder she has held her husband's interest for so long."

Edric whipped around at the sound of the feminine voice behind him, sour with malice and derision. The green-eyed woman glared past him at Avicia, her ever-present sneer fixed in place.

Several of the women tittered behind their hands. The duchess' pale expression concealed her thoughts and emotions.

Avicia's gaze dropped and her cheeks colored in the glare of sunlight. Soon, the sniggers around her gave way to peals of laughter.

Her horse bolted, a flurry of dust gathering behind them.

Edric tugged the reins of his mount and went after her.

CHAPTER 22

Rouen, Normandy
March 1064 CE

Edric caught up with her before her horse disappeared into the copse of trees. "Stop it. Do not be so reckless!"

He leaned forward in his saddle, grabbed the reins of her mare, and slowed the beast.

She slid off the horse's back and headed for the dangerous woodland. He followed and closed the short distance between them with ease, catching the trailing edge of her sleeve. She tugged but he held her. She whirled and raised her hand. He snatched her wrist.

"That is twice in the days since my arrival where you have raised your hand against me. Unless you wish a return of the gesture, I suggest you do not try it again."

Despite his fierce tone, his heart wrung with pity at the sight of her watery eyes. The other women had embarrassed her. Even now, he saw from his peripheral view how they stared across the expanse at him and her, and whispered behind their hands.

"You cannot wander the forest alone, Avicia. Do not run from them, or me."

"You do not understand what it is to endure such cruelty in this place! You are a lord with property, while my husband has no lands of his own. We are entirely dependent on his brother. All those highborn ladies with their wealth and estates – I am but a common servant among them."

Her words ended on a sob. Tears trickled down her cheeks.

Such naked pain inspired Edric's pity, but if he attempted comfort, he risked further gossip and humiliation. He would not cause her further hurt.

Avicia's friend stared at them from among the multitude of drawn faces and frowns. Hers reflected concern. Matilda of Flanders also looked in their direction, before she dismissed her ladies with an imperious movement of her hand. Avicia's friend searched Edric's face in slow appraisal and nodded to him, before she returned her attention to the falconer's efforts.

He spoke with Avicia again. "Those who speak ill of you are jealous of your charms. When they come to know you, they cannot help but admire you."

She swiped at her cheeks. "You knew me long before my arrival in London, yet you mocked me years ago, too. What was your excuse then?"

With difficulty, he met her gaze while recalling how he had caused her shame. He realized why the green-eyed witch seemed so familiar. She overheard him when he insulted Avicia in London.

"I am sorry for the past, but it cannot be undone."

"It cannot. Now, leave off." She struggled against his hold on her wrist.

"We must talk…."

Hooves struck the ground and warned of William's hunting party. Riders emerged from the trees. One rode directly at him, sword drawn. "Unhand the lady!"

Edric released Avicia. They both stepped back when the burly man drew near. His obsidian eyes and the edge of his upraised sword glittered in the sunlight.

Behind him, William and Harold approached.

"I can vouch for my man," Harold shouted. "I am sure he did not attempt to harm the lady."

"He could not harm anyone in my presence." Duchess Matilda's voice commanded attention. She approached with her attendants. She surprised Edric. He thought she had returned to her pleasure without a care for Avicia's suffering.

She continued, "The lady was upset. He tried calming her."

She wagged her finger at the man who brandished his sword. "I believe the lady can do well enough without your efforts to rescue her, my dear brother Odo. You shall sheathe your weapon. Or, do you wish to give my ladies a fright?"

When the man still brandished his blade, the duchess glared at her husband.

William smiled at Harold. "My brother, the bishop de Bayeux, fancies himself the protector of Christian virtue." While others in his entourage sniggered, William ordered Odo's withdrawal.

After a tense moment, Odo wheeled his horse around. He cantered toward a nearby fire, his shoulders hunched.

Satisfied, the diminutive Matilda curtsied before William before she addressed Avicia. "It seems you are no worse off than when I last knew you. I remember your knowledge of falconry. Mayhap you can aid my falconer, or shall I call him my fool?"

William guffawed at her comment.

Avicia whispered. "If you wish, Your Grace." She tugged her mare behind her and fell into place behind Matilda.

Edric stared long after they left. He avoided Harold's intent look.

The hunting party returned to Rouen just after midday. Edric dismounted in the bailey. Avicia and her friend cantered toward him.

"Milord, I wish to thank you for your service toward Sieur Philippe's wife," the elder woman began. "She is very dear to me."

Edric glanced from her to Avicia, who averted her eyes.

He replied, "Neither of you owe me such gratitude. My actions befitted any man of honor."

"I hope you shall be a guest at my table in William's hall. We shall feast tonight on the bucks the hunters have taken. Please tell me your name, milord."

"Edric of Newington," he offered, though certain she knew his identity.

"I am Alice de Beaufort, wife of the overlord of Avicia's husband."

"I did not recall your name, but we have met before, many years past."

"Indeed, we met in London." The bemused smile on Alice's face convinced him she remembered the circumstances of their first acquaintance, too well. His cheeks warmed again.

"We shall see you at the dinner hour, milord." Alice inclined her head toward him. With a nudge, her mare moved toward the stables.

Avicia stared straight ahead and avoided his eyes, as she urged her mount forward.

❧

In the afternoon, Avicia dined with Alice, her daughter and Edric in William's hall. Alice's light-hearted banter normally elevated her spirits but not now. She gripped the folds of her garment and wiped her shaking hands in it, before she reached for the wine.

Earlier, her gaze had lingered on Edric while he crossed the rush-strewn floor and joined them. Alice greeted him first. She introduced him to her daughter and namesake, who joined them in the absence of her father Hugh. Now Edric sat on one bench, while she occupied the other. How handsome he appeared in a russet-colored tunic. His pale yellow hair gleamed in the torchlight.

Since Alice dominated most of the conversation in her usual manner, Avicia kept quiet. She shivered too much and could not trust her voice not to reveal her anxiety.

197

Edric's muscular thigh had brushed her leg twice at the table. She knew he moved with purpose, for there remained adequate space between them. Then it happened again.

Despite his murmured apologies, her hand shook so badly she spilled liquid from the wine goblet. She stared at the red droplets staining the fabric.

She looked up and found he watched her steadily. Her cheeks grew flushed, heart lurching inside her chest.

When he said, "Lady Alice asked you a question," she hardly took in his words. Her concentration lingered on his mouth. She wanted those lips on hers again.

A harsh breath escaped her. Alice and her daughter also stared.

"I asked if you were unwell, my dear. Your cheeks are pink," Alice said.

"This hall is so stuffy, it is a wonder anyone can breathe." The younger Alice rolled her eyes.

Her mother leaned toward Edric. "Forgive my daughter's bad manners. She does not join me often and," Alice paused and glared at her child, "shall not be allowed to in the future unless she behaves better."

Edric smiled. Avicia stared at the crinkles around his mouth.

While minstrels and jongleurs entertained, she remained entranced by his presence. Alice's daughter openly displayed her appreciation for Edric. The little demoiselle practiced her flirting with him. Her eyelashes fluttered rapidly whenever she spoke to him. Her squeals and laughter rippled through the air whenever he said something she deemed humorous. She persisted more than her mother had in her inquiries about life in England. When Alice ordered her out, she protested and pouted sulkily. As she retired, Avicia sighed with some satisfaction.

Edric nodded toward Alice. "She reminds me of my daughter Deorwynn who is willful if her mother and I do not admonish her."

"Daughters can try a parent's patience," Alice said. "Tell us of your children."

He grinned. "I have two sons. There is my heir Leofsige and his brother Cenweard. Then, there are my beautiful daughters, Eanflaed, who is the youngest, her sister Deorwynn, and my eldest girl, Leofflaed. She shall wed in the autumn."

"I can see in your eyes that your children give you much pleasure."

"They are good children."

"You must long for home."

He swirled the contents of his goblet before he sipped. "I hope we may leave soon."

Beneath lowered eyelids, Avicia studied him. He spoke with affection for his family, but never mentioned his lady. He had five children, though that was no evidence of attachment to his wife, especially when the Church enjoined the procreation of children in marriage. Yet, here she had sat, sinful thoughts of him in her head. No good could come from her lingering desire. There was no hope. His family awaited his return to England.

She tightened her fists in her lap. "I am sorry, but I must retire." When his gaze darted to hers, she continued in a rush, "The hunt has left me tired."

"Please, do not go," he began.

She gasped and he fell silent.

He stood and nodded to her. "If you must, then I bid you a good night."

"And you. Good night, Alice."

She gripped the edge of the trestle table, unsteady on her feet. His hand alighted on her wrist. Flames leapt where his flesh brushed hers. She stared wordless. For too long, they regarded each other in silence.

He said, "Sleep well, milady."

She left the hall without a backward glance. Outside, she leaned against the door and gasped for air. Her heart pulsated deep inside her chest.

⁓

In the dim torchlight of the hallway, Avicia crept with a candle in hand. Peaceful sleep had eluded her.

Rampant images swirled in her mind, leaving her hot and stifled beneath her coverlet. She cast it off, donned the clothes she had worn earlier to dinner and left her room. She went to the mews. Perhaps she might find comfort in a familiar place from her childhood.

After the earlier hunt, Duchess Matilda had granted her permission to visit the mews any time she wished, against the falconer's objections. Avicia silently questioned her decision, especially given the disaster years ago with the merlin. She sensed a change in Matilda she had not anticipated. Marriage had tempered the duchess' natural inclination toward selfishness.

A silvery moon marked her progress across the bailey. Men-at-arms ignored their duties and slept. Some leaned against walls or animal enclosures, while others lay down in the dirt.

She reached the mews and tested the handle. With the candle aloft, she pushed the door. She pulled it closed behind her and stepped into the darkened room.

"Who goes there?"

A raptor trilled loudly at the introduction of noise and light into its space.

Her hand flew to her throat. Edric whirled toward her. His footfalls treaded across the dirt and straw, until he stood before her in the darkness. She licked suddenly dry lips.

"We must not be alone together, Avicia."

His words echoed her thoughts. She nodded, but her legs ignored the counsel blaring in her mind.

He exhaled in a long sigh. The candle flame sputtered once and extinguished. He took the beeswax stub from her grasp. It fell with a thud on the dirt and straw-covered floor.

His lips found hers. She returned his embrace with a silent plea. She sought his caresses, a balm for her wearied soul. Her hands roamed over his back down to his waist. Fingers slid under his tunic. Nails scored his flesh. He breathed a ragged sigh, broke their contact, and trailed a line of kisses down the column of her throat. Then, he sighed and released her.

"We must stop. It is a sin. You belong to another."

She tightened her arms around his neck and he held her. The length of her torso pressed against his. "*Non*, do not say it. This night, I belong only to you."

CHAPTER 23

Rouen, Normandy
March 1064 CE

She leaned back in the circle of his arms, her breath a harsh moan torn from her lips. Her heart thrummed in rhythm with his ragged sighs.

"You must remember," she said. "This is where we first met. Not this place, but in the mews at Lille."

His wide grin gleamed in the dimness. He loomed closer, kissed her face softly, everywhere but her mouth. She closed her eyes and trembled.

His hands caressed her, lips nuzzling the length of her throat. His fingers trailed over her back, across her waist and down her hips. She wound her arms around his neck and clutched him tighter. He tugged her further into the gloomy recesses of the mews.

What she could not see, she explored in bold caresses. Her palms slid over the coarse wool of his tunic and beneath it. Muscles bunched wherever her nails scratched. She marveled at his throaty response. His desire emboldened her. "I want to feel you, all of you. I want you naked against me."

Both discarded their garments. Cool air stung her flesh, soon replaced by the heat of his hands, the length of his body. He palmed her hips. His fingers glided and inflamed her skin. Now, he claimed her lips eagerly. His tongue teased at her mouth. She surrendered. A low moan escaped in her throat. His palm splayed across her warm belly. She groaned at his touch. She had always hated it when Philippe fondled her there, the flesh rounded from her pregnancies. Yet, she felt no shame in Edric's arms, only pleasure. She possessed a woman's body, and a woman's desire, not the timidity and maidenly modesty of her youth.

He grasped her at the waist and lifted her. Her legs around his hips, her limbs encased him. He pressed her into the wall behind them. She held him close, even though the rough-hewn timber jabbed into her back.

Somewhere in the darkness, a hunting bird trilled noisily before quiet descended. Her fingers mapped his countenance, the thick bushy brows, where they met the contours and planes of his forehead. Her hands smoothed over the flare of his nostrils and pressed at the curve of his mouth. He took the tip of one finger between his teeth. No words passed between them.

She touched a roughened, crisscrossed scar at his shoulder. Her heart wrung with sympathy at the thought of the whipping he endured. She kissed the reddened flesh, licked the edge of it. He pushed her against the wall. The wood creaked and splintered. His lips fastened on hers and she returned his forceful embrace. All desire for a gentle first coupling faded in heated longing.

"Edric! I can wait no longer."

Her throaty plea came in a voice she barely recognized. She cradled his face between her hands. He grabbed her arms and pushed them back against the wood. His body kept her pressed to the wall.

"Please, oh please." His lips fastened on hers and stifled her whispers.

One smooth, slow thrust joined their bodies. She moaned against his mouth, his heart in a steady rhythm with hers. This night, she truly belonged to him.

On the plush softness of his mantle, she clung to him, one leg draped over his hip. Her cloak covered them in the darkness. Not even the cool dampness of the sand and straw-covered floor, or the squeaks of the rats disturbed her. She gave a long sigh of contentment and burrowed deep into the warmth his body offered. His burly hand caressed the smooth contour of her hip.

"I am sorry," he whispered against her hair.

Her fingers curled tendrils of fine hair on his chest. "Why?"

"We should not have done this."

She tensed. Did he already regret this night?

"I mean, we should not have done this here, in this place. You are a lady. I treated you roughly. Can you forgive me?"

She relaxed against him again, as her heart slowed to its normal rhythm. "I wanted you. I do not regret it."

His hold on her tightened possessively. "Nor do I. Still, I fear the coming of the dawn."

"Hush now. We are in each other's arms, Edric. What more could I desire in life?"

"In my heart, you are my love. You are my true wife."

"Do not make such vows." She shivered against him. "Please, only hold me this night."

When he said no more, she closed her eyes and fought against tears. She loved him still. Did her sentiments make her a fool? She pondered this while he snored lightly beside her. She cleaved to him in silence through the night.

Hours passed, in which rainfall pattered on the thatched roof. What might the dawn bring?

His breath grew shallow and he stirred. He sat up and dragged the cloak from her shoulders. The tips of her breasts hardened under his heated stare. She touched his forearm. The muscle tensed beneath the skin.

"Please, morning shall soon be here."

His arm snaked around her shoulders. His lips found hers. She surrendered to his kiss.

"The night is almost over," she whispered. "A new day dawns, one in which you belong to another."

In his arms, she welcomed their union. Her thighs locked around his waist, gripping him tight. When her nails dug into his back, he pulled her hair, arching her neck almost violently. She cradled his body and delighted in the violent shudders that rippled through him. Tears spilled down her cheek. She surrendered to waves of pleasure and drowned in her desire.

He stirred and kissed her again. She trembled against him.

"You must go, Edric."

"I cannot leave you now!" His hold on her hip tightened.

"You must! We risk discovery. Your overlord may have missed you in the hall. Please, Edric."

Her words ended on a sob.

Then cold air stung her skin. He rustled in the dark. The yelp and squeal of a rodent followed. In the gloom, she listened while he dressed. His footsteps neared her and a bundle landed on her lap. Suddenly shy, even in the darkness, she stood and faced the wall, donning her clothes. She hugged herself tight. Tears threatened again.

His hand cupped the nape of her neck before he released her. When she turned to him, he retrieved his mantle from the ground.

He loomed before her, his lips covering hers again.

When he deepened their embrace, she drew back with a cry. "*Non!* We can never be together again."

His low chuckle disturbed one of the birds.

"This night is not over between us. It shall never be."

He left her behind with hot tears on her cheek. Not tears of regret, but joy at the determination in his voice.

Alone, she rubbed her arms beneath her cloak. She pushed aside thoughts of the future. This one night of pleasure must be enough, but her heart rebelled against the thought of turning from him again.

She dusted her robe, certain that straw covered her from head to toe. Fingers of light crept beneath the door of the mews, heralding the arrival of another day.

She peeked out from behind the door. When she saw Edric had left, a relieved sigh escaped her. It would be too soon to face him in the daylight. Her traitorous heart would reveal her secret love for everyone's view.

She stepped out into the bailey, her eyes focused on the ground. She lowered the bar closing the mews and pressed her head against the door with a loud exhale.

"Something troubles you, Lady Avicia?"

Odo's sonorous tone made her whirl. His dark eyes appraised her in the golden dawn light. She leaned back against the door and prayed Edric left long before the prelate could have seen him leave the mews.

"Did you pass the night here, milady?" Odo drew closer.

She sidestepped him. "I sought a moment's peace and comfort among the familiar sounds."

The bishop's hefty hand closed on her arm. "I would be your comfort, if you would let me. While I remember your fondness for the mews, you do not need to seek such unusual haunts when I am near."

She pitched her voice low. "You do not dare! Unhand me, Your Grace, for I do not like your familiar tone or the liberties you take with my person. I remember your attack on me in Flanders."

He released her with a hard jerk. She stumbled in the slick mud.

"You misunderstand me. I would be your confessor, milady. I never suggested otherwise."

His gaze scoured her form. "It is strange you only came for a moment's comfort, for straw covers you. One might think you rolled around in it all night."

She retreated to her chamber with her head held high. At every step, Odo's hot, merciless gaze trailed her.

❧

Edric always avoided Avicia at mealtimes or in William's hall in the days that followed. However, they often saw each other at Mass. On such occasions, he struggled with the order of service. His fingers curled into tight fists. He ached for her touch again.

On one occasion after the hour of Tierce, Harold insisted he accompany the rest of the Saxons for dinner, even if he refused food. Waiting outside the chapel for Harold, he overheard the conversation between Alice and Avicia as they passed by. Though she kept her eyes averted, he felt the tension radiating from her.

Alice said, "I have not seen you so happy in months, not since the Englishmen arrived."

Though Avicia hushed her, a thrill rippled through Edric's belly at the thought he might be responsible for her sudden joy. She gave him the same pleasure.

Harold and his men caught up with him. "I thought you would disobey me, again. I stayed behind to speak with William...."

"About Wulfnoth?"

"William campaigns against his enemies and he wants me to ride with him."

Edric turned from him. "Harold, you took me from my family, intent on gaining your brother back. We are no closer to that goal. Forgive me, if I say, if you do not discuss Wulfnoth, I do not care to hear of your conversations with William the Bastard."

"Or, to raid with us?"

When he glared at Harold, the earl shook his head. "Very well, but do not expect a share of the spoils."

He did not mind. If William's men left, he might enjoy some time alone with Avicia. He smiled at the thought.

As they walked to the hall, Harold asked, "Does your back still hurt?"

Edric nodded but he lied. His flesh burned where Avicia's nails scraped across the skin a few nights before. Lord, but she intoxicated his senses.

"While I am gone, you shall rest by my order," Harold continued, "I shall sway William to our purpose."

"Is he inclined to discuss the release of Haakon and Wulfnoth?" When Harold nodded, he shook his head. "I can scarce believe it. What does William want in return?"

Harold clapped his back and laughed. "You are too suspicious. I do not know what he shall say but I shall listen, if only to obtain the release of my brother and nephew. Wulfnoth has languished in this place for too long. Haakon may be my brother's bastard but Sweyn acknowledged him. He died on pilgrimage, never knowing his son's fate. I shall not leave Normandy without them, be assured."

When they sat at table in the hall, Edric snuck furtive glances at Avicia over the rim of his cup. She purposefully ignored him, except he realized each time he glanced her way, her cheeks flushed. If they were alone, he would have cleared the distance between the trestle tables and hauled her into his arms.

Harold and some of the Frenchmen engaged in a drinking contest. Edric joined in, determined he would best their captors. Though his head swam and his eyes glazed over, he never stopped. When the last knight surrendered, he claimed victory, though Harold's men dragged him off, barely standing, for his rest.

He craned his neck and found Avicia across the hall. She spoke with Alice, who rose and moved toward him. He wished she would stand still, for there seemed two of her in his blurry vision. He cursed the stout French wines and leaned on his fellow Saxons for support.

"Milord, it seems you have no head for our drink," Alice said. The insufferable woman and her phantom double smiled at him. If only both might stop swaying before his eyes.

She shook her head. "You may take one of the empty quarters where the men-at-arms sleep. The one who once occupied it died two weeks ago. I believe he had too much strong drink in him."

He growled at her and she laughed in his face. His companions proved more hindrance than help, for they struggled under his weight.

The ground swayed beneath him. Suddenly he sank into soft comfort. A woman's laughter sounded before his eyelids closed.

Sometime later, delicate fingers pressed something cool against his brow. He opened his eyes in a dimly lit space. A candle sputtered on a stool. His hands curled in the folds of a coverlet.

He tried rising, but a firm hand pressed him down. "You were a fool to undertake the challenge."

Avicia's voice seemed the sweetest sound, even when she chastised him. She hovered beside him with a cloth for his forehead, as she offered a wooden cup.

He frowned into the contents. "Not more wine?"

She grinned and pressed the cup to his lips. "It is not wine. Drink it." When he grimaced, she continued, "The barber-surgeon's wife Torfida brought it a little while ago. She said it would help you sleep and banish the effects of the wine. I trust her."

"Well, if you trust her, then I trust you," Edric murmured.

She offered the cup again. He caught her wrist. "Stay with me tonight."

Her fingers curled at his bearded cheek. "I would never leave you."

CHAPTER 24

Bayeux, Normandy
August 1064 CE

Perspiration trickled down Avicia's temple, but none of the other women seemed discomforted. They sat on wooden stools in a semi-circle around Duchess Matilda, their backs bent over embroidery meant for the abbey at Caen. In wedding his bride, William had flouted the Pope's prohibitions against the union. William worked on the abbey in penance for his marriage.

After Avicia had renewed their acquaintance, Matilda expected her companionship, as before. Avicia followed the court's progress from Rouen to Caen, and now Bayeux. Alice alone deemed it a veritable triumph, and delighted in the shocked expressions of the well-born Norman women.

Avicia remained reserved, and with compelling reason, in her opinion. Even now, whenever she looked up from the intricate fabric work, she caught the usual, unkind stares. Mabel de Belleme's green-eyed gaze riled her most.

She longed for nothing more than escape in her lover's arms. Almost every night for several months, she had made love with Edric. Her mind seethed with images of their shameless passion. They risked everything for their ardor, but even desire as powerful as theirs gave way to practical concerns. He worried for her if she should conceive by him. After their first reckless night together, they were careful afterward and ensured he never spilled his seed inside her body.

Yet she often daydreamed, as she did now, of bearing a child for him. Would a child of theirs favor him or her? A reckless musing, but it consumed her thoughts often.

"By all the saints!" The needle pricked the tip of her forefinger, for the third time. She sucked at the wound.

She whispered to Alice, who sat beside her. "How can you bear this torture?"

"I have my eyes focused on my work instead of glaring at Mabel de Belleme," Alice intoned. "The duchess does not want stains all over such costly materials."

Across the room, Matilda asked, "Is something wrong, Lady Avicia?"

"I have pierced my finger again, milady. It is quite tender now."

The other women tittered and shook their heads at her tender aches. Blood welled up, beaded, and trickled down her finger.

"Perhaps your lover might place tender kisses on your hand and make it better," Mabel muttered.

The vicious comment carried throughout the room, though spoken barely above a murmur. In the confined space, gasps of outrage and frowns followed from the other women.

The duchess rose and drew herself up her full height. "What did you say?"

Mabel's gaze swept over the room. Her mouth curved in a mockery of a smile, before she glowered at Avicia again. "You know I speak the truth. You cavort with one of the Englishmen. I have seen the looks pass between you two. Whore! Have you spread your legs for him already?"

Now stares of accusation focused on Avicia. She clenched her garments in both hands.

Beside her, Alice stood, her embroidery discarded. "How dare you slander her name? Her husband is my dearest kinsman. No one may call him a cuckold."

"Spare us your indignation!" Mabel sprang to her feet. Her embroidery fell from her lap. "You have long maintained a friendship with her, for reasons no one understands." She stabbed her talon-like nail at Avicia. "She is pretty, but it must be the extent of her charms. Since Hugh de Montfort and her husband have joined His Grace in his Breton campaign, the whore has all the time in the world to cuckold Sieur Philippe with her English lord."

Matilda ordered everyone out, except Avicia. In a flurry of garments and whispers, the women exited the chamber.

The breath raw in her throat, Avicia rubbed her arms through the fabric of her robe. When Matilda sat beside her, her heart pounded a tattoo of fear and betrayal.

Silence descended on the room and thickened. She jerked when Matilda touched her chin and turned her face so their gazes met. Her eyes watered and tears sprang forth in a torrent. She cried until her throat ached.

Matilda's arms came about her shoulders. Shocked by such kindness, when she deserved none, she succumbed.

When she calmed, Matilda smiled and patted her cheek. "Surely, you must know the tale of how William pressed for my hand in marriage."

She nodded, recalling the story of William's rough wooing.

Matilda continued, "It is a wonder I married him. Indeed, he met me with my attendants in Bruges one afternoon. He pulled me from my mare by my plaits and beat me. I despised him." A girlish giggle escaped her. "Yet I realized such a bold man, who desired me greatly, deserved my hand in marriage. I defied the Pope over William but, he was not my first love."

Avicia knew this yet she kept her silence.

Matilda took her hand. "I shall not ask if Mabel's accusations are true. Do you love your husband still?"

"Things are so different between us. I do not want him hurt."

"You know what you must do." The duchess rose. "I shall speak with Mabel de Belleme and the other ladies. If any of them repeat her accusations, they shall leave court permanently."

"Why are you so kind to me, Your Grace? After what I did all those years ago, I do not deserve your generosity."

"I loved an Englishman once, too."

Her ready protest died under the press of the duchess' finger against her lips. "His name was Brithric, son of the Earl Aelfgar of Mercia. He was an English lord who attended the Flemish court. He was beautiful, if such a word may describe a man. Hair of spun flax, *non*, gold and so pale, his people called him, oh, what was the word? I do not recall it now, long years it has been, but it was the English word for snow, I think."

"They called him Brithric Meaw." Avicia remembered Matilda's interest in the man, for whom she had waited for outside the church at Lille.

Matilda continued, "I loved him with all the youthful passion a headstrong girl can feel. His father had arranged his betrothal to another from the cradle. I sent my attendants to him, with tokens of my affection, but he rejected it all. I sent you with a letter professing my love. He did not want me."

Something hard glinted in the duchess' eyes and her lips thinned before curving in a smile. "I have not forgotten his slight, but it is in the past. He returned to England. I accepted life without him. I did not suffer because William wanted me more than all the lands in the world."

She looked at Avicia again. "None of this surprises you. You knew of my heart's true desire, and still you kept my secret from others?"

"When you sent me to Lord Brithric in the week before I left Lille, I knew your purpose, though I never spied upon the contents of your letter. I also knew you rejected Duke William's first suit because your heart sought another. I understood your sentiments."

Matilda smiled and patted her hand again. "Compose yourself. We are to dine in the hour. I expect you in the hall. Mabel shall not frighten you."

Avicia kissed her ringed fingers. "Thank you for your kindness."

When Matilda retired, Avicia clasped her hands at her bosom and bowed her head. "Please, my heart, listen to her advice."

❧

Later, she hesitated outside the entrance to the hall. Some of the women gathered at the trestle tables, her chief detractor among them.

Edric's distinctive footfalls rounded a corner. His grin widened at the sight of her. Determined strides brought them dangerously closer. Alice approached with the duchess and her attendants. Avicia shook her head violently. Edric's smile turned to a frown. She shrank against the wall, her gaze crestfallen. A light touch descended on her arm.

"*Non*, please go inside," she whispered.

"To wait upon you? I would rather not, for I am starved," Alice said.

Avicia turned, a sob caught in her throat. Matilda nodded in their direction, before she disappeared into the room with her train of attendants and maidservants.

"Why do you stand outside the hall? Are you worried over what Mabel de Belleme said? The duchess told her she would not allow such malicious gossip to besmirch you or your husband. Mabel looked ready to choke." A girlish chortle escaped Alice. "I wish she might, the wretched woman. Come now, no one shall look at you unkindly. The duchess would be displeased. I must say, you have made a favorable impression on her."

Alice tugged her into the room. When she sat, Duchess Matilda locked eyes with her, inclined her head, and smiled.

A tingle of warmth warned Avicia of the other eyes upon her. By instinct alone, she knew neither Mabel nor any of the other gossips stared at her. Her heart pitched. Poor Edric, he would not understand why she had warned him off. Could she risk seeing him again tonight?

"You dine without your duke?" William's strident voice cut off her worrisome thoughts.

He and his company entered the hall. Loud cheers erupted and the duchess rose with her goblet in salute. "Milord, you have returned! What news?"

"Victory, milady!"

Boisterous applause filled the room. William crossed the rushes and enveloped his wife in a hearty embrace. He lifted her off her feet and spun her around. Since he stood much taller than she did, it seemed as if he held a child. Open-mouthed, Avicia stared at them.

"Milady, it pleases me to see you again."

Philippe grasped her hand, bowed, and kissed it. Wordless, she shrank against the bench.

"I know my return is a great shock." He pointed to a roughened scar over his eye.

Hugh swept past them and kissed Alice soundly, despite her pretense at protests. All around them, the court welcomed its warriors, from the poorest man-at-arms to the noblest magnate among William's men.

Avicia dared look across the room, where Earl Harold embraced Edric. The pair towered above everyone else like golden gods. When Edric stared past his liege's shoulder at her, she avoided his eyes.

The mood at dinner turned festive. William ordered several casks of wine opened in celebration. He heaped praise on Earl Harold for a feat of considerable strength and heroism, for he had rescued William's men mired in the marshes of the Couesnon River.

All throughout the meal, Avicia remained calm. She ate despite Philippe's persistent, admiring stares. Yet, when his fingers alighted on her hand, she jerked in surprise and frowned at him.

"I did not mean to startle you," he said, "nor do I mean to watch you so. You are so beautiful. I almost forgot."

She swallowed against the bile rising in her throat. "You were away for some time. Your letter from the Breton countryside surprised me. I expected you at Montfort-sur-Risle for a month, not gone to war."

Her belly twisted in knots. In truth, she had received the missive with a glad heart. His absence allowed the illusion of her happiness with Edric.

By God's mercy, her lover had ceased his intent stares. The last time she snuck a glance in his direction while they dined, he refused her gaze.

"Now, I am here and we shall be happy again." Philippe raised her hand to his lips again and kissed her fingers. The spark of desire glittered in his silver gaze. Once, his passion would have thrilled her. Now her longing for Edric intruded.

Before the feast concluded, Philippe drew her from the hall. When he kissed the nape of her neck and removed her robe and chemise, she closed her eyes and pretended Edric's kisses heated her flesh instead. Her body responded to his skilled, familiar touch, but her heart cried out for another. In the throes of his passion, he kissed her lips roughly, bruised them, and demanded she open her eyes. The charade faded.

Later, when he rolled away and tugged her beside him, his hand possessively gripped the curve of her hip. She closed her eyes and wept. Philippe's snores drowned out her sobs.

♠

Three days after Harold's return, Edric rose in poor spirits. Images of Avicia in her husband's arms tortured him at night. Since Philippe's return, she had kept her distance. He wondered if she had known her husband would arrive at Bayeux from the moment she ignored him at dinner. Her startling rejection hurt, after so many months spent wrapped in her arms, tasting her pleasure.

With a curse, he hastened and joined Harold in William's hall.

"You look awful." Harold offered him a cup. Its dark contents soured his stomach. He shook his head.

Harold shrugged and downed the drink, wiping his mouth with the back of his hand. "More wine for me. Truly, you are different this morn."

"I am easily tired. I want to go home. It has been long months since I have seen my children." He tamped down the irritability from his voice but Harold's scowl told him he had failed. Yet, what difference did Harold's displeasure make? Nothing mattered anymore, since Avicia's rejection.

"Come, Edric, William awaits us at Bayeux Cathedral. At last, he has agreed to discuss my purpose. In light of my recent favor with him, by the Grace of God, Wulfnoth and Haakon may see their homes again."

As they approached the edifice of the cathedral, white dust warned of the constant hammering and chiseling of stone.

217

Harold pointed out the scarred remnants of the previous building, destroyed in a fire. "Odo's work continues. He has vowed this new cathedral shall be the most magnificent in Normandy."

Edric grunted, but made no other reply. When he and Harold's company dismounted, a guardsman greeted Harold, before leading him inside the cathedral. Edric gathered his mantle around his shoulders and followed with Harold's men.

In a chamber, William's retinue stood, among them Hugh. Edric glared at him simply for his resemblance to Philippe, until his gaze fell on William.

The sight unnerved him. William sat on a gilded chair, reminiscent of a throne. Two attendants clad in chainmail were at his side. Harold stopped short with the rest of his company.

"You brought your retainers, Harold. This is holy ground. Did you think I meant to kill you?" William twirled the end of his dark mustache. His comment produced the expected guffaws, before he imperiously held up his hands and called for silence. "Be at ease. I am prepared to discuss the matter of the release of your family members."

Harold nodded. "I am glad to hear of it. You have been a gracious host, Your Grace, but my company and I are eager for home. I pray I may leave with Wulfnoth and Haakon at my side. My aged mother would see her son again."

"I am sure she wishes it." William gestured to one of his retainers who brought forth a rolled parchment. "Before we proceed, I have certain pledges I require of you."

Edric frowned. The Frenchmen always wanted something. He had remained certain of this throughout their sojourn. Now, his fears might come true. His gaze narrowed.

"I understand you are not married, in the traditional sense," William paused when one of his men chuckled. "In view of the bonds of friendship we have established, I offer one of my daughters as a suitable bride. This union shall symbolize improved relations between England and Normandy, and foster goodwill between our families. I recall your late father did not have a good opinion of us, but I trust yours is different. A Norman bride would suit you well."

Edric gazed at Harold, who struggled for a response. "You are most gracious."

William cut him off. "There is more. I am sure you are aware King Edward spent his youth in Normandy. His mother Emma was kin and I mourned her death. Edward favored me when I visited his court some years ago, with the knowledge of the state of affairs in England. In particular, we spoke of the succession. Your family must worry because your sister Queen Edith has yet to provide the king with an heir. She may never give him a son."

Harold growled low in his throat. Mutters issued from his retainers. William insulted the queen of England. Whatever Harold's regard for his sister, Edric knew he would not let anyone besmirch her womanhood.

With his hands on his hips, Harold replied, "My sister may not be in the flower of her youth, but she has years left in which to produce an heir. By God's grace, she shall do so."

Cheers from his fellow Saxons followed his words, but Edric kept his attention focused on the Frenchmen. William's sudden glare and the stubborn line of his mouth held his gaze.

William muttered, "One can hope, but the queen is not in the prime of her youth, nor is Edward. He needs an heir."

"He has brought Edgar, son of his brother, to the court. Edgar is the atheling of England, a prince of royal Saxon blood," Harold insisted.

William scarcely hid his scowl, which matched Harold's glare. A dangerous undercurrent of anger broiled between the two men. Edric studied the duke's retinue. The men on both sides were evenly matched, eight of William's men to Harold's retainers of the same number.

William's gaze softened unexpectedly, "I had hoped, given our bonds of friendship, you might be more amenable to my interests in England."

Edric understood William's meaning. Harold sputtered, "You can have no interest in Edward's throne."

William grinned and leaned forward. "Not even if I hold your kinsmen? How badly do you want to see them returned? Would your aged mother's heart shrivel if her dear son never made it home?"

Edric gulped air furiously. William had laid a trap for Harold. He wanted Edward's throne. Wulfnoth and Haakon's lives were once more in the sway of a greedy, treacherous Frenchman.

"Think upon it, Harold," William cajoled. "I offer the freedom of your brother and nephew, and an alliance with Normandy, all for little except well-placed words in Edward's ear. Indeed, I think he already considers me a candidate to take the throne."

Silence overwhelmed the room, before Harold turned his back on William. "Leave us." His gaze flitted over his men.

"I shall not leave you alone with these people," Edric protested. "Harold, you cannot bargain with them. We have lost. They shall never return Wulfnoth and Haakon, you must know it."

"I said go! Do not question me. Go, Edric."

Edric followed the other men out of the solar. The rough-hewn door slammed shut behind him. He stood apart from his fellow Saxons, who argued furiously while he paced outside the door.

After an interminable time passed, Harold stepped out, and gripped the doorpost for a moment, before he nodded to his men. The portal closed on sniggers behind him.

With obvious effort, he forced a thin-lipped smile. "We leave within the week. William has agreed to release Haakon, but not Wulfnoth. We shall take my nephew home."

His men crowded around. Harold pushed past them. They fell into step behind him.

Edric stared resolute at their backs.

Harold spun on his heels and returned to him. "Well, it is what you wanted. You shall return home."

He turned away, but Edric grasped his arm. He did not care how Harold glared at his impertinence. He whispered, "What did you tell William?"

Harold shrugged his grip off. "I said what he wanted to hear."

Edric stumbled backward. "You promised him Edward's throne? Good God!"

Harold snarled. "I did not say that! I told him what he wanted to hear, what he needed to believe so we might leave this place. Now, come."

&

The court returned to Caen. Edric withdrew into himself, worry occupying his mind. He could never say with certainty what had happened inside that room within Bayeux Cathedral, but he knew Harold well enough to believe his actions would have dire consequences for England.

Later, in the darkness of the mews, he sensed Avicia behind him, before she spoke.

"Milord, are you here?"

Although he would have turned toward her, his feet remained rooted.

She came around and wound her arms around his neck. "I hoped you might be here. Forgive me. I could not see you after Philippe's return. We risked too much."

"It was a dream, Avicia, one from which we must awaken."

"Edric, please do not say it. Our love is not a dream. It is real. How else can I explain the tearing of my heart at the news of your leave-taking? I cannot bear parting from you again."

"You must accept it." He forced resolution into his voice. "We have no choice. I must return to England, and you shall remain here, where you belong."

She sought his eyes in the dim light, and tightened her grip about his neck. "You cannot mean it. You love me, as I love you. No matter what happens, we shall never be truly parted, not now."

The familiar scent of her intoxicated him. He hauled her tight against him. He sought her mouth greedily. She returned his embrace with fierce passion.

He allowed himself one last kiss and savored her lips, her full length against him. "I love you. I shall always love you, but you must go from this place. It is not yet sunset. We cannot risk exposure."

She held him in a viselike grip. He unwound her limbs and nudged her. "Go, please. For mercy's sake, if you love me, Avicia, go."

The birds trilled noisily, as her sobs filled the space. She would not move. Instead, he rushed from the mews and left her behind. He brushed at his watery eyes and headed for the hall.

The green-eyed woman who did not like Avicia stood in his path. Her mouth widened, in a poor imitation of a smile. She raised her hand and pointed across the bailey.

He turned, his stomach tied in knots of fear. When Avicia emerged from the mews, Bishop Odo de Bayeux grabbed her. His face purpled with rage. "Deceitful whore! I knew I would find you with him."

CHAPTER 25

Caen, Normandy
August 1064 CE

Edric stared straight ahead, his lips pressed tightly together. He had endured Harold's full anger since nightfall. In the wee hours, the earl's tirade continued.

Harold circled, hands clasped tight behind his back. His expression, scarlet and swollen with fury, showed no pity. "Damn you! I cannot fathom it, even after you have told me the full truth. You risked everything. Our return home, the boon William has given me, all for some wench to spread her legs for you. Look at me when I speak!"

Edric met his regard. They stood nose to nose, evenly matched in height. When Harold drew back his fist and rammed it into Edric's face, both men reeled from the impact of the blow.

Edric righted himself and blinked harshly in the torchlight of William's dining hall.

Harold's glacial stare, colder than the waters of the Channel, froze him in place. "Do you understand we are to leave at dawn?"

"I cannot go. You saw what happened. The bishop," he barely growled the word, "dragged Avicia here, and accused her of adultery in front of everyone. He has petitioned William for an ecclesiastical court to hear evidence against her. They shall condemn her. She cannot suffer alone."

Harold gaped. "You assume you have a choice in your leave-taking."

"I shall not abandon her!" Edric pounded the trestle table beside him.

"You would remain and give proof to the charges against her? You have a family at home. This woman bewitched you when you lay between her legs."

"You shall say no more of her!" His heart hammered inside his chest. He curled and uncurled his fists. "Though blood ties bind me to your cause, Harold, you shall not insult the woman I love ever again. She means more to me than you can ever know. Did I not tell you this night how it was between us?"

Earlier, after everyone had left the hall, he unburdened his heart to Harold. He confessed his long-held secrets, but found no sympathy in the earl's Nordic blue gaze. At first, Harold seemed incredulous and disgusted at turns.

Now, they stared each other down in silence.

Harold stabbed a finger at him. "You shall forget her! Do you understand me? You shall leave with us. We return home with Haakon. Forget the folly of this day."

Edric's fists bunched tight again. "I shall never forget her."

Harold's scowl darkened. "She belongs to another. Have you overlooked that?"

When Edric had re-entered the hall, Avicia's husband stood shocked with a blank stare on his face. He said nothing while she cried, not even when the guards led her to her prison. Harold's firm grip on Edric kept him from murdering all who manhandled her.

"We never meant for this to happen. Fate brought us together, in Flanders, in England and here again." He stiffened when Harold's hand pressed his shoulder. "You shall hear me, my lord. I do not know what power compels me, but please do not ask me to leave her."

"Edric." Harold paused and cleared his throat. "I understand how you must feel. I have loved Edith the Fair since she was a little village girl at Nazeing. She was free to give her heart. This woman is not. You heard the bishop's proclamation. She must prove her innocence at trial.

I doubt anyone here shall swear an oath and attest to her good character, in contradiction of Odo. He said he saw you leave the mews and she followed."

"Avicia is not without support. Her friend Alice shall not abandon her."

"You also heard Odo claim how he saw her leave the mews with her hair and clothes in disarray, on an earlier occasion at Rouen. He has suspected her for many months. They shall judge her. You must leave it to God. Perhaps He shall be kind and spare her."

Edric groaned. "I cannot leave her, again."

"If you do not, you must watch her suffer. Can your heart bear it?"

Harold's footfalls treaded from the room. Edric sank on the rush-strewn floor, and remained there until long after the servants had returned and removed the trestle tables. Embers from the torches sputtered once before they died. Alone in his misery, he cradled his head in his hands and wept.

Avicia stood in a darkened cell, in Caen's old Roman sewer. The only source of light came through the iron bars of the doorway. Rats scurried in the corners, where she hoped they might remain. Her eyes darted maniacally, picking out their movements in the gloom.

With great effort, she kept down the contents of her stomach. Beads of perspiration dampened her forehead and trickled down her temple. The stench of death, decay, and filth permeated dank straw on the ground. The slime and moss coating the walls kept her confined in the center of the room.

How had it come to this? Even before she asked it of herself, Avicia knew the answer to her question. She had been careless, and now, she must endure the consequences. Images flashed in her mind:

the bishop's monstrous glare and everyone's eyes on her, icy speculation in their pointed gazes. She shook her head. Not everyone showed the same expression. Alice had stared, transfixed with horror. Lips pressed together, Philippe never once met her regard. How her heart ached at his shame laid bare for public scorn.

Although she acknowledged her betrayal and the pain it caused Alice and Philippe, she clung to the memory of her last sight of Edric in the hall. He must have seen her silent plea echoing in her eyes: stay away, keep silent. His countenance, drawn and pinched, remained etched in her memory. When guards dragged her from the hall, a snarl of agony twisted his mouth. Now she suffered alone, in misery. She longed only for the comfort of his arms and his whisper in her ear.

Limp and weary, she swayed on her feet. Fear of the rustling vermin kept her awake. A gust of wind rustled the torch in the hallway. She clasped her hands together and prayed the light would not fade.

The days passed slowly and the nights seemed endless. No one visited her, not even Philippe. She would have accepted his recriminations easily, if only it meant a respite from the wearisome loneliness. Alice never visited, but she could not fault her. Surely, her friend felt betrayed and Avicia understood her sentiments.

With only the vermin for company, she ate whatever the guards shoved under the door, even when they spat on her food before shoveling the trencher inside. At least they had never pissed in it. The possibility of such a happenstance made her shudder. Despite it, she resolved to eat, no matter how she suffered. In the absence of friends and loved ones, she needed her strength and wits about her.

Without news, she never knew whether Edric had returned to England but guessed at it. She prayed wherever he might be, he remained safe. She vowed regret would never tarnish their love, despite the trial she faced.

When her cell door suddenly opened, she stood ready for the guardsman who brought her food once a day.

Instead of the insolent man, Odo de Bayeux stood in the doorway. In place of the livid glare he had last shown her, the veneer of a smile curved his lips. This did not make him less dangerous. She stood her ground in the center of the room.

She scratched at her wrists covered in fleabites. Her dirtied clothes clung to her and smelled of the same foul odors in the cell. So did her hair, grimy hunks of it clumped together. She hated that he would see her in such shameful circumstances, but swore her weakness and fear would not betray her. Instead, she stood tall before her enemy.

"What do you want, Odo?"

He chuckled. "You remain ever so proud, even after a month in this place. I am glad. I do not want your spirits broken yet."

She reeled. "It has been a month only?"

Odo smirked. "You are an adulterous whore and your due punishment is coming. I thought you might wish to know the ecclesiastical court shall convene in one week's time at Rouen. They shall hear the evidence against you and put you to the test. Alice de Beaufort and even Matilda have offered testimony on your behalf, but their words shall not avail you."

She nearly sobbed in relief at the thought that not everyone had abandoned her. Matilda's mercy shocked her, and she clung to the hope of Alice's friendship, even knowing she did not deserve their help.

"Have you naught to say?" Odo interrupted her thoughts.

She shook her head. "Not to you."

When he advanced, she held her ground, denying him a moment's showing of fear. "You are no righteous man. Lust rules your heart. I have never forgotten your assault upon me in Flanders. What angers you the most? Is it because I denied your evil desires, or your belief that Edric got what you wanted?"

She anticipated the blow, but not the powerful force with which the bishop clouted her. She collapsed on the ground and clutched her cheek. Blood stained her palm and the circumference of Odo's ring.

He spat in her face. "You shall learn the cost of your recklessness. Your lover is not here to protect you."

Avicia shrank back.

She regretted it when Odo smirked again. "He is gone, left for England the day after you were seized, the coward. Did you expect he would stay? He has deserted you."

He crossed the cell in brusque strides and left her.

Interminable days passed again. Then her cell door swung open and revealed another unexpected arrival. She sobbed into her hands at the sight of Alice.

"Hugh thrashed me more than once and confined me, but I am here now. Come, my dear, you must have a bath and some proper food. Duchess Matilda ordered it before you must leave for Rouen. I am sorry, but Philippe dismissed your nurse Biota, or I would have brought her with me. He blamed her. He said she should have watched you more carefully."

Avicia sobbed harder, that her nurse should have to leave because of her foolish behavior. On wobbly legs, she rose, with Alice's help.

"*Non*, do not soil yourself by touching me. I am dirty."

Despite all her struggles, Alice kept her upright with a firm hold. Her arms supported Avicia until she stood of her own accord.

Tears welled in her eyes and blurred her vision. "I am sorry, Alice. I lied to you and betrayed our friendship. My heart ruled my mind."

Her voice trailed off. Alice hugged her tight and whispered to her. "I was not fooled. I saw how happy you were with Lord Edric. It seemed the sun shone inside your soul. You loved him and your happiness gave me joy. How sad for you both to be apart, when you belong together."

When she drew back, she tried smiling, though her mouth trembled at the corners and her eyes shone with unshed tears. "Avicia, you are my dearest friend. How could I begrudge your happiness? I shall always treasure Philippe. Yet when I saw you with Edric, I understood where your heart truly lay. I do not fault you for it."

"I have sinned, Alice."

"Everyone sins, but not everyone seeks God's mercy. I believe you do. Now come, you must prepare yourself."

Alice threw her mantle over Avicia's shoulders and led her from the cell.

A guardsman came forward with manacles. Alice frowned in his direction. "Those are unnecessary."

"I have my orders. No prisoner is to walk freely."

Alice drew herself up her full height. "Do you think a mere woman, weakened by more than a month in this place can be a danger to anyone? Stand aside, you fool!"

Together, the women left the old sewer. Avicia mounted each step with painful, jerky movements, but Alice kept her steady. When they reached the landing, Avicia blinked in the sunlight that filtered through the doorway. She hesitated but Alice squeezed her fingers.

Stares and remarks followed her progress across the bailey. One person even spat in her direction and received a deluge of curses from Alice.

Shocked, Avicia stared at her friend, who shrugged. "I abhor unladylike behavior, but no one shall taunt you in my presence. Torfida has come from Rouen. I summoned her husband when they took you. I knew you would need care upon your release. Turstin is ill, but she can tend to you in his place. Good Lord, there are fleas in your hair."

In an empty hovel, Avicia stripped off the cloak and her grime and vermin-infested clothes. Red sores covered her body. Torfida set buckets of water near the doorway, and held the grimy garments at arms' length with metal tongs, as she went outside.

Avicia winced while Alice washed her skin, and when she put on clean garments for the first time in weeks, she sobbed with relief.

"Hush your tears, milady." Torfida re-entered the hovel, "You must eat. I have bread, ale, and cheese."

"This is the best rye I have ever tasted," Avicia said later, between bites, "or it tastes so good because I have been so hungry."

"Eat the cheese, milady."

"*Non*, the smell of it sickens me."

When she finished the bread and ale, Torfida and Alice washed her hair. "I have added pennyroyal oil, milady, it shall rid you of the fleas," Torfida said.

The chapel's bells sounded. Avicia inquired about the hour.

"It is Tierce," Alice replied. "You must be ready soon."

Avicia sat at the fire and rubbed her damp locks with a cloth.

Behind her, Alice commented, "For all your troubles, you seem no worse. If Mabel de Belleme saw you now, she might choke. She deserves it after all the trouble she wrought. We are all well rid of her."

Avicia swung toward her friend. "Rid of her?"

"You have forgotten, Matilda promised anyone who spoke ill of you would know her wrath. Whatever the bishop may have seen or said, the duchess saw him and Mabel leave the hall together before he dragged you back inside. The duchess ordered Mabel home to her lands. I daresay Roger de Montgomery was not sorry to see his wife go. He blames her for the corruptible nature of their sons, especially the young devil, Robert de Belleme."

Avicia dried her hair in silence. Alice and Torfida's continued stares startled her. "What is the matter? Do I still appear so frightful?"

"Strange, but you are truly none the worse, now you are clean." Alice drew closer. "Your cheeks have a rosy color and your eyes are clear. After all you have suffered, I am surprised."

Her voice trailed off and she nodded to Torfida, who asked, "Milady, did you have your show of blood last month?"

Avicia lowered the cloth in her hands. When she made no reply, Torfida said, "Your breasts do seem fuller."

"They were tender also. She could hardly bear my touch," Alice commented.

Understanding dawned, but Avicia shook her head. "I cannot be with child, not now."

"Matilda must be told. She will stop this trial," Alice said.

With a nervous glance at Torfida, Avicia pitched her voice low. "If I am with child, I do not know who sired the babe."

Alice asked, "Could it be Philippe's child?"

"He bedded me on the evening he arrived at Bayeux, and each night afterward until…. When I was with Edric…we were cautious."

"Let me go to Matilda. Torfida shall examine you."

"It is too soon to know the truth."

"If you have any reason to suspect you carry his child, you must be certain."

Before Alice withdrew, at her insistence, Avicia reclined on a pallet. Her pale flesh tinged with prominent bluish lines beneath the skin. Torfida palpated her stomach. She winced when the midwife touched her breasts and lingered at the budded area around the nipples.

When Alice returned, breathless, she clutched Avicia's hand. "I spoke to Matilda. William and Odo were with her. She demanded a halt to the proceedings. They are asking for the midwife."

Torfida scrambled off, while Alice took Avicia's hand. "I also saw Philippe and told him of the possibility you carried his child."

"What did he say?" Avicia worried at her lower lip with her teeth.

Alice smiled. "He made me promise you would eat well, for the babe's sake."

At least, he cared enough for the child.

Torfida returned, but Philippe accompanied her. He ordered Avicia outside.

Stepping into the glare of sunset, she averted her gaze. "Alice told you of the child?"

He cut her off. "I have news of your fate. They have postponed your trial. The duchess has swayed her husband, against Odo's objections, to wait three months for confirmation that you are…with child. If…the babe is mine, I cannot allow harm to my child's mother. You shall endure your confinement at the abbey of Montivilliers, in the north."

She sagged against him with relief. He never pushed her from him, but neither did he hold her. "You and the child shall be well in the care of the nuns. I shall ask Hugh to pledge an endowment for your upkeep, for my sake. When the child is born, send word."

⁐

Within the week, Avicia departed Caen for the abbey at Montivilliers. Philippe and Alice accompanied her, with a small retinue of men-at-arms. It rained often on the journey and the party sought refuge from the cold droplets. At length, they sighted the two towers of their intended destination.

A lone nun garbed in black stood outside the gates. When their horses halted, Philippe helped Avicia down. Alice dismounted and the women shared a fierce embrace.

Avicia kissed Alice's hands. "I shall think of you every day."

Philippe hung back when she thought of approaching him. Instead, she curtsied before the nun, who arched her black eyebrows, and with a strange, familiar glint in her eyes, glanced at Philippe.

He said, "Sister Felice, I commend my wife to your excellent care."

The nun's silvery gaze widened, but she made no reply. Avicia stared. The nun seemed familiar, though they had never met before.

Alice kissed her hand, before Philippe helped her mount. They rode for home. Alice glanced over her shoulders at times. Philippe stared straight ahead, his back rigid. When they faded from view, Avicia followed the nun.

She met with the abbess, the aged Beatrice de Montivilliers, and ate while Sister Felice prepared a room. Except for her gesture toward the meal on the table, the abbess avoided looking at her. Her shame increased.

She went to her room, small and dimly lit, with only a pallet and a table, on which Sister Felice set a candle.

She thrived in the care of the nuns. So did the child inside her. At the end of spring in the following year, when she gave birth to Cecilia, a babe with black wisps of curls like her father Philippe, Avicia wept.

CHAPTER 26

Montivilliers, Normandy
October – December 1065 CE

In the early hours of the morning, a cool mist condensed over the Benedictine abbey at Montivilliers. At the center of the small garden, Avicia and Alice stood outside the guest quarter, enshrouded in haze.

"You were very quiet when you returned from confession yesterday," Alice said.

"The chaplain spoke to me of the Final Judgment," Avicia replied. "He said the Lord would weigh good and evil works, while the devil tries to sway the scales in his favor. I wonder what shall happen when God considers my deeds. "

Alice drew nearer to her. "You must not think you are an evil woman."

"An inconstant one, then. None can deny it, not even you, dear friend."

Months of sorrow weighed upon her heart. In the attentive care of the sisters, life in the abbey offered some comfort. Yet, peace eluded her. When she closed her eyes before prayer, she never felt regret for her sins. Images of Edric crowded her mind. After this last separation, his visage remained clearer in her thoughts than ever before. Even within the abbey walls, she could not forget him.

"You are ready for the trial?" Alice asked.

She nodded. "I shall accept whatever comes to me. I should suffer."

"Why do you punish yourself? The bishop de Bayeux is more than eager to mete out what he believes is God's sentence for adulterers."

"I shall not deny the bishop any longer."

With brisk strides, she crossed the garden and returned to the guest quarter, a small, outlying wooden structure.

Alice followed her. "Wait! Why are you so eager to go now?"

She whirled and faced her. "Isn't this part of the reason you came to Montivilliers? To warn me of how Odo harangues his brother about my chastisement. I shall not wait for the bishop's men to drag me back. We shall go to Rouen, where God shall judge me."

"What of your daughter? What of Cecilia? She is barely six months old."

"The sisters are kind to her. They shall care for her in my absence, especially Sister Felice, who dotes on her."

"Well, it is only right for her to dote on the child, but have you thought of what may happen to Cecilia after this trial? Philippe has seen her. He acknowledged the child for his offspring. Indeed, anyone who sees her must accept she is your husband's child. Can you reconcile with him for her sake? What does your heart say?"

"Do not ask about my heart!"

Her traitorous heart still longed for a lover across the English Channel. When Cecilia came into the world, a piece of Avicia's heart shriveled. On sight, she knew the child belonged to Philippe. Her sons and now this daughter echoed the image of their father.

She continued, "I do not care what my heart says, Alice. Even the kindness Philippe extends to me is not without end. He has spared our sons the dishonor of my affair, but you did not see his fear when he visited after Cecilia's birth. He searched her features. He noted all the things that marked her for his daughter. Yet, he shall never look at me the same. I have dishonored my marriage vows and betrayed my husband. I deserve whatever Odo does."

"I beg you think of your children, Avicia."

"I do. How can I not consider them? My sons would be so ashamed of me if they knew what I have done, how I treated their father. We cannot delay longer. Shall you return with me to Rouen or not?"

Alice fell into step beside her. "Do I have another choice?"

They reached the cell she had occupied for over a year in exile. In the dim light of the small room, Sister Felice attended Cecilia. She soothed the fussy baby and oiled the pink patches on her rough, scaly skin. When they entered, the nun inclined her head yet said nothing in her usual manner. Soon Cecilia settled and Sister Felice nestled the child in the crook of Avicia's arms. The nun's silvery gaze offered the same kindness and comfort she had found after her arrival.

Avicia asked, "Was she crying?"

When Sister Felice nodded, she whispered, "Thank you for your thoughtfulness. I appreciate your continued attentiveness to her."

The nun smiled and left them. Alice kissed the baby's cheek. Cecilia chortled and wriggled in her blankets.

Avicia asked, "Would you like to hold her?"

Alice held out her arms. "It has been so long and my children are all grown now, even little Alice. Soon, I expect her father shall find her a husband."

She cuddled the baby and crooned against her cheek.

Avicia placed her possessions into saddlebags. "I must take leave of the abbess before we go. She has shown me exceptional kindness, all the nuns have. I do not deserve their generosity."

"Perhaps they see your true nature," Alice murmured.

Avicia ignored the comment. No kind words could assuage her guilt. "I have not thanked you for the endowment you provided me in these long months at Montivilliers. I have known only compassion here and I am grateful for it. Sister Felice helped me deliver the baby.

Cecilia's birth was not easy. When I remained weak in the days afterward, Sister Felice cared for her and attended me in the infirmary. She even found the best wet-nurse when my milk did not come in. She has been good to me."

"Sister Felice is the infirmaress of the abbey and has charge of the sick. Philippe commended you to her because he knew she would treat you well."

Avicia glanced over her shoulder. "Why would he have held such an expectation?"

Alice approached, eyes wide. "Surely, you understand why you are here. You must know the nature of their relations."

"Whose relations, Alice?"

"I told you, I remember I spoke of it. Of all the abbeys in Normandy, you came to this place. I cannot believe you do not understand the reason."

"Alice, please do not dither, not this time!"

Cecilia whimpered at the annoyance in her mother's tone. Alice scowled and soothed the baby again. After she placed Cecilia in the wood carved cradle at the end of Avicia's pallet, a look of exasperation altered her features.

With her hand clasped together, she frowned at her. "Have you not noted the resemblance between the nun and your husband? Sister Felice is Philippe's mother and Cecilia's grandmother. Upon your arrival in Rouen all those years ago, I explained the circumstances of your husband's birth. Philippe lived at Montivilliers for the first five years of his life. When his father knew of him, he came here and took his son. Philippe never forgave Felice. He does not speak with her unless necessary, but he does not deny she is his mother."

Avicia thought back to her arrival at Montivilliers. She recalled the familiarity of Sister Felice's features upon first sight. She remembered

Philippe's guarded expression, and the clipped tone with which he had addressed the nun.

Alice continued, "Sister Felice's nature suits the nunnery, but if she is kinder than you expected, now you understand why."

"She hardly speaks to me."

"She does not do it to be unkind. Surely, you have seen her and her fellow sisters communicate with hand signals. I suppose she speaks when required?"

Avicia nodded absentmindedly at the question. Thoughts swirled in her mind. She smiled. "I want to pledge Cecilia for the Church."

"What?"

"I wish my daughter to be a nun at this abbey. I ask for much, but I know the daughter of a minor Norman knight could never be a nun without an endowment. May I count on your support?"

"You know you may. If it is your wish to see Cecilia dedicated to God, I shall ensure Hugh provides for her. She is his niece by blood, after all. I must ask, though, what inspires you?"

Avicia buried her face in her hands. "Alice, you know no one else shall ever want her in marriage. Look at her!"

"I have! She is a beautiful baby who shall grow in the lovely spirit of her mother."

Avicia marched to the cradle and lifted her daughter, who loudly protested the disturbance. She moved the baby to the corner of the room where the tallow candle afforded the best light. "Look at her again, Alice! Who can accept her affliction?"

Sobs strangled her. She shrugged off Alice's hand on her arm and through blurred vision, stared at the large opaque eyes of her child. "No one shall marry her when they know she has been blind from birth. The morning she came into this world, I wept. God robbed my daughter of her vision because of me. She shall never see the world around her, or the beauty of her own reflection. You must understand,

Alice. I am to blame for my daughter's trouble. I should suffer, not her, never her."

She laid Cecilia in her crib again. She packed the last of her clothes. Alice kept to a corner and remained silent.

Just before Sext, Sister Felice arrived at the guest quarter and applied more oil to Cecilia's skin. At Avicia's entreaty, the nun escorted her to the aged abbess, Beatrice de Montivilliers. From Sister Felice, Avicia had seen no outsiders entered the abbey without permission, except where their stay required interactions with the abbess.

At Sister Felice's gesture, she waited while the nun knocked and entered the room at the abbess' entreaty. Sister Felice closed the door behind her and soon reappeared. She beckoned Avicia inside before she withdrew. Avicia curtsied before the abbess.

The female superior crooked her whippet-thin finger. She gestured to a stool beside the chair in which she sat. Avicia sank down and clasped her hands in her lap.

"You wish to leave us."

Though the abbess did not ask her a question, she nodded. "I must beg your permission to go. How did you know what I would say?"

The abbess' lopsided grin revealed timeworn teeth. "Sister Felice told me of the arrival of Alice de Montfort. I have also received the messages of Odo de Bayeux, who has demanded your presence in Rouen for months."

"He sent messages? Why did no one tell me?"

"The bishop may wait upon the abbess of Montivilliers. I wanted to know you would be ready to face the trial. It seems you are. I told my nephew William you would arrive in due course."

"Forgive me, abbess, but do you mean Duke William is your nephew?"

"Do you know naught of my circumstances, milady?"

When she shook her head, the abbess continued. "I am the natural daughter of Richard, William's grandfather. I claim kinship to the dukes of Normandy. I am sympathetic to the cause of those of unfortunate or low birth. William is a particular favorite of mine. His brother Odo, though he may be legitimate, is not."

Avicia nodded. "Your kindness knows no bounds. I beg your favor for my daughter to remain here in my absence. I must spare her what I face upon arrival in Rouen. I hope to dedicate Cecilia's life to the Church."

The abbess' glassy-eyed gaze darted over her face. "If it is your choice, Montivilliers would welcome her."

"May I take my leave of you, abbess?"

"You may. Go with God, child, He shall protect and guide you. Seek Him in your darkest hour and He shall grant you succor and strength."

When the abbess proffered her spindly hand, Avicia kissed her parchment-thin fingers, and received the sign of the Cross on her forehead.

∽

Avicia traveled to Rouen with Alice, under the protection of guards. Despite the chill in the autumn air, she relished the slow pace and the renewal of her friendship with Alice.

The peace that once eluded her at Montivilliers now washed over her. She experienced her first restful night of sleep in months. Philippe's disappointment and the wrath of Odo barely concerned her anymore.

On the outskirts of Rouen, Alice asked, "Do you not fear the ordeal by fire? Hugh witnessed it once, he said ..." Her voice wavered and her watery gaze sought Avicia's own. "How can you suffer this burden? How shall I bear the sight of your pain?"

Avicia recalled the abbess' last words and repeated them now for her friend's benefit. "Seek the Lord in your hour of need and He shall give you strength."

When they arrived at the *donjon*, it seemed everyone in the bailey stopped and stared. Mothers with children made the sign of the Cross and drew their offspring behind their skirts.

Alice scowled at the gesture, but Avicia soothed her friend's ire. "They do not trouble me."

Alice ordered one of the guards to fetch her husband and Philippe. Hugh arrived first. He drew his wife from the scene and spoke with her. He dragged Alice off to the *donjon*, despite her loud protests.

Philippe plodded across the bailey. Avicia gazed at her husband, but he avoided her stare.

Odo appeared on the steps. He left the *donjon* in long strides with his retinue close behind him, determination etched in his pitiless glare.

Philippe stood before her. She found the courage for words. "I have returned to face the trial."

"How does the child fare?"

"She is well, only a slight irritation of her skin but Sister Felice ..." Avicia noted how his nostrils flared at the mention of his mother's name. "The nuns care for her. How is Thorbert? Has he grown much?"

"He has missed his *maman*."

She sighed. With her selfishness, she had risked her children's happiness.

Odo's obsidian eyes fixed on Philippe. Her husband now avoided her stare. "Sieur Philippe, remove yourself, at once. This woman is under orders to surrender herself to the ecclesiastical court."

Philippe returned the bishop's glare. "Is my shame and dishonor not enough? Must you condemn my wife? She is mine, to chastise when I see fit."

Odo's face reddened and he drew back. "Not in the case of adultery. How dare you question me? You must know the power I possess, the authority with which God charges me to do His will."

Avicia laid a hand on Philippe's arm. He drew back but his disgust never altered her resolve. "Let them take me."

She followed Odo and his guards.

CHAPTER 27

Rouen, Normandy

December 1065 CE – January 1066 CE

"Confess!" Odo's exhortation pierced the rafters of the small room, where Avicia knelt before him and the assembled clergymen in the cathedral of Rouen.

For three weeks since her return to Rouen, the bishop harangued her with one constant demand: her full confession to the sin of adultery. While others celebrated the Christ Mass and looked toward the New Year, the bishop cajoled and demanded, begged and berated her.

Archbishop Maurille of Rouen, the senior prelate of the diocese stepped forward. "You are insolent, milady, and would do well to seek God's forgiveness. Do you understand your immortal soul is at stake? God damns adulterers to the hell-fire. You must confess and repent."

Her eyes fixed on the cold, stone floor, Avicia ignored him, though he appeared a more pious and patient man than the bishop de Bayeux.

The archbishop arrived the day after her return. He first commissioned one of his clerks who sought evidence among the Norman courtiers. Odo responded with outrage to the inquiry, when he had sworn Avicia emerged from the mews on the heels of her lover. Since ecclesiastical law offered any accused the right to a proper legal advisor, Maurille charged Odo with finding an appropriate representative. Fiery argument followed and the archbishop relented. Odo resented the loss of his power to the rightful authority, but he never wavered in his admonishments.

Avicia regretted the pain and shame Philippe endured. Memories of Edric's sustained her spirit. In her dreams, she heard the sound of his voice and felt his hand upon hers. Such recollections offered comfort on long and lonely nights.

His hands clasped behind him, Odo pronounced, "If she shall not confess, we waste our time. She shall not swear an oath to deny the accusation. I demand the clerk read the charge against her in preparation for the trial by ordeal."

The archbishop frowned at his fellow clergyman. "Have we come to that point, Your Grace?"

Avicia feared their choices: water or fire. She could not swim. Yet, drowning might be a mercy compared with the torrid heat of fire against her skin.

She glanced at Archbishop Maurille. He caught her gaze and held it. His countenance wavered for a discernible moment.

Odo said, "Your Grace, by ecclesiastical laws, if a woman stands accused of adultery, without proof to the contrary, she must prove her innocence by the ordeal of the iron."

They would choose the flames over water. She feared the test.

Archbishop Maurille frowned, but gestured to his clerk, who read the charge. Odo smirked. His beady eyes lingered on Avicia while the clerk spoke, until he noticed the archbishop glared at him. He ordered, "Take the woman from here."

"Not so hastily, if you please," Archbishop Maurille interjected. "I shall speak with the lady before she returns to her confinement. Everyone else shall leave."

Odo blanched. "You mean to be alone with her, Your Grace?"

The archbishop raised an eyebrow. "Surely, you do not suggest I am susceptible to the taint of her wickedness?"

When he dismissed everyone, Odo stalked from the room. Maurille paced before Avicia, while she kept her eyes averted.

"Bishop Odo has oft told me you have no humility, milady, and think yourself above God's judgment. He shows a strong interest in the outcome of your trial. Have you offended him in the past?"

She never expected such a question. It gave her the courage. She met the archbishop's kindly regard. Yet she acknowledged the malice Odo bore her could not absolve her sin. His past cruelties bore no relevance in her current predicament.

"You do not confess to the charge against you," the archbishop remarked. When she said nothing, he continued, "Yet, you do not deny it, or allow oath-helpers to aid you."

Though Alice and even Duchess Matilda risked perjury, Avicia would not let them hazard eternal damnation as her oath-helpers.

The archbishop continued, "My clerk could not find incontrovertible evidence against you, except comments from others upon the circumstances of your marriage. If your husband abducted you and then wed with you, the sin lies with him. You are no more inclined to sin than any highborn noble is.

"The ordeal attempts to secure a verdict where the truth is unclear. Without confession or compurgation, we rely upon the judgment of the Lord. I shall make a confession, milady, even if you shall not. I believe divine purpose may be misjudged. The courtiers of Rouen and the bishop de Bayeux think you are guilty. Have you considered life after this trial, milady?"

She dared glance at him. "Your Grace, what do you mean?"

His hands clasped together, Maurille replied, "Those allied with you, the good duchess, and your devoted friend Alice de Beaufort spoke especially of your love for your children. They informed me you birthed a daughter earlier this year, a child acknowledged by all to be your husband's issue. Have you considered how your refusal to answer the inquiry affects your children?"

Avicia closed her eyes. In her lonely hours, delirium almost overwhelmed her, and fear nearly drove her mad. Yet, each morning when she emerged from captivity, her resolve strengthened her. An oath offered temptation but her love for Edric remained. She would not swear a false oath but neither would she confess the adultery. Resigned to whatever pain-filled fate awaited her, she rejected all offers of aid. God alone would judge her.

Archbishop Maurille's sigh echoed through the room. "Still, you refuse to speak? Whatever judgment awaits you, your strength is remarkable. You shall go from this place and return to your confinement. You must fast and pray for three days. On the fourth day, which is the day of Epiphany, you shall return here. By the glow of the iron, God shall judge your innocence or guilt."

She stood on wobbly legs. When the archbishop called for his clerk, the young man took her to the soldiers who waited outside the cathedral. Her hands tied before her with a long rope, the soldiers mounted their horses. She kept pace with them.

Gray morning skies hung heavy over Rouen and blotted out the sun. Every day, Avicia endured humiliation. Everyone knew of her disgrace. Regardless of the sneers and muttered curses cast her way, she never weakened. Not even now, when the soldier jerked the rope hard, and she tumbled and slid in the mud.

❧

The next three days passed in solitude, where Avicia saw not even the guards or a priest. She guessed the Twelfth Day celebration occurred with feasts on the eve of Epiphany in her absence. Her stomach growled at the thought of food.

Weak with hunger, her back ached from hours spent on the dirt floor. Her parched lips barely managed a prayer but she sought God's mercy. She must bear the fiery metal when it seared into her flesh. She begged for strength.

On what she guessed was the fourth day, a knock came at her cell door. The guards never asked for entry before they came in, so she crawled across the floor weakly and pulled herself up, peering through the iron grate.

"Milady, it is Torfida!" A murmur rose on the other side of the door.

"How did you come here?" Avicia whispered. "Are there no guards at the door?"

"They change the watch. I must go before they catch me."

A hand slid through the bars and Avicia grasped it. Slick skin connected with hers and held fast. "We pray for you, milady. Have courage."

Torfida released her and the sound of her footfalls faded. Avicia closed her eyes and leaned against the wall. She hardly cared about the slime cover anymore.

Soon, the guardsmen arrived. When they brought her into the bailey, only a few of the courtiers gathered there.

Alice gave a sharp cry and struggled against Hugh, though he held his wife back. "Release me, husband. She is my friend. Avicia!"

Philippe also watched her. Lady Marian de Vernon hovered at his side. Avicia waited for the pang of jealousy in her heart, but it never arose. Her folly had brought them to this end. If Lady Marian gave him some measure of happiness, he deserved it. Her own heart yearned for another, too.

The guardsmen tightened the rope around her tender wrists. She winced and closed her eyes for a short-lived moment. They dragged her to the cathedral.

Inside, Archbishop Maurille waited before the altar, clad in his sacred vestments. Odo hovered, his gaze trained on Maurille like a hunting hawk. Other clerics stood ready.

She waited in silence, while the archbishop reached with tongs for a piece of iron the length of his hand.

He glanced at her before he made the sign of the Cross. "God, the just judge, who is the author of peace and gives fair judgment, we humbly beseech You to deign to bless and sanctify this iron, which is used in the just examination of doubtful issue. This woman, Lady Avicia stands before God accused of adultery, a dishonor to her husband and a sin against God's laws. If she is innocent of the sin of adultery, she shall take the iron hot from the fire in her hand and appear unharmed. If she is guilty, let God's most just power declare that truth in her, so that wickedness may not conquer justice, but falsehood always be overcome by the truth. Through Christ our Lord. Amen."

She swallowed. How might she hold a fiery piece of metal in her bare hand, yet appear unharmed? For the first time, she feared the pain and the consequences of the trial.

The archbishop sang a hymn and led the assembly from the cathedral, Avicia included. Curious onlookers milled around. A fire burned in the courtyard. It consumed the wood the clerks heaped upon it.

Maurille approached the flames. "Bless, O Lord God, this place, that there may be for us in it sanctity, chastity, virtue and victory. Sanctimony, humility, goodness, gentleness, and plenitude of law and obedience to God the Father and the Son and the Holy Ghost. Amen."

One of the other clerics who attended offered the archbishop a vial. He sprinkled the iron with holy water. Then the clergymen returned to the cathedral.

Avicia remained alone outdoors with the sentries from Rouen. From inside, the sounds of Mass drifted. She clasped her hands together in supplication and looked heavenward.

"Prayer cannot help. Everyone knows you are a whore." One of the guardsmen spat a white blob at her feet.

She returned inside and attended the communion at the archbishop's insistence. She received the bread and wine hesitantly. She glanced at Maurille. In his usual manner, his gaze held no censure, unlike the righteous fury in Odo's gaze.

Maurille took the tongs offered to him and plucked the hot, iron bar from the fire. He sprinkled it again with holy water. The metal emitted a loud hiss and sizzled.

"The blessing of God the Father, the Son, and the Holy Ghost descend upon this iron for the discerning of the right judgment of God." He paused and Avicia raised her gaze to his. Her entire body shuddered.

"Lady, if you are innocent of this charge, receive with confidence this iron in your hand and the Lord, the just judge, shall guide us, his servants to the truth."

Odo glared at her. "Adulteress, you shall carry the hot iron three paces to the cathedral door. Then you shall release it. The clerk shall bandage your hand and seal it for three days. If your wound does not begin to heal and bad blood is found, all shall know you for the whore you are!"

Archbishop Maurille pursed his lips. "God is the only arbiter of this trial. I shall remind the bishop de Bayeux that I alone act on behalf of our heavenly Father. The bishop shall withdraw."

A sneer of irritation slashed Odo's features, but he stepped back.

Avicia held out her hand. Fire shot through her palm to the very bone. She bit her lip against a cry of pain and walked in the direction of the cathedral door. It seemed the longest journey in her lifetime.

Her hand throbbed with fire. Burnt flesh and blood. Her own. Her throat arid, a scream died inside her. Her eyes watered. The pain became unbearable.

One last litany of prayer repeated in her mind. "Lord, if I have sinned by my love for Edric of Newington, mark me. If not, let this pain pass."

Her body crumpled.

❦

"Dearest, please wake. Avicia! Open your eyes, it is finished."

A familiar voice tugged her from oblivion. Alice hovered beside her. Tears ran down her face. "Thanks be to God."

Avicia tried speaking but her tongue would not work.

Alice offered her a cup. She drew back from the bitter brew, but Alice urged her on. "*Non*, drink it slowly now. Torfida brought it. Her husband promised it would dull the pain. Rest, you are in my care and no one shall trouble you. Believe me, they have larger concerns now."

Avicia raised her hand to the light filtering through a half-shuttered window. The bandage bound her palm tight. Wax sealed the cloth. Beneath it, the flesh throbbed, aflame.

"Do not concern yourself." Alice kissed her forehead. "The burn shall heal with time."

"Not…in…time." Tears splashed across her cheeks.

Later, when she had regained her voice, she asked, "Does Philippe know I…endured the trial?"

Alice stopped crooning. "He led a garrison to Montfort-sur-Risle after your return. He intends to remain there. I could send word to him if you wished."

She shook her head. "Please, do not. I do not want him…burdened."

She slept again, fitfully. Alice's supportive touch or voice penetrated her awareness at times. When she roused, Alice offered water and food, and she savored each morsel. It might prove her last meal, for her wounded flesh pulsed beneath the bandage. She feared the removal of the cloth.

Yet, she knew with love for Edric in her heart, she could endure anything. Despite the discovery of their affair, the subsequent cruelty she suffered and even the ordeal, his sweet visage remained in her mind. She regretted none of it.

❦

On the third day, she returned to Rouen's cathedral under guard, but Alice accompanied her. Together, they awaited the archbishop's pronouncement.

A grunt of frustration escaped Odo as the clerk revealed her hand. "Impossible!"

Avicia stared in wonderment at the pink flesh revealed beneath the bandage, puckered and reddened at the edges. A persistent soreness remained. No festering blood marred the flesh. She shook her head in wonderment. Had God answered her last prayer? Had He approved of her love for another man?

"God has revealed His judgment. This woman has not sinned," Archbishop Maurille pronounced.

Odo whirled. "She bears a mark! It may be healing but surely, the redness indicates some festering blood. This is absurd! We need further proof. She is guilty of her crime. She must be punished."

"Your Grace, you think too much of yourself!" Incensed, Maurille stabbed a finger at Odo. "How dare you appropriate the sentence for yourself, when God has granted us His wisdom? If you want further proof, we may seek it but I do wonder at your interest in this woman."

Odo sputtered, "I would see God's justice done!" Spittle flew in all directions.

"God's or Odo's?" The archbishop held his ground. "You live the life of a courtier, ignore chastity, and take pleasure in the hunt and warfare. And, you take far more than a Christian interest in this woman's guilt or innocence."

Odo raged, drew his dagger. Only the clerks who intervened between him and the archbishop prevented bloodshed. Alice pulled Avicia toward the door.

"I shall report your threat of violence against me to your brother, bishop," Maurille said. "One day, your lineage shall not protect you. William shall see the truth of what you are. Lofty concerns occupy your duke, yet you lust for this woman's blood. You should be ashamed."

The archbishop made the sign of the Cross toward Avicia. "Go with God."

Alice urged her from the cathedral toward their horses.

Avicia halted before she mounted. She still stared at her hand. "Torfida."

Alice asked, "Why do you speak her name?"

Avicia recalled the morning Torfida had arrived at her cell, how she grasped her hand through the bars. Her fingers were slick with something. Had she smeared some substance on that eased the trial? It seemed the only explanation for the miracle.

"Why do you wait? Let us return home and send Philippe the good news."

"Does he still care?" When Alice stayed silent, Avicia shook her head. "I wish only to return to Montivilliers, and my Cecilia."

"You are leaving me?" Alice pouted. "It is selfish, but I want you here."

"I must be with my daughter. I shall leave next week, but tell me now what the archbishop meant when he said William had greater concerns."

Alice said, "The morning after Epiphany, word reached our duke by messenger while he hunted in the forest at Quenilly. King Edward is dead. The English have crowned Harold Godwinson in his place."

"Godwinson? Edric's kinsman?" Avicia's heart thudded inside her chest.

"The same. William is furious. He abandoned the hunt and spoke to no one, not even his duchess. Only the seneschal FitzOsbern roused him. William shall press his claim to the English throne."

"William does not have a claim."

"Avicia, Harold swore on holy relics to support William's bid for the throne, my husband told me so. William has summoned a council of his nobles. His brother, Robert Comte de Mortain, Richard d'Evreux, Walter Giffard, William de Warenne, all the magnates shall be present. It is likely we shall go to war with England."

CHAPTER 28

Newington, Kent, England
May 1066 CE

Edric shaded his eyes against the glare cast off glittering shield bosses and swords in the noonday sun. Leofwine, the Earl of Kent, alighted from his horse and stood for a moment in the company of his *huscarls*. Edric approached and halted at his side.

They did not embrace. A tic, which pulsed in his cheek, forewarned Edric that his arrival boded ill.

Edric asked, "News of William the Bastard, my lord earl?"

Leofwine scowled. "I bring word of the traitor Tostig."

Since the death of King Edward at the start of the year and the ascension of King Harold, Edric had waited with trepidation for the invasion. Two years after his sojourn in Normandy, he never forgot when William, in his vain attempt, forced Harold's submission. Whatever Harold swore at the time, he made his statement under duress. His oath could not affect the *witan*, the principal council. Yet, it seemed the perfect pretext for the declaration of war.

Within weeks of the coronation, Harold bolstered England's southern defenses. He calculated William intended an immediate attack, but the new king underestimated his adversary. First, William sought the sanction of the papacy under Pope Alexander II. Though the selection of England's monarchs had never depended on Rome, whoever supported Harold now went against the perceived will of God. In the meantime, word reached the king of a meeting between his brother Tostig and William in Normandy.

"So, your brother shall ruin Harold because the king would not restore him as earl of Northumbria," Edric said. He slapped his thigh and cursed. "Tostig brought his people's rebellion down on his own head. He cannot blame Harold for it."

"He does. Now, he raids the Isle of Wight and all along our coast. He seeks alliances with our enemies."

"We have more than one enemy? I thought only William the Bastard desired the throne."

"In Norway, Harald Hardrada thinks England is a rich prize to add to his domains. My brother the king has spies among Tostig's retinue. The Flemings also support Tostig, whose wife Judith is aunt of the duchess of Normandy. Flanders shall not avail us in this fight."

"Norway, Normandy, and Flanders stand against England," Edric whispered. He nodded to Leofwine. "What would you have me do?"

"Come with me to Dover at the end of the week," Leofwine replied. "My *thegns* convene there this month. Harold needs all the support he can muster. The men of Kent shall stand behind him." He motioned to his retinue who remained on horseback across the yard. "We must trespass on your domain until our departure."

"What I hold is yours."

Leofwine patted his shoulder and waved to his *huscarls*, who dismounted. Edric led him into the hall. The occupants stared wide-eyed at Leofwine's unexpected arrival. Emmeline and Cynwise rose instantly, though Edric's mother deferred to her daughter-in-law as the lady of the hall.

Edric said, "Earl Leofwine shall stay awhile with us. See to the comfort of his retinue, my lady."

Cynwise's gaze darted from him to Leofwine, who bowed before her. She left the hall in a flurry of yellow skirts.

Leofwine sat in the chair Cynwise vacated. He stretched his legs out before him. "Your home seems a happy one."

Since Edric's return from Normandy, many changes had occurred at Newington. He reflected with pride on his grandchildren. His eldest daughter Leofflaed had married her betrothed, Heahstan of Elmton, in his absence. The couple named their firstborn for her father. The first time Edric held his namesake, he had recalled his own father never knew his first grandson. Tears misted his eyes at the memory of Tunwulf Grim, gone too soon from the world, long before Edric ever had the chance to tell him how much he had admired and loved him.

Now, Leofflaed and her little Edric played across the hall. Edric's eldest son Leofsige strode into the hall from the family quarter, with a twin boy and girl on his shoulders, and his wife Wynflaed beside him. Leofsige's handfasted bride was the daughter of Thorkel Redbeard, the only *huscarl* in Edric's retinue. Edric never approved of their union, for he knew someday Leofsige might have to put aside the girl for a more favorable match. Yet, he could not deny his son anything.

"Oh, I do wish you would not perch them so high!" Emmeline scolded her grandson. "Aelfred and Gytha are but a year old."

Leofsige grinned at his grandmother before he deposited the children in her lap. He and Wynflaed left the hall with hands intertwined.

Edric's younger daughters, eleven year-old Deorwynn and her sister Eanflaed played with their dolls. At least, they remained innocent children.

"I have more news of my brother Harold which may interest you." Leofwine drew his attention. "The queen is with child."

He did not refer to Edith the Fair. Though she remained loyal to him, Harold had sacrificed their love for an alliance. He had married Ealdgyth of Mercia, sister of Morcar of Northumbria and Edwin of Mercia, forging a union with the northern earls.

Edric wondered how Lady Edith fared, though he asked, "Is Harold pleased?"

"I think the earls are, for the queen may carry the atheling of England. I like Ealdgyth, but she is no Edith the Fair. No one knows this better than the king does. He pines for her. Now that Ealdgyth carries his heir, he may feel differently about her and his marital vows."

Leofwine trailed off. Edric withheld comment. He had also loved someone other than his wife, and understood Harold's predicament.

After his return to England, he had hoped in vain that memories of Normandy and Avicia would remain behind him. Yet, their stolen hours and whispered promises of love haunted him.

In the weeks after his return, Edric pestered Harold about her fate, but he refused any inquiry into events after their departure. Lingering guilt still plagued him. Once again, he had abandoned her to the wrath of her tormentors. Frustrated, he returned to his comfortable life at Newington. Yet, a piece of his heart remained with her in Normandy. She would hold it forever.

Cynwise re-entered and bowed before him. Edric averted his gaze, almost in a reflex.

She noticed, for her stare hovered on him, before she spoke. "The bower house is prepared for you and your company, my lord Leofwine. Shall I attend your comfort?"

Leofwine replied, "By your husband's leave."

When Edric nodded, Cynwise led their guest from the hall. Edric never noticed Aelfred cross the rush-strewn floor until his grandson chortled at his feet. With a grin, he lifted the child onto his lap. At the door, Cynwise cast a momentary glance over her shoulder toward him. Again, he avoided her stare.

�

When the week ended, Edric left Newington for Dover. A gathering convened in the great hall of Leofwine's estate with all the *thegns* of

Kent, including Edric's longtime friends, *thegns* Alwin of Buckland and Aethelwold of Teston.

"How long must we dally here?" Aethelwold grumbled. "I married just yesterday."

Alwin laughed and Edric clapped his friend on the back. "You are so eager to return to your new bride? Leofwine shall not keep you from her for long."

"Leofwine, is it?" Alwin whistled. "You live well with the Godwinsons."

Edric looked to where Leofwine sat. "They are my kin."

The trio jostled the crowd and found places near the earl. They listened while Leofwine spoke of the danger England faced from the north and south.

"Who shall attack us next? Irish raiders?"

Edric never saw who spoke, but everyone laughed at the comment. Leofwine called for silence.

Aethelwold stepped forward. "I heard the bastard duke seeks the papal banner. I shall not go against the Church."

Edric frowned and thumped his friend's shoulder. "Rome should not decide our fate or the kingship."

Assent rose up, but not from everyone in the hall.

A *thegn* whom Edric did not know raised his hands and called for attention. "I recognize your kinship to the Earl of Kent. You remind me of one of the Godwinsons. You care about their interests but I worry for my land and my family. You all saw it, the long-tailed star of fire last month. It glowed brighter than any other in the heavens did. It heralds a great evil. I say Harold's folly brought the wrath of God on us. He stole the throne of England."

Edric's hand rested on the pommel of his sword.

Leofwine stood purple with rage. "Harold is England's lawful king! I was at court when the old king died. Edward made his last will and testament. He held out his hand to my brother Harold and commended our sister Edith to his care. He made Harold protector of his domain and servants, including the king's *huscarls*. What better proof can there be of Edward's intent? The *witan* ratified Harold's kingship. Now, do you stand with my brother against the traitor Tostig and all our enemies?"

No one answered.

Edric stepped forward. "Men of Kent, are you bold *thegns* with courage in your heart or not?"

He stabbed a finger at his fellow *thegn* who had besmirched Harold.

"You think you are the only one with lands and a family? I hold the same dear to me. I want an England where my children and grandchildren are free to play at my feet. A Saxon England. No Frenchman, a bastard at that, or heathen Viking shall take my lands from me. I am glad to claim kinship with the Godwinsons. I am proud to share their blood, prouder still to call Harold Godwinson my king. He is the rightful ruler of us all. I shall meet any man in combat who claims otherwise."

In the summer, King Harold called up levies of the *fyrd* for the defense of England against its foes. When the harvest season came in September, he reluctantly disbanded the men. Kent's *thegns*, including Edric, thought they would return home and reap the year's crop. However, Harald Hardrada and Tostig sailed from Norway. The flotilla of longships first ravaged the eastern coasts of Yorkshire, despite Earls Edwin and Morcar's efforts.

When Leofwine sent word of the Saxon defeat to Edric, he also informed him of Harold's fury with Edwin and Morcar. Now, Harold would meet Hardrada with his *huscarls* and the troops of their brother

Gyrth, Earl of East Anglia. Leofwine asked Edric to follow him to London, where they would await news of the battle to come.

On the last morning, Edric stood with Thorkel and his men at-arms, and bid his tearful family farewell. He kissed the tiny foreheads of his grandsons and granddaughter, though they shrank from the sight of his armor. He embraced his daughters by blood and marriage. His daughter Deorwynn clung to him piteously, until she ran into the hall. Her noisy sobs echoed.

He tousled the raven-black hair of his second son Cenweard. The thirteen-year-old stared past him to his elder brother Leofsige, already mounted on his horse Bavo.

"Why can he go when I cannot? Thorkel Redbeard taught me to fight, too."

Edric patted his shoulder. "I need you to stay here, and protect your mother and this village. Can you do it for me, son?"

Cenweard mumbled something under his breath that sounded like resentful agreement. Father Alwine, now in his seventy-seventh year, blessed the men and sketched a stiff bow before Edric. Eanflaed and Emmeline approached with his grandfather's wolf pelt. They cast the ragged animal skin over his shoulders and, wordless, both women kissed his hands.

Cynwise stood nearby while the others said farewell. Now, her dainty feet shuffled forward. Bells tinkled at the ankles of her shoes. Edric recalled the same sound on the day they had wed.

She affixed the wolf's head pin to the pelt. Tears brimmed in her eyes.

He said, "Lady, we shall see each other again."

For a moment, she struggled for speech. She clutched his hands and kissed them. "I pray for your swift and safe return. I have never been the wife you deserved. You are a good man, Edric."

His culpability slammed him hard in the gut. She had warranted better than their passionless marriage. His heart had always belonged to Avicia. He had never given it to Cynwise.

"You are the best of wives. You have cared for my home and our family. I shall always honor you for it."

"Go with God, my lord. I pray He shall protect you and our son."

Leofsige's twins wailed for their father, despite Wynflaed's soothing kisses.

Edric mounted Elfhar. "To London, boy."

With a wave of his hand, he led his men out of the gates of Newington.

❧

During the swift-paced journey toward London, wary eyes tracked their progress wherever they rode. Fear gripped the Saxon people.

Edric never worried about his king meeting Hardrada in the north. He knew enough of Harold's wars against the Welsh in the west, and believed his strategies sound.

He dwelt on Avicia at intervals, when she remained far across the Channel. More than his Saxon heritage and the distance between them kept them apart. Her husband supported William the Bastard. When the Saxons defeated the Frenchmen, how might she feel? He chided himself for such idle thoughts, but still, he worried for her.

When he arrived in London, Leofwine awaited him at the king's palace with the king's nephew Haakon. The young man resembled his father Sweyn, dead now for more than fifteen years.

Edric vaulted from Elfhar's back. "What news of the king?"

Leofwine replied, "None, we do not know if the battle with Hardrada and Tostig has begun."

They embraced before Edric nodded to Haakon. "It is good to see you."

"And you, Lord Edric. I have never forgotten your kindness," Haakon replied in a gruff tone.

❧

The trio spent much time together in the next days. In the evenings, Edric observed the pale-faced Queen Ealdgyth. Her hand often palmed her rounded belly, where Harold's heir kicked. The queen eagerly awaited the birth of the atheling. Edric wondered whether Edith the Fair knew of the queen's pregnancy. Though pleasant, soft-spoken, and somewhat shy, Ealdgyth lacked Edith's charm. The differences between the women reminded him of the contrast between a steadfast but dispassionate Cynwise and the spirited, fiery Avicia.

One morning when Edric and his men neared the hall, Ealdgyth's terrified scream echoed through the palace. He entered the cavernous room, and found the queen's attendants comforting her though she wailed. A herald knelt before Leofwine.

Edric's heart hammered in his chest. "What news? Has the king fallen against Hardrada?"

Leofwine stared, almost catatonic at the floor. His words barely rose above a whisper, but Edric heard them. "The Frenchmen have landed at Pevensey and Romney. They have come to destroy Harold's kingdom."

CHAPTER 29

London, England
October 1066 CE

Cheers erupted in the streets of London when the king's herald arrived with word of Harold's victory over the combined forces of Harald Hardrada and Tostig Godwinson at Stamford Bridge.

The occupants of the king's great hall cheered, but knew they faced another formidable adversary in William, who ravaged the south. At the approach of the king, his family and retainers prepared for his return, and awaited his plans for the Frenchmen.

Edric's son stood beside him in the recesses of the hall. He said, "Leofsige, I want you to return to Newington."

His heir's black brows knitted together, his aversion clear. "I am no coward."

Edric grabbed Leofsige's arm and ignored the frown Thorkel directed at him. "I do not ask you to leave, I command it! I am your father and lord of Newington. You shall heed me. Take Thorkel Redbeard, and go home to your wife and children."

"I beg your pardon, my lord but I do not mean to overhear," the *huscarl* interrupted, "though I cannot help it, since you have taken no pains to hold your tongue. I shall not return to Newington either. I mean to remain here and fight the invaders."

Leofsige's determined stare matched the *huscarl*'s own. "I shall stay also, Father."

Disgusted, Edric watched for Harold's arrival, trumpets blaring announcement of his return.

A thin slash marred the king's right cheek. He strode into the hall, with the royal standard-bearer, Ansgar the Staller at his left, and his brother Earl Gyrth on his right. The men advanced on Earl Leofwine and Harold's retainers who waited at the forefront. Gyrth threw down a tattered red fabric, a ragged tear slashed through the black image inked on the cloth.

Harold said, "The remnants of Hardrada's war banner, the Land-Ravager."

Well wishes and applause erupted around them, but the king paled. Edric followed his catatonic stare.

Countess Gytha of Wessex lifted the hem of her garment above the rushes. Two women attended her progress. The clamor died with each of her footfalls. She stood before Harold. Her expression betrayed nothing. Silence descended in full.

"Where is my son Tostig?" she asked.

Earl Gyrth answered, not the king. "He is buried at York, my lady."

Harold struggled for words. His mother met his gaze and held it before she curtsied. She left the room, retaining her dignity and poise before she departed from view.

Murmurs thronged after her exit. Edric edged closer toward the royal family, and overheard Leofwine whispering with Harold.

"What did you say?" Harold demanded. The king's gruff tone quieted all conversation in the hall.

Leofwine avoided his brother's gaze, but Harold insisted he repeat his statement.

The Earl of Kent said, "Hugh Margot, a monk from Fecamp, has come. He is William's herald."

The king's face reddened. "And he wishes to secure William's throne, has he? If he wants an answer to his master's claim, I shall meet him now."

Gyrth touched Harold's arm. "Do not meet this man of God with rancor in your heart. Wait until the battle-blood has cooled, my king."

Harold raced from the hall. Gyrth and Leofwine trailed their brother. In their absence, the courtiers milled around. Edric turned to his son, again.

"You have heard the tales out of Sussex," he began, "where the Frenchmen pillage, rape and murder on Godwinson lands. They do not come for riches or plunder. They seek to destroy the Saxon way of life and kill all who oppose them."

"That is why I must stand with you, Father," Leofsige replied, "to defend all we hold dear. I am not afraid to fight for the people and the land I love."

Beside him, Thorkel nodded. "To the death, if need be."

❧

Edric remained in the hall with Leofsige and Thorkel, when a frightened scream rent the air. With others, they rushed outdoors and witnessed the uproar.

Gyrth and Leofwine restrained the king, who had drawn his sword.

He yelled at a rotund man in monkish garb who scrambled for his mount. "Run, you fat pig, before I stick you again. Warn the Bastard of the fate that awaits him! He shall never have my throne."

The monk whipped his steed in a furious haste and urged the beast through the gates.

Edric inquired. "My lord Leofwine, what happened?"

Leofwine released the king, who shouted obscenities in the monk's wake.

"Harold lost his temper and we suggested Hugh Margot leave."

"It was good you did so." King Harold faced them. "I might have killed the whoreson. He dared suggest that mine is a rival claim compared to the bastard duke! I am the rightful ruler of England, am I not, Edric?"

Edric replied, "You are, my king."

Harold grinned and swayed slightly. Edric wondered if he imbibed too much strong drink.

"My brothers, my kinsmen and advisors, come with me," Harold demanded. "We have much to discuss if we are to answer this new threat."

Edric joined the conclave of those around the king. Harold ordered the hall doors barred. No one entered or withdrew except by his permission.

The resultant discussions devolved into quarrels. Beside Edric, Haakon fidgeted, perhaps ill at ease among the magnates of England because of his low birth. Edric shared the sentiment. A minor *thegn* with an impact on England's future seemed unlikely.

"Where are the queen's brothers, the earls Morcar and Edwin?" he asked.

"They cower and lick their wounds after they accepted Hardrada's peace at the surrender of York. They could not hold the city," Haakon muttered. "Besides, they never forgave the king for his appointment of a deputy in the north, which is their domain."

"Such petty sentiments are unworthy now. England needs all its warriors."

"Indeed, since the king intends to fight against all advice."

Haakon pointed toward the brewing argument between Harold and Gyrth.

"My king, if you must engage them now," Gyrth began.

Harold slapped his thigh and stood. "If? If! Gyrth, William ravages my lands. He has been here on my soil for more than a week. He plunders my people and villages. What shall I do but answer him?"

"My king, your men are exhausted and battle weary! We marched nearly two hundred miles in eight days. Worse, some of the army has deserted you. Look around this hall! Where are Edwin and Morcar? They grumble because you did not distribute the plunder from the campaign at Stamford Bridge."

"My warriors clamor for riches while my kingdom faces annihilation?"

"Let me lead the first attack against the Frenchmen. Gather your earls and *thegns* here in London. Descend with the larger force to defeat our enemies."

"Why, so you can claim the flush of glory?"

"Harold, God damn you for a prideful fool!" A collective gasp filled the room at Gyrth's disrespect for the king's position. "I have ever served you loyally. Who was at your side when Hardrada fell and Tostig took up his banner? I did not fail you at Stamford Bridge. I shall not do so against the Frenchmen now."

Leofwine added, "Do not let Tostig's betrayal affect your judgment of Gyrth."

The king paced before the assembly. "I do not. I know he is loyal. The pair of you counsel me to wait but for what cause? Should I let William land more reinforcements? Do I ask my tenants in Pevensey and Hastings to suffer their crops and houses burnt, their women molested?"

"If you must!" Gyrth insisted. "It is William's cruel strategy to tempt you to a fight, but use it against him. Torch the earth around his base. Keep William in the south, without stores to raid, with naught for foraging. Weaken him, Harold! You can destroy his army. Send me in your stead to give battle to this bastard. Gather a strong force in London, not the wearied men force-marched from the north."

"Gyrth, I love you well for a loyal brother," Harold began. His murky gaze swept the room. "Yet, I shall not permit any man to suffer battle while I hide in London! Destroying the land shall not hold the Frenchmen. If the Bastard raids further into Sussex or Kent, or turns westward, shall I allow it? I am king of England and I shall suffer the Bastard's men no longer. We march today to meet our foes."

"For the love of God and England, Harold, wait for the levies!"

Gyrth groaned in his distress. When his shoulders sank, the king gripped them. "Stand with me now, brother. Let us drive these Frenchmen back and into the depths of the Channel."

Near Hastings, Sussex, England

In the arduous march south, Edric pushed aside his concerns about the imminent conflict. He fought for his land and those whom he loved. When he looked at Leofsige, in the prime of youth, with children and a wife who longed for his return, he saw a purpose for his presence on the battlefield. Thoughts of a vanquished enemy never stirred his blood. He desired only the safety of his family. The Saxons must destroy the Frenchmen to preserve their way of life.

They arrived after midnight, three days after their departure from London. Their bivouac formed below the woodland at Caldbec Hill. A contingent of *huscarls* claimed the old apple tree and lit their campfire near its roots.

Encamped southeast on the gorse and broom-covered slope with his son and Thorkel, Edric looked north to the king's tent. Ansgar the Staller had pitched the standards. Faint moonlight shone down on the Fighting Man, the king's own pennant, and the Dragon of Wessex, its wyvern design attached to a staff by its nose, tongue, jaw, and foreleg. A cool mist rolled inland. The king's standards fluttered in the autumn breeze for most of the night.

Edric gathered with *thegns* he did not know, but it hardly mattered when a common cause united them. Into the night, each man took up a portion of an epic poem about the Battle of Maldon, a fierce fight with the Vikings almost seventy years before, which the Saxons had lost. In the saga, the men of Essex faced implacable foes, and many met their deaths beside their fallen leader. They never abandoned the cause or fled before the onslaught of the Danes.

Edric spoke a few lines and the words weighed heavily in his heart. He embraced the prospect of death with a sole regret – leaving behind those whom he loved. He would fight and die, if only to ensure their safety.

He halted in the midst of speaking and looked beyond the fire, where Harold stood outside his tent, watching them from a distance. Then the king withdrew inside.

※

In the cheerless dawn, the Saxon army roused to the sight of French archers, advancing across the ridge from Telham Hill, intent on a hillock parallel to their position.

Bleary-eyed, Edric stumbled in his haste. Harold stood outside his tent. He spurred the *fyrd* on. They must take the position first. A clouded flurry of arrows rained down on the Saxons. Guttural screams from the stricken and dying filled the air. Volley after volley flew from the French bows. The *fyrd* engaged them. With swords, spears and clubs held high, even pitchforks, the Saxons pressed the enemy archers back. When morning dawned in full, they claimed a small triumph.

A surge of energy rippled through the camp. Buoyed by the boisterous victory chants of the *fyrd*, Harold commanded the ranks form up at the edge of the ridge.

Leofsige asked, "Father, why do you not cheer with the others?"

"There is more to this battle than this initial skirmish," Edric muttered.

He called for Thorkel, who aided Edric and his son when they donned the garments of war. Leofsige wore a shirt of black chainmail that once belonged to Tunwulf Grim. Edric put on a coat of leather with iron rings sewn on it. Sword belts wound about their waists. Edric grasped his blade and the spear of his father, Tunwulf. Leofsige carried the weapons of the *huscarls*, the battle-axe, and a spear. Helmets on their heads, Edric and Leofsige reviewed each other.

Edric ordered, "We take position with the *thegns* under Earl Leofwine. Whatever happens to me, remain with Thorkel. He shall protect you."

When his son nodded, he glanced at the *huscarl*. "Defend Leofsige."

"With my life," Thorkel replied.

Edric removed the wolf's skin pelt he wore and draped it over his son's shoulders. "I pray it shall protect you in my stead."

The wolf's head pin glittered in the dawn light.

They sought Earl Leofwine, who huddled with his brothers the king and Gyrth, their nephew Haakon and their uncle, Abbot Aelfwig Wulfnothson of Winchester.

Edric clasped his son's shoulder. "Hold off, Leofsige. It is a gathering of the king's close kin. Let us wait here."

When Harold saw them, he waved them over. "Join us. We are more than a people united against a common foe. If we die on this day, we do so together."

Leofwine grinned at Edric and patted his shoulder.

Harold continued, "We are kin. We stand with each other, no matter the end."

Edric nodded. "No matter the end."

CHAPTER 30

Near Hastings, Sussex, England
October 1066 CE

Edric stood on the southern ridge and watched the activity at the French encampment. His horse nudged him and laid its muzzle on his shoulder. He stroked Elfhar's forelock and leaned against him. The familiar scent and warmth of the stallion soothed the tension in his body.

"You cannot be with me this day, boy. I shall keep you from harm."

He dreaded their separation. At his signal, one of Harold's pages grabbed Elfhar's reins and led him to the rear. The stallion snorted its protest. Edric watched until the horse disappeared into the woodlands. Tears pricked his eyes. He feared he might never see Elfhar again.

The Saxons formed up their ranks on the high ground. Edric found Earl Leofwine with his *thegns* and *huscarls*. Leofwine's warriors stood in a dense formation behind a wall of rounded, wooden shields. The Dane Thorkel and Leofsige joined their ranks.

Trumpets echoed in both camps and roused the armies to battle. They faced each other after the earlier mid-morning skirmish. The marshy area at the base of the slope limited the Frenchmen to a narrow strip of earth. Their archers and infantry marched in staggered ranks, which preceded the cavalry. They formed up at the bottom of the ridge.

Edric asked, "Why do we wait? Why does the king hold our position?"

Leofwine's resolute stare remained fixed on the Frenchmen. He shrugged. "Harold is cautious."

Edric seethed inside. "It is folly to allow his enemies time to form up."

Leofwine glared at him. "Does your courage fail you now that they amass before us? Cowards shall not win the day for Harold."

If any other man but a Godwinson implied he lacked courage, Edric might slay the fool where he stood. He met Leofwine's stare. "I am no coward."

"I know it. Believe in Harold and we shall defeat the invaders."

The roar of his fellow warriors filled Edric's ears. The incessant pounding of their weapons against their shields vied with their battle cries. Leofwine shouted encouragement. Edric feared the loss of his hearing before day's end. The Saxons shouted "God Almighty" and "Holy Cross" while the chants of the Frenchmen rivaled them.

Edric noted the herald who carried the Papal banner before the enemy. The cross at the center and four smaller crosses, one in each quarter, shimmered on a white cloth background.

Pope Alexander in far-off Rome did not matter. Images of his beautiful daughters, his second son, and Cynwise filled Edric's mind. For them, he would fight and die if necessary.

He looked for his eldest son among the warriors. Leofsige stood beside Thorkel at the rear of the *huscarls*, but in advance of his father, recognizable by the wolf pelt on his shoulders. Edric never feared the outcome of the battle, but he worried for Leofsige in this first test of his manhood and Thorkel's teachings. If his son seemed anxious or fearful, Leofsige never showed it. Edric whispered a prayer for his safety.

Leofwine's guttural laugh jarred him. "Harold calls for the advance." He pointed with his spear. "Caldbec Hill shall bear the stain of French blood today."

The entire Saxon army stood at the ready. Across the field, the French infantry surged forward and broke into a run. Their archers drew back their bows and took aim.

Perspiration trickled down Edric's back. It left him cold. He held his shield before him in his left hand, his father's spear upraised. He gripped the weapon and stared straight ahead. Arrows whistled through the air, dipped and hurtled toward him. He raised his shield above his head with the other *thegns*, but the Frenchmen shot from a lower level. Their missiles struck Saxon shields with a thwack or passed over the heads of their intended victims.

A second volley followed. As a wave of arrows thwacked against shields, the *thegn* who stood before Edric staggered backward, gurgled, and crumpled at his feet. Bright red blood sputtered. A feathered shaft protruded from his throat. Edric gasped and drew back.

The French infantry pounded the earth beneath their feet. Leofwine's warriors marched with shields interlocked. They impaled most of the enemy in a hail of spears. A few reached the shield wall but met with the axes of the *huscarls*. Inhuman cries rent the air as blades cleaved flesh.

French cavalry prepared its uphill charge. Hooves rumbled and thundered across the earth toward Leofwine's men. Too late, the mounted warriors realized the strength of the interlocked rounded shields. They crashed against the shield wall. The *huscarls* withstood the brutal impact. Their heavy axes whistled through the air. Horses and riders crashed to the ground, dispatched with eager fury by the *huscarls* with swords, axes and spears, which penetrated chainmail. Wounded men screamed in agony, trampled beneath their own warhorses. The metallic scent of blood permeated the air. The cavalry line broke and scattered. Some among Leofwine's *huscarls* pursued them.

To Edric's horror, Thorkel plunged into battle and Leofsige followed him. Edric's breath expelled in sharp gasps timed with each blow from the *huscarl's* axe.

Leofwine jabbed his shoulder with the sharp point of his shield boss. He bellowed, "Leave your son be! Look to our defense."

Edric scanned the battlefield for his son and the Danish warrior. Bodies piled at Thorkel's feet. Leofsige brandished a bloodied axe beside his mentor. With a single swing of his battle-axe, Thorkel scythed both a destrier and its rider, a man who had aimed his spear at Leofsige.

Then, Thorkel slew another among the enemy. Leofsige remained at his side. Edric proudly observed how his son never shrank from battle. His bloodied weapon descended with fury on the heads and limbs of his attackers. Crimson blood sprayed the wolf skin pelt whenever he struck. Shrieks followed. The *huscarls* drove deeper into the fray and Edric lost sight of his son. He prayed wherever Leofsige might go, God would protect him.

French arrows shot uphill, answered by the *fyrd* who hurled slingshots, spears, and hatchets. The French knights mounted another assault. Their destriers shied away from the tips of Saxon spears. As before, Leofwine's *huscarls* pursued. Soon, the number of Danes who protected him dwindled.

Edric shouted to Leofwine, "Call your men back, my lord!"

Leofwine waved his shield toward the struggle. "You think I could stop them, even if I wished it? Let them whoresons come to us."

French infantry backed by knights attacked again. With exultant cries, the *huscarls* rushed headlong and sliced through their attackers. Blood arced and sprayed, coating men and animals. Everywhere, the sickened thud of the long axes crushing bone resounded across the battlefield. The remaining Frenchmen faltered and streamed down the hill.

When Leofwine's *thegns* followed, he howled a cry of bloodlust and waved his spear. "We take them now!"

Edric broke into a run. The *huscarls* and *thegns* in the vanguard shouted their war cries. They skewered and carved through the infantrymen who fled before them. Suddenly, the cavalry wheeled their horses around and met Leofwine's warriors. The bulk of his forces rushed forward, but could not save their comrades at the fore. The Frenchmen obliterated their foolish pursuers.

Leofwine yelled, "Re-form the shield wall!"

The remainder of his men followed orders. Enemy riders bore down on them, but could not penetrate their ranks. The *huscarls* hacked horses and men. Screams echoed across the battlefield. In their terror, the knights spurred their panic-stricken horses into full retreat. Yet one among them galloped forward, his lance upraised. He exhorted his companions who renewed their attack. The knight impaled a bloodied *huscarl* with his weapon. He drew his sword and charged. His battle cry echoed on the wind. He aimed for Edric.

The rider urged his warhorse onward. Edric drove the butt of his spear into the ground. His shield before him, he steeled his resolve. The destrier snorted and its nostrils flared wide in terror. Momentum propelled the animal. Edric's spear tore into its neck. Horse and rider toppled. The weight of his mount crushed the knight beneath it. His helmet rolled. Edric drew his sword and severed the fallen warrior's head.

Sharp, hot pain bit deep into his right hip. He howled and bashed his shield boss against the chest of an archer, who wore no armor. The man fell backward and screamed just before Edric drove his sword into his neck.

Blood splattered Edric's leather tunic. He looked down. An arrow protruded from his side. A viscous red trail leaked from the wound.

Wearied, he retrieved his father's spear with a ferocious twist of the weapon.

The remnants of the French cavalry retreated, but another knight rode for the fore. He removed his helmet and waved it in the air. Even at a distance, his curses and cries echoed. With his lance, he whacked at the men who fled.

"God damn you all for cowards! We carry the Papal banner. God is on our side. Return to the battle."

When the rider wheeled his mount around, Edric recognized William.

He pointed his bloodstained sword. "The Bastard! Cut him down and this day is ours!"

His companions followed his gesture and raced toward William. At his left, Leofwine whooped and hollered, urging them on. However, the knights rallied and shielded their lord, forcing the *thegns* back.

Leofwine removed his helmet, whipping hands through his hair.

Edric yelled, "What are you doing? Put it back on."

Leofwine grinned and smeared viscous blood from a gash across his cheek. "Look how the Bastard cowers behind his men."

A fusillade of arrows showered them. One struck Leofwine in the eye. He tumbled backward. Blood coated the side of his face where the arrow protruded.

Edric grabbed his shoulders. "My lord! My lord!" His gaze darted, desperate for help. "Look to the king's brother. The king's brother has fallen."

He shouted until he grew hoarse, in the midst of the screams and snorts of dying men and horses. He cradled Leofwine. "Stay with us. You must know of Harold's victory."

Leofwine jerked and coughed. Blood and spittle struck Edric's face.

In a haze of vibrant red, Thorkel and Leofsige appeared beside them.

Edric's joy at the sight of his son dampened when Leofsige gripped his side. Blood caked his fingers. "It was an arrow, Father. Thorkel removed it."

Edric nodded. "Help me get Leofwine to the king's tent."

Though his hip pained him, Edric and the other men moved Leofwine up the slope of the hill to where the king's men guarded their rear. A wall of *huscarls* below the standards parted for them. Edric shouted for Harold. One of the king's warriors showed them to his tent. They laid Leofwine on the ground. His breath expelled in a sigh. Blood trickled from inside his mouth.

Edric grabbed his hand. "My lord, your brother shall come."

Thorkel grasped his shoulder. "He is no more."

"Damn you, do not say so!" He hauled Leofwine against him, and listened for the intake of a lungful of air or the steady heartbeat. He howled in grief when no sound issued.

Harold burst into the tent and knelt beside his brother. "Not Leofwine!"

Edric laid the king's brother on the ground. "My king, we must remove him to the battlefield. Your standard hangs outside. If…if we do not survive this day, if the Frenchmen find him here, they shall desecrate his body, for hatred of you."

Harold sputtered, "You want me to leave him like carrion on the battlefield!"

Edric shook his head. "He is best preserved among the rest of the dead. We can find him later, after we have won the battle."

After some hesitation, Harold called for his *huscarls*, who took the body some distance from the tent, helped by Leofsige and Thorkel.

The king removed his helmet and buried his grimy face in his hands.

"God shall judge me. By my hand, two brothers of mine have met their deaths in a short span."

Alone with him, Edric grasped his sword and spear. "Leofwine died in your service. He loved you as his brother and his king. The other, Tostig, earned a traitor's death, for death is the only just fate for a man who would betray his family. Leofwine did not see your victory, my king, but he shall know of it."

Harold rose and clasped his forearm. "By Christ's blood, I vow he shall."

The king ordered the advance halted, and re-formed the shield wall.

In a brief respite, Leofsige removed his mail shirt and washed his wound. Thorkel broke the shaft and worked on the arrowhead from Edric's skin.

He gritted his teeth against the pain. Thorkel gripped the arrowhead with metal tongs and pulled. Edric growled in anguish. A torrent of blood stained his side. Thorkel cleaned the wound with water. Leofsige crouched beside them, his eyes wide with anxiety.

Edric gestured for his leather tunic. "Hurry, I am returning to battle."

Leofsige shook his head. "You cannot, let Thorkel clean and dress your wound."

"Boy, do not tell me what to do!"

Edric shoved both men aside. He stood and tested the strength of his hip. When he swayed slightly, Thorkel reached for him, but he glared at the man.

"Get away from me. I do not need a nursemaid."

Thorkel glowered and spat on the ground before he left them.

Leofsige frowned. "He tried to help you, Father."

Edric tore a strip of cloth from the tunic he wore against his skin. He wadded it at his hip and tightened the drawstring of his trousers.

He dragged on his leather tunic. Pain roared up his side. He struggled for breath, but warded off his son's help.

He hobbled toward the battered Saxon warriors who had re-formed their ranks. Leofsige and Thorkel readied themselves on either side of him. Kentish *thegns* remained but without their earl, Harold placed them under his brother Gyrth's command. They stood behind the *fyrd*, which readied for another attack from mounted knights.

Edric's hip throbbed but he ignored the pain. He swore vengeance for Leofwine's death.

Leofsige pressed his shoulder. "God be with you this day, Father."

"God be with you also, my son."

Trumpets heralded the second advance. Frenchmen galloped up the hill. One man at the center of their charge waved his mace and bellowed. Edric suspected William brandished the weapon.

Fyrdsmen preceded *thegns* and *huscarls* into the fray. The former did not bear the same armor or weapons as their noble counterparts. Many fell, but others bravely fought on.

Edric separated from his son and Thorkel for a second time. He pushed aside worry for Leofsige. He needed no distraction. Thorkel protected his son and for now, the *huscarl's* protection and strength must be enough. With renewed vigor, he stabbed with Tunwulf Grim's spear and thrust his sword into any Frenchman who challenged him. Sweat trickled beneath his helmet and stung his eyes. The steady ache in his side seemed well worth it. He slaughtered enemy knights and infantry without mercy.

The fighting straggled to a halt. The commanders of both armies called for a respite. Exhausted, Edric paused and rested. He raised a hand and wiped away the sweat on his brow. He prayed Leofwine had seen his retribution, looking down from Heaven.

❧

In the Saxon camp, Edric gathered with the remainder of the *thegns* nearby the king's tent. The body of Gyrth Godwinson lay beside Leofwine.

The grief-stricken king knelt beside his younger brothers. Lovingly, he swept a lock of Leofwine's hair back from his forehead, and closed Gyrth's sightless eyes. He rose, crestfallen.

Edric called, "My king."

Harold kept his silence. His distant gaze avoided everyone. He staggered to his tent with his advisors. Edric worried for the king's state of mind.

"It is a stalemate," Thorkel said at his side. "Harold knows it."

Edric muttered, "His fight is not over. Do not discount his strategy yet."

Shadows lengthened when the battle resumed in late afternoon. As before, French arrows hurtled through the wind and found their mark amongst the poorly armored *fyrd*. Pockets of knights harassed the Saxons on the slope, but withdrew when the shield wall approached. Edric recognized the tactics of feigned flight from earlier.

Each time the *fyrdsmen* broke ranks, William's knights wheeled around and whittled them to a handful of scattered fugitives. The warhorses trampled their bodies. The loss of the majority of *fyrdsmen* made the rest of the Saxons vulnerable. They lost ground steadily.

However, the bulk of the king's shield wall remained. The *huscarls* fought below the standards, which the Frenchmen desperately tried for on Caldbec Hill. Up the slope and from the west, French warriors surged again. His archers bombarded the king's loyal guardsmen. Each time the *huscarls* raised their shields for protection, the French cavalry bore down. They hacked off exposed limbs. Gaps appeared in the shield wall, which the enemy exploited.

Below their position, Edric fought on. In the carnage of the fallen and the heaps of the slaughtered, his compatriots swirled around him. Yet, the tide of battle changed. With the loss of Leofwine Godwinson, and the death of his brother Gyrth, morale slowly vanished. Some of Edric's fellow *thegns* deserted and fled to the woodlands.

Near dusk, dried blood clung to his hands, face, and garments. Weariness numbed him against pain and drained his last reserve of energy.

Beside him, Leofsige slid on a bloodied patch of grass. Edric grabbed him at the waist.

"Thorkel, watch out!" His son's shriek drove Edric forward. Sprawled on the ground, he rolled and protected Leofsige with his weight. Heavy hooves struck near their former positions.

A knight impaled Thorkel on a lance. The *huscarl* never uttered a sound. He sagged under his own body weight. The lance broke.

Leofsige pushed his father off and hurled his battle-axe. It struck the knight square in the chest. Arms flung wide, he fell backward.

Leofsige cradled Thorkel's head in his hands. Sobs ripped from his throat. "Do not leave me! What shall I tell Wynflaed? How can I tell her you died on this field?"

Edric's heart tore at the sight of his son's pain, but he dragged Leofsige from the body. "He is dead! Let him go."

He retreated. His sword arm weakened. He forced his weaponless son behind him and defended them with a discarded shield. The kite-shaped design indicated it belonged to one of the Frenchmen, but he did not care. Two new attackers rained blows with maces on the shield. A sharp pop and fiery pain in his forearm warned him they broke his bones.

Leofsige sprang from behind him. He gripped his grandfather's spear and drove it into the eye of one of the warriors. The knight crumpled, the spear stuck fast.

Edric urged, "Get back to the standards! Defend your king. Leave me."

"I will not leave you, Father." Leofsige brandished the fallen knight's mace and swung wildly. He deflected a spectacular blow swung at his head. Instead, the second mace crushed his arm. His howl of pain and fury echoed his father's own.

Edric pushed himself up on his knees and grabbed Tunwulf's spear. He aimed a sharp thrust at Leofsige's attacker. The knight evaded him. Leofsige swung the mace in his hand, again. He caught the man at the temple. Shattered skull bones expelled a cascade of blood and brains.

When Leofsige crumpled beside him, Edric cradled his son and covered him. A crush of bodies trampled them underfoot. The crown of Caldbec Hill rose above their heads. The shield wall had collapsed.

The remnants of the *huscarls* rallied around their king. The standards of the Fighting Man and the Dragon of Wessex billowed in the breeze.

Edric groaned before darkness enveloped him. "Harold."

CHAPTER 31

Montivilliers, Normandy
May 1072 CE

Under Avicia's watchful gaze, Cecilia picked comfrey and marigolds with Sister Felice in the central garden at Montivilliers Abbey. The nun guided the child's hands.

At the entrance of the infirmary, Avicia sighed and leaned against the doorpost. She wondered if it might help or harm her daughter, if she knew of her shared blood ties through Philippe with Sister Felice.

Six and half years ago, he had died on the bloodied battlefield at Hastings. When Alice brought the news to Montivilliers, Avicia never cried. She had wept in all the weeks beforehand, certain of her husband's death. His violent end pained her, but in truth, she had lost him years before.

Afterward, she remained with Alice at Rouen until the end of last summer. Now, Alice lived in England with her husband Hugh, where he held many estates. Alice entreated her often for a visit. She promised English estates and the prospect of re-marriage, but Avicia wanted none of those things.

With their baskets of flowers in hand, Sister Felice led Cecilia through the garden path to her mother. She whispered in the girl's ear. Cecilia giggled and ran toward Avicia. "Where are you, *maman*?"

Avicia caught the girl's hand. "Here as always, waiting for you, my lamb."

Cecilia offered her a marigold. "For you, *maman*."

"Thank you my darling. You are very sweet to your *maman*."

In the infirmary, Sister Felice set the baskets down at a table. Among her duties, she stocked the plants and herbs for the various ailments endured at the abbey.

She spoke in low tones to Cecilia. "Can you tell the difference by touch alone, my child?"

Avicia had so rarely heard the nun speak that her voice always startled.

Cecilia said, "I can, Sister Felice."

The child's lisp contrasted with the sonorous tone of her grandmother.

Sister Felice set Cecilia on a stool. The girl touched the turnip-like root and hairy, broad leaves of the comfrey. She selected a marigold and skimmed the ring of ray florets with the pad of her thumb. She set it apart from the comfrey.

Avicia sighed, pleased with her daughter's accomplishment, as she easily discerned the two plants by touch alone. She worried for her existence, in a world she would never see, but she also seemed a healthy and happy seven-year-old girl.

Avicia thought the abbey might suit her, too. Widowed and without Alice's companionship, she suffered. Rouen remained her home, but bad memories soured her life there. Without Alice, she could never reside at Montfort-sur-Risle. She recalled Philippe with fondness, but she could not live in a place so associated with him. At the abbey, she could be with Cecilia and perhaps, find the solace that so often eluded her.

Sister Felice interrupted her musing. "I forgot to pick some mint. Would you like to help, milady?"

A strange glint warmed the nun's silvery gaze, but since Cecilia remained absorbed in her task, Avicia nodded. She kissed her daughter's black hair, whispered that they would return shortly, and followed the nun outdoors with a basket on her arm.

Then Sister Felice strolled past the mint leaves.

"Wait," Avicia called out. "What you wanted is here."

"I know." The nun pointed to a twisted and gnarled tree, bereft of foliage except for a tiny bud. "See there? Life renewed." She turned to her. "You cannot wilt. You must begin anew, also. When a loved one is lost, the heart does not shrivel and die, even if you wish it."

"I do not intend to shrivel and die."

"Why do you haunt this abbey with your gloomy expression and sighs, milady?"

She drew back. "I did not think my presence so unwelcome."

"You are welcome here, but your dreariness is not. This is a place for the adoration of God and duty in His service. Your heart suffers grievous wounds. You cannot give it whole to God."

"What do you know of my anguish?"

"I understand pain, milady."

Silence descended with the sea breeze sweeping inland.

Sister Felice reached for her hand. "Resolve the troubles of the past. Only then can you give your whole heart to God's service. You must seek the source of your misery."

Avicia wrenched her fingers from her grasp. "How can I do this?"

"Heralds arrive from England for you every month."

"I thought those visitations were private."

"I have not spied upon them. I once loved and lost, milady. I also sought comfort in another's arms. It did not help. Even if you hide here, it shall not alter your history. You must absolve the sins of the past before you can claim your rightful future, wherever that might be. If your fate lies at Montivilliers, we will be waiting for you when you return."

Sister Felice took the basket and picked the mint leaves. Avicia stared at her, wordless. The nun returned to the infirmary.

Avicia twirled the marigold stalk between her fingertips, Sister Felice's advice echoing in her mind. She must embrace the past for the sake of her future.

❧

Saltwood Castle, Kent, England
September 1072 CE

Saltwood Castle beckoned from the extensive green woodlands. It reminded Avicia of the familiar motte-and-bailey structures in her homeland. The smoke of afternoon cooking fires drifted beyond its confines. She urged her mare onward, toward the comforts offered behind its timber palisade.

Guardsmen eyed her approach. Perhaps they thought it odd a lone woman arrived without an escort. However, she had traveled unmolested after her arrival at the port of Hythe, in the company of an English priest. Father Ulfer left her at the outskirts of an extensive village, where he ministered to the inhabitants. Before his farewell, he directed her to the castle.

When the sentry asked for her name and business, she provided both. His stone-faced visage relaxed when she greeted him in the Norman French language.

Beyond the tall gatehouse, the chaos of the bailey seemed reminiscent of Rouen. People thronged everywhere. Men drove livestock to stalls along the north wall. Children ambled behind their mothers and chased geese and ducks. No differences existed between the toil here or in Normandy.

Curious and unfriendly looks darted her way. A woman clouted a child who stared at her. She grabbed him by the scruff of his ragged tunic. He helped her with the fowl. The woman muttered something in the English language beneath her breath and spat in the dirt.

More sentries defended the bailey than even at Rouen. The clang of swords startled her. Other knights practiced on a southwestern field. She wondered at the necessity for so many guards and weapons.

The English avoided her, shooing small children out of her path. Perhaps they recognized the disparity between her fine robes and their coarse clothes. They marked her for one of their oppressors. She hung her head in shame.

A guardsman approached. "Milady, welcome to Saltwood. I have sent word to the lady of the castle."

She dismounted with his aid.

From across the bailey, Alice rushed from the wooden bridge and embraced her.

When they drew apart, she blanched. Alice seemed a shadow of herself, at a loss for words. In the past, she bombarded her with incessant conversation. She wavered slightly when a stiff afternoon breeze buffeted them. Dark circles colored underneath her eyes.

"At last! I thought you would never come."

"You are ill. Why did you never warn me?" Avicia accused.

"I am merely tired." Alice sighed. "The work of the chatelaine of Saltwood Castle is more tedious than at Montfort-sur-Risle. Come into the castle."

"What of my garments in the saddlebags?"

"A page shall retrieve them."

She leaned heavily upon Avicia much of the way. They entered the tower. Alice indicated the kitchen and storerooms on the ground floor. The heat and smells stifled.

Directly above in the hall, masculine voices issued from an unseen corner. Avicia viewed the magnificent tapestries and carved furniture in the room before Alice led her to the next floor, the family chambers.

Two female servants exited at the end of the hallway and curtsied, before they darted down the stairs.

Avicia commented, "They looked frightened."

"These English are a nervous people." Alice waved a hand in dismissal. "Do not concern yourself about them."

"Where is milord Hugh?"

"He is in the hall below. He entertains a petition from one of his tenants." Alice indicated a tapestry whose frayed edges trailed on the ground. "See here. Our sleeping and private quarters are just beyond."

Alice took her hand and drew her into a small room. Chests occupied two of the corners. Alice pushed aside her embroidery and sat on a long bench affixed to the wall, covered with red and green cushions. She patted the space beside her. "This is my bower, do sit."

Avicia did so, her hands clasped in her lap. "You have changed. I do not remember your being so dismissive of servants."

"I do not dismiss them. I simply do not trust our servants." Alice's sharp falsetto voice betrayed her annoyance. "We have less reason to do so than in Normandy. You would know if you were here."

When she paused, Avicia wondered if Alice resented her long-standing refusal. Before she could inquire, her friend continued, "King William relies upon Hugh and the magnates to subdue the rebels."

"We have taken English lands! How else should a conquered people feel except rebellious?"

"You do not understand what they are capable of, Avicia. Why, bandits ambushed my Alice and her husband Gilbert de Ghent when they visited us this spring. Gilbert is a fine warrior. He comes from Flanders, you know."

A thickened silence pervaded the room with each moment. Alice stared at the fennel and chamomile herbs strewn on the floor. She said no more.

With a sigh, Avicia took her hand. Tears pricked at her eyes. "I have missed you too much to quarrel with you."

Alice sobbed. "I have missed you so! Please, let us never disagree again."

They embraced. When Avicia swiped at her cheeks, Alice offered her a white linen cloth.

"So, your daughter has married. You said her husband's Flemish."

Alice blew her nose. "Indeed, he hails from Aalst."

Avicia frowned. "Is this Gilbert, the son of Count Rudolf and Gisele de Luxembourg?" When Alice nodded, she chuckled, "We are relations through our grandfather, Adalbert."

"Gilbert has grown to a fine man, with the reward of great estates in England. He fought well at Hastings."

She blushed, but Avicia patted her hand. "Those estates once belonged to Englishmen, but Gilbert bears no fault for the demise of their former masters. I am happy for your family, Alice, to know how they prosper."

"When you sent word of your approach," her friend paused and her countenance wavered for a moment. "I reminded Hugh of his pledge. He promises you two estates in Kent. He can secure the necessary consent."

Avicia shook her head. "I do not want them. I have come to see you, not to live in England forever."

A knock at the door interrupted them.

A servant stepped inside. "I ask your pardon, milady, but you wished to be informed when Seigneur Hugh and his guest finished their discussion."

Alice gasped and her hand trembled in Avicia's clutch. Though she could not understand Alice's reaction, she waved away the servant. "Tell Seigneur Hugh his wife is unwell."

"I am not," Alice protested. "Just overcome. We did not expect our guest until tomorrow, but he came a day beforehand. Oh, I thought I would have more time to prepare you."

"Prepare me for what?"

"To see him."

"Do I know this tenant of your husband's? Is he of some importance? Why should his presence matter to me?"

"Come with me." Alice grasped Avicia's hand and led her from the bower, down the stairs to the hall.

Hugh's baritone voice echoed from the chamber. "I tell you again, no good can come of your questions. The king shall never release the last of the Godwinsons now, so those who remain loyal to Harold might rally around him instead. Forget him and forget the Godwinsons. Wulfnoth Godwinson shall die in Salisbury Castle. The rest of his kin died in battle. Your oath of loyalty to Harold the Usurper ended on a blood-soaked hill."

Another voice issued from the room. "Do not speak of Hastings or my king. Your bastard duke shall burn in hell-fire for the lies he spoke of Harold. I was there at Bayeux. I know the truth of what happened. William has stolen Harold's crown and his country, just as surely as he stole Wulfnoth's life."

The sharpness of his familiar timbre tone sent shivers down Avicia's spine.

Alice hugged the wall and pressed her lips with a finger.

The voices drifted from the hall again.

"You asked for a boon and I gave it," Hugh said. "You know where King William keeps his prisoner. It must be enough for you."

"Wulfnoth is the brother of my king! I can never accept the fate William has planned for him."

"William is your king! It is time you accepted his rule."

Avicia extracted her hand from Alice's grasp. She stepped inside the hall.

Hugh stood in the center of the room. Anger quickened his breaths and reddened his features.

Another man, tall and hooded, stood before him with clenched fists. He wore a bedraggled wolf skin pelt on his shoulders.

"Your people may have crushed the rebellions at York and in the fens," he said, "but mine shall never accept a bastard for a king."

Hugh raged, "You dare speak against William. After I have offered your former holdings and a new bride, you show such contempt?"

"Milord," Alice interrupted the heated exchange and stood beside Hugh. "I pray you cease this argument, now that our kinswoman is here."

She gestured toward Avicia.

Even before he turned to her, she suspected the identity of the hooded man. His eyes remained the blue of a robin's egg. At first frosted with irritation, they sparkled at the jewel-like center.

She shook her head. "*Non.*"

"Please, my dear," Alice reached for her. "I can explain everything."

"*Non!* Do you hear me? I said, *non.*" She fled the hall.

❧

Edric glared at Hugh and his wife. "Why did you do this? You summon me here on a pretext to meet a French heiress. You wanted me to wed with her so my lands might again belong to my family. Yet, you brought Avicia here."

Stunned, he gripped one of the trestle tables behind him. Eight long years since they last saw each other. He had not anticipated the terror in her expression.

Alice pleaded. "Please fetch her before she does some harm. Milord, she is the bride my husband intended for you."

"Then, you should have prepared her before you gave her such a shock."

Nevertheless, Edric ran from the hall. He took two steps at a time to the ground floor. Outdoors, he scanned around the area but did not see her. He ran across the wooden bridge, which connected with the castle's courtyard. He spied her close to the gatehouse.

"Avicia, do not go."

She neared an unattended horse. He reached her first and yanked her hard against his body.

Her tiny fists pounded at his chest. "Release me, I pray."

"I shall never let you go." Her sobs tore at his heart, but he held fast.

"How dare Alice betray our friendship? How could she bring you here, and think it might please me?"

His arms dropped to his sides. The distance and time between them had altered her affections. She did not love him anymore.

"Why are you here, Edric?"

Her gaze stabbed at him. No love reflected in her watery eyes. Nothing resembled the ardent passion that had claimed his heart at their last encounter.

"Hugh de Montfort asserted lordship over some of my holdings," he began.

She gasped softly but he heard it nonetheless.

"After Hastings, I became his tenant at Newington. He wrote to me in the spring. He promised the return of lands I had held, if I would marry the heiress who now controlled them. I presume that is you."

"Hugh gave me no properties. Perhaps he intended to, but he did not. He makes sport of our lives to bring us together again, him and Alice. I shall never forgive her for this."

He struggled against the harsh breath torn from his lungs. When he had discovered the identity of his new overlord, shock at another connection to Avicia replaced his anger. He never thought she might re-appear in his life. After the conquest, when he lost so much, becoming the tenant of the land of his ancestors chafed at his very soul. The Frenchmen wrought too much destruction. Yet, he intended to survive and regain everything he had lost.

Still, Avicia was never far from his thoughts. He often wondered whether her husband had fought at Hastings, and whether he survived it.

Edric once wished God might allow them a chance for happiness again, a fresh start, though it seemed impossible. Now, her despair shattered the last remnant of his hope.

"This must be a great shock for you. I did not know you would be the woman Hugh de Montfort offered. I wished to wed simply to regain what I have lost. I understand your pain and shall trouble you no more with my presence."

He turned from her.

He could not blame her for the rejection. Too many times they had come together, only to separate because of his duty to the Godwinsons and his family. He vowed never to hurt her again. He would return home and never seek her out. She deserved the peace and happiness he could not offer her.

"Edric!" she called out to him. "Wait, please."

He continued in long strides to the castle and never looked back.

CHAPTER 32

Saltwood Castle, Kent, England
September 1072 CE – March 1073 CE

Avicia's heart sank inside her chest. The shock of her reunion with Edric could not compare to the pain of his sudden desertion. He abandoned her, as in the past, without another word.

"Edric!"

He remained oblivious to her cries, walking on with his shoulders hunched. He neared the entrance to the castle.

Fierce anger spurred her across the bailey. He disappeared behind the timber walls. She followed and sighted him at the top of the steps.

"How dare you ignore me after all I have suffered because of you?"

On the outskirts of the hall, he swung around. The cold glint of anger returned to his eyes.

"You suffered? Lady, you cannot know the true meaning of pain."

She mounted the steps and closed the divide between them. Her position at the bottom of the stairs offered him a superior advantage, but she subdued her fear and trembling.

She held out her palm. "Years ago, I endured the trial by hot iron rather than admit our sin before God. You returned to England and left me to bear the pain, alone."

He blanched and stared at her hand. "You undertook the trial?"

She smiled. "It surprises you to find no scar. It faded in time. Yet, the reddened stripes on my back remain from my girlhood. I took the whipping for the death of Matilda's merlin, instead of you. Twice, you have turned from me, leaving me in uncertainty to face the future alone. You shall not turn from me now, not until I have answers from you."

"As I would have of you. Your master spoke of marriage to an heiress, yet I find you."

Tears of regret pricked the corners of her eyes. She prayed they would not fall.

"My husband died at Hastings. He left me alone with our children, his sons…and a daughter."

He alighted on the step, drawing closer. She licked suddenly dry lips, but held her ground. His scowl deepened.

"When last we met, you did not have a daughter. You spoke only of sons, four sons."

"God blessed me with a daughter."

He smoothed a hand over the length of his hair. His ice blue eyes pinned her to the wall. She rubbed her arms against a sudden chill.

He snapped, "Well? Do I have to ask it, or shall you tell me the truth?"

"Do not speak to me in that manner! After everything I have borne for your sake, I shall not allow it."

He glared at her before the fine creases of his face smoothed. Her heart thudded, scarcely believing that she had finally held her own against him.

When he swallowed and looked sheepish, she felt mollified at last.

"She is not your child, Edric. She is the image of her father, as are my sons."

A skeptical frown marred his brow.

She shook her head. "I would never claim another man's child for my husband's own. Philippe did not deserve it. When Cecilia, that is her name, when she was born, I wept. Not tears of joy at the sight of her. Not in relief that her black hair and the color of her eyes proved she was Philippe's child, and eased the burden of my trial. There were only tears of foolish regret, sorrow that she was not your child. When you abandoned me, if I only had your daughter, it would have been enough to keep the flame of our love constant."

They regarded each other in silence. He swallowed audibly, so loudly that she could hear it.

"Now, I suppose, there remains nothing between us. Not even, regret. The conquest has changed everything."

His jaw tightened. "For us all."

She sighed, tears pricking her eyes. "I do not understand why Hugh chose you as a bridegroom. Please, tell me, where is your wife?"

Alice intruded before he could answer. "I heard your voices. I am glad you returned, Avicia."

"I tire of running."

Alice nodded and curtsied before Edric. "Please, milord, we dined before your arrival. May I offer you the comforts of the hall, now?"

When he nodded, Alice turned to Avicia, who shook her head. "With your permission, may I retire to your bower? The journey has left me weary."

"I shall send a servant to escort you."

ℝ

In the bower, Avicia sat on the long bench and cradled her head. Tears pricked at the corners of her eyes, but she wiped them away impatiently. She did not know whether she cried with joy or wept for sadness.

Her unexpected reunion fell short of the dreams she had once held. Memories of Edric had kept her sane and alive in the blackness, while she waited for trial by ordeal. In her darkest hours, she prayed God would reunite them someday. Her hope had helped her survive.

Now it seemed a foolish wish. The battle had changed more than just the fortunes of kings and countries.

When Alice rustled the tapestry and entered, Avicia reached for her hand.

Alice whispered, "Please forgive me, my dear. I thought only of your happiness. I remembered the love you bore for Lord Edric and presumed he still felt the same. I suggested the match to Hugh. While he resented your happiness after everything Philippe suffered, for my sake, he agreed to it."

"Do not make apologies for Hugh. Philippe was his brother, and he was right to think the worst of me. I thank you for your kindness of many years, dear friend. I know I did not always deserve it." Avicia sighed. "But you thought wrongly. I do not know how I feel for Edric. Too much time has passed. I am uncertain of his feelings for me. Once, I married for love but knew little joy at the end. I do not wish to marry again, not if it shall bring further unhappiness."

She wiped her wet cheeks. "When I last saw him, Edric was wed. What happened to his wife?"

Alice shook her head. "I do not know. When Hugh spoke to me of his tenancies, I learned of the change in Lord Edric's circumstances. Hugh said he petitioned him for the return of lands he once held from King Edward. He also inquired about the dower land of his former wife, but that belongs to Odo de Bayeux, now. Edric shall never regain it."

"Your husband thought to bind him as the under-tenant of a Norman, if he wed with me." When Alice nodded, Avicia chuckled ruefully. "Edric is too proud to submit."

"Or, he is too stubborn. He did answer my husband's summons, though."

"The promise of his ancestral lands lured him. He admitted it."

"If King William wants to rule this country, Englishmen and Normans must unite. Otherwise, the conquest shall never be over. For my part, I regret my stay in this country. You shall remember I did not like England on our first visit."

"I do remember. I liked it well enough."

Alice nodded. "At supper, you might try talking to Edric. He hated Hugh and me for not forewarning you of his presence, but he is not immune to you."

Avicia sighed and leaned on her friend's shoulder. "If only I knew he wanted me, not just the lands."

Hopeful yearning brightened Alice's sallow skin. "Does this mean you shall remain at Saltwood and find out?"

Avicia nodded. "I shall stay. Do you attend King William's court?"

Alice grimaced. "*Non*, but Hugh does. It is much the same as the ducal court and does not interest me. If Hugh agrees, I shall return to Montfort-sur-Risle. I grow old and England's weather makes my bones ache. Did you see your children before you left Normandy?"

"*Non*, not since I brought word of their father's death."

Avicia rose from the bench. "How they must despise me. I am a stranger to my sons. I have abandoned my daughter at Montivilliers."

"Where Sister Felice cares for her. I saw my sons last at my daughter's wedding. I hardly recognized Hugh and Robert, for they have not been at Rouen since their father fostered them. Robert has no interest in England. He shall inherit his father's estates in Normandy, but our eldest, Hugh, seems content here. We shall see him again at Christmas. I pray this shall be my last year at Saltwood. When I return home, you could come with me."

When Avicia looked at her, she added, "If Edric has not proposed marriage by then."

"You know Montfort-sur-Risle was Philippe's home, never mine."

"Has that sour-faced Mabel de Belleme returned to Rouen?"

"After the duchess, I mean, Queen Matilda, banished her, Mabel has kept to her husband's lands in Normandy."

Silence returned. Tears threatened Avicia's composure again. She did not belong in England any more than Normandy.

Alice commented, "You do not ask about Odo de Bayeux."

"I do not care where he is, so long as the lecher is far from me," Avicia muttered.

Almost in a reflex, she clenched the hand that endured the trial by ordeal.

Alice said, "He is earl of Kent and claims almost the same amount of land as the king. The magnates despise him. Hugh tells me they whisper about his aspirations to be king of England in William's stead. The English hate Odo, too. He tramples their crops underfoot when he travels to his various estates."

"I wish one day his horse might throw him, so he can break his neck."

A servant informed them of the supper hour.

Arm in arm, both women left the bower and headed down to the hall.

They met Hugh at the outskirts. His frown quieted both women.

"He is gone. Your Englishman has left us." He wagged his finger at them. "I shall never listen to you again, wife. You said he would want her and the land. All this trouble for naught, a fool's errand it has been."

He left them with muttered curses.

Avicia looked at Alice. "Does Edric still hold Newington? How far is it from Saltwood?"

"I do not know." Alice's gaze narrowed on her. "What are you planning?"

Avicia smiled in reply, but said nothing.

Alice groaned and cupped her forehead.

⁊

At the end of the harvest month, Avicia stood on the steps of Saltwood Castle.

Edric stalked across the bailey, his face a grim mask of fury.

She curtsied before him. "Milord, you are welcome here. Lady Alice is ill so I greet you in her stead. Please follow me."

He did so. Inside, he grabbed her arm. When she whirled and the wide skirts of her robe brushed his legs.

"How dare you? Remove your hand at once, milord and do not take such liberties."

"Do not speak to me like a churl. You think I do not know what you have done to bring me back here. At Dover, the townsmen speak of a beautiful French widow newly arrived at Saltwood, ripe for re-marriage with two new holdings."

She avoided his rapt gaze. "Hugh has explained the law which allows him to grant any of his manors in exchange for service. I live by his generosity, but I must have a husband to maintain the lands."

He loomed closer. "Those holdings belong to me. You knew I would return if provoked. Do you care about the lands?"

She stiffened. "I am not concerned with English tenancies. Did you return just for them, or for me?"

When he kept his reserve, she fought against the stab of pain in her heart. With a deep breath, she regained her composure.

She said, "Milord Hugh wishes to greet you."

When he followed, the wooden steps creaked under their weight. He muttered something in the English language she did not understand.

She held her spine straight, her head aloft, though painfully aware of his presence.

When a maidservant approached with Alice's summons, Avicia murmured her apology. She darted up the stairs. Heat flared along her back and warned of his harsh gaze.

When she reached the bower, she breathed, "He is here."

Alice endured a coughing fit before she asked, "Was he pleased to see you?"

"He is aggrieved about his holdings."

"I recall how he looked at you in Rouen, when he thought no one watched him. If he still regards you with such desire, love can begin anew."

"I asked him if he came for the lands or me. He did not answer."

"He is unsure of your feelings and his own. Give yourself and him time. Only then can you re-discover your true feelings and love each other, again."

Avicia escaped from the castle in mid-afternoon. She needed solitude and quiet, away from the boisterous occupants of the hall at dinner. Her empty belly gurgled.

She had not eaten, not when Edric frowned at her repeatedly. Unsettled, she headed for the mews across the bailey.

Barely a few steps from the castle entrance, she halted in mid-stride and turned around. Edric followed her. He closed the distance between them.

He commented, "When we last spoke, you said you were tired of running."

She licked dried lips. "I meant it."

His gaze strayed to her mouth. Desire warmed his expression.

Despite the thrill rippling through her body, she clenched her fists and tamped down her natural response.

A wry smile dimpled his cheeks. "Are you going to the mews? Is it as fine as the ones at Lille and Rouen?"

She blushed with remembrances of their time together. "I suppose."

"Show it to me."

She shook her head. His voice hinted with carnal promise. "I shall not."

She bypassed him and headed for the castle.

His hand closed none too gently on her wrist.

"Let me go, milord. You are hurting me."

His grin widened but it seemed a mockery of a smile. "You do not know what it is to hurt, Avicia, not truly."

She struggled against him. "The scars on my back and the burn on my palm tell the story of my hurts. Did I imagine those pains?"

"There are more devastating hurts. The loss of a son, a wife and daughter or the deaths of a beloved old woman and an old man who never harmed a soul, can torture a man."

She gasped. "You cannot mean you suffered so?"

He glowered and shook her a little. "Would I burden you with someone else's pain? Before England lost its rightful ruler, I had fought at his side with my eldest son Leofsige. I brought my son's broken body back to Newington after the battle. Greater horror awaited me."

She turned from him, but he held her tightly, despite the watchful gazes of others in the bailey.

"On its victory march north to Dover, the Frenchmen descended on Kentish villages in their path. They raided Newington. They slew my uncle Alwine and stole the golden chalice from his chapel. Frenchmen ravished my daughter Deorwynn, a mere child. When her mother tried to save her, they drew their swords. My wife died with the knowledge of our child's ruin. My grandmother died of her grief a few weeks later, starved and frail because we had nothing to eat. One full year to the day of the devastation, my Deorwynn drowned herself in the millpond. She left her daughter behind, a child sired by rape."

His dispassionate summary of the events after Hastings belied his tortured expression. Red-rimmed eyes met hers. His body sagged in anguish, from his drooped head to slumped shoulders.

She stared in disbelief. His grief overwhelmed her.

He continued, "So, when you ask me if I want you or the lands, understand those holdings are my rightful legacy. I shall do anything to regain them. With their prosperity, my family can survive the brutality of your people. They have taken everything from me: my son and daughter, my wife, and my properties. I have good reason to hate any Frenchman."

She fought against his grasp, and he released her. She stumbled backward. Tears blinded her. The foolish hope that he cared for her more than the return of his estates faded. He had suffered at the hands of her people. He would never forgive her for what the Normans wrought in England.

His fingers closed on her shoulders.

She buried her face in her hands, until he pried them away and grasped them in his.

"I have never hated you, Avicia, despite all I have lost, and the ways in which God has punished me for my pride and the sins I committed against my family. I shall always want you, more than lands, or old glories of the past. My lifelong duty to the Godwinsons took me from you often, always against my will. You were never far from my thoughts, and forever in my heart.

"I mourned Harold's ending. I have often wondered why God took him and my son, and left me alive, but now I understand. I am free to devote myself only to you, as I always should have. If you can forgive me for the past, you shall never regret it."

In her heart, hope unfurled like a falcon's wings. She wondered what a new beginning would mean for both of them.

∻

Six months after her arrival in England, Avicia bid Alice farewell. The two friends embraced fervently in the midst of Saltwood's hall.

Alice pleaded, "Promise you shall send word to me when you can."

Avicia kissed her tear-stained cheeks. "I shall. Be well and happy."

"Are you ready to depart for Newington?"

Edric's gruff voice sounded behind her. When she turned, he held out his hand. His pale blue eyes sought an answer in hers.

She extended her fingers for his grasp. Sunlight entered the hall's northern window and illuminated the filigree work of her wedding band.

They had married in the morning at the church door of Saltwood. Hugh obtained the necessary consents for their marriage. Father Ulfer presided over the ceremony, which only Alice and Hugh attended.

Four new additions to Edric's retinue followed him from the hall: Father Ulfer, whom he had appointed as the priest of Newington with Seigneur Hugh's blessing, and a mated peregrine and tiercel, with a new falconer for their upkeep.

After Edric helped Avicia onto her mount, both paused in admiration of the beautiful birds.

He said, "A generous wedding gift from your lord, to be sure."

She touched his shoulder tentatively. The heat of his body beneath the mantle and tunic brought long-remembered warmth to her hand. "It is said, they mate for life, milord."

His ice-blue gaze flitted to hers. His countenance never changed, but something in his eyes sparked, a secret fire flaming within. She snatched her hand back, as though burned.

They left the castle. He spoke little on the journey north to his village, but she suspected the reasons for his silence.

For so long, both despaired of happiness. She never dreamed of the day where she might call him her own. In the past, fate always drove them apart. Now, they both feared the future.

He avoided her stark gaze and focused on patches of bracken.

When the first drops of moisture fell, which signaled rain clouds, he addressed her. "Let us shelter under that copse of trees."

Later, he leaned against a tree. Under a canopy of wet leaves, she stared at the graying sky. She dreaded her arrival at his home. His family might view her as the enemy, a reminder of their losses.

His gaze fell on her face. When she shuddered, he moved toward her, but then he hesitated.

She took the final steps he would not. Her hand rested over his heart. The metal of her ring gleamed against his tunic.

He loomed closer and claimed her mouth hungrily. She leaned into the kiss and gave what he sought to take. Her hand traveled upward, her fingers cupping the nape of his neck.

When they drew apart, the sapphire glow returned to his eyes, his breath expelled in a rush.

Aware of Father Ulfer's discomfort, she stepped back. "The rain has stopped."

❧

Bleak, windswept trees lined the road to Newington. She expected the sights and sounds of villagers at work, but silence greeted her. No one stirred outdoors. Patches of land remained blackened and scorched. She hung her head in shame, knowing her people had wrought such devastation.

The far-flung doors of the hall beckoned. Edric rode ahead. She stared at his back. Her lips still tingled after their embrace under the trees. Full of demand, the kiss grew fervent when she surrendered. They needed more than passion. Desire faded with time. They needed trust and love, too.

A solitary figure placed dried flowers on five graves near the chapel. Avicia recalled Edric's account of his losses after Hastings, and knew these were the burial sites of his family members. How could love begin anew in this tragic place?

He dismounted first and approached the person at the graves, who whirled toward him. After they spoke, she nodded and approached Avicia.

"I remember you, the girl who bewitched my young son."

She spoke in the Flemish language. "I am Emmeline, Edric's mother. I bid you welcome, Avicia, Lady of Newington."

Edric joined them and reached for Avicia. "We are home at last."

The bright, eager faces of children peeked past the doorway. When she hesitated, his brow furrowed. She feared the reaction of his son and daughters to a stranger newly wed to their father, one among the people who had wrought such devastation and killed their mother. Yet, she knew she could not avoid the interaction forever.

In the instant before she found her courage and reached for him, he turned on his heel and greeted the children racing toward him.

Emmeline murmured, "A beginning is always hard."

Avicia's throat tightened. "What of the ending?"

Emmeline smiled. "Only you and Edric can decide it."

CHAPTER 33

Newington, Kent, England
December 1073 CE

In the company of two men-at-arms, Edric slowed his horse at the outskirts of Newington village. His heart burgeoned with hope. The coming year might bring prosperity. He wanted enough food for his family and the village, perhaps with a profit he might sell at Dover.

Edric leaned forward in the saddle and patted the stallion's neck. He never saw Elfhar or Leofsige's mount Bavo again, after Hastings. Within a year, he purchased a new horse, but never named it.

He sensed the animal's eagerness for the comfort of the stable, where water and dry fodder awaited it. Edric shared the same desire for home, but hesitated.

Rebellion against the conquerors continued. For three months, he had remained at Saltwood Castle with other Kentish tenants. With constant vigilance, questioning and unexpected summons to Saltwood, their Norman overlord ensured none of the remaining Saxon landholders conspired in support of the uprising. The Frenchmen would force peace on the embittered Saxons.

Edric wondered if it could ever happen, even in his own house.

'When there is peace between lord and lady, so shall Newington thrive.' He had hoped his great-grandmother's wish would become reality with Avicia at his side, but happiness remained elusive.

Before his departure, they had argued, though he could not remember the reason. He had felt glad for an escape from her unpredictably foul temper. Presumably, her sullen moods continued in his absence, for she had sent no messages, the only missives from Heahstan arriving weeks apart. He held a fool's hope for contentment. What joy might he and Avicia find in a world altered by the Saxon defeat at Hastings?

The riders followed the gravel path between barren fields. Wisps of clouds gathered overhead. Newington's chapel bells marked the hour of Sext.

In a sudden burst, showers fell and hastened the men to the hall. The horse whickered and shook off the droplets. Edric led his men past the gatehouse and into the palisade, where a stable boy led their horses away to the stable. They dashed for the entrance to the house. Frozen rain chased them indoors. The water soaked through Edric's wolf skin.

In a collective gasp, the occupants of the hall seemed startled by his sudden appearance. The pair of falcons he had brought from Saltwood Castle chorused cries of distress, before the falconer offered them morsels of dried meat. They settled on their perches, quiet again.

Heahstan and Leofflaed, heads bent together over a tafula board, dropped their painted gaming pieces when Edric entered. Emmeline, with her great-grandchildren around her, eyed him with an assessing gaze.

Eanflaed, his youngest daughter, launched herself at him with a jubilant cry. "You are home, at last!"

He kissed her cheeks and patted her thin black curls, reminiscent of her mother Cynwise. He greeted Heahstan, Leofflaed, and Leofsige's widow Wynflaed. His son Cenweard, a shy young man much like his mother, bowed beside Wulfstan, the old steward.

Edric also embraced his grandchildren, the most restrained being Deorwynn's six year-old daughter Cyneburh. With time, perhaps she might be cheerful, as her mother had been before the Frenchmen came.

Emmeline stood. "Wulfstan, tell my son's wife of his return."

Edric was not ready for a reunion with Avicia, especially when it seemed she shunned his family in his absence. "Why is she not here with you now?"

"I told her to rest," Emmeline offered.

He frowned. "Why should she need rest at midday? Is she ill?"

The concern in his voice irritated him more than her absence. He turned from his mother's speculative gaze.

A servant approached with a cup of ale. He reached for the drink. At the sight of his wife, the cup fell and cracked.

She crossed the hall. Her hand rested on her rounded belly, which jutted beneath her robe. She carried their child.

He scoured the hall for Heahstan. The young man had darted behind Leofflaed before Edric roared, "Why did you never tell me my wife was with child when we exchanged messages?"

"I asked him not to speak of it." Avicia's voice rang clear through the hall, above the alarm the falcons raised again.

"You did what?" He almost choked on his rage. How dare she keep such news from him? Had she been so angry when they parted?

"Damn you, woman, you shall not keep secrets from me! I am your lord and you shall honor me in the way a wife should honor her husband...."

He halted, with the realization that she had understood his conversation with Heahstan, and addressed him in the Saxon language.

Before he could comment on it, Emmeline nodded to Avicia. "You see, proud and savage like the wolf, in the manner of his father at times."

Edric frowned, but she ignored his grim expression. "Son, before you rail at your bride with unfounded accusations, I suggest you take her away from curious eyes and ears. You may be lord of this hall, but I shall clout you if you continue so before my great-grandchildren.

What must they think of you? A little propriety, it is all I ask from you. I never raised you with such bad manners."

Indeed, everyone stared. He stalked forward and grabbed Avicia's arm. Though she winced, he dragged her toward the family quarters.

She muttered, "Your mother speaks the truth. You are arrogant."

He swung on his heel. "I dare you to say that, again."

"And what can you do, strike me down with your fury while I carry your babe in my belly?" Her slender fingers settled on his forearm. "Indeed, you are overly prideful, have always been. When we first met, I was foolish enough to take Matilda's merlin out to impress you. Now, I know better how to handle your conceit."

"How do you propose to do that?" He hauled her against him, expecting they would continue the argument of months past.

Instead, she took his free hand in hers and kissed it. "When there is a thorn in my wolf's paw, I must soothe his savagery."

Her bemused smile disarmed him. With a shrug, he realized how foolishly he behaved.

His family gaped. Eanflaed giggled behind her hands.

He said, "It pleases me that you are learning the Saxon tongue."

"Father Ulfer is a good teacher. Our son shall know his English heritage."

He cupped the roundness of her belly. "He has your blood inside him, too."

She stood on tiptoe and kissed his cheek. Hand in hand, they left the hall.

Behind a partition, in a corner apart from the family, they sat together. He patted her abdomen and marveled.

A girlish giggle escaped her. "I am not the first woman in England to bear a child, Edric, nor to have your child."

"Why did you keep this from me, when you do not seem angry with me anymore?" When her brow crinkled, he continued, "Before I had left, we argued. I do not remember why it happened."

"We have argued often of late, even on our wedding night. I suppose we are both too strong-willed for each other."

"I can bend and not break. I can learn patience, with you for a wife."

Her brow furrowed. "Do I try your patience still?"

"You kept this," his hand cupped her belly again, "from me for months."

"I wanted to see the look of pleasure in your eyes when you knew of our babe. Sometimes, I despaired that you would never return on time, but I could not send a messenger to deliver such news. When you left, and I missed my monthly flow, I knew I carried your child even before Emmeline summoned the midwife to confirm it. Do you recall the day in the woods before you rode to Saltwood?"

Her voice trailed off and she blushed. He remembered the evening they rode alone before his departure. They had made love beneath the forest canopy. Despite the cold and dampness, they gave and took in mutual delight.

He asked, "You understand why I want a daughter?"

Avicia answered, "Emmeline told me of your pain when you lost Deorwynn."

He sighed, but she framed his face in her hands. "Whatever you desire, I pray to God that it should be so. If we have a daughter, I want to name her Emma, for your mother."

"Emma, she shall be. If it is a son, I want to name him Harold, for my king."

Her lips brushed against his. "Harold, he shall be."

⌘

In the Yuletide season, boughs of ivy, holly and other evergreens decorated the hall at Newington. Avicia's labor started. After sunset, the proud father stood at the center of the room. Everyone crowded around him for a glimpse of the twin babies, Emma and Harold.

"The lady of Newington rests after her travail." Emmeline emerged from the family quarters. She kissed Edric's bearded cheek. "I congratulate both of you. It was surely difficult bearing just one of your babies, son, much less two. She shall recover. It helped that she has had five children in the past."

A loud knock at the door of the hall preceded the sudden entry of three men and a small boy. The elder two, who wore the mail coats of Frenchmen, pushed their coifs back. The younger ones removed the hoods of their cloaks. Each revealed black hair shorn in the Norman style.

His jaw clenched, Edric gave his newborn children over to his mother and Leofflaed. He ushered everyone into the recesses of the room. He closed the distance between him and the arrivals.

One of the knights asked, "Is there a priest here who can speak Latin?"

Before Father Ulfer could step forward, Edric demanded, "Who are you to invade my lands? Strangers are not welcome here, especially Frenchmen. How did you get past the gatehouse without a warning?"

The knight seemed surprised at a welcome in Norman French, but he gathered his wits quickly.

"We do not mean to trespass at this late hour. Your sentries allowed us entry in the name of my liege lord, Seigneur Hugh de Montfort-sur-Risle. I am Sieur Geoffrey. Beside me are my younger brothers Baldwin, Simon, and Thorbert. We have come seeking the Lady Avicia, whom milord Hugh tells me resides at Newington manor. She married the English lord of this village last year. Please, we desire only to see her, and know that she is well and happy here. She is our mother."

Edric nodded. "I am the lady's husband, Edric of Newington. She has just delivered of our twins, a boy and girl." He pointed to the children snuggled with his family.

The quartet stared at him in silence.

Then Geoffrey said, "Seigneur Hugh never warned us. I did not know my mother had other children, except for us and our sister Cecilia at Montivilliers."

Edric wondered how much Avicia's children knew of her history with him. He studied Geoffrey's placid expression. No resentment or resignation soured his looks, but he neither smiled.

Edric said, "It was a shock for me when Avicia told me I would be a father again. I did not expect it. Like her, I was once married to another. I did not expect to wed your mother. I hope you and your brothers can accept our children. They are English, but Norman blood runs in their veins. Your mother's blood."

Geoffrey nodded and glanced at the babies briefly. "I congratulate you. I am also newly married. My wife, Gisela de Guines, gave birth to our first son last month. I named him Philippe for his grandfather."

Edric grinned. Would Avicia enjoy being a grandmother?

Geoffrey continued, "Milord Hugh's wife, Lady Alice, has spoken of your love and devotion to my mother. After my father had died, I hoped she might find happiness at Montivilliers, but it seems God has another purpose for her. If she is content with you, then I am grateful she has found what she deserves. I would be glad to know you better, and my new brother and sister."

Edric's smile widened. "You and your brothers are welcome in this hall. You shall always be welcome here, for so long as your mother is my wife. I intend that it should be forever."

While the family and their guests toasted the births of the twins, Edric went to Avicia, who slept on a pallet amidst sweet scented herbs. When he bent and kissed her forehead, she stirred groggily.

Golden lashes fluttered against her skin. "What is it, Edric? Are Emma and Harold well?"

He caressed her cheek. At last, she belonged to him, his to cherish forever. With her, he could begin life anew at Newington, united by the bonds of their love.

He said, "The children are well. Rest, and when you are full awake, I shall have a surprise for you."

"The twins were enough of a shock for one day. I never expected two babies at my age, a woman with grown sons." She stretched and yawned. "What is your surprise?"

"You are always eager and impatient, but you must rest for now. You shall like my surprise."

She cradled his hand against her cheek and closed her eyes. "Do you promise me?"

He kissed her brow again. "I shall always keep my pledges to you."

THE END

AUTHOR'S NOTE

On Falcon's Wings is a work of fiction, inspired by my fascination with the late Anglo-Saxon period in England. The historical figures (denoted with the symbol * in the list of Characters) are factual, and I have done my best to render them as history recalls.

William's marriage to Matilda of Flanders aided his cause at Hastings, as the Flemish contingent contributed to the Norman victory. William became king of England on December 25, 1066, a reign that lasted almost twenty-one years. Constant fighting in Normandy and rebellions in England plagued him. He died at Rouen at the age of fifty-nine on September 9, 1087. He left England to his second son William Rufus, Normandy to his eldest son Robert, and five thousand silver pounds to his youngest son Henry. After many years of feuding with his elder brothers, Henry became king of England in 1100.

William's advisor, Hugh II de Montfort-sur-Risle, received over one hundred English tenancies and remained a trusted supporter. In 1087, he divided his holdings in England and Normandy between his and Alice's sons, Hugh and Robert, before he took monastic vows and retired to the Benedictine monastery at Bec. He died shortly afterward.

Only Wulfnoth survived his Godwinson brothers. He remained a prisoner of the Normans until his death in Salisbury Castle, during the reign of William Rufus. Harold's uncle, Abbot Aelfwig, his illegitimate nephew Haakon and all of Harold's brothers but one, died with their king at Hastings. Harold's brother Tostig had died earlier, fighting against him at Stamford Bridge. If Harold had awaited reinforcements after the battle of Stamford Bridge, as I had his brother Gyrth suggest, the outcome at Hastings would have been very different. Controversy remains surrounding Harold's end. According to tradition, he died when an arrow lodged in his eye, just before four Norman knights beheaded and dismembered him, making it almost impossible to identify his body, until Edith the Fair found him. In the depiction on the Bayeux Tapestry, Harold's standard, the Dragon of Wessex appears alongside the figure with the arrow in his eye. The standard in such proximity suggests the person is Harold, hinting at an almost divine justice that rained down from the heavens.

William made a strong case for his incursion into England. His version of Harold's oath on holy relics in 1064 and his reliance on the blessing of Pope Alexander II before he invaded shows the importance of propaganda. For me, the Bayeux Tapestry is an example of history written, or rather stitched, by the victors. I do not think the legendary 'arrow in the eye' afflicted Harold, and instead had his brother Leofwine suffer that fate. In the end, it does not matter how Harold died, only that his passing forever altered England's future.

Avicia is a fictional character, but I hope she reflects the difficulties women faced during this tumultuous period in history. Her enduring love for Edric, despite their differences, mirrors the struggles many Saxons and Normans endured after 1066, as they then united to establish the English country we know today. Avicia is always dedicated to her beliefs, and unwavering in her love for Edric, despite the pain it brings her. I wanted her to be sympathetic; the kind of heroine I would admire.

Avicia also had to have her match in a hero who would always love her, despite the difficulties and distance between them, a man ready to prove himself worthy of her in the end. Edric is a distant relative of Harold, and his commitment to the Godwinsons always separated him from Avicia and his family. He is not a perfect hero, but I gave him heroic qualities, which he often shows in his courage in dealing with the Godwinsons, his dedication to Harold's cause and his own dignity as an English nobleman. Ultimately, these same traits led to his downfall. He had to lose almost everything and everyone before he could have an opportunity for real happiness with Avicia. I hope readers will think the lovers deserved a happy conclusion.

Edric is also a fictional character, though based on the true Saxon landowner of Newington near Hythe or Folkestone. Varying records for the Kentish village state, "Neuentone: Hugh de Montfort from Odo, bishop of Bayeux; Hugh de Montfort and Edric, the pre-Conquest owner, from him*….Edric held it of King Edward, and it was taxed at two shillings then, and now at one, because the other is without his division….The whole, in the time of King Edward the Confessor, was worth twelve pounds, and afterwards three pounds, now twelve pounds…."**

Newington's value before and after 1066 is one example of the devastating changes that the Norman invasion brought to England, but during the Domesday survey twenty years later, the property had rebounded to its previous value. Less than ten percent of the Anglo-Saxon landowners, like Edric, remained in direct control of their property in England. In the reign of King Henry, Hugh de Montfort's heir, Robert, lost the manor at Newington, and all his other English tenancies. The final fate of the real Edric is unknown, lost to history, as were so many other lives in the aftermath of Hastings.

*The Domesday Book: England's Heritage, Then and Now, Crescent Books, Thomas Hinde, ed. (1995)

**'Parishes: Newington', The History and Topographical Survey of the County of Kent: Volume 8 (1799), pp. 197-210. URL: http://www.british-history.ac.uk/report.aspx?compid=63474&strquery=Newington Priory

HISTORICAL TIMELINE

1049

Earl Sweyn Godwinson of Hereford comes to King Edward of England, seeking the return of property Edward had given away to Sweyn's brother Earl Harold Godwinson of East Anglia and Earl Bjorn Estrithson of Huntingdon. After Harold and Bjorn oppose this move, Sweyn meets with Bjorn on a pretext of reconciliation, but has him killed instead. Edward exiles Sweyn for the murder of his cousin and the *witan* declares him an outlaw. Sweyn flees to Flanders.

1050

King Edward of England pardons Earl Sweyn Godwinson of Hereford, who returns to England and receives all his previous holdings.

1051

King Edward of England appoints Bishop Robert Champart of London, former Abbot of Jumieges, as archbishop of Canterbury.

Tostig Godwinson weds Judith of Flanders, sister of Count Baldwin V of Flanders.

Edward receives a visit from his brother in-law, Count Eustace of Boulogne. When Eustace attempts to return home from Dover in Kent, his men become embroiled in a skirmish with the townspeople over a forced billeting of Eustace's men. After Eustace complains, Edward orders Earl Godwin Wulfnothson of Wessex, also earl of Kent, to punish the townspeople, but Godwin refuses. Edward exiles the Godwinsons. Godwin and his wife Countess Gytha, with their children, except Harold and Leofwine, go to Flanders. Harold and Leofwine sail to Ireland. King Edward consigns his wife Queen Edith, eldest daughter of Godwin, to Wherwell Abbey. Edward gives Harold's earldom of East Anglia to Aelfgar, son of Earl Leofric of Mercia.

Earl Sweyn Godwinson of Hereford leaves Flanders on a pilgrimage to the Holy Land.

1052

Earl Godwin Wulfnothson of Wessex invades England in May with his son Harold. They attack the Isle of Wight, Pevensey, Romney, Hythe, Folkestone and Milton Regis before sailing up the Thames River. They force King Edward of England to reinstate them in positions of power. Queen Edith returns to court from Wherwell Abbey.

Archbishop Robert Champart of Canterbury flees to Normandy upon the return of the Godwinsons, taking with him as hostages, Godwin's son Wulfnoth and Sweyn's illegitimate son Haakon. Edward declares Robert Champart an outlaw. Bishop Stigand of Winchester becomes archbishop of Canterbury.

Earl Sweyn Godwinson of Hereford dies at Constantinople in September, after completing the pilgrimage to the Holy Land.

1053

Earl Godwin Wulfnothson of Wessex dies at Winchester in April. Harold inherits Wessex and forfeits the earldom of East Anglia to Aelfgar, son of Earl Leofric of Mercia. Leofwine Godwinson becomes earl of Kent.

1055

King Edward of England declares Earl Aelfgar of East Anglia an outlaw. Aelfgar goes to Ireland and then Wales. Earl Harold of Wessex helps in the defense of England, against him but later assists his reconciliation with Edward.

1057

Earl Leofric of Mercia dies in October. His son Earl Aelfgar of East Anglia inherits Mercia. Gyrth Godwinson becomes earl of East Anglia in Aelfgar's stead.

1058

Earl Aelfgar of Mercia flees England, but soon returns in force with the help of Prince Gruffydd ap Llewellyn of Wales, who marries Aelfgar's daughter, Ealdgyth.

King Edward of England appoints Earl Harold of Wessex to the earldom of Hereford.

1062

Earl Aelfgar of Mercia dies. His son Edwin inherits the earldom.

1063

Earl Harold Godwinson of Wessex attacks Prince Gruffydd ap Llewellyn of Wales at Rhuddlan in January. Gruffydd's men kill him in August, and Harold brings his head as a trophy to King Edward of England.

1064

Earl Harold Godwinson of Wessex leaves Bosham in Chichester and lands in Ponthieu. Comte Guy of Ponthieu captures him, before releasing him to Duke William of Normandy. Harold later returns to England.

1065

The people of Northumbria overthrow Earl Tostig Godwinson and demand the appointment of Morcar, son of Earl Aelfgar of Mercia, to the earldom. At the behest of King Edward of England, Earl Harold Godwinson of Wessex confirms the wishes of the Northumbrian people. Furious at Harold's abandonment, Tostig and his wife Judith flee to her home in Flanders.

1066

Earl Harold Godwinson of Wessex marries Ealdgyth, daughter of Earl Aelfgar of Mercia and widow of Prince Gruffydd ap Llewellyn of Wales. King Edward of England dies in January. Harold becomes King Harold II of England.

Duke William of Normandy hears of Harold's crowning, and plans an invasion of England, asserting that Harold made a vow supporting his claim to the English throne in 1064. William secures papal support from Pope Alexander II.

Harold prepares for William's invasion in July. He disbands his army by September for the harvest season. Tostig Godwinson invades England in support of King Harald Hardrada of Norway. Earls Edwin of Mercia and Morcar of Northumbria engage Tostig and Harald at the Battle of Fulford Gate, a mile south of York. Following the defeat of Edwin and Morcar, Harold's army goes north, and kills Tostig and

Harald at the Battle of Stamford Bridge in September. William's forces land at Pevensey and Romney. They plunder the towns in their path.

Harold returns to London before engaging William near Hastings. At the Battle of Hastings in October, Harold dies, along with his brothers, the earls Leofwine Godwinson of Kent and Gyrth Godwinson of East Anglia. The Norman army pillages the countryside, before reaching London. Edwin and Morcar surrender.

William becomes King William I of England in December.

1067

In May, William's wife, Matilda of Flanders officially becomes queen of England.

Godwin and Magnus, the sons of King Harold II of England, sail from Ireland and invade England. The Normans defeat them.

1068

Rebellion against King William I of England flares in Northumbria. Earls Edwin of Mercia and Morcar of Northumbria also oppose William, but soon submit to him. Morcar forfeits his earldom as punishment.

1069

Godwin and Magnus, the sons of King Harold II of England, sail from Ireland and invade England again. The Normans defeat them again.

Rebellion against King William I of England begins at York. William destroys most of Yorkshire.

1071

Edwin of Mercia and Morcar of Northumbria revolt against King William I of England, making a stand at the Isle of Ely with Hereward the Wake. Edwin's own men kill him. William imprisons Morcar.

1072

King William I of England invades Scotland in June, where the remnants of the English royalty and the northern nobility have sheltered. King Malcolm III of Scotland surrenders to him and signs the Treaty of Abernathy.

ABOUT THE AUTHOR

Lisa J. Yarde writes fiction inspired by the Middle Ages in Europe. She is the author of two historical novels set in medieval England and Normandy, *The Burning Candle*, based on the life of Isabel de Vermandois, and *On Falcon's Wings*, chronicling the star-crossed romance between Norman and Saxon lovers. Lisa has also written three novels in a six-part series set in Moorish Spain, *Sultana, Sultana's Legacy*, and *Sultana: Two Sisters*, where rivalries and ambitions threaten the fragile bonds between members of a powerful family. Her short story, *The Legend Rises*, which chronicles Gwenllian of Gwynedd's valiant fight against English invaders, is included in Pagan Writers Press' 2013 HerStory anthology.

Born in Barbados, Lisa currently lives in New York City. She is also an avid blogger and moderates at Unusual Historicals. She is also a contributor at Historical Novel Reviews and History and Women. Her personal blog is The Brooklyn Scribbler.

Learn more about Lisa and her writing at the website www.lisajyarde.com. Follow her on Twitter (**@lisajyarde**) or become a Facebook fan (**Lisa J. Yarde**). For information on upcoming releases and freebies from Lisa, join her mailing list at http://eepurl.com/un8on.

www.ingramcontent.com/pod-product-compliance
Lightning Source LLC
Chambersburg PA
CBHW051010180726
48291CB00006B/2053